T0333443

THE DREAM
OF A TREE

THE DREAM OF A TREE

MAJA LUNDE

Translated by Diane Oatley

SCRIBNER

LONDON NEW YORK SYDNEY TORONTO NEW DELHI

First published in Great Britain by Simon & Schuster UK Ltd, 2024

Copyright © Maja Lunde, 2022

English translation copyright © Diane Oatley, 2024
Originally published as *Drømmen om et tre* in 2022 in Norway by Aschehoug

The right of Maja Lunde to be identified as author of this work has been
asserted in accordance with the Copyright, Designs and Patents Act, 1988.

1 3 5 7 9 10 8 6 4 2

Simon & Schuster UK Ltd 1st Floor
222 Gray's Inn Road London WC1X 8HB

Simon & Schuster Australia, Sydney
Simon & Schuster India, New Delhi

Simon & Schuster: Celebrating 100 Years of Publishing in 2024

www.simonandschuster.co.uk
www.simonandschuster.com.au
www.simonandschuster.co.in

A CIP catalogue record for this book
is available from the British Library

Hardback: 978-1-4711-8531-1
Trade Paperback ISBN: 978-1-4711-8532-8
eBook ISBN: 978-1-4711-8533-5
Audio ISBN: 978-1-3985-3045-4

This book is a work of fiction.
Names, characters, places and incidents are either a
product of the author's imagination or are used fictitiously. Any resemblance
to actual people living or dead, events or locales is entirely coincidental.

Typeset in Palatino by M Rules
Printed and Bound in the UK using 100% Renewable Electricity
at CPI Group (UK) Ltd

Longyearbyen, Svalbard
2097

On the day after the year's final night of midnight sun, a tree washed ashore on the beach of Longyearbyen. Tommy was five years old and alone in the former container harbour. He had been wandering around between the rusting metal walls for some time, and after sounding out the words *Tollpost Globe* on the side of a container, he sat down with his back against it to warm himself beneath the rays of the low-lying sun.

It was while he was sitting there and digging in the sandy soil with a stick that he noticed the leaves. They were sticking up out of the ground a short distance away, the green colour wholly out of place on the rocky, black shoreline of the fjord.

He got to his feet, gripping the stick tightly, one of the best sticks he had found in a long time – straight, long and difficult to break – and trotted down to the shore. A tree was lying there on the dark ground, parallel with the water line, the crown facing the river delta of the Advent Valley in the east and the roots pointing west, towards the blackness of Isfjorden.

'A tree!' Tommy shouted, as if saying it aloud made it more true.

Trees washed ashore in Svalbard all the time, large logs of larch, spruce and pine, propelled by the wind and ocean currents, travelling here all the way from Siberia. Bleached white by the sea and the ocean, stripped of bark, waterlogged and infested by hosts of small marine creatures from all the years spent in the ocean, they were no longer proper trees; they were mere shadows of what they had once been.

But this tree was different, because it was not a shadow – it resembled a living tree. The crown was large and bushy. The leaves were curled up and wilting, but many of them still clung to the branches, and even though the colour was sort of washed out and faded, they retained yet a decidedly green hue. Tommy took one carefully between his fingers. At the same time, he released his grasp on the long stick to which just a moment ago he had been so attached, because now, faced with the enormity of a tree that was replete with live branches, the stick seemed dry and dead.

The leaf came loose right away. He stroked the green surface with his fingertip and turned the leaf upside-down. He could see how it clearly had a back and a front, and how the green colour on the front was brighter than on the back. Pinching the leaf between his thumb and index finger in a tweezer-like grip, he held it up to the sun, closed one eye and saw with the other how the light filtered through the green surface, which resembled a thin fabric. The leaves grew in clusters on long stems, like small families. He broke off an entire stem and counted them. Nine leaves in all.

Then he walked down along the shore and squatted beside the trunk. He rested his hand against the greyish bark. It was gnarled and hard. He stroked it carefully, back and forth.

'Nice tree,' he said.

Afterwards he pressed his nose cautiously against the trunk, inhaling the scent.

'Bark,' he said to himself. 'That's how bark smells.'

Again, he got to his feet and took a step away from the tree to get a better look at the whole of it. He had seen pictures of trees and forests many times and he knew that trees came in all sizes. His grandmother had told him that the largest trees in the world had once grown in a place called California, mammoth trees that could live for more than four thousand years and grow to more than 100 metres tall.

Tommy knew that two of his steps combined made up a metre, so he hurried all the way to the top of the tree and started measuring.

It was difficult. He struggled to remember that each step was a half metre, rather than a full one. He counted aloud to keep it straight but got the numbers mixed up and had to start over again several times. But finally, he thought he knew how tall the tree was.

'Twenty-three metres,' he said. 'A tree has come to Svalbard that is twenty-three metres long.'

His head was buzzing from all the counting. He thought he should find Grandmother, because when something important happened in Svalbard, Grandmother was the one who knew best what to do. But first he needed to rest, so he lay down beside the tree, putting his left arm around the trunk. He found a relatively comfortable spot on the stony ground; he could feel the pressure of the trunk against the inside of his upper arm. He had no plan for how long he would lie this way, since he didn't know how to tell the time and there was nobody waiting for him – at least, nobody he could think of. And his relationship to time was still pretty abstract. Time was something that passed when he did something. And now he wasn't doing anything. He just lay there, while the sun shone as strongly as it always did this time of year, and he thought about the tree, about the trunk, about the leaves and about how tired he was.

And then he fell asleep.

The frail body of a child with his arms around a tree, on a black, rocky beach. There was a faint breeze and the wind whipped the water into small, steep waves topped with a delicate lace of white bubbles. Dark water broke against tall rock walls where recent landslides had created gashes in thin layers of vegetation. Small bushes grew on the lowlands, along with grass and hay, and pink and yellow veils of tiny flowers draped the slopes facing south. Seagulls soared above him, flying from the valley towards the fjord, and disappearing into the distance, in the direction of the bird cliffs. But the child saw none of this; he was fast asleep.

He was woken with a start by the sound of a girl's voice calling loudly.

'Tommy?' The voice sounded anxious, at its wits' end. 'Hello? Are you sleeping?'

He sat up and at first he didn't understand where he was. Then he turned his head and saw the chaos of branches around him. His body felt stiff and his arm was sore from embracing the trunk.

'Tommy, what are you doing?'

He turned around and stared straight at Rakel. She was standing a short distance away, with her hands on her hips, her head tilted and an expression of astonishment on her face. They were the same age but she was a head taller than him. She was thin and erect, with bony shoulders and hair that often looked greasy, at least since both her parents had been killed by a landslide not long ago. Now she came running towards him. Charcoal-coloured sediment and stones shifted beneath her feet, but Rakel didn't notice, because she moved lithely, almost silently, as if she weren't really in contact with the ground.

She stopped and stared. 'Did we get a tree? It's huge!'

Tommy climbed to his feet and stood protectively in front of the tree. 'I found it.'

'Yes, but it's not yours!'

She gave him a little shove. He could feel the strength in her hand, but planted his feet firmly on the ground, unwilling to budge.

'I found it,' he repeated.

Her eyes narrowed then, the curiosity and joy vanished.

'So, it's your tree, all yours?'

He nodded.

'And you hugged it,' she said slowly and now her voice was hard and teasing.

'I did not!'

'Yes,' she said more loudly. 'Tommy hugged a tree! Tommy hugged a tree!'

She started to sing *Tommy hugged a tree* in a jeering tune, as if she were singing about how he had kissed someone. Or wet himself.

'No, I didn't hug it,' he said. 'That's not what I was doing.'

But she just kept going: 'Tommy hugged a tree! Tommy hugged a tree!'

His heart pounded angrily and the anger expanded like branches through his body.

'No,' he said, his voice lower now.

'But I saw you doing it,' Rakel said. 'I saw you!'

'No!' Tommy said.

Rakel turned to face the tree, looking it over. 'And it's not a real tree even, it's as dead as dust, you can see that.'

He turned to face the tree as well, and now it seemed sort of more pitiful where it lay. The green colour was pale. Many of the leaves had already fallen off the branches and blown away.

Rakel moved closer, kicked at his tree, and as it trembled even more leaves fell off. 'You know you will never get to see a real tree, Tommy. Svalbard kid.'

She said it softly, sort of indifferently.

And then she walked all the way over to him.

'It's not alive,' she said into his face, so close that he could smell her breath, which was surprisingly sweet. 'It's just a corpse. Your tree is every bit as dead as the people they burn up in the cremation oven!'

His feet wanted to run away, but his hands wanted something else.

He raised one and struck her.

It was not a good punch. It was more like a thump.

But he meant to hit her. And she understood that. Rakel responded to the punch, or the thump, by thumping him back.

That was all it took. He lunged at her. He put his arms around her skinny girl body, as if he were hugging her, and waved one of his hands to grab hold of her bushy, black hair, while she reached for his face with ragged fingernails. She raked them down his cheek so hard that he heard a scratching sound.

'Stop it!' he howled. He released her and touched his cheek with his hand.

His fingertips were red.

He lunged at her again, thrashing, dragging, tugging, railing against her.

But she was quick and strong.

Although he didn't understand how she managed it, she knocked his legs out from under him. He fell to the ground, which was hard and stony.

'Ouch!'

Before he knew what was happening, she was straddled on top of him, and had grabbed his hands and pressed them to the ground above his head.

'You're creepy, Tommy.'

'No,' he said. 'No, I'm not.'

He snorted and tried to tear free of her grasp, but it was no use. She held him tightly in place and even though she was skinnier than he was, she was so heavy that he couldn't get her off him. He flailed his arms, kicked his legs, twisted his entire upper body, threw his head back and forth and howled.

And while he was lying there like that, he realised that he was not only distressed and furious, but that it was also nice, in a way. Nice to lose control, go wild, while she had him completely under control. Something inside him wanted it to continue.

But then Rakel was pulled off him by strong arms.

'Enough now,' said a voice Tommy knew well. 'That's enough!'

It was Grandmother. He caught a glimpse of her sparkling eyes under the brim of her knitted cap, of the dark fringe over her forehead, the green jacket she always wore. She was smaller than most other adults, but still the strongest person he knew.

Grandmother took hold of Rakel under her armpits and pulled her up. Then she hauled her grandson to his feet as well.

One of Rakel's cheeks was red; he must have hit her without noticing. He could feel blood running from both his nose and his cheek. Some of it found its way into his mouth and it tasted steely, metallic.

Grandmother glanced at Rakel first, then at Tommy. She slowly shook her head.

'Do you see the tree, Grandmother?' he said, and pointed behind him. 'A whole big tree.'

'Yes,' Grandmother said. 'I see it.'

But it seemed that she had not really seen it, because she took a few steps forward and her eyes widened.

'It's an ash tree,' she said, and walked all the way up to the tree to pluck off a leaf.

'It came from the ocean,' Tommy said.

'Yes,' Grandmother said. 'I assumed as much.'

She patted the tree trunk gently. 'It's been many years since I've seen something like this.' Then she turned towards the children. 'Was it the tree you were fighting about?'

'Yes,' Rakel said.

'No,' Tommy said.

'Yes, ma'am and no ma'am,' Grandmother said. 'Then we won't say another word about it.'

But afterwards, when they were walking home and Rakel had long since run away from grandmother and grandson, she had a few more words to say about it after all.

Grandmother's hand was thin and sinewy, but strong. She held Tommy's hand firmly in her own.

'I don't think you should fight with Rakel.'

'She said the tree was a corpse,' Tommy said. 'That it should be burned up in the cremation oven.'

'Rakel thinks about cremation ovens a lot.'

'She's dumb.'

'Maybe she was being dumb, but you must put up with it. From Rakel. You'll just have to put up with it, for now.'

'That's not fair.'

'No, it's not,' Grandmother said. 'But there are other things that are even more unfair.'

And then they walked on and he knew she was right. They would have to put up with a lot from Rakel right now.

Tommy
2110

'No! Stop!'

The ship is on a steady course headed west, towards the ocean. It is in the middle of the fjord, no larger than a toy boat against the backdrop of the mountains.

'Henry! Hilmar!'

It is moving at a solid clip. The hull covered with solar cells is pitching slightly, but it is stabilised by large, grey sails, which ensure that the boat cuts through the water on an even keel. The boat's windows are two narrow, dark strips, and the glass is covered with soot, so he can't see inside, can't get a look at the passengers.

'Come back! Turn around!'

Tommy stands on the shore, the water lapping around his feet. As he wades out, he can feel it seeping into his shoes, but pays it no mind and waves his arms.

'Please! Henry! Hilmar!'

But the ship moves steadily onwards and he would be but a tiny speck against the black beach. Even if he waves, jumps and screams, they will never notice him.

The waves of Isfjorden turn white, spreading across the

dark blue floor of water. The waves break against the cliffs in rhythmic collisions of water with land.

'Come back with my brothers!'

His voice is swallowed by the wind, but he keeps on calling all the same.

'Please, turn around, now, right now!'

The fog is rolling down from the mountain, misting over the fjord before him, and is about to engulf the ship. Soon the ship will disappear altogether and his brothers will be gone.

SvalSat, he thinks, turns around, tilts back his head and stares up at Platåberget Mountain. Up there, almost 500 metres above sea level, is the satellite station.

He starts to run, losing sight of the ship, and follows the road back along the fjord, passing the ruins of the Vestpynten lighthouse. He continues inland along Adventfjorden by Hotellneset peninsula. His heart is thudding in his ears, sweat is running down his back and his throat is burning. *They left without me, they left without me.*

Just after the disused airport, he finally reaches the fork in the road. One road leads towards Longyearbyen, the other towards the mountain.

The uphill route is agony. Every single stone is situated to work against him. Ten metres at a time, he thinks, just ten metres, while fixing his gaze on something directly in front of him to avoid looking at the top, which seems endlessly far away.

When he has finally scaled the summit, he stands doubled over, gasping for breath while keeping his eyes on the fjord. The fog has receded, but the ship is even smaller, no more than a white spot against the darkness of the fjord. It advances doggedly towards open sea.

Tommy turns towards the satellite station SvalSat. Ten

large antennas have been installed, scattered across a huge area on the mountain. The antennas are mounted on concrete bases and some of them are covered with tarps that gleam in white contrast to the brown and grey stone. They resemble enormous mushrooms in the landscape, alien elements that have pressed their way up through the ground, from spores spread by a UFO.

Many of the structures have been long since destroyed by the wind and weather, the tarps torn away or flapping in the wind. The remains resemble semi-mangled skeletons surrounding huge antenna discs.

He remembers how curious they were about the satellite station as children. Nobody was allowed to go up there, nobody was allowed to use the station. They told one another that the antennas on the mountain were magic mushrooms, and if you ate them, you would come into contact with another dimension. The satellite station was the portal to other people and other places.

But the place is most beautiful from a distance. There is nothing magical about the damaged rooftops, the rusty steel structures and the crumbling concrete.

He hurries over to the main building and tries to open the door, which is stuck, so he has to force it open. Then he runs through the filthy breakroom, where dilapidated sofas are pushed up against the walls and a cutlery drawer is hanging open. He continues into the corridor, and from there, into the control room. An empty semi-circle desk occupies half the floor space and huge computer screens hang on the walls. He checks the screen for the building's micro power plant and sees that it is on. The building has electricity. But he doesn't take the time to turn on the lights; in two bounds he is over by the door on the far side, which leads to a smaller control room. The radio equipment is there, the only communication equipment they have that still functions.

He digs through a pile of old notebooks on the table and finds a library book about shortwave radios. Rakel must have brought it up here.

The radio seems simple to use. It has power – a tiny bulb is emitting a green light. He pushes some buttons frantically, pulls on the headset.

'Tao!' he screams into the microphone before he has even got around to pressing the button. 'Tao, please, you have to turn around! You must come back!'

The only response is white noise, but he continues all the same. 'You have to turn around; you must bring my brothers back. Hilmar? Henry? And Runa! They're just children. You can't just take them with you. They belong up here, you can't just take them with you!'

He thinks he hears a sound on the other end. He clutches the microphone, notices that it is sweaty in his hand, tries to calm his voice, be an adult. 'Tao, listen to me now. You must turn around and come back right away.'

But nobody answers.

He pulls the chair out and puts the microphone down for a second to settle himself properly in his seat.

'Tao. The children are residents of Svalbard. They live here. With me.'

He hears nothing but a humming sound on the radio. And out there he knows that the ship is moving steadily forward, that it is headed for a completely different world, that the bow will soon meet the huge swells of the ocean.

Tommy winds the cord quickly around the index finger of one hand while clutching the microphone with the other.

'Come back with my family!'

The only response is silence. He is alone. Like the trap-per he was named after, stationed here in isolation for the winter. But the difference between him and all the trappers who came before him is that nobody will come for him in the spring, nobody will take the trouble to check on Tommy Mignotte, to see how he is doing.

He drops the microphone, pulls his feet up beneath him, and rests his head against his knees. The images of hundreds of memories of his brothers rush through his head. Finally, he finds peace in the very last one. His brothers in bed with their eyes closed; he poked his head in to check on them before he headed out to Bjørndalen. It was night-time. They were sleeping deeply. Henry on his side, curled up in a ball under the duvet, only his hair sticking out. Hilmar on his back with his arms behind his head, secure even while asleep. Tommy rests in the image: Hilmar, the calm, sleeping face of his little brother.

The first time Hilmar was placed in his arms, Tommy was so proud that he was shaking. He had yearned for a brother or sister for as long as he could remember. He knew no other only children, which made him involuntarily different, and when as an eight-year-old he learned that a brother was finally on the way, he started to cry. 'This is the most important event of my life,' he said gravely, and didn't notice his father turning away with a smile, or that Grandmother, half ironically, half proudly, mumbled, 'From what book did he pick up that phrase?'

Tommy followed his mother's pregnancy with great enthusiasm. Nine months turned out to be an unbelievably long time. He read books about pregnancy and at all times knew the size and developmental stage of the foetus. He studied pictures of life inside the womb with fascination. The placenta, the umbilical cord, the strange creature that increasingly resembled a human being and occupied increasingly more space. And he read about childbirth with huge eyes, about everything that could go wrong.

Hilmar was small and comely, while Tommy's hands were enormous against the tiny face, stubby and brutish, with dirty fingernails. Tommy had the feeling that his mother and father must find him repulsive. Compared to this soft, other-worldly creature, he was dirty, shabby and brutish. He started scrubbing his hands and combing his hair, but the feeling did not go away until his mother pulled him onto her lap one evening and hugged him for a long, long time without saying a word.

It also helped that after just a few days Hilmar began to demonstrate that he absolutely did not come from another planet but was decidedly of this earth. The nappies stank of sulphur. He peed uncontrollably while on the changing table. And the tiny body was capable of roaring so loudly that even Platåberget Mountain seemed at risk of tumbling down. But neither the roars, the nappies, nor the fear that his parents no longer cared for him caused Tommy to dislike his little brother. Because Tommy thought Hilmar *too* was worthy of love and he immediately felt a sense of ownership for the little one: the teeny-tiny fingers, the barely visible eyelashes, the wisps of hair on the nape of his neck, and the almost bald baby skull with its worrisome soft spot that at all times had to be protected from impact. And that everyone talked about how alike they were. My brother, Tommy often thought, you are like me. Yet the fact that they resembled one another did not make his love for his brother simple – it made it annoying, messy, ambivalent.

Once, when Hilmar was around one year old, Tommy was sitting in the living room waiting for his mother. It was the dark period of midwinter, and she was going to read to him. She used to read to Tommy every night after Hilmar had been put to bed, because during the winter they had plenty of time. It was their time, Mummy and Tommy's, on the sofa, without interruptions. But on this evening, she didn't come. At first, Tommy didn't mind. He was busy reading a dog-eared Donald Duck comic book, carefully turning the pages so they wouldn't be ruined.

'Mummy,' he called. 'Are you coming?'

No reply.

'Mummy!' Finally, he got up off the sofa and went out into the hallway.

The door to Hilmar's bedroom was ajar. The lamp on the bedside table in the room emanated a faint glow.

He pushed the door open and there he saw them. They were both asleep, lying curled up against one another. His mother lay on her side, with her face near Hilmar's head, as if she had been snuggling with him until the moment she fell asleep.

Tommy threw open the door and marched into the room. 'Mummy!'

He gave her a push, with all his strength, as hard as he could. 'MUMMY!'

His mother awoke with a start. Sat up, stared at him, at first confused, then furious.

'Tommy, hush!' she hissed between pinched lips.

But it was too late, Hilmar's soft, little body squirmed, he opened the two round eyes that everyone, Tommy included, found so 'lovely' and started to howl.

'Tommy!' his mother said, and she wasn't hissing any longer, she was shouting.

And he saw right away how upset and angry and tired she was, with dark circles under her eyes, and her skin as pale as it becomes only after the sun has been away for many months.

Tommy knew that she struggled to get Hilmar to fall asleep. He knew that his little brother cried during the night. He knew that the darkness confused Hilmar, and he had seen signs that it had got worse lately because, unlike before, Mummy could only bring herself to read one chapter every night, no more.

No chapters were read on this evening. She ended up walking back and forth in the bedroom lulling Hilmar to sleep until it was too late.

Little brat, Tommy thought, while at the same time he

wished he could be the one to carry him around and press his nose into his soft cheeks.

Little brat, get lost, he shouted at Hilmar every time he came to his door.

Eventually, he no longer needed to say it. Hilmar bolted away from his big brother's bedroom as if the mere sight of the door sent him scurrying.

When Hilmar started putting words together to form sentences, some of the first words he learned were these: Get lost. He stood by the doorway to Tommy's room and peeked in and even if Tommy wasn't in there, Hilmar would still shake his head and say these words softly to himself: Get lost. And then he waddled away, his nappy swaying.

Hilmar loved cucumbers but hated tomatoes. He explained to Tommy once that it was the runny part in the middle that was icky, and the seeds, yuck. Had the tomato been only the flesh around the middle, he would have willingly eaten the vegetable. It's a berry, Tommy said. What, Hilmar said. Tomatoes are not vegetables, they're berries. Sometimes Grandmother, who did not want to waste a single ounce of the precious food from the greenhouse, scraped off the seeds for him, ate them herself, and chopped the flesh up into pieces. Then Tommy laughed at him. When Hilmar was older, he tried to eat a whole tomato. His eyes narrowed and he swallowed it down as fast as he could, his gaze at all times fixed on his big brother. Did he see what he did? Did Tommy see what a big boy he was? Yes, he'd seen, but he didn't say anything.

Later Tommy hoped that Hilmar didn't remember any of this, even though he eventually learned from the psychology books he read at the library that bad experiences would become engraved in a child's mind like the grooves carved out of a hill by a landslide. Nothing would grow in these grooves, not for many years. But Tommy was just his brother. How dangerous could it be when it was a big brother who was responsible for the bad experiences?

Besides, Hilmar possessed great inner strength. He talked a great deal about their mother and Tommy thinks that he continued to carry her protectiveness within him. Everything rolled off Hilmar's back, like the raindrops on the yellow sou'wester he wore. On the rare occasion when Tommy screamed at him, Hilmar would tilt his head to one side and simply observe his teenage brother. It was as if he understood that hormones were raging inside him and was secure in the knowledge that it would soon pass.

'It's puberty,' he heard Hilmar say to Grandmother once. 'I look forward to the day when puberty comes to an end.'

At school, his brother was level-headed, talkative, happy. Hilmar is popular, Tommy thought, and he felt a jab of envy. And then he felt ashamed because Hilmar was not just popular; he was kind to everyone.

Hilmar's laughter, Tommy can still hear it, his lingering chuckle. He remembers Hilmar in the sou'wester on a rainy day. He had stopped on the way to school because Tommy had told him a joke. He has long since forgotten the punchline, but he remembers Hilmar's laughter and how several passers-by had stopped and laughed along with him. The sound was a sun in the light beneath the yellow sou'wester.

The echo of his laughter reverberates inside him.

Tommy lifts his head. He doesn't know how long he has been sitting like this in front of the shortwave radio, but he thinks it has grown darker outside. He runs out, looks towards the ocean. Fog is creeping in towards shore. The ship is gone.

Then he walks back, sits down again. Yet again he grasps the microphone, holds the button down, trying to breathe calmly.

'Mayday, mayday,' he says. 'Can anyone hear me?'

No ship can refuse to respond to a distress call, he has read, everyone out there has a duty to answer. That is at least how it was in the old days. He knows that only Tao's vessel is sailing in these waters, the sole ship in this maritime region for fifty years.

'Mayday, mayday, mayday. My name is Tommy Mignotte, and I have been left alone on Spitsbergen. My position is ...' He gets to his feet and checks the faded coordinates posted on the wall. 'Seventy-eight degrees north, fifteen degrees east. Mayday, mayday, mayday.'

He keeps saying the same words, over and over again.

Mayday, mayday, mayday.

Tommy Mignotte.

Alone on Spitsbergen.

And finally, he hears a crackling sound.

78° north, 15° east.

And then a click.

Mayday, mayday, mayday.

'Tommy! We hear you.' He leans heavily against the desk, feeling dizzy, and then collapses into the chair as waves of relief billow through his body.

He fumbles for the words. 'Tao, do you hear me, are you there ...?'

'We can hear you just fine,' she says, amicably, the way she always is. Always friendly, even now when she has taken his brothers with her. 'We hear you loud and clear. I hope you haven't been trying to contact us for a long time? We have just turned on the radio.'

He straightens up in his seat, gets control over his voice. 'I was in Bjørndalen when I saw the ship,' he says. 'I didn't think you were just going to leave. Tao, you have to turn around. Right now. Henry, Hilmar and Runa belong here on Spitsbergen, you can't just take them with you.'

'Is Rakel with you, Tommy? Can I talk to Rakel, too?'

His heartbeat accelerates. 'Tao, tell the captain that she must turn the ship around right this minute!'

There is a momentary silence.

He squeezes the microphone in his hand and leans towards the radio, as if this would enable him to hear some of the conversation on the other end.

Then Tao is back. 'Tommy, listen to me. The captain and I have talked. Mei-Ling is sitting here beside me. And, Tommy, she says it's not possible. I am so sorry. It's too late to turn around.'

'What!'

'The days are cold, the nights even worse. Even though the geographical pole has been without snow cover all summer, there is still a risk of it freezing over. We are afraid there will be ice floes in the water, Tommy. The vessel is not built to withstand hard collisions.'

'There aren't any ice floes so early in the year, certainly? And aren't you headed south? Listen to me, you have plenty of time to turn around.'

He hears a muffled, intense discussion on the other end, but can't make out the words. Finally, she is back.

'Listen, Tommy, we're sorry. But our departure was already delayed by many days, you know that, because we were waiting for you and Rakel. And it's not just the Barents Sea that worries Mei-Ling. It's the whole journey through former Russia and Kazakhstan. We spent almost a month on the trip here, the mountainous regions are hazardous. We must get home before the storms start in the mountains.'

'But what about Henry and . . .?'

'Henry, Hilmar and Runa are fine here on board. We will take good care of them.'

Tommy has got to his feet, he wants to rip the line to shreds, throw the radio onto the floor, but forces himself to keep his voice calm.

'What are the children doing now, how are they?'

'They've gone to bed. They're asleep. I can wake them up if you want to hear their voices. But it took a long time for Henry to fall asleep. He needs a little quiet time in the evenings.'

There is something presumptuous in her tone of voice, as if she were an expert on his brother.

'You can't talk about Henry like that.'

'What do you mean?'

'You don't know anything about my brothers.'

'Tommy . . .'

'Who do you think you are, really, just showing up here and taking three children?'

'Who do I think I am? Who are we?' She is speaking more softly now. 'You are the one who called us. Promised us the seed vault. We travelled halfway around the world to find you. Then you and Rakel ran away. Took off.'

'We didn't take off. That's not what happened.'

'I was left with three children. But no seeds. Four days went by, each day colder than the last. What was I supposed to do?'

'We didn't take off,' he says again.

'But where were you all that time then, Tommy, what happened?'

Her voice is gentler now, full of quasi-concern. He does not reply. She doesn't understand anything anyway.

'Were you at SvalSat the whole time? We went up there looking for you.'

'No,' he says. 'I was here and there. Mostly in Bjørndalen. Grandmother has an old cabin out there.'

'You and Rakel?'

'Yes. Yes, Rakel and I. She is still in Bjørndalen.'

'But why did you run away?'

'We didn't run away.'

He hasn't thought this through, doesn't know what to say, racks his brains for a good explanation. And finally believes that he finds one.

'We were looking for the seeds.'

'Oh?' Tao says.

He wishes that he could see her, doesn't know whether her brief reply is concealing interest or distrust.

'Tommy,' she says softly. 'Since you haven't said so yet, I assume you didn't find them?'

Is that all it would take? If he tells her what she wants to hear, would they turn around then? Would he get Henry and Hilmar back?

He sits down again, his body heavy against the chair. 'Would you come back? If . . .' he says, 'if we found the seeds or traces of them?'

There is silence on the other end. She clears her throat softly. 'Do you really know anything about the seeds?'

He places his free hand against his forehead, pressing his fingers against his skull so hard that it hurts.

'Tommy, are the seeds safe? Do you know where they are?'

I'm the thread, he thinks, the thread holding everything together.

He just has to pull himself together, the way he has always done.

He straightens up.

'No,' he exclaims. 'It was just something I said. We found no sign of them. The seeds were no doubt destroyed a long time ago.'

He hears her sigh in frustration. She has no idea what he's thinking.

He is the one in control and if he can just get his brothers back, they can go on as before, the four of them, all alone here in Longyearbyen. They don't need anyone else.

But Tao keeps talking to him, in her warm, gentle voice. She tells him they will find a solution together, that they will help him and Rakel, in one way or another they will manage to help.

No. To hell with her. He holds the microphone up against his mouth and speaks softly but clearly. 'We don't need help. You're right. It's late. I have to go. I have to get down to Longyearbyen before dark.'

'But, buddy, when will you be there again?'

'I'm not your buddy.'

'Can you contact me tomorrow again,' she asks. 'Tomorrow at ... five o'clock?'

'We'll see,' he says.

'Tommy, I'm here,' Tao says. 'I'll be waiting for your call tomorrow.'

Tao

The line goes dead. He is no longer there. Tao places the radio mike in its cradle and turns to Mei-Ling, who has been pacing the deck and listening to the entire conversation.

The first mate is waiting for them outside the wheelhouse. 'Finished?'

Mei-Ling nods to him.

'You can switch to manual.'

The first mate goes inside, and through the window Tao can see him switch off the autopilot and take the wheel.

Mei-Ling shudders against the cold and looks dejectedly at Tao.

'What he said about the seeds, what do you think?'

'I don't know.'

'You understand that it's just desperation over being left behind up there? We can't turn around, no matter what he says.'

'But they left to search for the seeds. Why would they otherwise abandon their siblings?'

'He's lying,' Mei-Ling says. 'He's been lying all along, just like Rakel. She hadn't even seen the seeds but promised us them all the same. Without knowing whether they existed.'

'You're forgetting how much they've been through.'

'No. That's exactly what I mean. They've experienced too much pain, too early in life. And are both equally confused.'

Mei-Ling stares vacantly out into space for a moment. Then she sighs heavily. 'That we even started all of this –' she waves her arms '– this expedition was madness. Driven by desperation. And now we are headed home from our great journey, and all we have to show for it are three orphans.'

Tao knows that Mei-Ling is right. But a strong tremor of uncertainty is buzzing inside her. She doesn't want to believe that it will end like this. And she doesn't understand why Tommy and Rakel ran away from them. She was never sure about what Tommy was up to but believed that Rakel at least was honest.

At the same time, there was an air of desperation about Rakel. She reminded Tao of the homeless teenagers who had attacked her once in Beijing, the teenagers who had lost everything and were willing to do anything, even commit the most inhumane acts, to survive. Tao doesn't know if those teenagers are still alive today. But *if* they are alive, the seed bank would be the salvation, both for them and for all their siblings: rippling, yellow wheat fields, grain, corn, rice, soybeans.

Svalbard is no more than a faint shadow on the horizon, virtually lost in the clouds. Otherwise, the sun is shining.

The cook sticks his head through the doorway and calls for Mei-Ling. The captain disappears below deck, and left alone, Tao walks over to the railing. She turns her face towards the ball of fire in the sky, which shines without warmth.

The sun was shining on the ocean as they approached Spitsbergen, as well. That was just eleven days ago, though it seems longer.

The first sign of land was a bird, white against a blue sky, a seagull, the likes of which she had never seen before. They were standing by the railing, she and the captain. Mei-Ling lifted a finger without saying a word and gestured towards something in the sky. Tao looked where the finger was pointing, found the seagull and steadied her gaze on it. Mei-Ling, who usually chattered away loudly and at length, for once was silent.

Dense clouds hung above Spitsbergen. The ship moved into the whiteness. The bird disappeared into the distance before them, as if someone had erased it with a rubber. And then the mountains emerged through heavy layers of fog. At first Tao thought that the high cliffs were even more clouds, but then she noticed formations that could not be anything but land.

Tao had lost count of the days spent on the ship, how many days it had been since they bunkered food and water in the almost deserted harbour in Archangel. The midnight sun played tricks on her; the hours passed in fits and starts. Sometimes she would stand in front of the old-fashioned wall clock in the mess room and wonder whether it was morning or night. She slept when she was tired, ate when she was hungry. She tried to read – the ship had an abundant library – but she often sat staring into space, waiting. She tried to ignore how fervently she hoped this journey would be a success, wanted to rid herself of the heavy burden of expectations from Li Chiara, the leader of the Committee, and from all the people back home.

They had left Sichuan on a gossamer summer day. Children waved flags and gave them flowers. Li Chiara squeezed Tao's hand in her own and tied a new, red scarf around her neck. A symbol of excellence. 'You will earn this,' she said softly to Tao, and then smiled brightly at all those in attendance and waved with a flat hand.

The ocean had helped Tao keep the expectations at bay. Life out there was one big *nothing*. The ocean and the sky, everything in movement, the clouds above them, the water beneath the keel, the ship gliding forward at all times, pounding against swells and drawn by the wind. The horizon was the only stable point, the only place to settle one's gaze.

But now the mountains were there, a palliative for the eyes. And the first thing Tao felt was a sense of relief over the change, an end to the monotony. Then they drew closer and the brutality of the landscape frightened her. Svalbard was a wall of stone. While on the ocean the size of the ship was relative, small when the waves rose high above them, large and heavy when the ocean was flat, the mountains caused it to shrink. It was as if the vessel's true dimensions emerged. The ship was not much larger than the toy boat Wei-Wen had once played with in the bathtub.

She lifted her head, gazed up towards the mountaintops. They had to be at least a thousand metres high.

The ship glided silently forward and a wide fjord appeared from between rock massifs. Tao turned to face the wheelhouse, where she saw the first mate change over to starboard, and soon his movement was transmitted down through the helm, which then altered the vessel's course by many degrees.

As they moved inland on the fjord, the swells ebbed away. The wind was blowing gently, churning up the water into small, sharp waves, but the further inland they sailed, the calmer it was.

The trip took several hours and Tao remained seated on deck. She was unable to take her eyes off the landscape, as ever more details came into view. What she had initially thought was bare rock proved to be overlain with a thin layer of vegetation. Undulating textures of brown, grey and green covered the mountainsides.

The ship sailed past an iridescent green area on the port side where the steep mountain slopes were teeming with life. This must be the home of the seagulls. The birds took flight and landed according to a system only they understood. They flew towards the sea, dived for fish and surfaced anew with their beaks full. Up there, in the bird cliff, there had to be thousands of nests in which tiny beaks reached towards the sky, instinctively, because the only two movements the small, down-covered creatures had learned was to tilt back their heads and open their beaks.

Soon the ship had passed the cliff and the vegetation became less bright green. There was less that was life sustaining here than under the bird cliff. But in some areas along the shore she could still see bushes, grass and hay.

Yet again they steered starboard and now it was Adventfjorden which lay before them. Tao had been studying the map again yesterday, trying to create a mental image of their destination, but there was nothing that could have prepared her for this. She got to her feet again and went to stand by the railing.

Mei-Ling came back and stood with her legs straddled even though the water was calm. She always stood like that, with her feet solidly planted on deck, far apart.

'Prosaic,' she observed and studied the landscape through a pair of binoculars hanging from a strap around her neck. 'Quite scruffy, actually.'

Tao smiled.

'But frightening,' Mei-Ling said, and shuddered. 'Not a single tree. There is nowhere to hide here.'

They saw more signs of human habitation now. Small

cabins along the fjord, most of them completely destroyed by
the wind and weather. Subsequently, a collapsed air traffic
control tower, and the remains of the tarmac that once upon
a time had been an airstrip.

Suddenly Mei-Ling laughed in surprise.

She handed Tao the binoculars. The strap was so short that
they had to stand with their heads close together.

'Do you see that?'

'Where? No?'

But then, behind the airfield, it appeared, a strange concrete structure on the hillside.

'Yes!'

A narrow grey roof. Solid edges. A damaged ornament
sparkled above the front door.

Tao had studied old photos of the vault, the facade of which
had once been radiant. An artwork of glass and light had
covered both the roof and the visible short wall. The building
was actually just a single doorway. Behind it a long tunnel
ran into the mountain and inside there were three storage
rooms. Long rows of shelves, all of them full of crates. In these
crates were the seeds, meticulously harvested from all over
the world, dried and placed in paper bags, a crate for each
country, containing its genetic materials. Seeds from plants
the world had forgotten, which the Anthropocene, the epoch
of human impact on the earth's ecosystems, had long since
obliterated.

In Tao's world, only the genetically manipulated generalists remained. But the origin lay in the vault. The seeds in
there would make it possible to turn back time, create the
agricultural diversity the human race had once had, find
specialised food plants suitable for all conditions, plants that
thrived in heat, drought, cold or damp and would tolerate

the current conditions of the world. It was the diversity that would save them, which would provide food for all those who were starving.

'Imagine. It's still standing,' Mei-Ling said. 'Who would have believed it.'

'Not you, at any rate,' Tao said and laughed with relief.

Nobody had thought that the seeds could still exist. The human race had had more than enough on its hands trying to survive all these years that had passed since the Collapse. Nobody had taken the time to check, nobody had thought it worth the trouble, since Svalbard had been out of touch with the world for so many years, in isolation. The seeds had been forgotten or written off. Until the children had contacted them.

'You were right,' Mei-Ling said. 'Now we'll find the children and empty the vault. I will give us two days up here, then we'll set our course south so we bloody well make it home again before the winter sets in.'

Tommy

He walks inland towards the village, passing old warehouses that have been invaded by seagulls. They are perching in all the windows. The building facades are mottled with their droppings and the gulls fly back and forth bringing food for their offspring. The autumn twilight descending slowly upon the landscape still feels unfamiliar. The sudden arrival of darkness every year continues to catch him by surprise.

He is not carrying anything, is returning every bit as empty handed as when he took off in the middle of the night four days ago.

The village that greets him is also deserted.

Tommy has always had the impression that Longyearbyen offers resistance to Svalbard's landscape. The buildings provide something upon which to train one's gaze and the people's movements counteract the stolidness of the rocky terrain. The buildings show signs of the battle they are waging at all times against the forces of nature. The boards are grey-washed from the wind and weather, some of the buildings in a state of collapse where the unstable foundation beneath them has crumbled. Old roads wind between the buildings, but they are all overgrown with green grass. Here and there, amidst all the buildings which nature has long since made its own, are houses that have been preserved. Damage and wear and tear have been repaired with patchworks of wooden cladding and driftwood. And everywhere traces of human life can be found. An abandoned planter crate, dried fish hanging under the eaves, a bicycle and a sled. In some places, curtains in the windows, paintings on the walls, knick-knacks and books can be seen.

But these signs of human habitation are now nothing more than artefacts. The emptiness has crept into the city to stay, the houses mere shells, abandoned snail's houses on a huge beach that will soon be washed away by the ocean. And with every snail's house that Tommy passes, emptiness oozes out of the shell, like invisible smoke, and penetrates his flesh, occupying his blood vessels.

Don't think, just walk, make it home.

When he opens the door, he realises how hungry he is. Dried meat is still hanging from the ceiling in the pantry and, in a basket, he finds a lone carrot.

He eats standing up. The sound of his teeth crunching on the carrot is deafening. The morsels have a difficult time finding their way down his throat. It feels like they will get stuck there, choke him. The *Heimlich manoeuvre*, he thinks. But if something were to lodge in his throat, there is nobody here to put their arms around him and force it up again.

After he has finished eating, he opens the door to the bathroom. The sight of his reflection in the mirror startles him. His face is dark with filth, with dirt and congealed clay. He looks down at his hands; they are just as filthy and full of scrapes and cuts. He peels off his clothes, leaving them in a pile on the floor, but he doesn't have the strength to wash. He drinks a glass of water and goes into his room, falls down on the bed, pulls the duvet over him and closes his eyes.

Sleep is a pit into which he disappears. Here there is not a streak of light, only the mountain's eternal darkness and dormancy.

He is woken by a voice. It is speaking to him, loudly, a voice unfamiliar, hoarse and deep. He sits up in bed, and for a few seconds thinks there is someone in the room, but then he understands that he's alone and it was his own voice he'd heard. But what he'd said, he can't remember.

It is so quiet. He tries to hum a few bars, 'Are You Sleeping, Brother John?', the song he used to sing for Henry. But the sounds his vocal cords press out are too feeble, they don't fill the room. He shakes his head – what are you doing, get it together. He goes into the bathroom, fills the sink with water, wrings out a washcloth and wipes off his face and body with decisive movements. He closes his eyes, wishing somebody else was holding the washcloth, that somebody else was touching him. Pull yourself together. He forces himself to open his eyes, throws the washcloth into the sink and leaves it there until it is soaked with water. He then wrings it out again so it may carry out its task. It is just a washcloth, I'm the one controlling it, it's just a washcloth.

His mother used to bathe him. She would put the washcloth in water that was so hot it was steaming. He never understood how she could bear to stick her fingers in it, but she always waved the washcloth to cool it before wiping his face.

She knitted the washcloths herself. Every evening she sat at her end of the sofa, her fingers moving quickly back and forth while the ball of wool at her feet steadily shrank and the garment in her lap grew.

Mother with the white, toy rabbit she is knitting in her hands. Her hands work quickly, she must finish in time, because her tummy is large and the baby is coming soon. But when Tommy goes over to her, she puts her knitting aside anyway.

'Come here,' she says. 'Come up on my lap.'

'There's no room,' he says.

'Yes, there is, there's always room for Tommy-boy.'

She lied. Because the place on her lap disappeared when she did.

He has always felt that he was missing something. Ever since Mother died, he has known what longing is. But longing isn't dangerous, he thinks, longing is just a feeling, just thoughts, electric signals in the brain.

Or a dolphin singing, vibrating notes that travel 50, 60 kilometres underwater, penetrating through everything.

No. Forget the dolphin. Tommy wrings out the washcloth, hangs it on the peg, takes out clean clothes, tugs a wool undershirt and jumper down over his head, pulls on long underwear and trousers, and walks into his brothers' room.

Their clothes are gone. The books, Henry's wooden horses and Hilmar's broken Legos. He pulls off the duvets. At the foot of Hilmar's bed, he finds one lone wool sock. That's all.

They were so enthusiastic when they were packing. Rakel started on the very afternoon they received word the foreigners were on their way. She laid her clothes out on her bed, looked them over, assessing, lifting every single garment, sort of weighing each one. Would it be good enough for the new country?

Henry stuffed toys into his father's old backpack. He helped himself from the neighbouring houses. Unlike Rakel, he was wholly without inhibitions. Only a few wooden toys were still whole, otherwise most of what he had found was hundred-year-old plastic.

'Are you sure you want to bring all of that?' Tommy asked as Henry shoved yet another broken toy car into the backpack.

'What if they don't have toys where we're going?' Henry said gravely. 'I might run out.'

'I don't think that will happen for some time,' Tommy said.

'You never know,' Henry said. 'Aren't you going to pack?'

'There's no rush,' Tommy said.

'No? Are you sure?'

His little brother peered up at him, knitting his brows.

He can see every detail in the tiny face.

Henry.

The dolphin sings, invisible in the depths below, and glides forward, casting a dark shadow across the seabed and pressing his song out with such force that it is impossible to ignore. Tommy sits on the edge of the bed, wants to sleep, but is wide awake, alert. It's just a sense of longing, he repeats to himself. I am used to longing.

When his mother was still alive, family life was full of frivolous things, of dancing in the living room, of guests around the kitchen table, of his father's nimble fingers on the guitar strings or on Tommy's stomach when he tickled him.

His father, David, was easy-going back then, quite adventurous. He found expression for his creativity in the kitchen. He often got in over his head, making ambitious plans. He could carry on for hours, rattling the pots in frustration, but then he would beam with pride when the meal was finally on the table.

Life was full of outings, expeditions solely for pleasure. Trips out on the boat at night, in October, when the weather had become cold and dark, just to see the reflection of the moon in the water and the marine phosphorescence flickering around the oars. Trips on foot up towards the glaciers, or under the ice, to see the caves the rivers had created there. Ski trips in the bright March sunshine when the snow cover was thick, gliding calmly forward and basking in the small shock of the sun's rays waking the body from its hibernation.

Life was filled with his mother. He remembers how she held him close under the Northern Lights. He was afraid of the green waves in the sky above him. They produce so much light, he said to his mother, how can they be so silent when they are making so much light?

Once upon a time, the Northern Lights, *aurora borealis*, had been feared. The light was the souls of the dead, it was said, and should not be spoken about. If one sang beneath the Northern Lights, they would see you, reach down, twine their shimmering arms around you and pull you up into the sky. Don't whistle, Tommy whispered. We must remember to be completely silent. Yes, we must, his mother whispered back, and remember I will always take care of you.

Some memories shine with a particularly strong light. Father waking him, late at night. Tommy was in a daze, and tired in the way one is after having just slipped into a deep slumber, but his father tousled his hair gently until he awoke.

'There's something I want to show you,' Father said.

For weeks there had been heavy rain and fog, but in the past few days the temperature had dropped below freezing and they had had clear days of sun and frost. Ice formed on the mud puddles, thin frozen water paintings, which the children made sure to stomp to pieces as soon as they discovered them, for the sheer joy of hearing the sound of the ice crunching under their feet.

Tommy sat up in bed.

'I was about to turn in,' Father said. 'But then I discovered that it had started to snow and thought you would want to see it.'

Tommy got out of bed, went over to the window and pulled back the curtains. It was pitch dark outside, but in the light from the living room windows Tommy could see that the ground was white. The family lived in Gruvedalen, the most landslide-safe area in Longyearbyen, in an old, terraced house with crooked walls that shifted to accommodate the unstable ground on which the house was built.

But now the ground was frozen and silent.

Tommy turned around and looked at his father, who was smiling.

'Are you thinking what I'm thinking?'

'I don't know,' Tommy said. 'What are you thinking?'

'That we should go outside,' his father said. 'And see whether the snow is any good?'

'Yes,' Tommy said. 'I think so too.'

'But look at you,' Father said. 'You're wearing nothing but your pyjamas. Come with me.'

His father lifted him up in his arms. Tommy was actually too big to be carried, but his father carried him all the same, down the hallway and over to the hooks where they hung outdoor garments.

'Look at this.' He held up the old snowmobile suit he usually wore when it was really cold. It was patched, but clean and warm.

His father pulled the suit onto his body. It was so big that he was almost unable to move. Tommy sneezed.

'Hush,' Father said, chuckling, and held his index finger to his lips. 'Mother's sleeping.'

Father pulled on ski trousers and his heavy jacket. He dug

out gloves and hats for them and then they opened the door carefully and went outside.

Tommy's eyes slowly adjusted to the darkness. He stood still, trying to make out his surroundings.

Then he walked down the stairs and out into the snow, towards the yellow square of light from the living room window. His gaze came to rest on the ground, on his own footprints in the snow. The snow crystals were light and dry, the snow almost weightless. With every movement he made, small clouds rose into the air, mingling with the snowflakes falling to the ground.

'Shall we make snow angels?' his father asked, walking over to stand in the middle of the yellow square of light.

'Mm-hm,' Tommy said and dropped down into the snow.

His father lay down beside him. They flapped their arms and legs a few times and then climbed to their feet.

Tommy and his father considered the impressions in the snow. One small, and one large.

'We managed to make them almost perfect,' Tommy said.

'Yes,' his father said. 'We didn't trample on them at all.'

'It looks like they are inside the house,' Tommy said.

'How so?' his father asked.

'Look.'

Tommy pointed out how each of the angels was situated in its own respective square of light on the ground.

'They're inside looking out at us.'

'What do they see, then?'

'You and me, of course.'

'Yes. You're right. You and me.'

This father, the one he was on this particular night, also disappeared when Mother died.

His mother passed away when Henry came into the world. The third son lay twisted in the birth canal, unwilling to emerge. His mother pushed, and Berit, who was both a midwife and a doctor and whom they all trusted, pushed. When nothing helped, she tried to perform a caesarean section.

Afterwards, nobody sat down with Tommy to talk to him about what had happened, but he understood there had been a lot of blood and that no human being could survive losing as much blood as his mother had done. She was not the first Svalbard woman whose life had ended in this way. He later came to understand that this was one of the local government's greatest ethical challenges. Svalbard needed to increase its population, but giving birth was so dangerous that there was always a risk of the loss of human life, either the mother or the child, if not both, in the process.

There are many children's graves in the cemetery, gravestones on which the date of birth and death are the same. The gravestones seem so dependable, appear so innocent, as they stand watch over the piles of gravel covering the urns. His mother is also buried in the cemetery. Tommy has never gone to see her grave; his memory of her has nothing to do with the moss-covered stone. The person she was remains in his hands, in his body, a warm pressure against his stomach, where she once embraced him, a sensation on his cheek from her kisses, a faint echo of her voice in his ears and a shadow of a scent in his nostrils. Her presence remains like a feeling in his heart, of security, of unconditional love, of belonging together.

More than fifty years ago, Longyearbyen had had a proper hospital, with anaesthesiology equipment, antibiotics, painkillers, blood pressure cuffs, an ultrasound, catheters, defibrillators. When Harry was born, the available equipment consisted of knives, boiled water for sterilisation and liquor to numb the pain. But most illnesses couldn't be cured by hunting knives, melted snow and moonshine. Blood poisoning, for example, sepsis or pneumonia. Cancer. Viruses.

Perhaps mother would have died anyway. Nobody blamed Berit or the lack of equipment at any rate. Nobody blamed Henry, either, who tried to press his soft skull out of her body.

Henry, little Henry. Tommy reaches his hand towards his youngest brother's bed and tugs the duvet into his lap. He holds it against his face, trying to recover the smell of Henry.

He looked like an old man during the first years of his life, with his bald, bulb-like skull that gleamed from Grandmother's arms. He was sort of always small. Tommy recorded heights and ages by making pencil marks on the kitchen doorframe. Henry would never catch up with his two big brothers, never shoot up and grow taller than them.

But while Hilmar's ambit was large – he had no fear, because he knew he had always been looked after, he didn't stop, walked away without looking back, disappeared constantly, ran towards the ocean, towards the landslide risk area in Nybyen, had to be held firmly by the hand when they were out walking – Henry usually stayed in close proximity to the others. For while Hilmar was whole and strong, the loss of his mother was a weakness in Henry, like a clear crack in a sheet of drift ice. He started crawling at an early age, moving like lightning across the floor, and took his first steps before his first birthday. Tommy thinks he learned out of necessity. It was wholly essential for him not to lose sight of the others. Especially not Tommy.

Tommy has few memories from the period just after his mother died. But he remembers coming home and hearing Henry crying. He sees his father sitting in the living room, his face in his hands, rocking, sort of matching the rhythm of the tender sobs from the next room. Grandmother is nowhere to be found.

Tommy runs into his parents' bedroom. Although the noises Henry is making are faint, they are still more intense than anything else he has ever heard. The baby is red in the face, forcing out the tears. He picks up his brother and can feel that his nappy is soaking wet. He holds him against his chest, rocks him, soothes him, there, there, Henry, little one. He takes him to the changing table, removes his wet nappy, dries him carefully with a washcloth, finds a clean nappy, pins it into place on his brother, lifts him up, holds him against his shoulder, are you hungry, let's find you something to eat, there, there, it's all right.

He sees himself standing there with his brother over his shoulder and is struck by the practised nature of his movements, by how quickly he changed the nappy, the way he picked him up, soothed him. He can't remember all the other times, but he knows that there were many.

And he will never forget the infant's crying, the feeling it awakened in him. I will do anything to make you stop crying, anything to get you to stop. The most frightening sound was not the crying itself, but that there was something in it that said that the baby was about to give up. That had Tommy not come to pick him up, Henry would have eventually fallen silent, turned inwards, into himself, to a darkness found only in those who are abandoned and without language.

You must trust that I will always come, Tommy would sometimes whisper in the little one's ear, don't give up, I will always come and pick you up in the end, I am always with you. If you just call for me long enough, Henry, I'll be there.

His father alone in his chair in the living room, his face

in his hands, rocking, that is an image that takes up a lot of space. Tommy doesn't know for how long his father remained seated in his chair like that. But he does know that at one point he must have got to his feet, that he felt a sense of duty that kept him from giving up.

It was necessity that fuelled his father's activities, not desire. It was necessary to hunt, it was necessary to slaughter, and deal with the carcasses, dry, smoke, preserve. It was necessary to make sure the children went to school and did their homework. It was necessary to mend clothing, do the dishes, scrub the floors, keep everything more or less spick and span. It was necessary to pull his children onto his lap now and then, or to read to them so they would fall asleep. It was necessary to hug the children, stroke their heads, tell them how important they were.

'You're a good boy,' Father might say when he put him to bed. 'Goodnight, Tommy, sleep tight. I love you.'

Father remembered to say these things. His voice spoke the right words, but neither his eyes nor his body participated. Father's hugs, especially during the years immediately following Mother's death, were distanced, as if he held himself at arm's length while he embraced Tommy.

Tommy knew that his father read books about child rearing, about having children and about adolescents. The book *Living with Teenagers* lay on his bedside table for a period of time, along with *How to Connect with Boys in Puberty*. Father could often be indirect in the way he gave orders, saying things like *I would like you to* or *I would appreciate if you would* instead of *do this* and *don't do that*. With time, Tommy understood that he had picked up these phrases from one of the books. If one has brought a child into the world, one must do it properly. It was a duty.

This is also how Father was as a citizen of Svalbard. He wanted to be a proper resident, who deserved to live there, who was respectable. Father felt both a sense of duty and gratitude about the island and people of Spitsbergen. Tommy believes that his father, perhaps until the very end of his life, felt that it was Longyearbyen that had raised him, Longyearbyen that had given him love and all the structure a child needs.

David seldom said no when asked. A request from the governor of Svalbard and he would drop everything he was doing and come running. In 2105 an avalanche descended upon a settlement in Haugen. Father was in the middle of making dinner when he received the call. He left the house without turning off the stove and the smell of burned fish remained in the kitchen walls for a week. It was April, so it was light twenty-four hours a day. Late in the evening, Tommy walked up to the avalanche area. There, in the distance, he saw his father holding a spade. Red in the face from exertion, he dug the spade into the snow, again and again. Brett called out to him, wanted him to take a break, but his father shook his head and continued. Brett walked down to join Tommy, smiled at him and said that David was a truly wonderful man. He used exactly those words, a truly wonderful man, and Tommy felt proud, the way he often felt when he saw his father through the eyes of others.

But at home, Father could be forgetful. Tommy's packed lunch, the socks in Henry's boots, he could forget about dinner, birthday presents, saying goodnight. He was unable to create routines for caring. His love did not find spontaneous expression.

That's why it was so important that he, Tommy, took care of the packed lunches, the socks, the dinner, that he reminded his father about birthday presents or that he lay down beside Henry in the evening and sang 'Are You Sleeping, Brother John?' softly into his round, protruding ear.

On the sofa in the living room lay a tattered, burgundy blanket, the fabric worn as thin as silk from years of use. In several places it had been mended with red thread, the colour a little too bright. Tommy used to trace the weave with his fingers. I am the thread, he thought, without me this family will unravel.

The house is cold. All of Tommy's movements echo in the rooms and he can't find any fresh vegetables. Without bothering to eat breakfast, he throws on his jacket and shoes and rushes up to the greenhouse.

It is located on Hilmar Rekstens Road, just above the library, built on the foundation of a former shopping centre, Grandmother told him once. As a child, Tommy had had difficulties understanding the concept. Why didn't everyone simply *receive* what they needed?

'Money,' his grandmother tried to explain. 'It was absolutely not the most foolish idea humankind has had. Quite a creative system, actually, which functioned very well for quite some time. Some people called it a religion, but a religion requires magic, something supernatural. The money in itself was not supernatural, although much like a divine being, it only existed because people believed in it.'

Tommy opens the door to the greenhouse, steps into the heat and light of the Four-season Room and takes a deep breath.

Trees and bushes in pots and tubs are lined up along the walls. Grandmother never dared to plant any of these plants directly in the dirt floor; she was afraid the roots would eat their way into the building.

Several of the fruit trees are many years old. Their branches knock against the ceiling and want to get out, don't know what's good for them, don't understand that all that's awaiting them outside is death. Previously, the leaves and the branches were pruned zealously every autumn to prevent them from blocking too much of the artificial light from all the lamps in the ceiling. In the past year they have grown far too much; he needs to have a go at them with the saw.

This part of the greenhouse replicates the seasons out-doors, but the climate is not like that of Svalbard. In here the winters are mild and the summers comfortable, the condi-tions favourable for apples, pears, grapes, berries and nuts. Tommy walks over to an apple tree, picks a ripe apple and crunches on it as he moves into the Summer Room.

Eternal summer. The light timer is set at thirteen and a half hours a day, the least common multiple for daylight hours, as Grandmother put it. The temperature is maintained at a stable eighteen degrees. The humidity in the air confirms that the watering system is in working order. Tommy knows that the facility can operate on its own for months. But if he stops sowing, and stops harvesting, it will gradually become wilder in here, the plants will bolt, wither, some will scatter seeds and grow anew, while others will disappear altogether.

While the colours of the landscape outdoors are muted and cold, in the greenhouse the colours explode against the retina. He sniffs, inhaling the sharpness of the herbs, the sweetness of the carrots, the cabbage plants' singular aroma and the soil's own fragrance, which he cannot describe for himself, but which smells unlike everything else. It smells of Grandmother.

The plants are arranged on platforms at a working height. Three rows, one along each wall and one down the middle. All the way in the back of the greenhouse, carrots, cabbage, beans and onions are planted directly in the ground.

He absent-mindedly pulls a few carrots out of the soil, tosses them onto the bench so clumps of dirt shower off them, picks four tomatoes and some beans, and slices off a head of broccoli. That's enough for him. The greenhouse never produced enough for all of Longyearbyen. But he is alone now in the Garden of Eden. The thought causes a smile to spread across his face.

He opens a peapod, allowing the peas to roll around in his palm.

'Do you know what a seed is?'

It was Grandmother who asked him the question. He remembers they were standing side by side in here. He was fourteen years old, thin and ungainly, awkward and ill at ease in his own body. It was Saturday. He had actually wanted to go to the library, but Grandmother had grabbed him by the arm and dragged him here.

She stood with the light from a lamp behind her as she thinned out carrot shoots. The light created a soft halo around her head, making it difficult to see the expression on her face. This was often how she was, close, but nonetheless blurry, so completely different from how Mother had been.

'A seed? Yes,' he said. 'Of course I do.'

'What is it then?'

'It's something you put into the earth that begins to sprout and turns into a plant.'

'But a seed is also something you can eat,' Grandmother said. 'Like wheat, corn or nuts.'

'I know that,' he said.

'It's important that you know these things.'

'Why is that?'

She did not reply. Instead, she just continued: 'A seed is a shell, and inside the shell nutrients and the germ of a new plant are hidden: a plant embryo. The germ contains the makings of the root, the stalk and the seed leaf. And the nutrients in the seed provide the energy the seed needs to sprout. These are the nutrients humans are often searching for, starch, fat and proteins.' She glanced at him. 'Did you know all that?'

'Yes. Or ... no.'

'Do you know how the seed begins to sprout?'

She thinned the bed with adept hands. They had sown the seeds liberally, and now she weeded out mini carrots to make space for the others.

'No. But you probably do.'

She ignored his sarcasm.

'The seed often needs to rest,' she explained. 'It lies under the tree or the plant it came from and maybe needs cold conditions before it will sprout.'

'Fine. Can I go now?' Tommy said.

When he looks back at his former self, he can't understand how he could have been so obstinate, that he couldn't see even back then what Grandmother was doing, teaching him, in preparation for the role she would later assign to him.

And Grandmother seldom allowed herself to be dismissed.

'No,' she said. 'You can't go ... Sooner or later water will find most seeds. Water seeps in, trickles and drips and slowly penetrates the shell and dissolves it. And then the seed needs oxygen. Oxygen and water will cause the seed to begin fermenting. And then, when the shell disintegrates, the great miracle takes place.'

She paused for a moment, walked over to a tray of newly sown cabbage, plucked out one of the small sprouts and held it up in front of him. At the bottom, the remains of the seed dangled, with spindly roots below and a thin sprout above.

'The great miracle,' he wanted to mimic, making a face, but instead he nodded politely while his grandmother continued.

'A small root forces its way out of the shell and immediately pushes down towards the earth, and soon a stalk also emerges, with one or two leaves, which pushes upwards. Some seeds want light, while others only sprout in darkness. The seed, with its rootlets and its tiny shoot, resembles a creature with long tentacles as it expands ever so slowly through both the soil and the air, and occupies more and more space in the universe. It *is* miraculous. You have to admit.'

'Yes. For sure.'

'And then the plant grows. Some plants grow slowly, others quickly, but sooner or later the plant will want to reproduce. And then, light is important. Because all plants flower. They will attract insects, they will spread their pollen and produce their seeds, which fall to the ground as newly fertilised, plant embryos.'

He studied her. Her cheeks were red, from both the heat of the greenhouse and her enthusiasm, and she smiled at her own words. Suddenly she glanced back at him slyly.

'For a person so hungry for knowledge you are surprisingly lacking in curiosity, Tommy,' she said.

'I *am* curious,' he said.

'It is your hunger for knowledge that makes you the person you are. That is something you must never lose.'

'No, of course not.'

She observed him for a moment, her gaze a spotlight. It warmed him and made him feel special. Suddenly he didn't feel like leaving after all.

She gave the cabbage sprouts a quick once over, plucked away a few of the most shrivelled and threw them onto the compost heap. Then she walked over to the cold-storage chamber where there was a row of old apothecary cabinets. All the small drawers were labelled, each dedicated to a specific plant, a specific seed.

Grandmother searched for a bit before coming back. Then she rolled four peas out of a paper bag into her hand.

'Can you imagine anything quieter than a seed, Tommy?'

He nodded eagerly, wanting to show her what he knew now.

'Quiet, yes, they are quiet and motionless.'

'No,' she said. 'They're not motionless.'

'No?'

'Because seeds travel.'

And then she continued explaining and this time Tommy allowed himself to be transported. Grandmother spoke about how the seeds' development depended upon physical movement. The seeds travelled on the wind, or with animals, birds and humans. She told him about the cultivation of grain, which started in the Middle East and Egypt and slowly spread throughout the world. Rice, soy and peaches originated in China, while the potato, tomato and strawberries came from South America. The seeds adapted to their new habitats and the cultivators selected seeds from the strongest plants for breeding. The journey was the development and the development was the journey. Many of the seed and plant collectors were also travellers. Carl von Linné, the father of taxonomy, who systematically collected and described different species and the connections between them, started his career on a journey in his own country. And Darwin, of course – where would he have been without the HMS *Beagle* expedition?

'While poor Gregor Mendel limited himself mainly to the garden of the monastery where he lived, with all the pea plants. But perhaps such peace and quiet was necessary to lay the foundation for modern-day genetic research,' Grandmother said.

'I've read about both Darwin and Mendel,' Tommy said, eagerly.

'Vavilov – have you heard of him?'

'No.'

'A grave omission, the rectification of which I will take upon myself.' She spoke the words with an exaggerated pathos and winked at him.

Nobody travelled more than Nikolai Vavilov, she explained, the father of modern-day seed collectors. He grew up in Russia during a difficult time, when one period of starvation followed the next. At an early age, Vavilov set a goal for himself: he would solve the problem of famine. He wanted to breed species of grain that could grow throughout all of Russia and thrive everywhere. An important part of this work entailed gathering seeds from every corner of the earth. Hundreds of thousands of tubers, nuts, roots and seeds. And the collection of seeds is found in our vault right now.'

'Here, in Svalbard?'

She nodded. 'Vavilov's entire collection was moved up here in twenty forty-five. Just before the Collapse.'

Grandmother placed the peas in a can of water so the shells of the seeds would soften, accelerating the process of germination.

'Seeds,' Grandmother said. 'It's such an inadequate little word, don't you think? It doesn't roll off the tongue, has no elegance. I prefer *nucleus*. The little word *seed* is perhaps suitable for its referent – every bit as insignificant and minuscule as that which the word is meant to describe – but it does not exactly express the ovule's potential.'

She peered down into the can, added a little more water.

'I know where the word comes from,' Tommy said.

'Which word? Nucleus?'

'No, the Norwegian word for seed. *Frø*. It comes from the Norse word, *frjó*.'

She nodded. 'Do you know the roots of that word?'

'No.'

'The Germanic word *fraiwa*,' Grandmother continued. 'And the linguistic building blocks for the word *fraiwa* are *fra*, which means "forward", and *aiwa*, which means "life" and "time". Originally the word may have meant something like "future life". *Fraiwa*,' Grandmother concluded. 'That's a beautiful word. Maybe we should call our vault the *fraiwa* vault instead?'

Then she stepped nimbly away, disappearing into the germination room to check whether the baby plants in there had grown so tall that they now required additional light.

Our vault. It wasn't until later that he thought about how she had used those words specifically, and pronounced them with such entitlement, as if the seed vault belonged to him and Grandmother alone.

Everything moved quickly around Grandmother. She had so much movement inside her; her thin, sinewy body was seldom at rest, except when she was reading. She alternated between Norwegian, English and French when she spoke. But Tommy was the only one who tried to understand the French.

He wanted it to be their secret language, to create a space that was theirs alone. But he never learned enough, or perhaps Grandmother Louise never stood still long enough. She found rest only when in movement and seldom did he see her more relaxed than when she was in the greenhouse. With time he gave up on his French studies and followed her there instead.

But sometimes she abandoned all of them. The family had a little rowing boat in the harbour, and on good days, when the water was calm, she untied the mooring line and rowed out to sea. Sometimes she fished, returning with a fat mackerel or a huge cod with staring eyes and a beard under its chin. But usually, she just rowed out into Isfjorden, further and further away, a tiny pinprick amidst the immensity of blue, which from a great distance appeared motionless.

Louise hadn't told him much about her childhood, but he knew that she had lived in a house beside a canal without water and that a sailing boat had been in the canal. Louise had loved that boat and she'd believed that one day water would fill the canal and she would sail away. But the water never arrived, she explained. Grandmother's childhood world was a desert, with a boat that was never launched.

Even though Grandmother had lived by the ocean for many years, she never dared venture out to open sea. She stayed between the mountains of Isfjorden. She never learned to sail, never managed to steer by the forces of nature, as she had dreamed of as a child. The oars would have to do, she said, the little rowing boat. Making a dream come true need not be exactly as one has wished, Tommy. When I am out there alone in my rowing boat, on bright summer nights or dark autumn evenings, then I am as close to my old dream as I can get and I am satisfied with that.

He was not certain that she meant it. She was often smiling when she returned from her trips on the fjord but he thought he could also detect a trace of longing on her face.

It often came to pass that Grandmother did not dare to go out because the weather on the fjord was too stormy. Then she would pack a knapsack instead, throw a rifle over her shoulder and disappear for several days in a row. Father said that it wasn't strange. She had been wandering her entire life, she needed to wander again. It doesn't mean she doesn't love us, only that she has the need to be in movement.

Sometimes they could see her from a distance. She walked as if she were headed somewhere, as if she had a destination, even though she went no further than to Bjørndalen. Out there, on the shores of Isfjorden, she had her preferred trails. But she was not content on flat ground, by the old, collapsed cottages. She wandered along the ridge of the mountain that had once housed Mine 3. She moved through the unstable slopes where remnants of old ventilation shafts were the only surviving relics of human activity. And she had her cottage out there in the valley, the cottage that was hers and hers alone. When the weather was bad, she sought refuge there.

'Have you been inside the mines?' Tommy asked her once when she returned. 'Have you tried to get in?'

Then she smiled. 'I think you're overestimating the abilities of an old woman, Tommy. I think your assessment of my powers is flawed.'

He looked at her inquisitively.

'You don't see me packing a crowbar when I leave?' she said. 'You don't see me packing an ice pick and a shovel?'

'No.'

'The mines are sealed,' she said.

'I know that,' he said. 'But can't you just remove the boards?'

'The mine is sealed by both humans and nature. Behind the concrete barriers the mining people installed when they closed the mines for good, is a wall of ice. Water has run down into the tunnels. Every summer drops from melted snow have found their way in there and the more the permafrost has thawed, the more water there has been. And so, in the winter, the water has frozen into ice plugs, and the plugs don't melt in the summertime, and especially not those furthest in, where there is still frost in some places year-round.'

She started unpacking the few items she had brought

along in the knapsack. A blanket, a bag of beef jerky, an extra sweater, an old plastic container holding her rifle ammunition, which rattled hollowly against the sides.

'No, Tommy,' she said. 'The mines belong to the mountains now, only the mountains.'

This was who we were, my family, Tommy thinks. A brother who could run away from him without looking back, who was without cracks, secure that the care he needed would be forthcoming. Another brother who doubted, who measured and weighed his words and love, who picked up on everything that happened, who never released his grasp on Tommy. A father driven by a sense of duty, who was present, but disappeared nonetheless, who forgot the most elementary things, but who could suddenly remember and assign unnecessary importance to random details. And a grandmother who was a wanderer, who followed her own path, and who had such authority that nobody considered questioning whether she should be allowed to come and go as she pleased.

But they all did the best they could. For as long as Tommy can remember, he has thought this, specifically: I can't be angry at them because they are doing the best they can. And he also knew that it wasn't good enough. For that reason, he had to do *everything* he could. This became his job from the moment he got up in the morning until he went to bed at night and he never questioned the nature of this work, he never expected time off.

There was only one place where he allowed himself to forget his role in the family: at the library. He rested in the books' world, in the stories they gave him, in the people he met, the places he could travel. He worked his way through one shelf after the next, starting as a young boy with children's books, but moving on from these at an early age, undaunted by genre or subject matter. Every book was a new country he would conquer. As he read, his pulse rate slowed, his vigilance relaxed its grip; while he was reading, he found peace. For a few minutes or hours at a time. Until once again he was interrupted.

Henry used to come looking for Tommy when he was at the library, with snow in his hair in the winter, or moss and straw clinging to his wool sweater in the summer. Henry often brought a bit of nature indoors with him and showed signs of having not merely strolled through the landscape on his way home from school, but of having rolled around, jumped up and down, fallen – he seldom hurt himself – and clambered to his feet again. And in his hand, he often clutched the knitted toy rabbit.

'Is this where you're hiding Tommy,' he shouted one afternoon, as he opened the broken glass door that was repaired with a piece of cracked plywood.

And without waiting for his big brother to reply, he would enter the big room, bringing with him the scent of the day outside.

'What are you reading today?'

Henry came over to stand directly in front of him, breathing loudly from the run he had just finished, because he preferred to run, with light and somewhat staggering steps, as if he couldn't quite decide where he was headed.

'A book,' Tommy replied.

'But which book?' Henry asked and held the rabbit over the cover, as if it too were reading.

'A book about the seed collector Nikolai Vavilov.'

Tommy held the book up reluctantly to show him. A picture of a bearded Vavilov wearing a hat graced the cover.

'He was strange,' Henry said.

'He was smart,' Tommy said curtly.

He demonstratively held the book up in front of his face. Tommy had been deeply immersed in the text, but now the words refused to form sentences. Henry stood directly in front of him, kicking his feet restlessly against the floor. And then Tommy discovered that the shoelaces on Henry's right shoe were untied. They were soiled with mud and flopped against the floor.

Tommy decided not to do anything about it and stared at the book again.

Henry walked a few steps across the room. It was impossible not to notice the shoelaces dragging behind him. If he were to run with them flapping like that, he could step on them and trip.

Tommy put down the book. 'Come here.'

Henry's face lit up. 'Why?'

'Your shoe.' Tommy pointed.

Henry obediently held out his foot.

'Pretty soon you must learn to tie them yourself,' Tommy said, as he took the muddy laces between his fingers.

'Yes,' Henry said.

'You can ask Dad. Or Grandmother.'

'Mm.'

But Tommy knew that if anyone was going to teach Henry how to tie his shoes, it would have to be him.

Encouraged by the shoelace tying, Henry sat down beside Tommy, picked up the book and studied the picture of Vavilov again.

'He *was* strange.'

'He was wise. And a hard worker. He and his people travelled all over the world collecting seeds. They found three hundred and eighty thousand.'

'Three hundred and eighty thousand!' Henry said. He loved big numbers.

'Vavilov went to Colombia, Canada, Ethiopia, Japan; he went to South Korea, Russia, Guatemala, Germany.'

Henry nodded quizzically.

'Come on, I'll show you,' Tommy said and led his brother over to a globe in a corner.

'Look, here is Algeria. He was there. And here, in Italy, he collected seeds there. And here, in Ecuador. Vavilov gathered seeds from every continent.'

Henry's breath misted in the air as he exhaled, and he nodded, breathing heavily and with deep concentration.

Then he spun the globe a bit and considered.

'You can't see Svalbard,' he said and pointed at the plastic arm holding the top of the globe. 'Svalbard is almost missing because of that piece of plastic.'

'But *we* know that we are here,' Tommy said.

'What did he do with the seeds, then? That guy, Valivov?'

'Vavilov.'

'Yes. Him.'

'He stored them in the world's first seed bank. It was located in Russia, in a city that was called Leningrad at the time.'

'But did he just store them? He must have used them for something?'

'He did research on them. He tried to breed plants.'

'Breed plants?'

'Vavilov wanted to put an end to all famine. He wanted to create new seeds that produced better crops and thereby more food for the people.'

'Did he succeed?'

Tommy sighed. 'Do you really want the full answer?'

'Yes!'

Fine. You asked for it, Tommy thought as he began to explain to his little brother how Vavilov had done investigative research in the tradition of Gregor Mendel in the effort to identify plants and seeds that through natural selection were especially well suited for their environments. Tommy spoke in a rapid, steady stream so his little brother would not interrupt him. He explained to Henry how Vavilov monitored the plants for many generations and then cultivated those plants that had such deviant, positive features. But the work took time and time was something Vavilov did not have to spare, because Russia was afflicted by severe and widespread famine. And Stalin, who was the ruler-in-chief of the Soviet Union, was impatient, even though he was personally responsible for the fact that people were starving, because he obliged all the farmers to hand over their grain. In addition to this, the conflicts in Europe were growing like vicious weeds and another large-scale war was on the horizon.

'So the answer is no,' Tommy said, finally. 'Vavilov did not quite succeed.'

Henry gazed at him, his eyes glassy. 'Oh, no.'

Tommy felt a stab of guilt. 'You can read more about it when you get older.'

'Sure. But what about now? Do you have any fun books?'

'You know I do,' Tommy said. 'Come with me.'

He led his brother over to the shelves holding their favourites. Lindgren, Jansson, Dickens, Verne, Ende.

'E for Ende,' Henry said. 'E is nice. But not as nice as H.'

'H for Henry,' Tommy said. 'I agree. It's the nicest letter of all.'

Outside Rakel and her gang of friends walked by. Tommy heard Rakel laugh long and hard, and he noticed how she was the centre of attention. He watched the young people jostling against each other, putting their heads together and making plans for the evening ahead of them.

He leaned over the book and started reading to his little brother: 'Long, long ago, when people spoke languages quite different from our own, many fine, big cities already existed in the sunny lands of the world. There were towering palaces inhabited by kings and emperors; there were broad streets, narrow alleyways and winding lanes; there were sumptuous temples filled with idols of gold and marble; there were busy markets selling wares from all over the world' (Ende 1983).

Henry, dear Henry, come back to me.

Tommy is a planet without a satellite, a moon. His brother has always moved in an orbit around him, stayed so close that he has always had complete knowledge of his whereabouts; he has either been able to see him or hear him or known exactly where his brother happened to be.

He tries weeding in the greenhouse – he has always liked weeding, the process of transforming the chaos of a box of plants into orderliness – but his fingers betray him, he keeps stopping as he works, and the vice grip around his head tightens.

He gives up, walks outdoors into the cold, into the dwindling light, wanders aimlessly between Longyearbyen's empty snail houses. Time is without system, it congeals into clumps, dissolves. It is September, every day is twenty minutes shorter than the last, the light draining out of the sky confuses him. Tommy constantly checks the watch on his wrist, wondering whether it is running correctly, if he has remembered to wind it, whether he can trust the 150-year-old timepiece. When the sun finally begins sinking towards the mountains, the movement confirms the accuracy of the hands on the wristwatch. Still, he doesn't trust the watch. He rushes up the hills, afraid he will be too late, that he will miss her call.

When he arrives, he sits and waits, spinning impatiently on the office chair, lifting and lowering himself up and down on the mouse-eaten old seat cushion. He rises halfway to brush decaying foam rubber off the seat of his trousers, sits down again. He waits.

She calls at five o'clock on the dot. Her voice sails through the air, loud and clear.

'Can you hear me, Tommy?'

'Where are you?' he asks, without preamble.

'Almost halfway to Archangel. It's snowing today, we are staying inside. How's the weather where you are?'

'I couldn't give a rat's arse about the weather. You have to turn around.'

'Tommy,' she says, again with her usual gentleness. 'Can't we talk about the seeds?'

'No.'

'No,' she sighs heavily. 'But perhaps ...' She hesitates. 'Then perhaps you can tell me what happened when you disappeared? You and Rakel. Or perhaps I can talk to Rakel? Is she there with you today?'

The questions about Rakel hurt his body, cutting like steel blades against flesh. He squirms. He has to get Tao to stop asking questions.

'It's cold here, too,' he says. 'I need to get a heater in this room. I am freezing to death.'

And it is really cold, he notices it now, he is shivering.

'Do you have a blanket?' Tao asks.

'What?'

'You said you were freezing. Do you have a blanket? Or maybe you should see if there's a heater in the building some-where. The electricity is working, isn't it?'

'Yes.'

'I'll wait while you go have a look.'

He gets to his feet, walks out into the large control room, and searches quickly until he finds a portable radiator that is probably one hundred years old, rusty and with legs of cracked plastic. He walks back to the radio room, sticks the plug into the outlet and soon hears a crackling sound commence. The odour of burnt dust spreads through the room, while a faint warmth penetrates his shoes.

'There,' he says to her. 'Now I'm back.'

'Is it warmer?'

'It will get better.'

'I asked about Rakel.'

'She's not with me.' He answers a bit too quickly.

'She's not?'

In that one short phrase alone, he feels like he can hear that she doubts him.

'I came up here all by myself today as well.'

'So she's home, in your house?'

'Yes. She's at home.'

'Can't you ask her if she'd like to come up there with you? Tomorrow?'

'Climbing the hill is difficult for her.'

'But you can ask, surely?'

'Yes. Of course.'

Tao falls silent. He winds the cord around and around his finger, so tightly that the fingertip turns white.

'Tommy ... how is Rakel, really? How is she feeling?'

'She's fine. Okay?' His voice cracks. He collects himself. 'Can the two of you please talk about this one more time? It must be possible for you to turn around?'

'Tommy, you have to tell me what happened. Why you and Rakel disappeared.'

He doesn't reply, doesn't know what to say. There must be some way that he can use this to his advantage?

'I can tell you what happened if you come back with my brothers,' he suggests.

She is silent. For a long time.

'Does this have anything to do with the seeds?' she asks, finally.

'The seeds,' he says. 'That's all you care about.'

'If the seeds are gone,' she says, her voice low and tense, 'or destroyed for good ... that would be a catastrophe.'

'"Catastrophe."' He spits out the word.

'Yes, Tommy. A catastrophe.'

'For whom?' he says.

'What do you mean?'

'For the human race, maybe,' he continues. 'It would be a catastrophe for the human race. But not for the rest of the planet.'

The radio crackles and he wonders if he has lost her. But then she is back.

'Three years in a row, the fruit crop where I live has failed,' she says. 'The first year, the spring was too cold, the second, the summer was too dry, and the third it rained far too much. And this spring? Cold and drought. Just a few, small fruits hang from the tree branches. I often go walking out there in the fields and it is a miserable sight.'

'The majority of human beings throughout history have been poor,' he says. 'Living has basically been, during every era and in most places, pretty awful.'

Again he hears her sigh. 'Tommy, if you know where the seeds are, you have to tell me.'

'The seeds are gone. You saw it with your own eyes. And I have no idea where they are.'

'But do you think that your grandmother took them?'

'If she was the one who took them, she had a reason,' he says. 'And it was no doubt a good one.'

He expects her to keep pestering him, but Tao doesn't say anything.

For a long time neither of them speaks. The heat from the stove is not enough to warm up the entire room. He pulls it closer to him, and it makes a scraping sound as he drags it across the floor.

'Tao?'

'Yes. I'm not going anywhere.'

'Where are you now?'

'I don't know, we are sailing in pitch darkness, the moon is hidden behind the clouds. There's an icy wind on deck, and the black ocean blends into the sky.'

'What are you doing, what are my brothers doing?'

'Right at this minute? A card game, I believe. And playing. Would you like to speak to them? Shall I fetch them?'

'No.' He blurts out his reply quickly. 'Let them play. Don't bother them. It's better for them if they aren't forced to speak to me.'

His chest tightens, making it difficult to breathe. It's just pain, he thinks, just longing, neurological signals from the brain to the chest, muscles contracting, fluid being produced.

'I understood that you didn't want to leave Svalbard,' Tao says. 'But why didn't you at least say goodbye to your brothers?'

She insists warmly, as if she wants to coax and cajole him with her maternal voice.

'I didn't know that you were going to leave.' He can hear how frail and childish his voice sounds and tries to deepen it when he says: 'Rakel is asking about Runa – she misses her sister. You have to come back!'

'There's no way. We don't dare. I asked Mei-Ling again. I am so sorry, Tommy.'

'I don't believe you. I don't believe you've asked her.'

'Yes, I did, Tommy. And I know that she's right.'

They're not going to turn around. She means it. They are going to keep going all the way back to Sichuan, where she comes from. She is going to take Henry, Hilmar and Runa with her to a place he can't even imagine. A city? A palace? A prison camp?

They are going to rescue us, Rakel had said, they're coming to rescue us.

It's Rakel's fault, all of it.

They'd been fine, the five of them, they had plans, they would manage it, a reconstruction, a new family, a new society.

He gets to his feet and stands in the middle of the room, his body trembling from the cold, his teeth chattering uncontrollably. He wants to hit something, pound his fists against something or other, hammer long and hard on something until he sheds the cold, like ice water sliding off a glacier.

'You don't know what it's like to lose someone,' he says.

Tao is silent for so long that he thinks she has disappeared.

'Yes, Tommy,' she says, finally. 'I do know.'

Tao

Her life is divided into three parts. All the years before he was born are one part. The next part, and the shortest, are the few shining years she had with him. And then there are all the years after that. The years numbed with grief. The years of indifference, without fear, without wrath. These feelings went away with him and she can no longer remember how it feels to be furious. Sometimes she misses the energy it gave her and tries to tell herself that she should be angry, deranged, desperate because she has lost a child, because the world is the way it is. But all she can feel is this numbness which she can't find her way out of, the distanced view of herself, the sluggishness in her body and thoughts. She moves through life like a body through water.

In the years afterwards, Tao has been first and foremost a mother who lost a child. She has been *the Mother* incarnate. The woman who lost *the Child* – her son, her boy. They call him that often: *the Boy*. In the beginning she tried to say Wei-Wen, he has a name. But eventually she started calling him that also, just the Boy. It was simpler.

And she has long since accepted that her child will never be anything more than that, a boy. A man will not grow out of his little body. His size is unalterable. Three and a half years old, one metre and four centimetres tall, 16 kilos. The only thing that has changed is the pictures of him. Sometimes he is just a profile of a face, at the bottom of a brochure, a symbol of the new era. Other times it's his whole body, in detail, spanning several metres on a banner or a placard, or as a living image, running towards the world with open arms. They have manipulated his image so many times that Tao doesn't recognise him, taken the few photographs of him that exist and made him run, jump, smile, dance, read, play, sing.

His singing voice is as clear as a bell.

In recent years they have also begun producing images of Wei-Wen as he would have looked today if he had lived. His birthday is commemorated with another manipulated photo: today the Boy would have been ten, today he would have been twelve, fifteen. The photographs are astonishingly good, she recognises many of her son's features in the pictures. She can see Kuan in him, his father, and herself as well. But still, it *isn't* Wei-Wen. She knows that the appearance of the child who was once hers would have been different. The images aren't hers, they are everyone else's.

Tao's memories are not connected to photographs and films, but to the feeling of him, his hand in hers, her nose pressed against his neck. And to the scent of him, the scent of the child and the scent of herself, the way he also used to smell like her, because their bodies spent so much time so close together, back when they were just a wholly ordinary mummy and a wholly ordinary child.

It's been twelve years since Wei-Wen played in the forest behind Field 748, twelve years since Kuan found him lying lifeless on the ground, twelve years since the venom from one bee spread through his tiny body and in the end killed him. Wei-Wen's death, the bee sting that killed him, became the symbol for the end of silence, for the new world. The bees had been declared extinct for decades, but now they were back. Now the entire forest is full of buzzing bees, both wild and domestic in hives and with them the birds have also returned. The pollinating insects proliferate, along with a number of other species, humans occupy less space on earth than before, and once again wild creatures can breed, the natural world is theirs. Human beings also grant them the space they need; only a small minority of the human population have two children. The cost of raising children is too great in terms of both money and judgemental eyes. Tao herself has only the one child, a boy who is only found in memories and fiction.

He would soon have turned sixteen, and maybe that is why she also feels relief about being far away. Maybe they will give him more prominent jaws now, higher cheekbones, thicker eyebrows. She can't imagine them not making him beautiful, because he remains forever flawless. Not a single blemish will press its way to the surface by the root of his nose, not a single irregularity will they draw on the perfectly proportioned face. But now she will be spared seeing the pictures hanging from the roofs, projected onto building walls and she will be spared doing all the usual interviews on his birthday, where she is supposed to publicly share her grief, squeeze out a few tears, but not too many, emphasise how much she misses him, but transmit that the feeling is nonetheless eclipsed by pride. Because Wei-Wen is the child who changed everything. He was the beginning of the new era. He represents hope, goodness, everything revolves around him.

'The return of the bees will always be connected to Wei-Wen's death. The hope is bright green, the hope is a shoot, but before the shoot comes the seed,' Li Chiara said to Tao the day it was decided that they should make the trip. And

Tao thought that as usual Li Chiara was masterful in the creation of clear-cut images, and that here she already had her next slogan.

'The seed is the core of hope. And you, Tao, are the living carrier of our hope. It goes without saying that you must make the trip to Svalbard. You are the one who must lead the way to the vault. Into the world's most important room.'

There was no possibility of refusing or negotiating the terms. Over the past twelve years, she has seldom said no to Li Chiara's requests. Li Chiara does more right than she does wrong and perhaps one can't expect more than that from a leader. Tao doesn't know if Li Chiara's actions are driven by a longing for glory or from goodness. Probably both.

And Tao wanted to leave. It was as if for twelve years she had been asking a question, without knowing what that question was, but that the seeds were the answer. She believed in the vault, did not allow herself to be discouraged by Mei-Ling, who in gloomy periods claimed that the seeds must have rotted long ago.

On the journey north, she tried to think as little as possible. She focused on the mission, on the seeds, on the time it all took, all the days along the way, hour by hour, minute by minute. She focused on all the obstacles they met on the twenty-five days they were travelling by land, first in ancient military vehicles all the way from Sichuan, through the veritable wasteland of Kazakhstan and then onwards to Russia and the harbour in Archangel. Terrible roads, breakdowns, power shortages, flat tyres. And the attacks by people who were destitute. She was not frightened during the journey. Instead she was thankful that something was happening, that a shift had occurred in that which had become her life, the monotonous series of identical days in which she had to make an appearance for the general public, offering the usual combination of grief and pride, and the not equally monotonous but all the more difficult series of nights when she lay alone in the big bed she had once shared with Kuan, in the apartment that had felt too small for three people, but was now large and empty and where the hollow echoes off the walls were all she had to keep her company.

Once upon a time, Tao had been a sound sleeper. She had laid her head on the pillow and fallen asleep immediately, her body heavy from the day's work, exhausted in every muscle. Because it had been a difficult life, physically, but also emotionally. She worried so much, about Wei-Wen's future, about the next child she hoped she and Kuan could have, if only they managed to put enough money aside. But her anxiety seldom clawed its way into her sleep; during the night she was left in peace.

She has many times thought that she hadn't really known what difficulty and grief were before Wei-Wen died. The nights became a time for restless wandering, the anxiety disappeared along with her son, the hope of another child vanished the day Kuan no longer desired her, and she no longer desired him.

During the first months following Wei-Wen's death, they really tried, they thought it would be possible to find their way back to each other, she was certain that she would manage to focus her attention on the world and forget her child. Kuan talked constantly about how time heals all wounds. But as long as they were together, it became impossible. The other's face was an eternal reminder of the boy who was no longer there, they saw him in each other's eyes, cheeks and eyebrows, in the other's knees, shoulders, neck, gait or manner of raising the head, they heard him in each other's voice, laughter and tears.

The trip to Svalbard was a departure from everything familiar and she had slept well while at sea, better than she could remember having slept for twelve years. On a boat one is in movement all the time, making small imperceptible adjustments to keep one's balance. The movement, combined with the sea air, made her pass out from exhaustion every single night. She slept through the nights and woke every morning with no recollection of her dreams.

Tao had only thought about the children up here from time to time, the young people who had summoned them. She had, perhaps, tried to avoid thinking about them.

The ship is so big that they can hardly feel the movements of the sea. Only now and then does the ocean make its presence known, a faint jerk, a sudden rolling movement, a reminder that something is different, an instability.

The children are in bed below. They have been given two cabins side by side, one for the boys and one for Runa.

The ship lurches as it collides with a wave. The movement shakes Tao's body awake. She gets to her feet. She hangs the radio microphone in its cradle and leaves the wheelhouse, where she has been sitting alone while the autopilot has had control of the helm.

She opens the door to Runa's cabin a crack. It is dark inside the room and she can just make out her body in the strip of light. The girl is lying curled up on her side. Her face is smooth and peaceful while she is sleeping. It is good to see her rest, to be spared having to smile the way she does all the time, a gentle and entreating little smile.

Tao continues to the boys' cabin. They have forgotten to

turn off the light, the bedside lamp shines a cold light onto their faces. They are both sleeping in the same bunk, it is far too narrow, their bodies are entangled. Henry's cheek is tear stained.

She leans over them and switches off the lamp. But then Hilmar wakes up.

'No,' he whispers.

'But it's shining right in your face,' she says, and hopes he understands what she means.

'Henry needs it,' he answers in a broken attempt at her language. 'Turn it on.'

And then he worms his arm loose and presses the switch himself.

'Go away,' he says. 'Please.'

'Yes,' she says. 'I'm leaving now. Sleep well.'

He doesn't reply. She closes the door behind her and stops for a moment in the hallway. Then she grasps the door handle again, wants to open it anew, go inside, pick Henry up out of the bed, carry him with her to the bathroom, crouch beside him, find a washrag, wipe his cheeks, remove the traces of tears, before they become a part of him, invisible burns he will carry for the rest of his life.

But she doesn't open the door. Instead she releases the door handle, walks to her own cabin, takes out her jacket and climbs the ladder up onto the deck.

The faint vibrations produced by the engine spread through her body, trembling through her arms and legs.

A wave breaks over the hull, giving her an ice-cold, salty shower. She can't see it but can tell from the air that the sea-water has begun to transform, the drops join forces, expand, thicken, becoming fog.

She moves abaft, finds shelter behind the wheelhouse,

sits on a tall crate holding life jackets, her feet dangling. The salt has created a pattern on the white cover, white on white, the way Svalbard must look in the winter. She moistens one finger with saliva, draws roads in the salt, a landscape where all the roads are headed away.

She is about to lose all feeling in her dangling legs, pulls them up and tucks them beneath her, leans against the cold wall and feels a seam-welded metal splice bore into one shoulder, but she stays seated where she is all the same, shuddering with cold.

Beneath her the passengers sleep in the boat's interior, as if it were a mother, pregnant with all the children.

Tommy

The first snowfall of the autumn. Tommy is sitting by the window in the sitting room and looking out. The sky is covered with cotton plants, the roots reaching for the stars and the plants for the earth. Then the seed capsules with all their white fibres are released, flying through the air in search of soil. But when they hit the ground, they don't spread their roots, they don't grow up out of the earth into cold plants, but instead melt immediately, leaving only wet splotches in their wake, which gradually accumulate and darken the colours of the rocks and the soil.

Tommy leans his back against the sofa, rests his head. At all times Rakel's face is there, the surprise, the fear. He closes his eyes, but she doesn't disappear.

He is so tired, his body aches, but he knows there is no point in lying down, he won't be able to sleep, not until his exhaustion is so extreme that it drowns him.

Then he remembers something. He puts his hand in his pocket, pulls out a small cloth bag and opens it, pouring some of the contents into his hand. Ten grapes, once upon a time plump and full of fresh juice, now dried into raisins. He takes one raisin at a time between his fingers, chews them slowly and lets the taste of sunshine and grape sugar

spread through his mouth. The taste brings with it memories of Christmas.

They used to put raisins on their Christmas porridge.
Peppermint tea and barley groats porridge with raisins.

After the meal there would be a torchlight procession
out along the fjord, a glowing serpent twisting through
the darkness. On the Christmases when there was snow,
the light of the torches reflected off the white ground, but
there were also winters when they were caught in a sudden
cloudburst. Then the rays from the torches were even more
intense, every torch its own little world in the pitch darkness. Christmas was not white, but both black and luminous
all at once.

In the past, one hundred years ago, the children used
to leave letters to Father Christmas in a mailbox up by
one of the old mines near Nybyen in the Longyear Valley.
They called it the Father Christmas mine. Back then, the
torchlight procession went out there. But nobody lived in
Nybyen any longer. The steep hillsides along the valley were
not secure, everything was loose, often the rocks creaked,
sometimes there was a landslide. And in the wintertime,
huge drifts of snow accumulated up there. The mailbox was
moved to the square by the Polar Hotel and the procession
went along the shoreline, past the Bykaia section of the
port, in the direction of the old airport and Bjørndalen. But
neither was it safe there; a landslide risk hung over them
as well from Platåberget Mountain. Be that as it may, they
would walk in the procession. Children and adults, hand
in hand, completely silent, so they would not startle the
snow into action, bring it to life. If the avalanche took one
of them, it took them all. Sometimes a critical voice dared
to speak up. Were they really planning to go through with

it this year? Because wasn't this madness, really, that they walked this way, just for tradition's sake, because the children pestered them?

When Tommy was a little boy, he couldn't imagine Christmas Eve without the torchlight procession, any more than he could imagine the period leading up to Christmas without the lighting of the home-made tree of driftwood on the square by the Polar Hotel or the Christmas jumper party on the third day of Christmas.

He remembers the last normal Christmas Eve best of all: 24 December 2108. The landscape was white, the polar night clear, and an almost full moon dipped towards the mountains in the south. The moon shone cold and strong, and for the people of Svalbard, who'd had time to forget what daylight was, the moonbeams sweeping across the landscape created the illusion of just that.

An icy breeze was blowing from the northwest, the mercury approached 15 below. The weather had grown colder over the past twenty-four hours. Tommy and his brothers got dressed in a mayhem of mittens, boots and scarves. They armoured their bodies against the cold, wool against skin, huge jumpers, knitted leggings beneath their snowmobile suits, two scarves, the outer scarf covering the face entirely. Their bodies overheated, they spilled out of the house and jogged towards the centre of the village, while Tommy urged them to hurry, they were running late.

They cut a path through the crowd to Emily, who was responsible for handing out the torches.

But her basket was empty.

'Sorry,' she said as she handed Tommy a single torch. 'This is the only one I have left.'

'I don't need it,' Tommy said quickly.

Her eyes sparkled joyfully under the brim of her thick hat. Emily had no children of her own, but often looked after the children of others while they were out hunting or fishing. She took assignments like this very seriously and wanted to do everything right, to really *see* the children. Now she turned to face Hilmar.

'Then you can have it, since you're such a big boy.'

Hilmar grabbed the torch greedily and hastened to light it.

Henry didn't protest, but Tommy's heart pounded harder, because he knew what was going to happen.

His little brother's whining began as a soft murmur. *Not fair*, Tommy heard, *a rotten thing to do*. But eventually the murmuring increased in volume. *Why does he get one if I can't have one? He always gets what he wants, I never do, not fair, not fair, not fair.*

Grandmother was speaking animatedly with Gerda and Brett, while Father was standing with the governor and her people discussing security measures for the procession. Nobody else heard what had happened.

'Be quiet,' Hilmar said. 'It's not unfair. She gave it to me because I'm older.'

'No,' Henry said, and stomped his foot against the ground and howled. 'I never get anything!'

Tommy's heart was beating hard. Not on Christmas Eve, he thought, please, not a meltdown on Christmas Eve.

'But Hilmar,' he said quietly to the middle brother. 'Maybe you can take turns with Henry? Can't you?'

And then he stared at Hilmar pointedly, trying to fill his eyes with as much severity as he could muster.

Hilmar mumbled something. Waved the torch in the air in front of him, just looked at it.

Henry looked back and forth, first at one and then the other, silent now, and he produced a long, drawn-out sniffle.

'Hilmar?' Tommy could hear his voice trembling.

'The one time I actually get something...' Hilmar murmured.

'What?'

'And then I just have to give it to him? And he just bawls, look how he's bawling!'

'Yes,' Tommy said. 'Yes, yes.'

But though his words were calm, the expression in Tommy's eyes, focused on his brother, remained firm.

Hilmar buried his head beneath his large scarf and shrugged. 'Fine,' he said, and turned towards Henry. 'We can take turns. OK?'

Henry sniffled again, wiped his nose with a mitten and nodded.

'Come on, then,' Hilmar said.

And then he started walking, quickly. Henry trotted to keep up with him but didn't say a word.

The two brothers were almost at the head of the procession; Tommy had to stride along briskly to keep up. He had long since lost sight of his father and grandmother. He noticed that Henry was out of breath from the pace, but still he stayed at his older brother's side, glued himself to him, never more than a metre away. Hilmar held the torch high above his head, and his little brother stared at it constantly, saying nothing, not for a long time.

Tommy wondered whether he would have to intervene again, but refrained from nagging in the hope that Hilmar would come to his senses.

Finally, it was Henry who spoke up.

'You said that we were going to take turns.'

Hilmar didn't reply.

'Hilmar? Wasn't the plan for us to share?'

'We can't share a torch,' Hilmar said. 'Only one person can hold it at a time.'

'But it's my turn now.'

'Not yet.'

'Yes, it is!'

Tommy stared at the back of Hilmar's neck, hoping he could imbue his gaze with the force of an angry mamma bear. Behave now, Hilmar!

But Hilmar just kept walking, raising the hand holding the torch even higher.

Then Tommy cleared his throat, almost inaudibly. Behind the tiny 'ahem' he placed all the power he hoped he had over his brother. And finally.

Hilmar sighed and whirled around to face Tommy. His lips were pursed but he didn't say a word, merely jabbed the torch towards Henry, who jumped away.

'Hey, be careful!'

'Do you want it or not?'

Henry's hand flew out and he quickly grasped the torch.

'Hold it up high,' Hilmar said. 'And don't wave it in any-body's face.'

'I won't.'

And Henry held the torch high in the air, stretching his arm far above his head, as if he were leading a military parade, an army, Tommy thought, or as if he were a marathon runner in ancient Greece, bounding into the arena to light the Olympic flame.

'Like that?' he asked, without turning towards Tommy.

'Yes, like that,' Tommy said.

They kept walking. Behind them someone started singing.

'We Wish You a Merry Christmas'. Henry sang along because he knew the words, more or less, and waved the torch.

'Be careful,' Tommy said.

'I am being careful,' Henry said and his face shone.

He marched in time and sang as loudly as he could in his halting English, and the glow from the torch cast a quivering light over his eyes, which were shiny from the cold.

Tommy leaned towards Hilmar and nodded.

'Look at that,' he said. 'See how proud he is.'

'Sure,' Hilmar said.

Tommy calmed down. It will be fine, he thought, nothing will be ruined, it will be a nice Christmas.

They walked for a short distance, Henry's steps quick and short. But he struggled to hold his arm up as high as before.

'Is it heavy?' Hilmar asked.

'No,' Henry said.

'Let me know if you want me to hold it.'

'I can do it myself,' Henry said. And then his shoulder jerked a little, as gravity pulled his hand closer to the ground. 'But if you want, I can share for a while.'

Come on now, Hilmar, Tommy thought.

'I don't need to share,' Hilmar said. 'The torch isn't all that important to me.'

Come on, Hilmar, please.

'Oh no,' Henry said and his arm sank even lower.

'You're tired,' Hilmar said.

Behave, you brat.

'No, I am not tired!'

Again Tommy had to glare fiercely at Hilmar. He hoped the torch flames were reflected with blazing fury in his eyes.

'Fine,' Hilmar said.

'Yes, fine,' Tommy said.

'What's fine?' Henry said.

Hilmar turned towards Henry and tried to smile.

'I. Really. Want. To. Hold. The. Torch,' Hilmar said. 'I want you to take turns with me. It would be *great* if you would take turns.'

Tommy nodded at Hilmar in encouragement – that's it, there you go.

'And I can take turns!' Henry said.

They switched again and Henry shook out his arms and jumped up and down a few times in relief.

They continued walking towards Hotellneset peninsula. The wind from the fjord stung their faces. Tommy didn't say anything more to his brothers. There was a lot he could have said. You see, he could have said. That wasn't so difficult, was it. And doesn't it feel good, he could have said, to be nice to your brother. But now it was a matter of keeping the peace. He hoped that it would last until the evening.

They walked on in silence and now it was too late to say anything. Now they had to listen to the mountains. They towered above them, enormous, white ghosts.

'It looks like The Groke,' Henry whispered, and pointed. And Tommy nodded. This was the Moominvalley, and the mountains were The Groke and all her sisters, dressed in white. They stood side by side with their backs to the people, but they could see them all the same. The people of Longyearbyen never escaped the mountains. And each individual human being was so infinitely tiny in the enormous landscape that they were almost devoured. Only when they were together were they visible.

A rumbling sounded in the distance, from far up in the mountains and a faint gasp passed through the procession. But they kept going even so, one foot in front of the other.

The glowing serpent was the only movement in the peaceful snowy landscape. All that could be heard was the sound
of footsteps squeaking against the snow. And fortunately, no
further sounds were issued from the mountains, they were at
rest, listening to the people with the same intensity as when
the people listened to them.

Maybe the mountains listened especially well on that final
Christmas Eve, Tommy thinks, and maybe they already knew
it was the last. Maybe the mountains knew, maybe the snow
knew, maybe the stones and the earth knew that time would
soon run out on the glowing serpent far below by the fjord?

Afterwards, everyone gathered in the great hall at the Polar
Hotel. The seals on a couple of the big, old glass windows
were punctured and the windows fogged up, but the largest
picture windows in the middle were still intact and recently
cleaned for the occasion. Tommy could see the mountains
and the fjord from his seat in the fifth row, where he sat
together with his brothers. Grandmother was standing with
Paul closer to the front, while Father was chatting with Emily.
    Outdoor garments were noisily removed; underneath
everyone was wearing their Sunday best. Tommy looked
around him. People were chattering and laughing, com-
plimenting one another's painstakingly patched suits and
dresses recently sewn from leftover fabric. The neighbour's
girl Wilma sat down beside Henry. She eagerly showed him
a new slingshot she had received in her Christmas stocking
and the two children ducked behind the row of chairs when
she sent a lump of coal flying through the air towards the
winter-pale neck of an elderly man seated towards the front.
Tommy wondered whether he should intervene, but at that

moment Wilma's stern mother stepped in. She confiscated the slingshot without a word. Tommy sent her a look of thanks.

Then everyone sat down, the lights were switched off and calm settled over the assembly. An infant started crying but found comfort in its mother's breast. Only the sound of the baby nursing softly could be heard in the otherwise silent hall.

Svalbard's 527 residents sat quietly for a while as their eyes adjusted to the darkness, all their faces turned towards the glass windows in front of them. And there, in the sky outdoors on this evening, was not the Northern Lights, but a huge, round moon that painted the mountains blue.

The governor walked to the front and stepped up to the rostrum. She was a woman who usually had a smile on her face, but today she carried herself with a decorum befitting the holiday. Chairs scraped against the floor as everyone stood up. She waited for a moment with her back to the hall and looked at the mountains, the sky and the fjord, before turning to face them. With a warm solemnity, she began reciting the prayer of thanks.

> We thank the ocean,
> for all that you bring us.
> We thank the earth,
> for your abundance.
> We thank the glacier,
> for your life-giving water.

Hilmar squirmed in his seat beside Tommy.

'Behave,' Tommy whispered to his little brother. 'Sit still.'

'Tick tock tick tock tick tock,' his little brother whispered back.

The governor continued and the villagers joined in:

We promise to live
with respect
for every animal,
for every plant,
for every single creature around us.
The value of the bird
is that of the reindeer,
that of the whale,
that of the human race.

Hilmar stuck out his tongue. 'Respect.'
'Please,' Tommy hissed.

We vow to live so that which gives us life,
will continue to give life to our children,
and to their children in turn.
Because we will not
repeat the errors of the human race,
but live everyday with love
for all living things.

Everyone sat with their heads bowed, in deferential silence.
Tommy elbowed Henry. 'Aren't you supposed to go up there now?'
'Is it now?' Henry whispered.
'Yes, hurry up.'
Henry jostled his way past the others and rushed forward to the large plate glass windows along with the other members of the children's choir. Anders, their teacher, took position in front of them and signalled that they should begin.

Tommy waved to his little brother in encouragement as he saw Henry open his mouth and prepare to sing. 'Dashing through the snow', the children sang in unison, 'in a one-horse open sleigh. Over the woods we go, laughing all the way.' The children of Svalbard, who had never seen a horse or woods.

Had Rakel been there, this last Christmas, he asks himself. Yes, she had been. She and Runa had sat right behind Tommy, both of them also all dressed up. Rakel carelessly dressed, Runa with a freshly ironed frock and a bow in her curly hair. She looked even more like a doll than usual. In her hand she held a folder; she was going to sing a solo. The sisters had had porridge with Anders's family, who had taken them in for a time, and they would be having dinner in the home of Louise and David afterwards. On the way out of the hotel, Rakel found her group of friends from school. She led the way, talking loudly and laughing, gesturing, planning a party. She seemed unaware of the gazes of others and had apparently forgotten her little sister, who was walking alone a short distance behind her, carrying her music folder. But when Runa stepped out into the winter evening, her legs slipped out from under her. The road was covered with ice and the ice with a thin layer of snow, and Runa slipped and fell backwards. Her head hit the ground with a thud. Rakel broke off her conversation mid-sentence and in two steps was at her sister's side. She held her in her arms while Runa cried, took off her hat to see whether a lump was forming, comforted her softly. Tommy could not hear clearly what Rakel was murmuring into her little sister's ear, but he thought he caught the word *sorry*.

It is, however, not the two sisters whom Tommy remembers

first and foremost from this Christmas evening. It is Henry waving the burnt-out torch in the middle of the sitting room; it is Hilmar opening Tommy's gift to him and unable to respond when he sees all the new flies Tommy had tied for his fishing pole. It is Father shoving yet another log of driftwood into the fireplace and smiling at him over the flames; and Grandmother, in the middle of the sitting room, short and thin and strong and large, singing with a surprisingly deep voice that fills the entire room. 'Deck the halls with boughs of holly, she sings, Fa-la-la-la-la, la-la-la-la!' And then she lifts her hands as if she were a puppet master and they were marionettes and they all get to their feet and start to dance. They run around the cramped house, from room to room, in a line and holding each other's hands. Around and around, until Henry shouts that he's getting dizzy, I'm spinning all over! And Hilmar laughs that bubbly laugh of his that always makes him seem younger. He laughs so loudly that his entire body shakes.

The following winter was darker and wetter than any winter Tommy can remember. The rain poured down and the fog unfolded across the mountains. It was as if he had crept inside a wet wool mitten and remained there.

Life was defined by routine and ordinary events. The children went to school, Louise and her helpers in the green-house cultivated plants beneath the light of the grow lamps: they sowed, watered, fertilised, pollinated. Most of the other adults went hunting and fishing. And in the evenings, in the lamplight, they busied themselves with productive tasks such as handiwork, the casting of bullets for hunting weapons, or repairs.

These were the daily skirmishes they all fought through-out this winter, battles against things that fell apart and had to be fixed, battles against animals when out hunting, battles against the carcasses that had to be quartered and transformed into something edible. The battle against the weather, the rain that forced its way into the houses, the mud upon which the houses were built, the faulty foundation. The battle against the landscape's movements. Because Svalbard was always in movement. From a distance the mountains appeared to be stable, enormous formations of stone, partly covered with silent ice. But nothing stayed still. On top of the permafrost and in its uppermost strata were layers of loose sediment, stone and gravel, in some places soil. The vegeta-tion spent decades putting down roots and there were few plants with roots that extended deeply enough to secure the ground underneath. And the plants, moss and grass were constantly being uprooted by small landslides. Because when the water infiltrated the underlying sediment, the gravel and stones were inexorably pulled downwards by gravity.

It did not help when the cold weather finally returned, because when the precipitation became snow, it piled up into huge snowdrifts. The risk of a landslide or avalanche hung over their heads year-round.

Hundreds of years ago, Svalbard had been an arctic desert, with scarcely any precipitation. But this aridity, the scarcity of water, no longer existed except in the form of records.

The snow, however, gave them something they longed for throughout the rest of the year: it gave them freedom of movement. Some of the old electric scooters still functioned and they were stored indoors and coddled like babies. The Svalbard residents took turns using them, signing up on a list for the next snowfall. The villagers had a few huskies as well. The dogs were kept in the kennel near Isdammen reservoir and Ivar and Henrik took good care of them. There was an annual discussion about whether they would permit themselves the expense of keeping the fourteen dogs, enough for two dog teams. The animals consumed large quantities of meat, were expensive to maintain, but it was worth it all the same, the majority felt, both because the dogs were good draught animals and because of the intrinsic value of flying across the snow on a sled pulled by joyful dogs instead of a motor. But this winter, the snow never stayed on the ground for long, the scooters were left idle and the dogs wandered restlessly around in the kennel.

The people longed for daylight. They argued so the noise reverberated through the wooden walls and was passed around by the neighbours; they gathered in the bar of the

Polar Hotel, drinking and laughing. They talked about the reindeer stock (was it dwindling?), they talked about a she-bear with two cubs that someone had spotted further inland in the Advent Valley, and which seemed a bit too curious about humans (a problem bear?), they talked about the wind, about the small wind and solar power stations providing electricity for the houses, about the capacity of the old Musk batteries (were they of poorer quality?), about whether the sun of last autumn had provided them with enough stored energy to cover the first months of darkness and if the wind was strong enough to get them through the entire dark season. They talked about the mackerel, there was so much mackerel this year, the more the temperature rose around the equator, the more the fish sought their way north, the adults sang the mackerel's praises while the young people talked about how sick they were of mackerel, *sick to death*, was the phrase they used, especially of mackerel fried in seal blubber. And when the children talked about seal blubber, the adults began to speak with concern about the seal population, which was diminishing all the time. And then they talked about butter and oil, and butter and oil were usually the opening – the perfect opening – for talk of the things they used to have. In the old days. Like chocolate, coffee, like cheese and crème fraiche, beef and honey. Like motorways, helicopters, airports and new clothes of wool, cotton, viscose and Gore-Tex. And sugar!

Everything they had once had was deteriorating. Tommy's sheets were threadbare and patched several times over, the soles of shoes were repaired with rubber from old car tyres, the synthetic nylon ropes they used to moor the boats in the quay frayed and unravelled. The people of Svalbard recycled the remains of remains, they mended, cobbled, darned and patched. And they knew it was only a matter of time before all the remains of what had once been called the modern world had completely disappeared, before the nylon had disintegrated into teeny-tiny fragments of plastic and disappeared into the ocean, until the rubber in the soles of their shoes was worn away and turned into the kind of granules they found on the football pitch, before the bedding was nothing more than cotton threads, before all the glass panes in the houses were broken, before storms had knocked over the windmills on the roofs and smashed them, before the solar cells no longer functioned and the batteries could no longer be charged. They lived on the rubbish heap of modern civilisation. They had made themselves dependent upon the goods in which modern civilisation had revelled, but they knew that they had to free themselves. And they were well on their way. They prepared themselves for the time ahead, the time when they would have to find everything they needed from nature, like *true* hunters and gatherers. They sewed more of their clothing from animal hides, they had long since built a forge, they saved every single bullet for recasting, they used absolutely every part of the animals they slaughtered. There were constantly creative minds at work on inventing ways to replace everything they were lacking with something new. Motors that ran on driftwood, chalk made of eggshells. Some people even tried to spin thread out of cotton sedge, but the fibres were too short, and they had to give up.

But food, the most important thing of all – that they had. They hunted, fished and sowed, both inside the greenhouse and outdoors. They created potato beds beneath layers of moss. They harvested long pieces of moss and cut it into pieces, which they used to construct long, tunnel-like shelters. Beneath the moss, the South American plant had favourable growing conditions. And goutweed, nettle and different types of green cabbage thrived on south-facing slopes.

But food was not enough. It could not replace everything they'd had. Like red wine and grapes and internet access for eight billion people. Like paper and pens and computers. Like sewing thread and super glue and nails that were straight. Don't start, someone said, but then they started all the same, creating long lists of all the objects they missed. The young people, too – the young talked probably for the thousandth time about how tired they were of hearing the adults talk about things they used to have and mumbled that if the adults were so dissatisfied about not having any of these things, then they should get the hell away from this island. And there, there they had suddenly talked their way into the crux of all of it.

To stay or not to stay.

The majority claimed firmly that they belonged up here. But Longyearbyen never escaped the dissenting voices. There is life out there, they said, there's a whole world south of the seventy-eighth parallel. A world that is gentler, kinder, a world where there is maybe still an abundance of everything we are missing. And we can make contact again, we have Svalsat.

But the dissenting voices were in the minority and the decibels this choir had the power to generate varied. The volume also depended upon the growth cycle. After a harsh winter they would often shout loudly, after a benevolent summer they were silent. Sometimes the dissenting voices formed political parties: PPCW (Party for Promotion of Contact with the World), the Openness party, and the party that had proven to be the most viable – One World, One People (Rakel's parents had been active members until they were killed by the landslide in 2097). But none of these parties caught on. The Svalbard Party always won the majority in elections and never held less than 75 per cent of the seats in the local government. The political fronts in Svalbard were as black and white as the light conditions of the region. Tommy read Marx and Engels, he read Locke and Burke, but the texts did not resonate with him. The terms conservative, socialist, liberal did not hold much significance in Longyearbyen. The people were in agreement about how they should live, that they should share, that they should take care of the most vulnerable. They agreed that they should build on Svalbard's deep ecological values, as these were designed after the mining period came to an end, that they should harvest from nature's surplus, that people were on an equal standing with all the other species on the enormous island of Spitsbergen. Distribution policy was not a subject of discussion. Everyone felt solidarity with the most vulnerable. But if one were *too* vulnerable, one would not survive and the majority accepted this, in the way they accepted the isolation in which the population chose to live.

What do we need the world out there for, Grandmother used to say, though it wasn't actually a question. They don't need us, we don't need them. We live the way one should live, the way humans always should have lived and as long as we don't destroy anything or change the course of natural history, we can just keep on living on this island, in harmony with one another and the elements. We are achieving something up here, she would sometimes say, something people have never managed before. We should be proud of ourselves, of how we manage to conserve the environment, even though we exist. And then she would often use terms that came from Savage: We should be proud of how we managed to put *the great love* for the world, for nature before *the little love* we have for ourselves and the few individuals with whom we share a genetic makeup.

She didn't say: We are better than them. She didn't say: We are superior to all the other people who live or have lived.

But she did say: It is difficult. We are at the mercy of our own drives, instincts, it doesn't take much for us to lose perspective, forget history, put our own needs first, see only our own, minor history. But as long as we live here, isolated, as long as we continue to follow our principles and our laws, the nature around us is safe. And consequently those who live in nature and from nature's bounty are also safe.

Tommy walks through the slush up towards the greenhouse, trying to reproduce his grandmother's gait, the quickness, the slight rocking of the body. The slush settles onto the upper vamps of his boots, the moisture penetrates through the seams. He usually greases his boots every Sunday, to prepare them for another week, but this time he must have forgotten. His feet get wet, cold, and he starts shivering.

Grandmother could also be careless in this way; things were seldom important to her, only that which was alive mattered to her.

He has pulled his hood over his head, it gives him tunnel vision and every time he takes a step, the hood dips a bit in time with his head. They often walked this way in the morning, climbing side by side where the road was destroyed. She could have been here now, beside him, her voice ringing out loud and clear.

Grandmother, who usually walked down the roads beneath the Northern Lights and whistled. She loved the *aurora borealis*, the way she loved Svalbard.

He pulls off the hood, has to climb across a spot where the road is washed out, and continues climbing as large, wet snowflakes sneak down the back of his neck. He does nothing to stop them, just keeps walking while the sound of his footsteps becomes more and more deafening. A sound he wants to escape from.

He quickens his pace, starts to jog. It is as if he can hear something behind him. Rakel, he thinks, it's her footsteps, quick, light.

But when he turns around, there is nobody there.

Finally he opens the door to the greenhouse, moves into the warmth inside, in Grandmother's greenhouse, with her plants, which she tended so carefully, and which gave Svalbard's residents protection from scurvy.

He doesn't know much about her.

Louise and David arrived in Svalbard when David was just five years old, towards the end of the 2060s. They were on one of the very last boats that travelled to Longyearbyen, before the island severed all contact with the rest of the world. Louise had been on the move for as long as she could remember, like a dandelion seed whirling through the air. It wasn't until arriving here that she found a place where she could put down roots, she once told Tommy, in response to which he commented that it was typical of her to use a plant analogy about this in particular, and she said yes, just as typical as it was for him to comment upon it. Louise went ashore, holding little David's hand in her left hand and a suitcase in her right. In it was everything they owned, she said, even though Tommy had a suspicion that there must have been a trunk or two in the cargo hold; sometimes Louse would exaggerate for dramatic effect. She stood on the wharf, leaned back her head and looked up towards the mountains Sukkertoppen and Sverdruphamaren. She looked inland towards the Advent Valley in the southeast, where a large swamp area filled the entire floodplain, where the river carried soil and sediments and gave the innermost section of Adventfjorden a muddy colour. She looked towards The Longyear Valley in the south-west, where in several places the river had carved gashes out of the landscape when violent floods had overflowed the banks and forged new pathways. She took in the sight of the rough, stony landscape and knew that this was where she wanted to stay. Right here, where no trees put down roots, she would finally find peace, here she and David were safe.

Norway, where Louise had spent the previous four years, on increasingly longer trips north, was a land of outlaws. But Louise, who was actually French and had always been on the run, did not look back. Life in Svalbard was challenging. The threats were large and tangible, landslides sweeping away entire mountainsides, polar bear attacks, storms rolling across the landscape and taking with them everything in their path. But maybe the tangible threats from nature were liberating, Tommy thinks now, simpler than her previous life, in spite of everything, where an eternal vigilance and lack of trust in other people had demanded so much from her. In any event, Grandmother had liked Svalbard from the first moment, something she would confess to anyone willing to listen. She began gardening in the greenhouse, never found herself a man, did not have any more children, and passionately threw herself into politics. For many years she was a representative of the Svalbard Party, and one of the most pronounced voices in support of continued isolation.

Even though she was small and trim, slim shouldered, people listened when she talked. She had gathered knowledge throughout an entire lifetime, both from everything she had read and all her experiences, and she substantiated her claims thoroughly and with a natural authority. This earned her respect. It wasn't strange that they allowed her to start working at the seed vault, that she was one of the few granted access.

In the beginning she was only an assistant. Then, when the director died, she took over. It had been standard practice for the director of the seed vault to have at least two assistants, but Grandmother hadn't wanted any and, because of the local government's faith in her, she was allowed. Twice a year she let herself into the vault – on 12 March and 12 November. Her movements were hurried and a bit abrupt on these mornings, as she packed food and drink and donned her outdoor gear. She would be gone the whole day. For a long time it was not altogether clear to Tommy what exactly Grandmother did inside the mountain there for so long. He imagined that she walked around patting the boxes of seeds, as if she were taking care of them.

Once, but only once, was he allowed to go with her. He was fifteen years old and he remembers all the details.

On that morning he was woken by a weight against the mattress, another body. Slumber held him snugly in its warm grasp, and he was unwilling to open his eyes, so he just mumbled to the person who had sat down on his bed: 'Did you have a bad dream? Come lie down here, then.'

Then, without checking which of his brothers it was this time, he moved aside to allow the fearful little boy's body find peace and security nestled against his back.

But neither of his little brothers climbed into the bed. Instead, a hand lifted the duvet away from his face.

'Tommy?'

Finally, he opened his eyes. Grandmother hadn't switched on the light and was sitting on the edge of the bed, her body creating a dark shadow against the light from the hallway. She gently patted his feet which were sticking out from beneath the duvet. They were long and had grown much more quickly than the rest of his body. He pulled them under the duvet, but that didn't help, because then she started tousling his hair.

'Tommy,' she whispered. 'Can you wake up now.'

The word order was that of a question, an imploring 'can', but as was often her wont, she'd omitted the question mark at the end of the sentence. Abruptly he was awake.

He sat up. 'What is it? Did something happen? Has something happened to Henry, to Hilmar?'

She smiled. 'No. But it's time to wake up.'

He looked at her in confusion. 'What time is it?'

'Ten minutes to six,' Grandmother said breezily.

'Ten to six,' he groaned. 'But school doesn't start until half-eight.'

'You aren't going to school today,' Grandmother said.

He smothered a yawn, his drowsiness wrestling against his curiosity.

'Oh?'

'You're coming with me.' Grandmother handed him a jumper from the pile on the floor. Almost all the clothes he owned lay in the same place where he'd dropped them after removing them, the trousers inside out, a sock in each leg, and on the periphery, three pairs of randomly deposited unmatched wool socks with holes in them. 'Get dressed now.'

Inside the jumper was a T-shirt; he had also taken these two garments off at once. Now he pulled them on at the same time, too. Grandmother smiled.

'It's practical,' he said – he who always insisted that his little brothers put *their* clothes away neatly before they went to bed.

'No doubt,' she said and then announced without preamble, 'It is March the twelfth today.'

And then he finally understood where they were going. He looked at her inquisitively, but didn't dare say anything, fearful that she would change her mind. She responded to his gaze with an almost imperceptible nod. 'Dress warmly. It's freezing out.'

He pulled the socks out of the legs of his trousers, registered that they smelled bad but could not be bothered to find clean ones, pulled them onto his feet, then wool socks on top, pulled on his long, woollen underwear and squeezed himself into his trousers. Then he stopped.

'But what about the boys? They need breakfast. They always dilly-dally so much in the mornings.'

She looked at him inquisitively. 'David's home.'

'Yes, but . . .'

'Get ready now.'

In the past few weeks, the winter had tightened its grip. After weeks of rain and fog, snow had finally arrived, a thick blanket that turned Longyearbyen white. March was the sunny period of the winter. The amount of daylight increased by almost twenty minutes every day and now a reddening sky above Advent Valley bore witness to the fact that the sun was about to rise.

Grandmother started walking. Tommy followed behind her. She was shorter than he was and had a knapsack on her back but she still walked so fast that he had to jog to keep up. Every step she took hit the ground with strength and focus.

They left Longyearbyen behind them. Grandmother turned around and viewed the village.

'Would you ever want to leave here, Tommy?'

'What do you mean?'

'Have you ever thought that it's possible to live somewhere other than here in Svalbard?'

'No,' he said. 'Of course not.'

'No,' she said. 'I guess you haven't.'

'You've asked me that question before.'

'Have I?'

'Yes. Many times.'

They walked westwards in silence beside the fjord, passed the collapsed buildings after the Store Norske Spitsbergen Coal Company and approached the container harbour and the shore.

'That's where it washed ashore,' Grandmother said and nodded towards the beach.

'Yes,' he said.

That's where it had lain, the ash tree he had considered his own.

They continued down the beach, Grandmother first, Tommy behind her. They reached the harbour. The fishing boats lay on shore where they'd been pulled up for the winter. The smallest boats were in a row, upside down. He could just them make out, like a series of arches under the snow. The largest were elevated, perched on cradles, covered with worn tarps, and securely bound with rope mummified by frost.

They walked into the wind and he shivered.

'Cold,' he said.

'It's colder inside,' Grandmother said.

They reached the old airport and followed the road

upward towards Mine 3 and the mountain. In the mountainside, a distance beneath the mine, lay the seed vault, sharp and quadratic against the curved landscape, with two windmills on each side that supplied it with electricity.

Tommy was warm now from walking, and breathing hard as he followed his grandmother.

'Do we have to walk so fast?'

She turned to face him.

'You sit on your behind too much, Tommy.'

He rolled his eyes in response, even though he knew that it had no particular impact on her. Everything rolled off Grandmother's back; she seldom dwelled on painful feelings. It was as if she, when encountering something difficult, lifted the feeling up, held it in front of her, examined it, acknowledged it, and then turned around and kept going.

'You know that it once was lit up,' Grandmother said as they drew nearer.

'Yes,' he said.

'The roof and the area above the doorway were once covered with a work of art,' Grandmother continued. 'Triangles of steel, prisms, mirrors and light, protected by Plexiglass. It was compared to a glittering, polished diamond of light.'

'How beautiful,' he said.

'Perpetual repercussion,' Grandmother said.

'Huh?'

'That was the name of the artwork. It means something like eternal after-effect or infinite reverberation.'

'Awesome.'

They continued in silence. She stepped lightly, leading the way while he followed, his steps dragging in his oversized boots.

'Do you wonder about what happened to it?' she asked.

'Happened to what?'

'The artwork.'

'No. Not really.'

They had finished climbing and walked out onto the square in front of the vault. She stopped and stood looking at it.

'I will tell you anyway,' she said.

'Of course you will.'

'The Plexiglass shattered, people have helped themselves and used the steel and the prisms for other things. The weather has probably done away with some of it as well.'

They walked all the way up to the shiny steel door, which was apparently free of rust, because it still looked new. She put a hand in her pocket, jangling a set of keys.

Then she unlocked the door, first the top, then the bottom lock. She turned towards him. 'Are you ready?'

Without waiting for an answer, she grasped the vertical steel door handle that ran from the base of the door to the top and pulled.

The first thing he felt was the cold. It surged out of the interior as she opened the door.

'Welcome.' She gestured grandly at the doorway with her arm and let him into the dark freezer box.

'There's a switch inside there,' she said and pointed.

He pushed it and the fluorescent light on the ceiling immediately began to tick. Above them hung rows of white lamps.

'They're still working.' Grandmother smiled in satisfaction. 'They're the originals. We use them so seldom that they don't break.'

She entered and closed the door behind them. Their breath formed clouds, which froze into crystals in the air. The crystals descended slowly to the ground and merged with the carpet of frost that covered both the ceiling and walls.

The source of the cold was a number of enormous and roaring ceiling fans. Grandmother nodded at them.

'And they're still functioning too. Like clockwork.'

Before them was a long hallway leading straight into the mountain. The sound of their footsteps was drowned out by the noise of the fans.

Above them were thousands of tons of rock, he thought. The deeper they went, the more rock there was.

'We're entering the permafrost now,' Grandmother said. 'It's still intact, deep inside here.'

'But why are the fans needed, then?' Tommy asked.

'The temperature of permafrost is only a few degrees below freezing. Ideally, it should be colder for the seeds. In here it is eighteen below.'

'I can tell,' he said and noticed that his teeth had started chattering.

'I told you to dress warmly,' Grandmother said.

They walked a few more steps.

He had wanted to ask Grandmother why she had taken him along and why today, exactly, but he didn't dare. He was afraid it would remind her of something, that maybe she had made a mistake, that young people or untrained individuals or amateurs weren't allowed in here and that she would suddenly turn around and take him out again, before he had the chance to see what was hidden at the end of the hallway.

But they soon arrived and Grandmother apparently had no intention of changing her mind. She pressed yet another light switch and a cross corridor appeared.

They turned the corner and could no longer see the exit behind them. He felt as if the mountain above them was pressing against his chest.

'You'll get used to it,' Grandmother said. 'Think about the

miners, every single day they crawled several kilometres inside, many of them had to work lying down because the space was so narrow.'

'Was that supposed to help?' he asked. 'Now it feels even worse.'

Grandmother smiled. 'I'm sorry.'

'No, you're not.' He smiled back.

She stopped in front of a door in the wall to the right.

'Here it is. The middle hall,' Grandmother said. 'Most of the countries are in here.'

'What about the other two halls?'

'They never got around to filling them.'

She stuck the key in the lock and grasped the door handle. When they walked inside, the din from the roaring fans was even louder. Grandmother pressed more switches on the walls with self-assured movements, and the sudden white light stung his eyes.

'Yes, Tommy,' she said. 'Here you have Svalbard's pride and joy.'

He didn't know what he'd been expecting. He was aware that it was only a warehouse, that there were only boxes on the shelves, that nothing in the packaging suggested the uniqueness of the contents, but all the same he felt disappointed.

Before them were five, wholly ordinary warehouse shelves of steel. They had once been painted blue and orange; now the paint had peeled off. The standard shelves were full of equally standard-looking boxes of plastic or wood, and also some made of old, brown cardboard.

Tommy began walking along the rows of shelves.

'The air is drier inside here,' he said, because he noticed that there was no longer any frost on the walls.

'The seeds don't tolerate moisture,' Grandmother said.

She followed him, smiling with childish pride. 'What do you think?'

'I don't know ...'

'I understand,' she said. 'But try to picture a plant ... picture a cotton plant.'

'I've never seen cotton,' he said, and heard how petulant he sounded.

'*Gossypium hirsutum*,' Grandmother continued. 'American Upland Cotton. It came from Mexico, but with time was responsible for ninety per cent of the world's cotton production. The cotton plant is like a small tree. It has round leaves and yellowish-white blossoms that resemble hollyhocks and hibiscus.'

'I've never seen a hibiscus plant,' he said. 'Or a hollyhock.'

'Cotton is self-pollinating,' Grandmother said. 'And it develops a protective case called a boil, which contains between twenty-five and thirty seeds. The case splits into several pieces and then the seeds are exposed. What is unique about precisely these seeds is that they are covered with fuzzy fibres from two to five centimetres long and made up of a single cell. And why do you think the cotton plant produces hairy seeds, Tommy?'

He could feel how the words *hairy seeds* made him blush but hoped it wasn't visible in the cold. 'I have no idea,' he mumbled.

'You're not trying,' Grandmother said. 'They grow seeds that can be spread by the wind. That is the purpose of the hairs. The purpose of the cotton for humans, however, was something else altogether.'

'Clothing?' he said, in an attempt to contribute.

'Money,' Grandmother said. 'Cotton was money.'

Again she smiled and he could see that she was enjoying herself. 'The Industrial Revolution, Tommy, was spun like a thread from the cotton plant. People wanted to weave finer fabrics, faster, the steam engine was introduced because there was a need for more power for the machinery, slavery was consolidated because there was a demand from England for cheap raw materials from America. And the American Civil War ... Martin Luther King, the civil rights movement, Black Lives Matter, you can trace the thread all the way back to the little cotton plant. And the plant in turn, it started with a ...'

She looked at him expectantly.

'Yes. It started with a seed,' he said.

'Good, Tommy. And here ...' She threw out her arms in an overly dramatic gesture, wholly aware of what he thought of her pedantic enthusiasm. 'Here you have a million of them.'

'A million seeds?'

'No, a million *different species*, Tommy!'

Her eyes sparkled. The frost turned the dark tufts of hair sticking out from beneath her hat white and she was in truth quite beautiful, his small-boned, petite, yet also large and strong grandmother.

'Okay,' Tommy said. 'I'm a little impressed.'

'Look at the boxes,' she said. 'And imagine that every box holds several thousand plants. Picture the land, the forest, the fields, the savannas or the steppes where the seeds come from. And imagine all the time spent, all the energy invested in collecting this.'

He nodded and did as she said, as he walked between the rows of shelves. 'Chad, Chile, China, Columbia ...'

United States of America, he read on a plastic box. Russia on another.

'They were put here, side by side, in the cold,' Grandmother said. 'While humans were warring among themselves outdoors in the heat, their genetic materials were put on ice in here.'

She walked all the way to the end of the hallway and waved at him. 'Look at this.' She pointed at a box.

'ICARDA. International Center for Agricultural Research in Dry Areas,' he read aloud.

'Originally this centre was located in Aleppo,' Grandmother said. 'They collected seeds from the entire region. But then Syria was torn apart by civil war and the vault was destroyed. There were a hundred and thirty-five thousand species inside, many of them from the region we think of as the cradle of agriculture, and many of them were strong species, resistant to both heat and drought. When the war prevented access to the vault, duplicates were extracted from here. In twenty fifteen, ninety thousand seed samples were withdrawn and these provided the foundation for the new gene banks in the countries that back then were called Lebanon and Morocco. Some of the seeds were also planted to produce new seeds and these were sent back here. They are in the box there, as you can see. This was the first time in the course of the last century that local gene banks made withdrawals from here due to unrest and war, but not the last. Before the Collapse, many people were involved in this work, maintaining contact with the different banks, withdrawing seeds and replacing them ... the thirties, those were the vault's glory days.'

'And then what happened?'

'After twenty forty it became too difficult. People had enough on their hands just staying alive. One by one the gene banks around the world shut down operations. Some collections, such as the seeds in Vavilov's vault, were sent here. Others were just abandoned. When I came to Svalbard, they had contact with very few other seedbanks. Then we lost contact with those as well. I don't know if there are other seed banks any more. Based on my knowledge of the world, what I saw of it in the last century, I don't think so.'

'But what does the work involve now? When you're inside here, I mean?'

'What's involved?'

'Yes?'

She laughed. 'I don't do a thing. Check that the electricity is functioning properly, that the cooling system is up and running. That's it.'

'But don't you ever check the seeds?'

'This is a bank, Tommy. Every nation owns its seeds. Or owned them. All we are supposed to do is make sure they are stored safely.'

'But couldn't we use them? Try to plant them? It would give us more species, more food.'

'And what if we don't succeed? Let's say that we took all the seeds of one species and sowed them ... let's say that we tried to sow a species of German barley.'

'Yes?'

'And then we failed because the conditions are not exactly optimal up here. No plants were germinated, or those that were germinated wouldn't produce new seeds. Then we would have used up the seeds for no reason. And when Germany—'

'Germany no longer exists.'

'And when someone who felt they came from the place that was once called Germany, arrived to retrieve their seeds, when they arrive, in twenty or fifty or one hundred years, then there wouldn't be any left.'

'But if we were careful. If we selected seeds from cold regions, from countries that were like Svalbard.'

'Arctic species.'

'Yes, arctic species. Or if we tried to grow them in the greenhouse?'

'There's a list, Tommy, everything is recorded. Every nation, every single local gene bank or agricultural centre has received a receipt. We have promised not to touch the seeds, promised that they would be safe in here, and that we will take care of them, because it could be that one day they will need them again.'

'But what if there's nobody else out there any longer? What if we are the only ones left? Then we are just squandering all of this.'

She nodded slowly. 'I have also thought about that.'

She beat her arms against her body to warm herself, brushing a faint layer of frost off her coat. 'But as the years have passed, I have also begun thinking to a greater extent that there is another reason we shouldn't touch the seeds. Even though we have managed to survive up here, we are still part of the species *Homo sapiens*. Our natural state is chaos, everyone warring against everyone else, an eternal battle for own survival. And this vault was created precisely for that purpose: to ensure survival of the human race.'

'You mean we don't deserve it? Even though we are the ones who have created the vault?'

'I mean that the human race, in every possible way throughout the course of the past two hundred years, no, the past two thousand years, has demonstrated that it is not worthy ... A million species, Tommy.' She threw out her arms to indicate all the boxes of seeds. 'And humans are just one species. This vault is worth infinitely more than us.'

'So what do we do then, if someone comes?'

'I don't know, Tommy. It could be that time will be on our

side because all species evolve, also humans. It could be that *Homo sapiens* will, in the end, learn from their mistakes, if they only make the most of their time. But the people I met during all the years I was on the road ... there were few among them who convinced me that we were on the path to improvement. There were few who deserved this legacy, who deserved help to ensure procreation.'

She spoke the words lightly, as if it were amusing.

Tommy searched for words, suddenly feeling that he had to defend the human race.

'But isn't it possible that ... you were unlucky? With the people you met, I mean?'

She laughed. 'Or else it could be that desperation reveals our true nature.'

They stood for a moment in silence. Grandmother observed him from beneath frost-covered eyelashes.

'Are you cold?'

He nodded.

'One can start to feel pretty cold in one's heart when discussing the human creature's shortcomings,' she said.

'You get cold when it's eighteen below, too.'

She nodded. Then she tilted her head to one side and looked at him with an expression he couldn't read.

'Are you wondering why I brought you here, Tommy?'

He hesitated. 'Yes?'

'I'm thinking that maybe you can take over one day, that you can be a seed custodian.'

'Oh?'

'Not yet, of course. But when I'm no longer here. If you want to, that is.'

'Erm,' he said. 'I mean, of course.'

And that was all he could manage to say. But there and

then all her stories fell into place inside him, the greater story, her persistent instruction. The whole time she had been thinking that it would lead up to this.

Grandmother nudged him in his side. 'That's good. Then it will become your responsibility. All of life in your hands, Tommy.'

He sits in the greenhouse, looking down at his hands. She gave him all the responsibility and then she disappeared, the way she has always done.

She could have refrained from dying, she could have been in here with him now, standing in front of him with a pair of scissors in her hand, pruning the plum tree, carefully trimming away the unripe fruit, to liberate more growing space.

It wasn't my fault that I died, she would certainly have said.

Nothing has ever been your fault, has it, he would have answered.

Are you angry with me, Tommy?

No. I am not angry.

It sounds like you're angry.

I just want to talk about responsibility.

Her scissors would have made sharp clipping sounds as she pruned.

We were lucky we had you, she would have said. She often said, we are lucky to have you. We were lucky we had you, because you were wired in such a way that you could take it, a bit stronger than most everyone else.

Could I?

We would never have put the responsibility on your shoulders if you couldn't bear it.

But isn't it true that the more you can bear, the heavier the burdens others will place on your shoulders?

She would have put the scissors down again and tried to look him in the eye.

I still think you seem angry.

Then she would have drawn closer, shorter than him, but strong and erect, with a ringing voice that filled the room and one's head.

We human beings hurt one another, she would have said, she used to say, especially people who are fond of one another, we hurt each other again and again, and because we invest so much in one another, we also expect too much *from* one another. It is one of our species' many weaknesses.

But look at me, then, he would have replied, loudly. Look where I am now. How things have turned out for me. For everyone.

You have always be willing to shoulder responsibility, Tommy. We are lucky to have you.

No, he says. No, because things have not gone well.

Gone well with whom? For whom?

Everything has always gone away, disappeared. The first thing he lost was the tree.

It remains imprinted in him in the form of two bodily memories. The one is that of his arms around the trunk, sleeping in that position, with his hands against the gnarled bark. The other is craning his neck to see, because adults were standing crowded together in front of his tree and he couldn't get past the wall they created and it didn't help that he craned his skinny, little boy's neck as much as he could. But finally he found a space where he could slip through the wall of people, made it to the other side and saw the tree lying there, every bit as helpless as a stranded whale. But it wasn't *Tommy's tree* any longer; now it was the *village's* tree.

'A gift for us from the sea,' he heard their neighbour Pål mumble. He had a fondness for elaborate symbolism.

'It shouldn't be possible, in theory,' Emily said. 'A tree should not be able to travel all the way here without losing its leaves.'

'Why not?' Brett said. 'There's no ice to stop it in the summertime. With the right wind and ocean currents, a tree can quickly drift here from Russia.'

'Forget about how it has got here,' Pål said. 'The most important thing is that it is here. The most beautiful gift the ocean has ever given us.'

'Strictly speaking, it's the forest that has given us this tree,' Gerda said. 'And now we must put every single bit of it to good use.'

At that moment, someone came running with an axe, then a saw, and they started to attack the ash tree. They stripped off its branches. The leaves fell off and to the ground, were trampled and blown into the ocean. And the tree was quickly reduced to a trunk, to logs and lumber. It was as if someone had undressed it, pulling off one garment after the next, until it was left naked.

The ash was made into axe handles and oars, because the wood was hard and strong, resistant to wear and tear. The tree was allowed to live on, but Tommy didn't understand this until much later. He cried himself to sleep two nights in a row and, on the third night, Grandmother came into his room and sat down.

'Hi, Tommy,' she said.

He didn't reply, merely pressed his face hard against the pillow.

'It was a nice tree,' she said. 'A shame we couldn't keep it.'

He nodded uncertainly, his face still turned towards the pillow. He was starting to have difficulties breathing.

'Look here,' Grandmother said. 'If you turn around, I will show you something.'

He didn't move, would have preferred not to look at her, to show her his reddened eyes, would have preferred not to speak with her, either, because he was afraid he would sob loudly, and it was embarrassing to cry, he thought, just as embarrassing as hugging a tree. What kind of creature was he, really, who hugged trees, who cried over trees?

'Tommy?' Grandmother said.

'Hmmph.'

'Can you just look up for a second?'

At long last, he rolled over onto his side and lay facing her in a foetal position.

'What?' he said.

'Look at this,' Grandmother said.

Then she opened her hand.

'Something from the tree,' he said.

'Seeds,' Grandmother said. 'Seeds from your ash tree. *Fraxinus excelsior.* That's the Latin name.'

He sat up and studied what she held in her palm. 'The seeds have wings,' he said.

'So the wind can carry them,' Grandmother said.

The next day they brought the seeds to the Four-season Room. They planted them in a pot in a corner, between grapevines and a feisty hop plant, and soon four small shoots sprouted.

Seeing the shoots grow helped. They let them grow until they were several centimetres tall before thinning them out. In the end, only the very largest and heartiest remained.

It was Tommy's responsibility to water the little tree, his responsibility to make sure it was fertilised. The tree and the boy grew up side-by-side, the tree reaching for the sky, its branches stretching upwards and entwining themselves around the life-giving lights in the ceiling.

The greenhouse runs like a well-oiled machine, all on its own.

Every day consists of so incredibly many hours, minutes, seconds. He would like to sleep more, but can't manage it; spend more time on meals, but food has no taste; read more, but there are no books that hold his attention.

Tommy doesn't know why he goes back. At all times he hears Tao's voice in his head, simultaneously beseeching and with a pretence of compassion. He knows what she wants and he knows she is trying to manipulate him. She thinks that if he remains long enough in the soft light of her voice, he will give in.

That is something he will not do. It is not because he needs her that he keeps returning, he tells himself, it is because he has nothing else to do.

As he approaches Svalsat, the light begins to fade. The polar night will soon be here and there will be darkness around the clock. It will become even more difficult to keep the days straight. He must find a watch that works. He doesn't trust the one he has, takes it off all the time, winds it and holds it up against his ear to assure himself that it is still ticking.

It is warmer in the radio room now. He left the heater on. The Svalsat power plant has enormous capacity and now that the wind is blowing so much, it supplies the rooms with all the electricity he needs.

He takes a seat at the desk and lays his hands in his lap but sitting still is difficult. He closes his eyes, inhales air deeply into his lungs, holds his breath and releases it slowly. I am in control, he tells himself, of course I am in control.

Finally the radio crackles.

She says hi, asks whether he is cold.

'No.'

'How are you doing?' she asks.

'Why do you ask?' he says. 'You know I won't be doing well until I get my brothers back.'

She hesitates. 'Rakel, then, how is she?'

'She misses Runa.' He tries to make his words sound credible.

'But she's not with you today, either?'

'If she were she would be talking to you now.'

'Doesn't she want to talk to me?'

'No. Maybe. I don't know. Why are you so concerned about Rakel all the time?'

'I just want to be sure that the two of you are all right.'

'How are Henry and Hilmar?' he hastens to ask.

'They're asleep. We're a couple of hours ahead of you now.'

There it is again, time is passing and he isn't in control. Time has taken his brothers. They were abducted by a watch someone wound too tightly, that is racing away, the hands spinning as quickly as the windmill on the roof above him.

'Do you want me to wake them?' she asks. 'Do you want to talk to them?'

The small bodies under the duvet, mouths open, breathing deeply, peacefully.

'Tommy? Are you there?'

'Yes.'

'Shall I wake up Henry and Hilmar?'

He pictures them waking, shuffling drowsily up to the wheelhouse, shivering against the winter night, standing with the microphone between them and listening to him. What would he say? How would he explain to them what has happened, what he has done?

'No.' His answer comes quickly. 'No, don't wake them.'

Sorry, sorry, sorry. If you find out, you will despise me, hate me, for as long as you live.

She falls silent. Then it's as if she summons her strength: 'Are you crying, Tommy?'

'No, of course I'm not crying!'

'Excuse me, it just sounded like—'

He interrupts her. 'This is pointless.'

'What's that, Tommy?'

'Stop saying my name all the time . . . Talking. You and me talking is pointless.'

'Please, don't hang up. I want to get to know you better, Tommy.'

And he doesn't hang up, he takes the bait, even though he knows that she isn't interested in him, that she is just trying to butter him up, using her voice and words as a truth serum he won't be able to resist.

'I am trying to understand both you and the place you come from,' she continues.

'Is that right?' he says. 'So now you're interested in me and in us. Better late than never.'

'I've been interested all along. I'd read everything I could find about Spitsbergen and Longyearbyen before we left. I like to read.'

'I have understood that.'

'Just like you.'

'Oh, shut up. I know what you're trying to do.'

She ignores him, keeps talking instead, tells him about the old photos she studied before the trip, of colourful houses, snow-covered mountains. And the aerial tramway pylons from the mining era which were still found throughout the landscape.

When he doesn't reply, she starts talking about their Environmental Act, that she thinks it is strange, how they had declared 1946 the end of history.

'Everything that was created before this year was preserved, while everything that came afterwards was trash?'

'Why do you find that strange?' he replies. 'You have to draw the line somewhere.'

'Yes, I understand that. But what's even stranger in a way is what you did with everything dated after nineteen forty-six.'

'What do you mean?'

'Like the mine on the Svea Bay. Assessed and found to be too easy, too new. That's why you sealed it up and removed all the infrastructure, the runway, the houses, the warehouses, the aerial tramway and the harbour. Every trace of human life erased, as if there had never been people there.'

'They restored the nature.'

'Yes, *restoration*, I've always thought that word was used when one talks about removing nature's footprint on something manmade, but now it was nature that was to be restored, reconstructed, reclaimed, by removing every trace of human impact ... A strange operation, don't you think? And beautiful. Humans are, I guess, the only species that actively goes about removing every trace of itself?'

'It wasn't beautiful,' Tommy says. 'It was political.'

'Yes, Tommy. I know that.'

'No,' he replies. 'You know nothing about us.'

Tao

She is unsure whether the signal has failed, or if he hung up.

She tries calling him again, but he doesn't answer.

Tao could have told Tommy more about his island. Because of course she knows that there were also political reasons for removing all traces of the mining operations and infrastructure. That it was better to remove the runway and the harbour than to leave them in place, because this would prevent others, such as China or Russia, from taking control of the bay. But the history books have told her that *others* attempted, even though Svea had disappeared. The last residents of Russian Barentsburg didn't disappear until 2039. And immediately afterwards, her people founded a settlement in the former mining town of Pyramiden. They moved into the houses, which had been occupied by seagulls, cleared away nests, shooed out the foxes, cleaned, painted, restored the old school. All they did was operate a research station, but the population of Longyearbyen was nonetheless sceptical. The Norwegian half of the population feared that Norway would lose its sovereignty over Svalbard; they claimed that China was challenging the Svalbard Treaty. The other half didn't care. It's no longer of any importance, they said, the old game is meaningless.

And in the end, it wasn't nation states who challenged the treaty and Norway's sovereignty, it was nature. The Svalbard society was too expensive for Norway. The emergency government of 2050 surrendered its dominion. Longyearbyen was not even allowed to be a final outpost since the borders were on the mainland and it was meaningless to try and retain control over the barren territory just south of the North Pole. But the Chinese community in Pyramiden stayed. With time they collaborated better and better with the people of Longyearbyen. In the summer they arrived by sea and in the winter made the trip on snowmobiles or dogsleds. And when China at long last shut down the research centre in Pyramiden in 2052 and pulled out its people, many of them chose to stay. They moved into Longyearbyen and became a part of the population. They also brought their customs with them, and the books from Pyramiden's library were given their own shelves in Longyearbyen's library. And it was decided that the students were to learn Norwegian, English and Chinese at school. Soon a mixing of the three languages occurred. People borrowed words from one another, said *wân ãn* instead of goodnight, *záijián* instead of goodbye and *qîng* instead of please. This was why the children were able to communicate with Tao.

This was all that had been written in the history books and all she had managed to dig out from the library's archives before her departure. For the last forty years, she found nothing. In 2069 all contact with the society in Longyearbyen came to a halt. The place faded into oblivion.

She tries to recreate an image of Tommy's face, picture him sitting there in the radio room. The wind was blowing so hard where he was today that she could hear it, as if it had made its way through the ether and hit her on the cheek. She pictures him walking home alone, head bowed against the wind, with his scarf pulled up over his nose. His face is still childlike and soft, but with eyes that have seen far too much. This was also how he had looked the first time she met him.

Even before the anchor had been dropped, they saw them. The children came running towards the water. Two girls and three boys. The sisters Rakel and Runa led the way. Rakel ran with determined strides, Runa a bit more uncertainly. Behind them came someone she assumed had to be Hilmar, eager and unafraid, eyes gleaming with curiosity. The shortest of the boys, Henry, was last, together with his big brother Tommy. Henry stumbled a little over his own feet. Tommy took hold of him, supported him. Henry wanted to run faster, but Tommy held back, hesitating, glancing quickly in the ship's direction, clearly sceptical.

They lowered the lifeboat. Tao took position astern with the ship's doctor, Shung. The first mate rowed with long strokes of the oars. Mei-Ling sat all the way at the front with her face directed towards shore.

The children waited. The boys and Runa sat motionless on their respective rocks. Rakel paced back and forth impatiently. As they drew closer, Tao could see each of them better. Only the girls were smiling. Rakel's smile was faltering, Runa's broad and welcoming.

'Remember,' the ship's doctor said. 'Maintain sufficient distance between you and them at all times. At least three metres.'

'Yeah, yeah,' Mei-Ling said impatiently. 'But if the children had been sick, they would have died a long time ago.'

Shung sighed. They had discussed this several times already. 'I am just trying to do my job.'

'Me, too,' Mei-Ling said.

There was a scraping noise and the boat's forward-gliding momentum was halted as it ran aground.

Mei-Ling jumped onto shore clutching the mooring line in one hand.

The captain pulled in the oars and Tao jumped overboard with the others following right behind her.

It was difficult to breathe beneath the mask.

Runa took a step towards them. Mei-Ling backed up ever so slightly and the girl must have noticed, because she did not come any closer. We don't exactly inspire trust, Tao thought, with our white suits and covered faces.

Ever since they had made contact with Rakel, ever since they heard the crackling, thin voice and understood that the seed vault was still intact, Tao had had a perception of how the children would look. Dirty, with clothing full of holes, like unkempt street children from a nineteenth-century European novel and maybe with dust on their faces from the coal found in the mountains up here. Now she was abruptly ashamed about her own preconceptions.

Rakel hid her body inside an oversized jacket, but her clothing was clean and neatly mended. Holes in the jacket sleeves were covered with patches the same size, nicely stitched. The leather of their boots was worn but polished to a shine with shoe grease.

Runa was different from her sister; she wore a floral print skirt over her boots, her hair was neatly combed and braided, her facial expression gentle, polite, and her smile was unwavering.

The boys all had the same colour eyes and hair, dark

brown. They were so similar that it looked as if they were the same person at different ages. But while the two youngest, who were still just children, walked towards her with searching expressions, the eldest stayed in the background. All the same, he was the one she studied covertly. His jacket was of animal fur, on his feet he wore a pair of knee-high walking boots, the patched trousers were of some kind of synthetic material, which had once been orange, the colour now faded by the wind and weather. The smallest boy walked back to him, tugged his sleeve a bit, pointed at Tao's entourage and said something, and the big brother took him protectively by the hand.

Rakel placed her hand over her heart and nodded hello.

'Welcome. I am the one you have spoken to.'

The children co-operated, let Shun check them, one by one. The doctor asked them to open their mouths wide, examined their eyes, ears, checked their pulse, took their blood pressure. Then she took both saliva and blood samples.

The children chattered while they were being examined, making no attempt to conceal their curiosity and excitement. They had lived in such isolation and had probably been raised to look at other people, the outside world, as a threat. Still, Henry, Hilmar, Rakel and Runa were trusting. Only Tommy's expression was difficult to read.

The children's language abilities surprised Tao. Among themselves the children spoke mostly Norwegian – a language which, as far as she knew, was not spoken much in the scattered settlements on the mainland and primarily belonged to the past. But the children spoke a mixture of English and Chinese to them and had no trouble making themselves understood, even the three youngest.

Tommy didn't say much. His head kept dropping between

his shoulders, as if he wanted to hide, and then caught himself, and straightened up again.

Tommy told them that he was eighteen years old, but he looked younger. He still didn't have any beard stubble on his face and his eyes were childish and round. She couldn't stop looking at him, this tall, thin boy who was born not long before her own son.

Tommy

The head torch has run out of power by the time Tommy heads home, but the moon hangs like a yellow ball above the mountains, lighting up the road for him.

It's not snowing, but his footprints on the road have long since been whisked away by the wind.

Eliminating all traces of oneself.

Tao thought it was beautiful.

He should have objected more forcefully. The restoration project was not about nature, it was about people. It was about practical rather than ethical considerations, not morally significant but rather opportunistic.

The hill becomes steeper. He starts to run, his legs moving on autopilot beneath him, finding a rhythm.

And the project was short-sighted, he thinks, based on a fear about what might potentially happen to the residents of Svalbard in the coming thirty years.

It was Grandmother who had told him thirty years. 'The planning horizon for the human race only extends that far into the future,' she explained. 'There hasn't been any point in thinking much beyond that, because there, in the relatively near future, death has basically awaited.'

'Why do you have to bring up death so often?'

'Because the only thing we human beings have always known with absolute certainty about ourselves is that we are in fact going to die.'

'Fun.'

'Death is always a part of us because it comes from the body itself, Tommy, from the brain, which stops working ... this is at least how death was defined. But actually it is easier to explain what death is by speaking about cessation.'

'Cessation?'

'Yes. When life ends, an organism dies. Death is the absence of life.'

She made it sound so easy. As if death were simple.

As if 'absence of life' was an adequate description of the tragedy that had struck them.

The first people to get sick were Manfred Iversen and his family, his wife Mari and their two teenage boys, Georg and Martin. The boys were in Tommy's class at school. Georg was one year older than Tommy, Martin a little younger. They were for the most part happy, they laughed loudly with their mouths open, were big, strong, healthy, had rosy cheeks and few blemishes. They ate healthy food, a lot of protein, because Manfred was one of the most driven egg collectors in Longyearbyen. Every morning throughout the entire breeding season, he took his feather-covered baskets, which resembled small nests, and went out to the bird cliff. He was every bit as big and tall as his sons, with powerful fists, and it was strange that he had chosen an occupation such as egg collector. But his big body concealed an aptitude for circumspection. Tommy had seen him out there at the foot of the mountain, among the nests. He moved carefully between them, watching every step so he didn't trample

anything, and chose eggs with diligence, just one egg per
nest, because he lived in accordance with the prevailing
principles in Svalbard: harvest only from the surplus, do not
cause undue impact, do not put a species at risk. It looked
like Manfred was dancing between the nests, as he twisted
and turned, tiptoed or stepped to one side, and from time to
time he would bend over and reach towards a nest, ignoring
the furious mother bird standing beside it and scolding him,
to pluck out a single egg with the utmost care. He returned
to Longyearbyen with eggs large and small, beige, brown,
spotted, which he traded for everything both he and his two
ravenous, rapidly growing boys might need. And when the
breeding season finally came to an end, he returned to the
nests and filled bags and old duvet covers with the down
shed by soft baby bird bodies. Every night the villagers slept
on pillows filled with Manfred's feathers. He gave them their
nightly slumber.

It was not fair that Manfred and his family were the first to
become ill, Tommy thinks now, but then stops himself when
he remembers something Grandmother used to say: neither
life nor nature has a predisposition for fairness.

The first symptoms of the illness were a headache, quea-
siness and a fever. Then came the muscle aches, followed by
vomiting and diarrhoea, Finally, a blood storm would rush
through the body, a tempest of such dimensions that it was
no longer possible to contain it, and the red life-giving fluid
was pumped out through all the orifices.

People gathered outside Manfred's house, one of the newer
buildings in an area without landslide risk, down by the delta
in the Advent Valley. With them they brought food, things
that should be easy to eat, such as dried meat and boiled
potatoes. Tommy also made the trip out there one evening,

or perhaps one night, he didn't look at the time, it was light around the clock in July anyway. A fog hung over the valley, a drizzle beading on the tall-growing grass along the south wall. Drops of blood dripped off the white coat Berit peeled from her body when she exited the house. A small crowd of people stood before the front door. Rakel was among them, in front as always. Tommy stayed a few metres behind the others.

Berit lifted her head and stared at them.

'This is no ordinary illness,' she said softly.

The doctor's statement was repeated like a kind of mantra in the days that followed. This is no ordinary illness. No, it is different, worse, this is something we have never seen before, have never experienced. They said it as if it were meant as a kind of apology for their impotence, as if they owed someone an apology.

People backed away at the sight of Berit's bloodstained coat.

'Yuck!' Rakel said.

'It's just blood,' William from Lia said. 'You've seen blood before.'

And they had all seen blood, those who slaughtered, those who quartered, those who would even drink fresh, warm blood straight from an animal in the wintertime to prevent scurvy. But this was death's blood, a red speckled pattern, the Last Days' batik on white, threadbare fabric.

That evening, when he was on his way to the kitchen for his supper, Tommy heard Father and Grandmother talking. They were standing in the kitchen, their voices subdued, but not so subdued as to prevent him from understanding every word from where he stood in the hallway, peeking through the half-open door.

'It's not that I'm not listening to you, David,' Grandmother said. 'I have always listened to you.'

Sunlight shone through the kitchen window, the midnight sun producing sharp shadows. Tommy was amazed that they hadn't heard his footsteps across the wooden floor, but perhaps his wool socks had muffled the sound or perhaps they were so focused on the conversation that they didn't notice anything else.

'You're my son,' Grandmother continued. 'Your opinions mean a lot to me.'

Father did not answer right away. Tommy could hear him moving, the faint creak of his clothing.

'Enlightened despotism,' David said, and his voice was hushed but contained an unusual intensity. 'You are the empress of this kingdom and you listen to advice when it suits you. Some advisers are more important to you than others. Yes, I am perhaps one of them, but still, when push comes to shove, you are the one who makes the decisions. Alone.'

'No, David, child, that's not true—'

He cut her off. 'Don't call me "child". I will soon be fifty years old.'

'You will always be my child. You, Tommy, Hilmar and Henry. And that is why I am asking you to leave now. We must get out of here, before more people contract this illness.'

Her voice was suddenly thick with tears, a rare and unfamiliar sound. Grandmother, Tommy thought, wishing he could hug her, embrace both of them and get them to put their arms around each other.

'We are staying here,' Father said. 'This is where we belong. This will pass, we are healthy, in a few weeks it will all be forgotten.'

Three days later, Manfred and his entire family were gone. Berit passed away soon afterwards. She was one of the few

single women among them. Apparently, she could not have
children and when she understood that she was ill, she got
into a boat and rowed to Hiorthhamn, an abandoned settlement on the other side of the fjord. The last words she spoke
were an earnest plea to all of them to stay away. For two days
people saw smoke rising out of the chimney of the cottage
where she had sought shelter. Then all signs of life ceased.
Nobody dared approach the cottage to check, nobody dared
cross the fjord, even though they usually found peace in
Hiorthhamn's hunting cabins. We must wait, they said to one
another, until the illness disappears. As though they believed
that Berit would also disappear and take the infectious dis-
ease with her if they just waited long enough.

For a few days, the illness was the first thing the villagers thought of when they woke, the last thing they thought
about before going to bed, but the night gave them no respite,
because the illness accompanied them into their dreams, per-
secuted them in their nightmares. A few of them discussed
whether they should self-isolate elsewhere in Spitsbergen, the
way Berit had done, not to spare the others, but to prevent the
infection from spreading. The idea was quickly dismissed:
we must stand united, everyone said, take care of each other,
the way we have always done, because who are we if we
begin to fail one another, no better than the people in the
world we once upon a time chose to abandon.

A short time after the smoke stopped rising from Berit's
chimney, it became easier to breathe. People thought they
would be spared, that the illness was a powerful wave that
washed inland and took with it only those who were closest
to the ocean. The majority clung to the conviction that it was
over before it had actually begun and in the midst of their
grief over having lost people they loved – some of Svalbard's

best, it was even said, the way it often is when someone dies; he or she was one of Svalbard's very best – in the midst of their grief they were even joyful, in the midst of their grief they permitted themselves to celebrate. Not an outright celebration; they would not dream of being so disrespectful, but more people than usual gathered in the bar of the Polar Hotel, and there were many who staggered home late in the evening after having had far too much to drink, who smiled, who laughed, who sang.

The villagers felt more like a single, large tribe than they'd done for a long time. When Tommy thinks back on this time, it is almost as if he can glimpse an aura of immortality hovering like a shining halo above Longyearbyen. People raised their glasses, toasting their strength, their health, people toasted having managed without the help of modern medicine, some even held that it could be they had evolved into a stronger variant of the human species, who survived even the most gruesome of illnesses, that life up here had inured them, given them thicker shells, or more powerful wings.

But no wings could carry them through this. The illness returned. This time it was the men who had been responsible for taking the corpses of Manfred and his family to the crematorium who were infected. The villagers still cremated their dead. The shifting soil in the churchyard was not suited for the burial of large coffins, which could pop up again when the ground shifted. The remains were transformed into carbon in a large, coal-burning oven by the old power station. They shoved the dead bodies inside and shovelled in coal remnants gathered on the shores and from beneath the old aerial tramways.

The coal was high quality. It burned with a heat so intense

that the human body, its large water content notwithstanding, quickly succumbed. The ashes they swept out afterwards were dry and grey, resembling the cold dust that stained the beaches black.

It was the fishermen Kenneth and Adrian who were responsible for transporting the deceased. Tommy believed there was never any discussion about whether Kenneth and Adrian should also attend to Manfred and his family. They just turned up, the way they always did. How stupid they were, he thinks now, never to have questioned, just stepping up, blindly, to help others. Kenneth and Adrian were family fathers with children in school, both of them tough and strong. They dressed in protective garments, scarves over their faces, gloves on their hands and transported the corpses on a wagon drawn by dogs, the same vehicle that was always used for this purpose, unless there was snow, at which time the huskies would be harnessed to a sledge. Tommy stood on the roadside and watched them pass with the first load, two bodies under a large, spotted sheet. Grandmother stood just behind him. When the small procession approached, she laid her hand on his shoulder and squeezed it gently.

'Don't go any closer,' she said.

The undercarriage of the wagon creaked, the men toiled, their faces florid under their scarves.

They stopped before a hole in the road.

'Can we drive it around?' Kenneth who was driving the wagon asked.

'No, just drive straight through,' Adrian said, who was pushing.

Kenneth began to pull.

'Come on,' Adrian said as he leaned forward, clearly summoning all of his strength.

The wagon lurched violently as Kenneth pulled, Adrian suddenly lost his grip and the wagon's right back wheel slid into the hole.

Adrian cursed under his breath. 'I said to pull.'

'I pulled,' Kenneth said.

The vehicle was now lopsided and the two corpses slowly began to slide.

One man ran forward to stop the movement, but Kenneth raised his hand.

'Stay back!'

The man stopped while Kenneth took hold of the body that lay closest to the edge. Turning his face away from the corpse, as if trying to avoid getting too close, to avoid breathing from behind his scarf, he pushed the body back onto the wagon bed. The sheet slipped off. A bare, purplish-blue foot peeked out. Kenneth hastened to push it back under the sheet.

Tommy didn't know whether it was in this situation that Kenneth was infected, if it was when he lifted the corpse up onto the wagon bed, or when they reached the oven and unloaded it again. He imagined that Kenneth and Adrian must have pushed the wagon up against the platform in front of the oven and from there rolled the corpses over, before pushing them into the fire together. Yes, it could have been there, as they stood before the burning coal, in meeting with the bodies and the illness that was still alive in all the dead flesh, that it happened.

But Kenneth could also have been infected the minute he entered the house. Manfred and his family's little wooden house, with the open, safe location, far away from the threat of the active mountainsides; the contagion must have been everywhere in there, invisible fields on all the surfaces, drops of blood on the floor and walls, reddish brown puddles in the beds.

The illness was of the efficient variety. It spread through all types of body fluids and was steadfast. It could survive for days, resistant to both cold and heat. But it did not survive the cremation oven, everyone was certain of that. It could not contend with Svalbard's coal. No virus or bacteria survives the flames, at least none that Tommy has read about. And he has had time to read a lot, trying to find answers, to understand the difference between viruses, bacteria, parasites and fungi, trying to understand what it was that was afflicting them.

Svalbard had been invaded by illness before, by a parasitic tapeworm carried by mice, which slowly destroyed the human liver. There had been an outbreak of rabies, which spread from infected foxes, and there had been an anthrax scare, which hid in dead, frozen animals. But that was a very long time ago. They had actually been safe, up until now.

'Where does death come from, Grandmother?'

He lowered his voice when he asked the question and she did not reply. They were walking towards the ocean. Grandmother had asked him to accompany her and he was happy to take the boat out on the ocean with her, away from the invisible ghost that hovered over Longyearbyen.

They walked in step on the frozen road. He adapted her footsteps to hers. He glanced at her; her face was closed.

'Grandmother, can we talk about the illness?' he tried again.

Then she flinched, as if he had woken her. 'The illness? That's not why I asked you to come with me this evening.'

'But I've read that it helps to talk about difficult things. That you can talk things through.'

'You shouldn't believe everything you read, Tommy. That talking about things helps? I have always preferred working. Digging in the earth. And to be quiet.'

'To be quiet?'

'Yes.'

'I don't really think that you're usually quiet.'

She laughed, suddenly and loudly.

'Nobody knows where death comes from,' she said. 'And I don't know if it matters.'

'Do you think it came from the ice?' he asked. 'From the meltwater caves?'

They had reached part of the shore where her boat had been pulled onto land and was lying upside down. She grasped the boat resolutely and tried to turn it over but lost her grip and cursed softly.

'Can you help me?'

He hurried over to stand beside her and together they flipped the boat over. She grimaced as she lifted. He was taken aback. She had never before needed help turning the rowing boat over. They leaned down and pushed it across the crunching frozen sand towards the water.

'Glaciers can hide everything,' Grandmother said. 'Preserve everything. Have you heard of Dumoulin?'

He shook his head.

They pushed the boat through the frozen water surface along the shoreline, and it rocked gently when it reached open water. Grandmother hopped on board and signalled that he should wade out and give it one final push. And as they rowed out, Grandmother told him about the married couple Marcelin and Francine Dumoulin who in 1942 left their house in Switzerland to milk the cows in the mountains, and never returned. They had five children and disappeared without a trace. Their bodies were not found until 2017, mummified in the Tsanfleuron Glacier, 2,900 metres above sea level. Their identity papers were still in good condition, as were their boots and their hair. The seventy-nine-year-old daughter Marceline, the youngest of the children, had never given up the search for her parents and was happy to be able to give them a proper burial.

Grandmother also told him about Ötzi, the Iceman, 5,500 years old. He was found in the mountains between Italy and Austria. Ötzi had long held the title as Europe's oldest mummy, but that was before the thaw period of the twenty-first century, before the really deep layers of ancient ice were affected, before the Ice Sisters from Mont Blanc were found in 2029, and the Tyrolean hunting party in 2038.

Grandmother held the left oar aloft and turned the boat using only the oar on the right.

Then she leaned back and rowed slowly out. Her movements were confident and practised, but Tommy noticed all the same that the rowing put a strain on her.

'But we're not going to talk about mummies now,' she said, a bit breathlessly. 'We're going to talk about ice. And none of these mummies can rival the seeds when it comes to age. Packages of genetic material, hidden far, far beneath us in all the world's glaciers, so tiny that you can scarcely see them, innocent, insignificant until they are unpacked, until we open the package, thaw them out, place them in the soil, water them and nourish them. A couple of innocent plants on a table in a laboratory, they sprout energetically, they blossom and release seeds.'

She stopped rowing for a moment and looked straight at him as she explained intently and with such feeling that he could picture it. A sunny day, it is warm inside, the assistant opens the window, a few seeds on the plants come loose, the wind carries them away, they fly through the air, descend to the ground, a weed-covered area, just below the laboratory. And there they take root, spread. In the beginning there are only a few plants, it takes time, but through small modifications, the plant adapts to the present, and then suddenly things move quickly. The plant covers flowery meadows like a blanket, stifling other species. It spreads both through off-shoots and seeds, has provided well for its own descendants, only a small remnant of a root is required for a new plant to sprout, only a few millimetres and then there it is, resolute, indomitable. It is perhaps the worst kind, it takes over the entire landscape, thrives everywhere and the little plant experiment on the windowsill has become Iceland's lupines, planted to prevent erosion in the early twentieth century, or the ground elder introduced in Norway as an edible plant in the monasteries during the Middle Ages. Or, perhaps even worse, perhaps it has become a tree that suppresses all the other plants, like the eternal darkness caused by the treetops of the explosive Sitka spruce, which squelched all other life on the forest floor when the species spread across Northern Europe in the last century.

While she spoke, Tommy forgot about everything that was happening on land. All that existed was the two of them out here in the boat and the illness was not sinister, but rather something abstract about which the two of them could theorise one chapter from a long history.

'So it's the glaciers, then,' he said finally, 'that are responsible?'

'A glacier can never be held responsible, Tommy.'

'You know that's not what I meant.'

She started rowing again. 'Only human beings can be held responsible, only human beings can feel ashamed. That is perhaps the most important difference between us and other species.'

'That and that we try to explain to each other what death is?'

She studied him from beneath the brim of her blue knitted hat. 'You're no fool, are you.'

The boat glided smoothly across the water. There was no wind, not a sound to be heard except the rhythmic movement of the oars and a seagull screeching high in the sky above them.

'But the ice is not the only possibility,' Grandmother said, and her eyes came to rest on the bird. 'Death could also have been brought by the migratory birds. With the sound of spring, in huge V-formations in the sky, a sound and a sight we have been taught to adore, or it could be we adore it by nature, yes, perhaps we are genetically programmed, selected to love the V-shaped echelons in the sky and the sound of a hundred geese honking in unison.'

'Yet another thing that separates us from the animals?'

'Love for V-formations, the need to explain, and shame?'

'Yes, perhaps precisely those three things.'

Again she stopped rowing. She was breathing heavily, even though she had been rowing slowly.

She tugged at the oars, but did so clumsily, and one of the oars slipped out of

the rowlock.

'Do you want me to . . .' he said and motioned towards the oars.

She nodded. 'Yes, perhaps that's just as well.'

She lifted the oars so they rested on the floor of the boat. The two of them stood up at the same time and changed places while the boat rocked perilously.

'Two people should never stand up in the boat simultaneously,' Tommy said. 'You're the one who taught me that rule.'

'The exception proves the rule,' she said.

'Yes,' he said, and started rowing.

Grandmother rowed Grandmother's boat. Always. This was also a rule.

She leaned back and observed the seagull as it sailed above them, hovering over the boat, in hopes of receiving scraps of fish.

'One of them may have brought death with them,' she said. She was breathing normally now. 'Hidden beneath their feathers, grey or brown, green or reddish. It may have come with any one of the migratory birds, with the insect-eating ruddy turnstone, the monogamous dunlin, or the round little ringed plover. It may have come accompanied by accelerating trills, *kviti tritritri, kviti tritritri*, or rolling lure sounds, *krrry, krrry krrrry*, or a soft, rising whistle, *tu-ip, tu-ip, tu-ip*.'

'Whistling is not your greatest talent.'

'I'm trying to bring it all to life for you, Tommy. You could at least appreciate the effort.'

He smiled at her. Grandmother, he thought, can't we just stay here in the boat for ever, can't we just row and row and never return to the fears of Longyearbyen?

'Death may have arrived in May,' she continued. 'Or perhaps, even before that, because the migratory birds arrive in Svalbard earlier with every passing year. It may have been carried here by birds from the countries that were once called Denmark, Germany, Spain or maybe even from the Congo or Uganda. And the birds are hosts for mites and ticks, which in turn can be hosts for viruses.'

'But you don't know which bird? Which species?'

'No, how in the world could I know that.' She looked at him gravely. 'You overestimate my abilities, Tommy. But I believe it was actually the birds that gave us the illness. No man is an island, you know. No, no island is an island ... Actually, there's no such thing as an island.'

They fell silent. The only sound to be heard was that of his rhythmic oar strokes. Grandmother's gaze swept across the water, was never at rest, as if she were searching for something at all times.

'Grandmother?'

'Yes?'

'Do you want us to leave Longyearbyen?'

'Yes,' she said. 'And that was why I wanted to take you out here with me this evening.'

He didn't know what to say.

'What do you think?' she asked. 'Tommy the seed custodian. What do you think about leaving?'

'I don't know,' he said and noticed a growing feeling of discomfort in his stomach. Because he wished she hadn't asked him that question.

'We would be safe,' Grandmother said. 'The illness wouldn't be able to reach us.'

'Mm,' Tommy said and then he was unable to say anything else.

'The most important thing for me is that all of you are safe,' Grandmother said. 'You, your father and your brothers.'

'What about the seeds?' Tommy asked.

Because, despite his discomfort, he could not help thinking about what she had just called him.

'When we are safe, the seeds are safe.'

The very last day of school. Everything felt almost normal early in the day. He remembers that some of the kids were snatching hats off each other's heads, sending them sailing through the air and that it didn't matter, because the weather was warm with only a gentle breeze. And then he remembers how the pupils poured into the school building after recess, every bit as noisy and distracted as usual. Rakel spoke loudly about a party she had been to in an abandoned house and several of the others laughed when she described how drunk she had been. Tommy rolled his eyes to himself. Bragging about being drunk, wasn't that incredibly childish? At the same time, he listened to every word Rakel said, and couldn't help imagining himself staggering around with Rakel, that for a short while he had forgotten about his brothers, his responsibilities, the illness.

Greta, their teacher, sat behind her desk, facing the class. Some of the desks were already vacant.

Then she clapped her hands. 'You don't need to sit down,' she said. 'You can pack up your things and go home.'

'Really?' the pupils cried in unison. 'No more school today?'

'The local government approved it unanimously yesterday evening,' Greta said. 'The school is closed until further notice.'

Immediately the class burst into cheers. The other pupils always cheered when they were given a day off from school, regardless of the reason. But then somebody shushed them.

'You must all go straight home,' Greta continued. 'Do not congregate. Do not dawdle.'

'What?' Rakel said. 'Why?!'

'Until we gain control, we must ask you to do as you are told.'

The children groaned, but their complaints died away quickly. Only Rakel protested.

'Just go home and wait? Why don't they try to do something instead? Ask somebody for help?'

'Help?' Greta said. 'What do you mean, Rakel?'

'Maybe there's medicine for the illness, somewhere else in the world?' Rakel said.

Tommy couldn't help smiling at the suggestion. He raised his hand and without waiting for Greta to call on him, and started talking. 'It's not up to us to have that discussion,' he said. 'It isn't exactly our mandate.'

'"Our mandate,"' Rakel mimicked. 'Good God. Speak Norwegian.'

'Tommy is right,' Greta said. 'The local government has no doubt thought this through. And now you must go home.'

She was pale, with dark circles under her eyes, and Tommy thought she didn't look well, but perhaps he was just imagining things.

He stuffed the old slate into his knapsack along with the dog-eared textbooks from the drawer of his desk. Without speaking to anyone, he took his jacket and left.

'Well now, Tommy,' Rakel called to him. 'You must be happy, now that you don't have to meet the rest of us idiots at school.'

Again she mimicked him. '"Our mandate."'

He turned around. She was standing with a group of other children, a crooked smile on her face.

Tommy didn't reply. What could he say?

'Run along to the library, now Tommy,' she continued. 'Maybe you can cure the illness with all your books.'

Glenn pulled her by the arm and mumbled that they should take off, but Rakel continued to stare at Tommy.

Rakel was the only one who said things like that. The others were friendly, but seldom reached out, knowing that Tommy would say no, regardless, and they accepted it.

Rakel had seen him sitting alone in the library. She thought he preferred books to the company of the other children. And she was right, but it wasn't because he didn't like them, but because he didn't know what he should talk to them about. The stories they shared, weren't relevant for him, nor interesting. Parties, sex, breakneck joyrides on borrowed snowmobiles that ran out of power far out on the mountain plateau. He had never taken part in any such escapades. And the questions he asked himself, how to comfort Henry when he'd had a nightmare, how to make a packed lunch tasty enough that Hilmar would eat it, how to mend socks, make gravy without lumps, remove the stains from the knees of Henry's trousers, how to talk to Hilmar when he had been fighting with a friend, were all questions to which none of them could give him answers.

Tommy turned away from Rakel. He suddenly saw himself from the outside. His knapsack full of books, his bowed head. Just Tommy, always alone.

But then he ran into Henry on his way out of the school building, his jacket open, scarf untied, his knapsack hanging over one shoulder.

'Hey,' Tommy called, and hurried over to him.

'Tommy,' Henry said, his face lighting up.

Tommy squatted before him.

'Look at you. I think you've forgotten something,' he said.

'No, I brought all my things, like the teacher said.'

'But what did I tell you about your scarf?' Tommy said and wound the scarf snugly around his brother's neck.

'That it has to be tied.'

'And your jacket?'

Henry made a face as Tommy started fiddling with the zipper.

'And then there's your knapsack.'

'It's so heavy!'

'It's even heavier when you carry it on just one shoulder. Besides, that could make your back crooked.'

'Yeah, yeah . . .what does that look like? When your back is crooked?'

'Like this.' Tommy raised one shoulder up beneath his ear and hunched over while making a face. 'Do you remember the Hunchback of Notre Dame?'

Henry laughed.

'Come on. Pull it on now.'

His little brother reluctantly pulled the knapsack straps over both his shoulders. 'But it's so heavy.' He walked a few steps. Then he stopped and looked up at Tommy. 'Really heavy.'

Tommy sighed. 'Fine. Give it to me, then.'

He held the knapsack in one hand and Henry's hand in the other, and together they headed home.

Yet another night, yet another argument in the kitchen, but this time he was woken by their voices. He heard them shouting at each other and got up immediately.

'It doesn't help to wash your hands, practise safe distancing, exercise caution, nothing helps as long as we're here,' Grandmother said.

'But does running away help?' Father said. 'That's your solution again now, isn't it, Mother? Because you don't need anyone else, do you now?'

Tommy walked all the way over to the open kitchen door, squinting against the light from the window.

Grandmother placed both her hands flat on the kitchen table. Father stood in the far corner by the stove, with the table between them, but the way Grandmother was pressing her weight against it made it look like she wanted to shove it against him, drive him into a corner.

'Tommy,' his father said, and looked towards the door.

Grandmother turned around for a moment, and saw him out there in the dark hallway, but she didn't care.

'I know that you think I've run away,' she said to Father. Her voice was lower now, hoarse. 'I know you think the first years of your life were horrible. I know you had experiences on the road that no child should have, that you are carrying memories of events that will affect you for the rest of your life. I thought I had managed to protect you, David, I tried at all times to spare you. But I was perhaps naive in believing that my caring for you would be enough. And you're right that

I haven't needed many people, but you know I have always needed you.'

Mother and son just looked at one another. It was as if Tommy wasn't there. Or perhaps they both wanted him to hear.

'I don't blame you for fleeing,' Father said. 'But I think there were places you could have stopped along the way. I think there were opportunities for the two of us in many places along the way, and I think, I know, that if you had stopped in one of these places, then I would have been spared that which happened later. But you just kept running, or moving, as you call it.' He spoke the last words with contempt. 'You couldn't find peace anywhere and you can't deny that you put your own need for movement before my need for security.'

'As a child you had perhaps an exceptional need for security, David. I'm sorry I didn't recognise that.'

'No,' Father hissed. 'Don't speak about this as if my needs were unusual. I had no "exceptional needs". I was just an ordinary child! And even though you believe I was too young to remember anything, I know that there were also other people in our life once upon a time. I remember another woman, she was almost a mother for me, and I remember an older girl, whom I thought of like a sister, but you forced me to leave them. I didn't even have a chance to say goodbye. You woke me up one night, we left under the cover of darkness, ran away. Because you didn't dare to stay, is what I think now. Because you couldn't bear to face the obligation, the responsibility involved in taking care of other people, of living in a community. You have always been a loner. I don't know where your solitariness comes from but I refuse to allow you to pass it on to me, to the boys.'

Then Father turned to face Tommy again and he

understood that everything his father said now was actually directed at him. Father wanted him to know, to understand what had shaped him. Tommy didn't know what he should do. In meeting his father's gaze, he would be showing his support, by looking away he created a distance. He cleared his throat, blinked, noticed that one of his eyelids was trembling.

Finally, it was as if Father noticed his helplessness because he turned away. As Tommy drew air down into his lungs, he noticed that he had been holding his breath. Father took a step towards Grandmother, placed his hands on the table, leaned over it and stared at her intently.

'You've always said no to society, Mother.'

'But there was no society along the roads we travelled,' she replied.

'Not until we got here, at the end of the world,' he continued. 'Not until you were compelled to stay did you take part in something resembling a community.'

'I wanted to stay here,' Grandmother said, but her voice was faint.

All of a sudden, she crumpled and put a hand to her stomach, as if racked with pain.

'What's the matter?' Father said.

'Nothing,' Grandmother said, and straightened up again. 'I chose to settle down in Longyearbyen. I chose it, because I saw that it was a good place for you to be.'

'Rubbish!' Father said. 'You didn't choose to stay. You wanted to leave all the time. The planes stopped coming, they were grounded in other places in the world, the runway was long since destroyed and no ships left Svalbard any longer. You came to a society that had chosen to protect itself through isolation and when you realised that also this place would be too cramped for you, that also these people demanded too much, there was no longer anywhere else to go.'

Grandmother released the edge of the kitchen table with first one hand, and then the other. Then she took a step backwards. She turned her head and looked at Tommy. Her eyes were shining.

'Don't you want to go to bed, little one?'

'Yes,' Tommy said. 'I don't know ... it's hard when the two of you ...'

I must say something else, he thought, something that will make them stop, they must become friends again, I must make sure they are friends. Because otherwise everything will fall apart. He was the thread and when he was pulled from both ends, when he was stretched taut between them, it was painful.

His father too had turned to look in Tommy's direction. There was an unfamiliar fortitude in his gaze.

'It is impossible for him to sleep, you understand that certainly, when we're yelling like this.'

He spoke the words with kindness, didn't he, as if he wanted the argument to be over?

Grandmother looked towards Tommy, half-heartedly threw up her hands, tried to explain. 'I never wanted to leave Svalbard, I felt at home here, from the moment I came ashore on the very first day.'

'Yes,' Tommy said. 'You told me that.'

But now his father made a scoffing sound. 'I remember how you carted me around. It must have been the summer after our arrival. It was pouring, as usual, my feet were wet, water was leaking into my boots, but your hand was warm, as I recall you were short of breath all the time, as you searched frantically for someone who could take us away from here.'

I must say something, Tommy thought. He has to stop, I must make him stop.

'You're lying,' Grandmother said. 'You were a little boy. Your memory is playing tricks on you. You are mixing up situations, confusing events. You are remembering our time in Troms. What you are describing never happened in Svalbard.'

Father didn't reply, he just stared at her until she looked down.

'At the very least you can't say that I didn't become a part of the community here, in the end,' she said. 'That I didn't take responsibility just like everyone else. Yes, maybe more than many others, maybe more than most.'

'Are you talking about the seeds?' Father said, enraged now. 'The custodian role? That makes you so "special"?'

He never heard them argue again. After this night, for a few days they attempted to go on living as before. Vain attempts to carry out routines, a couple of dinners at five o'clock, Tommy who sang 'Are You Sleeping, Brother John?' to Hilmar and Henry or sat them down at the kitchen table with all their schoolbooks spread out like a fan before them.

'You must try,' he said to his brothers. 'Please.'

Grandmother had found a blackboard for them. She must have taken it from the school, pulled it down the muddy road, because the wheels were caked with dirt. Sometimes she would come into the kitchen to see how they were doing, write something on the blackboard, he can't remember what, the letters would not join into words. Once she crouched over and placed a hand on her stomach, the same movement he had witnessed during her late night argument with Father, but she straightened up again almost immediately with a quick glance in Tommy's direction, probably having noticed that he was watching her. He didn't meet her gaze. Instead he looked at the books, suddenly bashful, as if he had observed something he wasn't supposed to see.

The two younger brothers didn't notice a thing, were consumed by restlessness. Henry leaned over the table, groaning. Hilmar got to his feet and walked over to the window.

'Hilmar, sit down,' Grandmother said. 'We aren't finished.'

'I want to go outside,' Hilmar said.

'You can't,' Grandmother said.

'Look, there's Mikkel,' Hilmar said.

He raised his hand and waved at his friend. 'Mikkel is alone.'

'Yes,' Grandmother said. 'Indeed he is.'

'I want to go out and see him.'

'No,' Grandmother said.

'But he's not sick. He looks completely healthy.'

'Sit down!' Grandmother shouted and her voice was so loud that everyone jumped.

That same evening, Brett knocked on the door. Grandmother opened it a crack, peered out, his brothers standing behind her. Brett stood three metres away. He told her that now also Mikkel's family was dying.

'Yes,' Brett said. 'That's all I wanted to say.'

'Thank you,' Grandmother said, through the crack.

'Good luck, then,' Brett said, and his words sounded small and out of place.

All the rest, the chronology of events disappears, time breaks up into fragments, miscellaneous puzzle pieces that Tommy can rearrange, and that can be put together in a way, but all the same cannot, because nothing actually makes sense; sense has evaporated. It has been thrown like drops of water onto Svalbard's hot coals, sizzling momentarily before it vanishes.

A yellow house, mottled by the wind and weather. He stands outside, the window is open. He can hear sounds from inside, long, drawn out howls. The deepest pain, the kind of torture that makes people stop being human, turns them into animals. It is the sound of being in the throes of death, of giving up.

Tommy and Henry on the roadside, hand in hand, black shadows. The sun shines relentlessly, it hasn't rained in weeks. The mud has dried and turned to dust that stings the eyes, settles in layers inside the lungs, makes Henry filthy. The washrag, every evening he must wash that little face and the skinny arms and the washrag always becomes grey with dust.

The dogs have been released from the kennel and run inland in a pack, through Advent Valley, away from the village.

The bed, it is uninviting, hard and cramped. He can hear his brothers breathing deeply in their sleep. He gets up, gets dressed, goes outdoors. He meets no other human beings. The library is silent, dusty and empty. He moves soundlessly along the shelves, runs one finger across the spines of the books. Stops, pulls out a book, opens it to a random page, reads a few words. *Now*, he reads, *here*. Puts the book back, moves on. Thank you, books. Farewell. Then he closes the door and hurries home again, the only living shadow in the sun-filled night.

Rakel and Runa on the wharf. He sees them from a distance, does not approach them. The hissing sound of the fishing line when Rakel casts with the pole, the dogged expression on her face as she reels in the empty line. Runa sits on a rock, she lifts her hand to her head, tries to straighten her bow, but the ribbon is loose and wrinkled. Where are you living, he wants to ask, who is taking care of you? But they are too far away, his voice will not carry. And he doesn't dare to walk any closer.

The neighbour's girl Wilma, who is standing outside her house, crying.

'Where's your mum?' Tommy asked. 'Where's your dad?'

She points at the house. 'They're just lying there. I called out to them, but they can't hear me.'

Wilma has only one shoe, the other is missing. In one hand she holds the slingshot she got for Christmas. She keeps winding the rubber band tightly around her wrist, while the tears stream down her cheeks, which are dirty, covered with brown splotches of blood.

'Could you come inside with me? Please?' Her voice is high pitched.

But he backs away, hurries off, up the hills, home to their own house and closes the door.

His voice, the way he tries to keep it calm while an unfamiliar tone vibrates inside him. He is standing in front of his brothers who are sitting on the sofa, and he sees how they creep towards each other, that his voice is scaring them.

'Don't talk to anyone. Stay away from everyone,' he says. 'We can only be with each other. Only the family. Do you understand?'

The healthcare workers dressed in old survival suits used for protection out at sea, homemade face masks and gloves, rushing down Hilmar Rekstens Road, one taking the lead and two others following behind him, heads held high, gazes full of importance, the most important people among them now, even though they must know that they will soon be gone, that soon everyone will reach an unspoken agreement that there is no point in trying to help the sick, because there is no way out other than death.

Grandmother in the greenhouse. She pulls turnips out of the soil, replants cuttings that are so small that they should have been left in the seed tray a little while longer. She is oblivious to her surroundings, wholly absorbed by her work. The artificial lamp light from the ceiling casts hard shadows on her face and darkens her eye sockets.

The sound of the cart on dusty roads. Emily's face appears when the wind catches hold of the sheet. A twisted grimace and staring eyes in a face covered with haematomas. Tommy rushes to pull Hilmar close to him, forcing his face into his own chest. Hilmar protests, no, I want to see. You're not allowed, Tommy says, and holds him tightly.

The metallic odour of blood, a smell that is familiar from hunting and slaughtering, but all the same so completely alien.

Their view from the sitting room: the smokestack on the crematorium, the smoke rising, always rising, glutinous, thick, almost brown. Nothing can stop that smoke.

The sound of wailing from the yellow house also rises, becomes a part of the smoke, a howling mist hovering above all of Longyearbyen.

*

And the dreams at night. Hilmar falls ill, his contorted face, the death wail. Or Henry, lying on his tummy, the way he usually sleeps. Tommy tries to wake him, but his little brother does not respond. He takes hold of his tiny body, turns him over. The face screams at him mutely, nothing but a pool of blood.

Night time. Tommy is awake. He looks at the clock, half past one. He squirms, the bedding is damp, the pillow too hard, too flat. He tries lying on his stomach, but his arm is in the way and he twists over onto his back again. For a short while he finds rest in this position, but then his shins start to itch and he can't stop himself from twisting and turning.

He is so tired when he eats breakfast that his hands are shaking and the number of hours ahead of him seems endless.

The food has no taste. He chews slowly. Swallowing is difficult. He remembers Henry as a one-year-old, how he constantly got food stuck in his throat. Tommy watched over him at mealtimes, attentive to the strange choking sounds he would make when the food wouldn't go down. He would often have to go over and pound Henry on his back. A few times he even took hold of the boy's feet and held him upside-down, shaking him, until whatever was stuck came loose and, once, he put his fingers down his throat to extract a piece of potato. He can still remember the feeling of the smooth surface inside there, the mealy piece of potato he grasped between his fingers, and how afterwards Henry howled for a long time, trembling in his lap with fear and shock.

He chews and chews. Ensures that every single mouthful is ground to a pulp between his teeth before daring to swallow. A tough piece of meat tries to trick him, almost goes down the wrong pipe. He coughs, grabs the water glass, drinks down huge gulps and swallows the morsel, while images flood through his mind. How he gets down on his knees, emitting faint choking sounds from his throat. How his face gets red, then blue, until he ends up lying on the floor with his eyes wide open. Nobody will come to help him, nobody will come to find him. More alone than ever before.

If only Grandmother had been here, with her quick footsteps, her enthusiasm and her many stories. He needs to hear her voice, let it calm him down, needs to disappear into a story.

She could have told him the story of the wheat. She loved telling him about the wheat. Every time she told the story, she embellished it a bit and it didn't help if he told her *I've heard it before*, or if he turned away, saying *yeah, yeah, Grandmother*, because she would keep going anyway. This is the most important story, Tommy, and it is important that you, you in particular, know it.

Tell me about the wheat, Grandmother.

He feels like he can hear her breathing, softly, calmly, the way she used to breathe before she got sick.

Think about everything the human race has accomplished in just a few thousand years, she says. They have settled on huge tracts of land, which they made their own, they have created societies where before there was wilderness, they have conquered the air also, done the impossible, spoken with people on the other side of the globe. And everything they have accomplished started with a piece of grain, a seed. People thought of themselves as the masters of the seeds. But it was actually the opposite.

Here she adds a dramatic pause to give him the chance to ask a follow-up question.

The opposite? Opposite how?

Well, I will tell you.

For several thousands of years the wheat, corn and rice,

the rye, barley, oats and soy were the actual masters of the earth. The seeds in the vault, the crates from Israel, from the Middle East, einkorn and emmer wheat are the predecessors of the wheat types we have today and in the same family as the very first wheat seeds. They are in the same family as the seed a young woman picked up from the ground and held up to the light. She studied the grain for a long time before putting it into her mouth and eating it, and the grain of wheat, which at that exact moment was crushed between the woman's teeth, had no way of knowing that it would become the seed that would change everything. The woman picked more wheat grains and later that day told her family about the grain she had eaten. Her daughter began gathering the grain. She brought it home with her and then she ground it in a mortar and made porridge. And the porridge, and later the bread, was tasty and nutritious. From that point on things happened quickly. A thousand years later, grain no longer grew wild in the region. Human beings had long since settled here and conquered the land. But it wasn't actually humans who conquered the land: it was the plants that in fact ruled. Human beings had become slaves of the plants.

Slaves, Tommy replied, come on ...

The human beings called themselves the rulers of the world, saw for themselves how they became the species that changed everything, but actually it was the wheat which changed the earth. Imagine, picture it, that you are an ear of wheat.

An ear? Grandmother ...

Don't be so difficult. Imagine that you are an ear of wheat, with two or three or maybe even five grains on the ear, imagine that you are standing in a field at some time in the beginning of the last century, between thousands of other ears, you grow at the same pace as they do, reaching for the sky and the sun at an identical rate, as if you are all one, large organism. You dance in the wind in time with the others, you all move back and forth simultaneously. If you look up and observe yourself from the outside, from above, you will not see yourself, you will see the whole of you. From up there in the sky you discover that combined, you are enormous. All of you are a thin veil of tiny shoots on black soil in the spring, you are green blankets covering long and narrow plains in the summer, you are golden and vigorous in the autumn. You grow so closely together that nothing else can intrude, a dense, impenetrable carpet. And you cover the world. Every day millions of people walk out into the fields to cultivate you, first to sow, then water and fertilise, finally to harvest. The people build their houses, their roads, their schools, railways and airports adjacent to where the wheat will grow. Human beings have learned how to interpret the wheat's language, the ears do not need words, because they understand you anyway, notice every little sign, every wish and requirement, are more attuned to signals from you than from other members of their own species. And the wheat takes control of the world, it slowly eradicates other species, where previously there were forests, where thousands of species once lived in interaction, now only a single type of grain is growing. The conquest occurs because the wheat has a faithful servant, a servant who gives the ear everything it asks for. With the help of human beings, the wheat spreads silently but powerfully and once it has started it is impossible to stop. The wheat is the most powerful. Because while human beings are individuals and alone, vulnerable due to their limited scope, easily slain, the fields, due to their magnitude, are hugely powerful.

Yes, but Grandmother, we were the ones who began cul-
tivating wheat, after all. We were the ones who controlled *it*.

Yes, that's what we have been told. But actually it was the
wheat that tricked us into abandoning our greatest strength:
our mobility. The wheat made us every bit as attached to one
place as a plant, caused us to forget that it is not we who need
the earth, who need roots, to survive. Do you understand
what I mean, Tommy? We forgot that we are able to move
around, that we can escape when things become difficult.

I miss you, Grandmother.

I still don't understand how to live without you. Or without Father.

David, Father, who was he, really? If Tommy's family were
a forest, Grandmother and Mother were the trees, powerful,
towering, occupying all the sunshine. Father was just the
underbrush. He stayed close to the forest floor, one metre
above the ground. It was never Father people noticed, it
wasn't the wind rushing through his treetops people heard,
or his trunks that were so large that people had to make a
detour around him to get past. One could step on him without noticing, one could trample his opinions into the dirt
without being aware of it. But he never gave up; he grew
steadfast, in the semi-darkness, stretching towards the light
with a clear goal: that one day he would be seen and heard.

Tommy believes that Father, perhaps up until the very end,
felt it was Longyearbyen that had raised him, Longyearbyen
that had given him love and all the structure a child needs.
And that it was therefore right for him that he died along with
the place that he loved.

It was right for Father. But it was not right for Tommy. Or
for Hilmar and Henry. He put us second, Tommy thinks,

and repeats the words to himself. He put us second. But they are only words, he alone can decide whether he wants to ascribe them with meaning. No father can save him now, no father tried to save him back then. Father made a different choice.

The details from the last day at home are ingrained in his memory. His brothers' shoes on the floor in the hallway, tossed onto the floor helter-skelter, their glasses on the kitchen table, the almost invisible marks on them from their lips, Hilmar's clothes in the bathroom, the socks that remained stuck inside his long underwear, which in turn were stuck inside his trousers and the jumper and undershirt, both inside out. Hilmar's little world, built from old plastic blocks, in a corner of the sitting room, several small houses of different colours, a wharf and the beginnings of a ship.

And the traces of Father, a forgotten bullion cup on the chest of drawers in the hallway, a stack of books, bookmarks sticking out of some of them, on the coffee table in the sitting room, his fingerprints on the shiny watering can on the windowsill.

Father had gone out while everyone was still asleep and taken his fishing gear with him. When dinner was on the table, he had still not come home and they started eating without him. Tommy remembers the soft beans on the plate in front of him, the smoked reindeer meat he struggled to chew, the overcooked cauliflower.

'But where is Daddy?' Hilmar asked.

'He'll be back soon,' Tommy said.

'Has something happened to him?'

'No, I'm sure he's fine.'

'Imagine if he has fallen ill?' Henry said breathlessly.

'No, no,' Grandmother said. 'He was fine earlier today. Eat your dinner now.'

They did as she said, but Tommy noticed that Henry and Hilmar just picked at their food.

'He is often a little late,' Tommy said.

Nobody replied.

Finally they heard the back door open and the sound of the fishing gear being put away in the cupboard.

'Hello,' Father said from the hallway.

'Hi,' the children said in unison.

'Where have you been?' Henry asked.

'Sorry I'm late. I'll be right in,' Father said.

They heard him hang up his jacket on its hanger, place his shoes on the shelf, put on his sealskin slippers and walk, the faint sound of leather against the floor. Immediately it seemed to Tommy that every sound was too loud, too upsetting, and he jumped when Henry's fork hit the plate and when Hilmar set his glass down on the table.

Father came in, walked over to the kitchen counter, rolled up his sleeves, turned on the tap, and washed his hands for a long time. The soap foamed around his fingers and he washed his forearms too, as far up as he could without getting his jumper wet.

Then he sat down at the table, poured a glass of water and helped himself to the meal.

'Well?' Grandmother said, watching him.

'Gunnar and his mother, too,' Father said.

'Poor Mari,' Grandmother said. 'But it's odd that they contracted it, all the way out there.'

Mari and her adult son Gunnar lived alone at the kennel, far out in the Advent Valley, yet they had been infected.

Father didn't reply.

'But where have you been?' Henry asked.

Father took a bite of potato, chewed slowly.

'I have signed up to work at the cremation oven,' he said.

'What,' Grandmother said.

'Somebody has to do it.'

'No,' Grandmother said, standing up abruptly. 'No!'

'We can't just leave the bodies lying there.'

Grandmother spooned the last piece of cauliflower out of the pot, and onto Tommy's plate.

'I'm full,' he said.

Nobody was listening. Grandmother threw the pot into the sink, put the plug in and turned on the tap.

'Who is it that can't just lie there?' Henry asked.

'The dead, you dope,' Hilmar said.

'Hush,' Tommy said.

Grandmother had started doing the dishes. She snatched the glasses off the table before they were finished drinking, threw cutlery and pots into the soapy dishwater at the same time. That's in the wrong order, Tommy thought.

'We can't just leave the bodies lying there,' Father repeated and then he looked at his sons. 'To get rid of the illness it's important that we cremate them as soon as possible. You understand that, right?'

They nodded, Henry eagerly, presumably trying to show he was a big boy, Hilmar and Tommy more reluctantly.

'They understand that,' Grandmother said. 'But they don't understand why you are the one who has to do it.'

'Everyone has to pitch in, right, children?' Father said.

Grandmother threw the frying pan into the utility sink with a clatter, rinsed it off with water and scraped the iron surface with the dish brush. Then she cleared off their plates and put them in the sink.

That's the wrong order, Tommy thought. The glasses must be washed first. The grease from the dinner coated the water like bubbles, bobbing on the surface, gaping at him.

The empty eyes of dead bodies.

He never saw his father at the cremation oven but is still unable to rid himself of the images of him, with the heat glaring like a stage light into his face, his singed fingertips, the soot on his forehead. He lifts, carries, lugs, hauls. Nothing is heavier than a dead human being, nothing is more unwieldy than limp arms, limp legs, knees and wrists, than a head hanging and dangling. And the bodies Father is moving never have time to become stiff, he gets no help from rigor mortis. It's a matter of getting them into the oven, quickly, quickly. Because everyone is depending on David, that he is willing, that he can bear it. Everyone is looking at him now.

Tommy lay in bed waiting for sounds from the kitchen, for shrieking voices and loud shouts or subdued hisses bent on keeping the argument out of earshot of the children. But the silence of the afternoon extended into the night. He heard Grandmother go to bed first, then Father, the familiar sound of footsteps moving across the floor of the hallway, the creaking floorboard in front of Grandmother's door, the blackout curtains being pulled down to keep the midnight sun from disturbing their sleep. A dark silence settled in the rooms. Tommy pulled the duvet over his ears to escape.

The next morning the rooms were still occupied by silence. Henry was sitting at the table holding a cup between his hands, his feet dangling. He was too short for a grown-up chair. Grandmother was still home, usually she was out the door before the children were up, now she had heated up meat bullion for them, the steam from the pot settling like dew upon the windows.

Hilmar got up right after Tommy. He glanced around him.

'Where is Daddy?'

Grandmother poured bullion into cups with calm hands. 'He left around six.'

Hilmar went over to the window. Henry got up and went to stand beside him.

'There's smoke,' Hilmar said and pointed at the smokestack of the crematorium. 'Is he down there now, do you think, is he lighting the oven?'

'Yes, he is probably there now,' Grandmother said.

For a while, the two boys were silent.

'But can people burn up?' Hilmar asked.

'Everything burns, if it gets hot enough.'

Then Grandmother pulled the corners of her mouth into a semblance of a smile.

'Today you can take the day off from your schoolwork.'

'Yes!' Hilmar said.

'You can go down to the beach and gather coal,' Grandmother said.

'No! Do we have to?' Henry said.

'You remember what your father said about pitching in?'

'That somebody has to do it,' Hilmar said, looking small.

'Right.'

When they had eaten and dressed, Grandmother took out three old hessian sacks and gave them to the children.

'Fill them up as much as you can,' she said.

Her gaze lingered on Tommy. 'Look after the two little ones.'

'What do you mean?' he said. 'I always look after them.'

'Thank you,' she said.

I would let a bear kill me to protect them, you know that. I always take care of them, until my shoulders are stiff and my stomach aches. Why are you even asking me that?

'What are you going to do all day?' he said. 'Why can't you come with us, if it's suddenly so important to gather coal for the stove?'

'Go on now,' Grandmother said.

And then she closed the door behind them.

They walked to the beach by the airport and gathered lumps of coal for several hours. The coal had once been trees, a wetland forest from the Cretaceous Era, or deciduous trees from the Palaeogene Period. The black fragments lay on the ground like reminders of the forest that long ago had covered these tracts of land, when they were located on another place on the globe. Tommy wished he could have seen every single tree, he wished they could rise up out of the dead lumps on the beach, that thick trunks could grow all around them, protecting them, that they could walk into the forest and disappear amidst green leaves.

It was warm. They needed neither mittens nor hats. While they gathered coal, Tommy thought about all the hands that had been out here, that the pieces of coal he now picked up and weighed in his hand to assess whether they were worth bringing home with him, perhaps had already been held by somebody else. And that these people had neither been wearing gloves, and there was already illness in their home and they brought it with them out to the beach and left it behind on the rocks, on the coal. The illness was like an invisible creature that crept on tiptoe through Longyearbyen and ran its fingers of death over all of them.

Henry and Hilmar gathered almost no coal whatsoever, but when Tommy's sack was a quarter full, he decided that they should go back.

'I'm hungry.' Henry fretted and took his hand.

'You'll get something to eat later,' Tommy said.

'Why can't we walk on the road?' Henry complained when he led them down the hill to walk home along the shore.

'There might be people up there,' Tommy said.

'And the oven,' Hilmar said and pointed. 'The oven's there.'

'Is Daddy there now?' Henry asked.

'How should I know?' Tommy answered.

They continued walking for a bit. Tommy carried Henry's light sack, while Hilmar dragged his own behind him.

'Don't do that,' Tommy said. 'You'll rip it.'

'I am so tired,' Hilmar said.

'You've barely gathered anything at all,' Tommy said.

'I'm hungry,' Henry repeated.

'Why do we have to carry all the coal home with us, anyway?' Hilmar said. 'Why can't we just bring it up there?'

He pointed up towards the old power station where smoke could be seen rising out of the smokestack of the crematorium.

Tommy stopped, looked at him. For a moment, he was tempted. The sack of coal weighed heavily against his back, he was sweating and it was going to be taken up there anyway.

There was also something else that was drawing him there. Up to now, all he had seen of the illness had been bodies covered with sheets, bloodstains on Berit's white doctor's jacket, Emily's dead face on the trolley, just details, hints. It was up there, at the oven that one saw everything, he thought. Hell was up there and he wanted to see what the kingdom of death looked like. He wanted to see what his father had volunteered to do. Were the corpses stacked on top of each other? Did they have a stoker who was responsible for shovelling coal into the hot, blazing oven while the other two loaded in the bodies? And the illness, was it really as hideous as he had understood it to be, did it turn its victims into bleeding flesh wounds, bursting them open from the inside out?

Hilmar must have noticed his hesitation, because he seized his chance to weigh in: 'For sure it's not that dangerous,' he said. 'We'll just walk up and leave the bags there. And maybe we'll see Daddy.'

'I want to see Daddy,' Henry said.

'No,' Tommy said. What was he thinking was he couldn't take the two little ones to hell.

He started walking again. 'Let me take your bag instead. I'm used to it.'

'Daddy,' Henry whined.

'Shut up and walk,' Tommy said.

Henry flinched. He swallowed his tears, sniffling hard. Tommy had frightened him, as if the world were not already frightening enough.

'Sorry,' Tommy said. 'I didn't mean it. Come on, let's go.'

He took both sacks in his right hand and offered his left to Henry, who immediately grasped it.

Grandmother was sitting on the stairs when they came back. Her cheeks were red, and she looked sweaty and agitated as she drank water from a bottle.

'There you are,' she said.

Tommy held up the sacks of coal. 'Has Daddy come home? Will he need these right away?'

'No,' Grandmother said. 'We will take them with us.'

'With us? Where?'

'Into Todalen. To one of the cottages there.'

'Huh?' Hilmar said.

'But what about Father?' Tommy said.

'He'll join us there later,' Grandmother said.

She took the bags of coal and poured some of the contents from Tommy's into Hilmar's, so they weighed about the same. Coal dust filled the air and her fingers got soiled. Tommy glanced down at his own; they were also black. His face was probably covered with coal dust, too.

'I don't want to,' he said. 'I want to wait for Father.'

Grandmother stopped and looked at him. 'None of your foolishness, Tommy. You understand this.'

'No,' he said. 'I don't understand anything. The only thing

I do understand is that we must stay together, all five of us. The whole family.'

'Yes,' Grandmother said. 'I know that's what you want. But now we must go.'

'But Father,' he said. 'Please.'

Hilmar and Henry stared, their eyes moving from Grandmother to Tommy and back again.

'He'll come later,' Grandmother said.

'But how will he know where we are then, if we're just going to some cottage or other.'

'We have agreed on which one.'

'Which one then?'

'Really now, Tommy.'

'Which cottage, then?'

'The red one.'

'The red one? Half of them are red!'

She shot him a stern look and took out an old cloth bag which she offered to Tommy. 'If there's something you need from your room, some books you would perhaps like to bring along, then you must hurry and pack them now.'

'I don't want to bring anything,' he said.

'Fine,' she said. 'Probably wise. We have a lot to carry as it is.'

Then Tommy saw that she had packed a backpack for each of them. They were lined up and ready along the wall, together with Grandmother's rifle.

'Where's Father's backpack?' he said.

'What?'

'There's only four.'

'He'll pack his later.'

Hilmar tugged at Tommy's jacket. 'Will you stop,' he said softly. 'Can't we just go?'

'But she's lying,' Tommy said and felt a pressure on his chest. 'Don't you understand that she's lying?'

Grandmother took a step towards him, placed a hand on his arm and squeezed it gently.

'Please, Tommy, do as I say. You are still a child and I am the adult. You have to trust me.'

'No,' he said, but softly.

Giving in felt like dropping something large and heavy, as if he had been holding a stone high above his head, so heavy that he almost couldn't lift it, but all the same, he had held his arms up until his muscles burned. Now he released the stone and it slammed against the ground with a bang.

He took the cloth bag Grandmother had put down on the ground, ran up to his room and threw a few random books into it, mostly to demonstrate that he'd done as she said, that he had actually packed something. Then he went downstairs again. Hilmar and Henry were ready to leave and had their backpacks on their backs. They had each been given a piece of dried meat which they were chewing on. There was something ordinary and familiar about the chewing that made Tommy despair, the rhythmic movements of jaws in round children's faces.

'Good,' Grandmother said. She smiled and stroked him lightly on his cheek, a gesture he quickly shrank away from.

Then she helped him put on his backpack. It was as heavy as lead.

'What did you put in here?' he asked.

'Food,' she said. 'Enough food for a long time.' Then she picked up the rifle that was leaning against the wall of the house. 'We'll take the path. And then we will walk along the side of the mountain, above the water.'

She started walking east. Tommy felt faint, dizzy, and tried to keep his eyes focused on her back, ignoring everything else. But they had only walked a few metres when they heard a shout behind them.

'Mother? Tommy!'

They turned around.

'Damn!' Grandmother whispered.

Father came running down the road towards the house and he saw them, he saw everything, understood everything immediately.

'Mother?! What the hell?'

At that moment Grandmother shoved him aside. 'Move, Tommy.'

She pushed past him and took position in front of the children, holding up her arms, as if to protect them. 'Don't come any closer, David. Not one step closer.'

'But Mother,' he said. 'You can't ...'

'I have four children, David,' Grandmother said, and her voice was hushed and compassionate. 'But it seems that I can only save three of them.'

'No,' Father said. 'No.'

He shook his head in disbelief, turned to face Tommy. 'Son, this is no good, you see that, don't you?'

Tommy tried to say something, but his voice wouldn't work. Father, he thought, what is it that you've done?

Then Father took yet another step towards them.

'No, David!' Grandmother said.

She quickly lifted the rifle to her cheek.

Father didn't move, his arms hung limply at his sides. He was not carrying a weapon, never did when he wasn't planning to leave the village.

'Where are you going?' he pleaded.

'I'm not telling you,' Grandmother said.

'Please . . .'

'No,' Grandmother said, and now Tommy could see that she was shaking. 'I can't tell you, David. When you left home to go to the crematorium this morning, you lost us.'

Father raised his hands slowly, as if giving himself up.

'Say goodbye now,' Grandmother said. 'Say goodbye to your boys.'

Father looked at Henry, then at Hilmar, then Tommy.

His eyes were full of incredulous despair.

'Can't I just give them a hug?'

A short bark of laughter escaped from Grandmother and she quickly raised the rifle to her cheek again.

'We have to go now,' she said. 'We should have left a long time ago.'

Was there anything Tommy could have said or done? Something that would have changed his father's mind, that would have chipped open a crack in the wall of Grandmother's uncompromising determination?

He relives the scene over and over again. The dinner when Father told them about his decision. The day they gathered coal. The separation from Father. And the hours afterwards.

Yes, there *were* many things he could have said. He could have begged his father to change his mind about the job. For our sake, he could have said, for your children, for Henry, Hilmar and me. You're going to die, we will lose you and, before that happens, you could infect us as well. Please, stay with us, don't do it, let somebody else take care of the corpses. They're dead anyway, we aren't responsible for the bodies, we are only responsible for those who are alive.

Or he could have pleaded with Grandmother, begged her to find another solution, asked her to give Father a chance.

If she had thought about it, for sure she would have devised another plan. Father could have self-isolated and then come out to join them, once he was sure that he wasn't ill. Father should have been given a choice. If he had understood that working at the oven meant giving up his own children, he would not have said yes. He wouldn't have, certainly?

Tommy walks uphill towards Svalsat. His legs are heavy from sleep deprivation, and his tummy is growling with hunger. He dreads trying to eat, has only had some bullion for lunch, every single meal is worse than the last. It could be there's something wrong with him, since swallowing has become so difficult, perhaps something or other is actually stuck in his throat, preventing the food he eats from going down.

He is obliged to stop halfway up the hill. His head spins, he leans forward and crouches over.

He takes three deep breaths.

Then he straightens up. The road stretches into the distance before him, a long and laborious climb towards the mountain. The fjord lies below, far away, and on the other side, glaciers and mountains. He can see for many miles. Except for a few, small cottages, there is no sign of human life anywhere.

How did he end up here? Was there a point when he could have stopped and made a different choice? During all the weeks they stayed in the cottage and the months afterwards in Longyearbyen, the time spent alone and when the foreigners first arrived? If only he could turn back time.

But it wasn't my fault, he says to himself. I did the best I could. I am not the person I should be angry with.

'Hilmar has told me what your father did,' Tao says.

Is he supposed to answer her?

'Perhaps you are angry with him,' she says. 'I think I would have been furious.'

Her voice is compassionate and confrontational all at once. It fills his arms and legs with restlessness, makes it difficult to sit calmly, but he manages to hold his tongue.

She clears her throat. 'I understand if it is difficult for you to talk about this. But it made an impression on me, and I just wanted to tell you that. That I would have been furious.'

'It is none of your business,' Tommy says softly. 'And I don't give a toss about your opinion.'

She ignores him and continues. 'I would have been furious for a while. But the brain is very good at forgetting. The memories soften. And then you forgive. You forget or you forgive, or both. I think that forgetting and forgiveness are two sides of the same coin.'

Tommy wants to stand up, remove the headphones, doesn't understand why he came up here today. But her voice pins him in place.

'Once upon a time, I was also angry with my parents,' she says. 'I stood out as a child, was gifted, learned to read when I was three, picked up the characters, surprised the teacher by reading fairy tales to myself in a corner, but never for the other children. I stayed away from them. I dedicated my entire childhood to books.'

'I am not like you,' he says sharply. 'Just because I read a lot doesn't mean I am like you.'

'I was ashamed of my thirst for knowledge,' she says, without answering him. 'It made me different from the other children, confused my parents. They didn't want to help me when the opportunity for admission to a better school arose. They looked at me like I was an alien, they said they couldn't afford it, they felt I had to stop dreaming. I was angry with them up until the time when Wei-Wen was born, angry because they didn't allow me to be who I was.'

'Stop it,' he said. 'Stop what you're doing. I'm not angry. I have never been angry. And I have never been denied knowledge. I have always had access to an entire library and a grandmother who never stopped teaching me new things.'

She doesn't reply and it feels good to have struck a nerve, to have seen through her. 'You are trying to demonstrate how similar we are,' he continues. 'As if that would help. The only thing that will help is for you to come back with my brothers. Do you hear me? I don't give a damn about you, Tao, you don't matter, all that matters are Henry and Hilmar.'

For a while she is silent. He waits.

'Do you wonder about whether *they* are angry? With you?'

'With me?'

The question blindsides him; it's as if it gives him a shove, threatening to knock him down. 'Of course they aren't angry.'

This lingering silence of hers, as if she wants him to break down, sob into the microphone, tell her everything, tell her where the seeds are, what has happened to Rakel, talk about the epidemic, talk, talk, talk. She is probably one of those people who thinks talking helps.

'I can't be bothered with this,' he says.

He gets to his feet, still holding the microphone in his

hand, pulls at the spiralling cord, stretching it as far as it will go.

'What do you mean, Tommy?'

'I can't be bothered to talk to you. There's nothing in it for me.'

'But Tommy?' She speaks more loudly now.

'"But Tommy." Shut up! There is no reason for me to have conversations with you. Come back with my brothers! I can't be bothered with this any more!'

'Try to stay calm, love, can't we talk about it?'

'That's just what I'm saying, that I can't be bothered to talk about it!'

Tao

'Tommy?'

She tries one more time but gives up when he doesn't respond.

Tao is certain that he will contact her again. The radio is set on listening mode. There will always be someone who will hear him. And she will personally keep trying to reach him every day, just as she has promised.

Before going to bed, she stands for a while by the railing. The moon is shining, illuminating contours of land. No lights are shining there, the majority of the houses are abandoned. Mei-Ling has said they will arrive in Archangel tomorrow. The military vehicles are standing by in an empty warehouse by the harbour. The journey home seems endless. Tao fears for the children. They have cried so much since leaving Longyearbyen, especially Henry. He never stops asking for his big brother, but sometimes she has found things to distract them. A visit to the wheelhouse, a story about the constellations in the sky, a particularly tasty dessert.

This evening, when it was Henry's bedtime, she sat with him and started telling the story of the beginning of the world, the way she remembered the story from her

own childhood, about Pangu and the egg. But he turned
away from her.

'I don't want a fairy tale,' he said. 'It doesn't feel right now.'

'No,' she said, feeling childishly spurned. 'But let me know
if it feels right one day, okay?'

Sometimes she tries asking them questions, tries to get
them to talk about what they have been through. If the children become aware that they are talking about the illness,
they shut down, but when she listens to them and is simply
present, every so often fragments of what they have experienced will crop up, associations originating in trains of
thought she is unable to follow.

As more and more scraps of the story emerge, the image
under construction in her mind of the nightmare they have
been through becomes increasingly clearer.

Tao was not surprised by her own fearlessness regarding
the illness as they travelled north. But she caught herself
missing a feeling of passion, the way she missed all the active
emotions that had disappeared along with her son, the joy
and the aggression.

She remembers the first time she became aware of the
absence of fear. It was a short time after she had lost Wei-
Wen, an ordinary situation. She was about to cross the
road by their house when a silent car driving far over the
speed limit approached. She didn't see it, didn't hear it,
until it was right beside her and the brakes squealed. Even
when she actually noticed the car, she didn't respond by
jumping away.

Afterwards she stood on the roadside for a while and could
feel her own heart beating calmly as if nothing had happened
and she realised that in the same way she was no longer capable of feeling anger, she was neither afraid of dying.

Sometimes, in recent years, she has even thought of death as a friend, because although she knows that there is no life after this one, death would still connect her to Wei-Wen, put her in the same category as her son. Deceased. She likes the word, the distance it creates.

When it was decided that they were to travel to Svalbard, she was indifferent to the precautions that were taken, the warnings had no impact on her.

Li Chiara appointed a group of physicians and epidemiologists to study the risk of infection. Tao was summoned to the last meeting, along with the ship's doctor Shun and Mei-Ling. Li Chiara sat at the end of a long table, surrounded by a number of experts. One by one they presented reports on the risks of such a journey, they lectured on various known viruses and bacterial illnesses.

There was not much to go on, one of the epidemiologists said, only what Rakel had told them. But the group claimed that it was probable that the virus that had afflicted Svalbard was in the filoviridae family, or a mutated norovirus. Epidemiologists were uncertain about the origin of the virus but believed it could have been transported by a migratory bird from an African country, such as the Congo, Liberia or Sierra Leone. There had been little contact with these African countries in the past forty years and they didn't know whether there had been serious outbreaks of the same virus there, or whether this was a mutated variant of a known virus, such as Ebola or a comparable RNA virus, of the kind the world had experienced in different forms in the 2000s.

The twenty-first century. One of the epidemiologists called it the century of the virus.

'There have to be some benefits after all, for those

of us living in the twenty-second century, don't you think?' Tao said.

Nobody laughed.

'Pardon me. That wasn't funny. I apologise.'

Mei-Ling glanced at Tao, a grimace of disapproval on her face, before asking the epidemiologists how the virus is transmitted from birds to humans. This was the second time Tao had met her and she was surprised by how submissive and anxious Mei-Ling seemed. The first time they'd met, she had been loud, swaggering and confident, eager for adventure.

A parasite, was the answer Mei-Ling received. Like a tick. The virus lived in a pouch of blood carried by a parasite, the parasite moved from birds to humans and then entered the new host's bloodstream.

The experts spoke in turn, the words bouncing towards them like rubber balls. Tao observed how attentively Mei-Ling listened, while for her own part, she failed to absorb all the information. A filovirus, one scientist said, threadlike virus particles. Illness in both primates and humans, another said, transmission of the illness between species. Crimean-Congo Haemorrhagic Fever was mentioned and the even more fatal Sapovirus of 2048.

Mei-Ling's eyes were as large as saucers. Tao noticed that she kept rubbing her hands and was restless. Her own heart was beating with a corresponding calm.

In conclusion, the head of the epidemiologists outlined the challenges of the expedition. She said that she did not want to put the crew in danger, and although they had to be aware of the risk, she assumed that there were no longer any existing carriers of the live virus, at least not among the survivors.

She did, however, emphasise that there was a chance that the virus could survive on a host up there, a bird, or an animal, because the smaller something is, the more difficult it is to eliminate.

A tiny seed on a damn blossom, Tao thought, ready to jump out and spread like weeds when you least suspect it.

Tommy

He gets up at 7.15 a.m. every day. He bathes, gets dressed and forces down some breakfast. At exactly 8.00 a.m., he makes a list of tasks to be done and what he will read in the course of the day. What does he feel like reading? No, *feel like* is not the phrase he uses. He always says *should* to himself. The phrase *feel like* suggests a choice. There are no choices in this life because a choice can also bring about a change. And he can't permit himself to change the structure he has created. Eat, sleep, work, read. Eat, sleep, work, read. Every day exactly like the day before. Routine, Tommy says to himself, that is what is important now, the routines. The time is the closest he comes to a god, the routines are his religious practice. He has to laugh at the similarities between the words: *routine* and *ritual*.

The darkness eating its way into the daylight is a daily reminder of how the weeks are sliding by. October comes, the daylight is on the verge of capitulating altogether. He does not return to Svalsat, is done with Tao and her painful questions.

The time he spends with his books is the best part of the day. Tommy has gathered all the literature he could find about Vavilov and his seeds.

Vavilov was a brilliant child, hard-working, bright. As a

young man he studied in England, France and Germany. In 1916 he left on his first important expedition and in 1921, just thirty-four years of age, Vavilov was appointed the director of the Agency for Applied Botany in Leningrad. He was unstoppable, an inner drive kept him working without cease, never allowing him to rest.

In 1924 he left on a long expedition to the Middle East, the cradle of agriculture. Vavilov was searching for the common origin of agricultural plants. If he found it, he would be able to decipher the language of life, understand how it changed over time and would thereby have the knowledge he needed to create new plants, crops that tolerated frost, drought, illness.

In five months, Vavilov travelled 1,500 kilometres on horse-back. He brought with him seeds from fruit, cotton, rye, but the real jewels of his treasure were the different wheat seeds he found. No other country had as many types of wheat as Afghanistan.

*Rather difficult,** were the words Vavilov chose when he later described the trip. He was a master of understatement. Entering the country alone was a struggle. Afghanistan feared that if the Russians were allowed entrance, other foreigners would follow suit and soon the land would be overrun by Germans, the British and the French. To be granted an entry visa, Russia had to grant Vavilov and his men diplomatic status. He was given the title of trade representative and his men couriers. This made the British suspicious and they monitored Vavilov's movements closely.

He made his way through the country with the help of

---

* Pringle 2008, p. 108.

an interpreter who was basically intoxicated at all times, so Vavilov had no choice but to learn Farsi. He began getting up early every morning to study the grammar and picked up the language quickly.

To ensure the safety of the caravan, it was accompanied by a military escort, but the soldiers were a gawkish group who constantly complained that Vavilov demanded far too much from them. The mountain trails in Hindu Kush were so treacherous that even the horses and mules balked. The baggage therefore had to be carried while the animals were led. This was too much for the soldiers, who went on strike several times or simply ran away.

Vavilov suffered bouts of malaria, the fever came and went. He slumped, half asleep on the back of his horse, exhausted and sick. He was not the only one to fall ill. One of his closest subordinates had a sensitive stomach and almost everything he ate gave him food poisoning.

But Vavilov viewed such problems as nothing more than minor irritations. He was more interested in the landscape, the plants, the seeds. He wandered around in the fields picking barley, crab grass, winter cress, broad beans and wheat, while the gardens supplied him with apricots, pears, plums, figs, pomegranates and peaches.

Around him, everywhere, was the world's largest seed bank, nature itself. On the ground, flying through the air, in the soil he walked on, in the stomachs of animals and birds, beneath the shoes of human beings – trillions of seeds.

Tommy decides to do a proper tidy up of his own, living seed bank: the greenhouse. He gathers seeds. He sows. Every morning the trays of seedlings are the first thing he approaches. Tomatoes, lettuce, carrots, celery, broccoli – completely different plants, though the shoots are similar in appearance, the way the embryos of mammals also resemble one another in the very early stages. The same light green colour, the single pair of leaves at the tip. Tommy strokes the seedlings lightly, a soft carpet that tickles his palm.

He prunes, trims and harvests. The greenhouse contains enormous quantities of fruit and vegetables and a good deal goes straight into the compost. It feels bad to allow so much to go to waste, so after a few days he starts preserving everything that cannot be stored. He gathers empty jars for pickling. He dries apples, puts potatoes and carrots into cold storage, layer upon layer beneath dried grass. The stockpile of food grows. When his brothers return, piles of food will be waiting for them.

Imagine how thrilled Hilmar will be about the jars of pickled tomatoes. And Henry, when he sees the ropes of dried apple wedges.

Unless Henry is angry with him.

Had Tao meant to imply that Henry is angry with him?

And is Tommy angry with Father, with Grandmother?

Or has forgetfulness settled into his mind, the way dead leaves gradually cover up gashes in the landscape, creating new, fertile soil?

No, he has not forgotten.

Because he keeps the memories sharp and clear by reliving them, over and over again. There are no dead leaves in Svalbard and it takes forever for gashes in nature to heal.

He can see them, Henry, Hilmar, Grandmother and himself, as they moved through a landscape that Tommy knew as well as his own reflection in the mirror. All the same, it seemed unfamiliar. The large delta in the Advent Valley was endless, the aerial tramway pylons reached for the sky like threatening fingers.

Grandmother walked quickly. The children had to scurry to keep up with her.

But his legs resisted, the ground was a magnet holding his feet in place, every step required force of will.

Behind him he heard his brothers. Hilmar's slightly scuffing steps as he carried the heavy backpack. Henry's tears.

'Daddy,' Henry sobbed and clutched his rabbit. 'My daddy.'

I should have taken his hand, Tommy thinks, should have squatted down and comforted him.

'Daddy. Daddy, Daddy, Daddy.'

'Shut up,' Hilmar said.

'No,' Tommy said and turned around. 'We don't talk like that.'

'You said it. Earlier today.'

'And it was wrong of me.'

Henry released one more sob. The tears ran down his cheeks, creating trails in the coal dust.

'Now we have to walk,' Tommy said, and turned towards Grandmother's back, which was becoming smaller as she outdistanced them.

'Come here.'

He held out his hands to both of them. Henry immediately grasped one of them. Hilmar reluctantly took hold of the other.

They took shelter in a cottage at the far end of Todalen, an area without landslide risk. The cottage had not been cleaned in a long time. The floor was covered with tiny pieces of dried grass that had crept under the door and a thick layer of dust. But the windows were intact. The electricity was connected to a windmill and the solar cells on the roof were in working order, as was the coal-burning stove and there were enough beds for all of them.

'You take one of the bedrooms,' Grandmother said to Tommy. 'And Hilmar and Henry can take the other. I will sleep on the sofa.'

A room of his own, just like at home. He could retreat, close a door. But what about Henry and Hilmar? He should be closer to them in case they had nightmares. Or in case a fire broke out or a polar bear appeared.

'I don't mind sleeping on the floor with the boys. Then you can take the bedroom,' Tommy said to Grandmother.

'No. It's fine. I'll take the sofa.'

He wanted to protest again, but she stared at him once more with that gaze that told him that he was a child and had no say in the matter.

They could not see Longyearbyen from the cottage but needed go no further than out onto the road and walk a short distance towards the village to see the smoke from the crematorium oven.

'You can keep watch,' Grandmother said as they stood down there. 'See if anything changes.'

'What about the smoke from our cottage?' Tommy asked. 'What if someone comes, if someone wants to hide, just like us?'

'They are not hiding from other people,' Grandmother said. 'It's the illness.'

'But isn't that the same thing?' he said.

She didn't reply and started walking up towards the cottage again, where Hilmar and Henry were playing outside.

Grandmother's hands moved quickly as she unpacked the backpacks, at all times giving Tommy instructions.

'I put the jars of cured meat in the shed, they have no odour, so the bears won't be able to sniff them out. In the shed I found a few good snares, by the way. Come out with me and I will show you how to set them.'

And a bit later: 'See, I'm putting all the fresh vegetables in this cupboard. I think they will keep well out here in the hallway, where it's a little cooler than in the sitting room. We must be sure to eat all the tomatoes while they are still good.'

She showed him where the tinderbox was and she asked him to light the stove, so she could be sure that he was able to do it by himself.

Henry collapsed on the sofa while they were still working. He was too heavy for Grandmother to carry him to his bed and she let him sleep where he was.

'I can sleep in his bed instead,' she said. 'Just for tonight.'

She sat for a moment on the edge of the sofa by her grandson and stroked his dirty face with her hand.

'Bye now, little Henry.'

Then she went in to say goodnight to Hilmar. She sang a French lullaby. She didn't normally sing for the boys any more.

Afterwards, Tommy could hear them speaking softly on the other side of the wall. He heard Hilmar asking for Father. And he heard her answer in a reassuring tone of voice. Then the room was silent.

The curtain on his window was made of an old, red and white checked dishcloth and did not block out the light. Tommy lay awake for a long time, with a strip of light from the midnight sun in his face. The glare stung his eyes. And Father's gaze was there the whole time, torn by conflicting emotions, at the moment Grandmother aimed the rifle at him.

The next morning, Tommy awoke to the sound of migratory birds. He lifted the dishcloth curtain and peeked out. In the sky he saw geese flying in a V-formation. They were out practising formation flying now. Soon the birds would head south. They just had to ensure that the youngest would be able to keep up and find their spot in the huge formation.

He watched the birds for a few seconds before he remembered.

It felt like a blow, taking his breath away. The illness, Father, their forced isolation in the cottage. Soon we will have neither a mother nor a father. Henry and Hilmar are orphans.

My brothers. Are they up? It's so quiet. They must be hungry?

He slid his feet onto the floor, registered how cold it was, and pulled on a pair of thick socks. Then he opened the door and went out into the sitting room. Henry lay on the sofa staring into space.

'Hey,' Tommy said.

'Hey,' he whispered without looking at his big brother.

'Are the others asleep?' He nodded towards the bedroom door, which was ajar.

'Hilmar's asleep,' Henry said.

'And Grandmother?'

'She's not here.'

'Isn't she here?'

Henry twisted over onto his side and now he finally looked into Tommy's eyes.

'No. I went to see if she was awake and she wasn't there.'

Tommy walked the few metres to the bedroom door and opened it. Hilmar was just waking up. He sat up in the top bunk and looked at Tommy drowsily. The lower bunk beneath him was empty.

'Where is Grandmother?' Tommy asked.

'What?' Hilmar yawned.

Tommy poked her duvet, as if she were hidden beneath it, and then he turned on his heel, left the room, grabbed the anorak hanging on a hook and pulled it over his head. He shoved his feet into his shoes and ran out of the door.

His shoelaces flapping around his ankles, he ran around the cottage and into the valley.

'Grandmother? Grandmother?'

The valley's response was silence.

He kept running. His dangling shoelaces constantly threatened to trip him and he stepped on them, so at all times he was on the verge of stumbling.

He headed for the road.

'Grandmother, where are you?' he called. 'GRAAANDMOOOTHER!'

He stopped in the middle of the road and kicked hard at the gravel. Then he sat down on the ground, rested his head against his knees, and wailed.

'Bloody hell, bloody hell, bloody hell.'

He should have known, he thinks now. There had been many signs the night before. But he had allowed himself to slack off for a few hours. She stood there holding the rifle, taking charge and he'd felt that he didn't have any choice.

Of course he'd had a choice. Of course he should have done a better job of paying attention.

He tries to understand himself, the person he was last summer. A seventeen-year-old boy, his brain not yet fully formed, according to the books. And he was in shock, he had lost his father and wasn't thinking clearly. But that was no excuse. He should have understood what was about to happen. That she was going to leave them. And he should not have behaved the way he did afterwards.

He remembers how Henry and Hilmar followed him outside. Walked quietly over to their big brother, standing beside him, one on either side. Henry rested his little hand against his head, patted him tentatively.

'She probably just had to take care of something,' Henry said. 'For sure she'll be back soon.'

Tommy lifted his head, saw Hilmar standing there, his arms hanging limply at his sides, as if he didn't know what he should do with them. But then he too raised one of his hands and patted Tommy's hair, the way Henry had done.

'We'll be fine,' said Hilmar. 'We have loads of food.'

Tommy registered the weight of their small hands on his head for a moment, before Hilmar pulled his away. Then Tommy stood up abruptly, so Henry's hand also fell away. Without a word he walked towards the cottage where the door had been left wide open.

'Tommy?'

He heard their steps behind him but didn't turn around. Instead he went into the room he had already begun thinking of as his own, closed the door and kicked off his shoes.

It was cold. He shivered and crept into bed, where he pulled the duvet resolutely over his head.

A couple of seconds later there was a knock on the door.

'Tommy? Are you there?'

It was Henry.

He didn't reply.

'Tommy?'

Hilmar now.

'Of course I'm here! You saw me walk in here!'

The door slid open without a sound and he heard feet clad in wool socks shuffling across the floor. It irritated him, the sound of wool against the wooden floorboards, as if his brothers were unable to lift their feet properly.

'Tommy?'

He could feel them pulling at the duvet and allowed them to drag it off, but simultaneously turned abruptly onto his side, so he lay facing the wall.

'I'm just tired, okay?'

'Sure,' Henry said. 'Okay.'

'Okay,' Hilmar said.

Tommy squeezed his eyes shut, but knew that they were still standing there, watching him.

'Will you please just go away?' he said.

'Yes,' Hilmar said.

Tommy heard him take a deep breath, long and trembling. 'Come on, Henry. Let's see if we can find something for breakfast.'

'Yes,' Henry said.

The sound of shuffling wool sock steps faded away again, and the door closed behind them as quietly as it had opened.

'Let's see,' he heard Hilmar say to Henry out there. 'Shall we see what we have?'

'Yes,' Henry said. 'I'm hungry.'

'That's not strange,' Hilmar. 'So am I.'

Tommy pulled the duvet over his head again but was unable to shut out the sound of them and soon he put the pillow over his head as well. With one ear against the mattress and the other covered by the pillow, the sound of their chatter was reduced to a garble. The sound of their high voices in the kitchen rose and fell, rose and fell, a steady song with a desperate undertone. I can't do it, sang through his head, in unison with their voices. I can't be all alone.

Tommy doesn't know how much time passed before they fell silent. And it was a while before he noticed.

He pushed the duvet away, listened.

Nothing.

Had they gone outside?

He sat up, his heart pounding. They had no weapons.

The bear. It was silent and could attack their small bodies before they were even aware of it.

He rolled out of bed and stood in the middle of the room, which started spinning. He took hold of the ladder up to the upper bunk and waited, until the dark spots in front of his eyes gradually faded away.

Then he rushed out into the sitting room, noticed that they had lit the stove, that there was food on the table, that his boots were placed neatly in the shoe rack.

Then he heard their voices.

They were playing by the brook behind the house. He walked closer to the corner, so he could make out what they were saying.

'Ready or not, here I come!' Hilmar shouted as he ran towards Henry. 'I'm gonna get you now!'

'No,' Henry shouted. 'Because I have a rifle and now, I'm going to shoot you! Bang! Bang! Bang!'

'But you can't hit me,' Hilmar said, running closer to his brother. 'Because I'm so small that you can't do it. I'm invisible and the bullets just vanish into thin air!'

'But then I run!' Henry said. 'And I'm so fast you'll never catch me, never!'

He jumped over tufts of grass, running through the field. Hilmar followed behind him, was actually faster than his little brother, but Tommy could see that he was holding back.

'Yes!' Hilmar shouted, as the distance between him and Henry increased. 'You're so fast! And I am getting weaker. Because without a human being to inhabit, I can't survive. I lose all my powers. I can't move and now I'm falling down. Now I'm falling down. And then I die.'

He threw out his arms in a mock crucifixion and made strangling noises. And then he fell back onto the grass. Dead.

Henry released a ripple of laughter, turned around and discovered Tommy standing there.

'Hi, Tommy. We're playing Virus. Do you want to play?'

'Okay,' Tommy said. 'Of course I want to play.'

After Tommy had prepared the boys' supper, got them into bed, tucked them in and sung two lullabies, he went outside.

The sun was low in the sky, dipping towards the mountains. Go down, he thought, go away, let us have darkness, but the sun did as the sun wished, as reliable as ever, and there was nowhere to hide.

He started walking, aimlessly. He knew he should have brought a firearm, that it wasn't a good idea to be so far from the cottage without any protection but couldn't be bothered. Soon he began walking more quickly, broke into a jog, registering how his cheeks grew warm and sweat formed on his back. He kept going until he reached the road, and when he had flat ground under his feet, he began running even faster, headed straight for Longyearbyen.

He was perhaps 15 kilometres away from the village. It wouldn't take him all that long to get there. Grandmother had to be there, she must have gone back. To rescue Father? But if she wanted to rescue him, why had she aimed her gun at him? There must have been another reason for her abandoning them. And maybe she wasn't even in Longyearbyen, but his feet nonetheless carried him there, because he didn't know where else he should run. There was only this one road, only this one village, only these few remaining human beings. And Father was there.

He gasped for breath. Father, Father. He tried to keep the image of him at a distance in his mind, his eyes when Grandmother pointed the rifle at him. And the same eyes in a bed while pearls of feverish sweat formed on his forehead and his body started to turn against him. He would contract the illness. And he had chosen it, he had chosen the illness over his children.

Tommy stopped suddenly and stood doubled over in the middle of the road.

Breathe. You are in control, you can do this, fill your lungs with air, think about Henry and Hilmar, they need you. Breathe. Breathe.

He lifted his head, his gaze sweeping across the landscape, and then he noticed a figure in the distance.

Somebody was on the road. A swaying figure, walking towards him. Grandmother?

He straightened up. Squinted. The figure had the sun at its back, and was moving oddly, sort of erratically and then he understood that what he was looking at was the silhouette of two people, not one.

The smallest was thin and short, the tallest shapeless, almost hunchbacked. A few more seconds passed before he realised that the hump was a huge backpack.

And then he recognised the gait. Long strides, feet being placed solidly on the ground. It was Rakel. And the little one had to be Runa.

For a moment he considered taking off, pretending that he hadn't seen them, turning around and just running away. But then Rakel raised her hand in greeting.

'Tommy.'

The sound was carried to him by the wind.

He ran his hands over his face, drying his tears, got control over his breathing and took position there on the road, sort of casually.

The sisters started walking faster. He didn't know what he should do and started walking slowly towards them.

When they were approximately ten metres from him, they stopped. Rakel raised her hands above her head, as if she were surrendering.

'We're not sick,' she said. 'We haven't seen anybody else for over a week.'

'Neither have we,' Tommy said.

'I know,' she said.

'Have you spoken with Grandmother?'

She nodded.

'It was Aunt Louise who said we should come and join you,' Runa said and smiled at him.

Aunt Louise. He wanted to say something about that, that she was his Grandmother, not their aunt, it was meaningless to call somebody aunt if one was not a blood relation – he didn't understand why Grandmother had gone along with this, or perhaps it was Runa who had come up with it, all by herself. She probably wished she had an aunt, wished she had a family, any kind of family.

The sisters approached him.

'When did you talk to her?' he asked.

'Early this morning,' Rakel said. 'She woke us around six and said we should pack up and walk out here. She said that you would be here, that you had found a cottage that was in good repair and that you have food.'

'Not enough for many people,' he said. 'At least, not if we are planning to stay here for a long time.'

Runa observed him uncertainly. Her colouring was lighter than her sister's. She had green eyes instead of brown and golden hair. Yes, everything about Runa was sort of lighter, her disposition too. He had never seen her be anything but friendly. She smiled all the time. *Like me,* the smile said, *don't reject me.*

'But it was Aunt Louise who said we should come here,'
Runa said.

'Where is Grandmother now, then?' he said. 'Why didn't
she come back with you? If she went to get you, she should
have come back with you.'

Rakel shrugged. 'She just said there was something she
needed to take care of. She said we would have to manage
on our own for a while.'

Her words stung because this was more than Grandmother
had told him.

Rakel looked him up and down, in the way she always did,
while her eyes narrowed.

'What are you doing out here, anyway, on the road. Were
you on your way back to the village?'

'No,' he said and started walking in the direction of
the cottage.

Rakel stepped forward to join him, walking beside him
with those long strides of hers, as if carrying the backpack
required no effort whatsoever. She was strong, he knew
that, had always been strong and wiry, with long muscles in her arms and legs. On the hottest days she would
sometimes wear shorts and a vest. And sometimes she did
cartwheels, or handstands, and then nobody could take
their eyes off her, himself included, even though he wished
he could. Her body could do whatever she wanted it to do.
Once, when she was doing a handstand, her vest slid down
and he saw her torso. You could count the rows of muscles.
Rakel was a child of Svalbard, her body full of restlessness,
made for hunting and fishing and long treks, not for the
classroom, where she was easily distracted. She was powerful, alert, quick, the kind of child Svalbard wanted, *one of
Svalbard's best.*

Runa's face twisted into a yawn which she tried to conceal. 'Sorry.'

Tommy looked at his watch. It was almost midnight.

'It's that one over there,' he said and pointed at the cottage.

They tiptoed inside. The cottage was silent. Hilmar and Henry were sleeping deeply in their respective bunks. Henry's mouth was open. He breathed through his mouth, snoring lightly. Tommy closed the door behind him and pointed at the sofa.

'You two can sleep there.'

'Both of us?' Rakel asked. 'That will be cramped.'

'That's all that's available,' he said.

'I'm sure it will be fine,' Runa said.

In two strides, Rakel was over by his bedroom.

'But there are two beds in here, too.'

'That's where I sleep.'

'You don't sleep in both beds, do you?'

'No.' Tommy could feel himself blushing.

It's my room, he wanted to say. The only place I have right now.

Rakel yawned again, a long, drawn-out yawn with her mouth wide open.

'I suggest that we take this room, we girls,' Rakel said. 'And you take the sofa.'

I suggest ... It wasn't a suggestion, it was an order.

The sofa was hard and uncomfortable. It creaked every time he turned over. The curtains in the sitting room were even worse than those in the bedroom. It was impossible to find a restful position.

Rakel and Runa had long since fallen silent. They were probably sleeping heavily already. In his room.

Tommy had been invaded. Abandoned and occupied all at once. And he was so angry that his heart hammered, so distraught that the muscles in his diaphragm were tense, as if his body stood at attention, anticipating an attack. He inhaled deeply, pulling the air down into his lungs, again and again, hoping for relief. But nothing helped.

Grandmother came and went, she had always come and gone and they were not allowed to ask questions about her actions. They were just supposed to accept them, apparently, accept that restlessness compelled her to leave them, and that whatever she did, it was usually a little more important than what the rest of them were doing. There was something high-minded about Grandmother, which made it impossible to question her. Enlightened despotism. *Something she had to take care of*, was supposed to be an adequate apology, *something she had to take care of*, supposedly sufficient explanation for why she could permit herself to abandon him and his brothers out here and on top of everything send that bossy Rakel and damn baby-doll Runa here to join them. *Take care of* – it was such a modest phrase, but there was nothing that could be taken care of right now or fixed. Everything was already ruined and now they could only wait. That was why they had come out here, wasn't it, to wait, to grieve over Father and everything they had lost? But Grandmother apparently still believed that things could be fixed.

He can do this. Every morning he gets up at 7.15 a.m. He winds the watch, makes sure it is working so the time doesn't get away from him. At 8 a.m. he writes his lists. Then he goes to the greenhouse. He spends all day there, from 9 a.m. to 9 p.m. Lunch at noon, then a short walk to take advantage of what little daylight remains. Supper at 5 p.m., a simple evening meal before he goes home again. He goes to bed at 10 p.m.

Sometimes, at two o'clock, he drops by the library to look for something new to read. He never sits down in there; he does not allow himself to stay longer than one hour.

In the afternoon, when his back is aching and his feet are tired, when his body is asking him for a break, he tries to read.

The reading often goes slowly. He sits with a book in his hands, unable to concentrate, rereading the same sentence over and over again. Only the books about Vavilov offer him an escape. He travels with the botanist around the world, taking pleasure in Vavilov's success.

Vavilov worked around the clock, had a large and dedicated staff and soon became a well-known scientist not solely in Russia, but all over the world. Life must have been good, Tommy thinks, secure. For a few years. Until the pressure on him increased. Stalin was not satisfied with the progress of his research, and with time also began questioning the theoretical foundation. Trofim Lysenko, Vavilov's competitor, was more to Stalin's liking. Lysenko claimed that only acquired traits could be passed down, that plants and animals could be trained. Think of the giraffe, Lysenko said – and referred to the French eighteenth-century natural scientist Jean-Baptiste Lamarck's theory: if a giraffe spent its entire life reaching upward for leaves, its neck would become longer and its progeny would inherit the long neck. Lysenko denied the core of all genetic research, the idea that permanent change occurs through mutations. But his theory suited Stalin very well. In Stalin's Soviet Union, everyone was to have equal opportunities for improvement.

Research, biology had become political.

Stalin was particularly enthusiastic about Lysenko's experiments with the winter hardiness of seeds, which he claimed would yield large crops in just three years. Vavilov could not promise anything comparable. He spoke the truth: breeding a species took a long, long time.

In the course of the 1930s, life became gradually more difficult. While Lysenko was awarded with the Order of Lenin, Vavilov was increasingly criticised.

One morning, in a corridor of the Kremlin, Vavilov accidently collided with Stalin. Vavilov had as usual an overstuffed briefcase in his arms. Stalin took one look at the briefcase and in his paranoia thought it was a bomb. He glanced at Vavilov in terror before dashing into his own office. Vavilov was left standing in the hallway, equally terrified. He knew the seeds of discomfort he had sown in Stalin would not disappear.

What followed was a period when everything went downhill for Vavilov. He was undermined and discredited, publicly denounced, but he still didn't give up. He did not leave the country. Instead, he responded to the critique with even more work. His former success and all the international respect he enjoyed must have made him believe he was invincible. He must have thought he was safe.

*

Outside, the November polar night has descended upon Longyearbyen. Tommy needs to rest but looks forward to working again. At work he is also safe.

But safe, has he ever, since his mother died, really ever been safe?

Tommy never confronted Grandmother about her disappearance. He knows what she would have answered: I knew the little ones were safe with you. Not looking him in the eye, and waving her hand, as if she wanted to dismiss the entire issue.

He should have cornered her and told her she was wrong. He should have raised his voice with her. The little ones, he should have said, you always call them 'the little ones'. Even though Hilmar is nine, and older than I was when he was born. I changed nappies from the time I was ten – have you forgotten? I rocked a crying baby to sleep every single night – has that memory been completely erased from your mind?

She would without a doubt have tried to dodge his questions. Yes, yes, Tommy, the youngest children in a flock will always be called the little ones. Is that really something to get so cross about?

Cross. She loved that word. It was a reductive word, it made him smaller than he was and always made him give up.

I am not cross ... But you could have told me what you were up to, instead of just disappearing.

But Tommy, you could take it. You can take so much. More than anyone else I know.

She said that many times. You can take so much, Tommy, you are different from the others, you are mature, you are special. That's why I give you additional responsibility.

Besides, she would have said, my disappearing makes no difference now, as long as you are safe.

He looks around him in the greenhouse.

Is he safe?

Yes, she would have said. Inside here, you are safe. Completely safe.

And she would have been right, he *is* safe inside here.

The word safe, that brings her back again, a clear memory. He is twelve, maybe thirteen, yes, he must have been thirteen because he remembers how his voice was always cracking and how she, instead of smiling at him, ignored it completely. Maybe out of kindness, or maybe because she basically didn't notice such changes in him. For her, he remained the same, regardless of whether he was five years old or almost a grown man. And maybe she had already then started thinking of him as the seed custodian. Maybe she had begun his training, even though he hadn't understood this himself.

They had just come inside from the winter night outdoors. Snow on their shoulders, cheeks red from the cold. Grandmother hung up her jacket and smiled with relief, before throwing out her arms.

'Our own biosphere, Tommy. Aren't we lucky?'

'Huh?' he said.

'So you don't know what a biosphere is?'

She stuck her hands into the bed of artichokes and pulled out one after the next.

He shook his head.

'The biosphere is the oceans, the forests, the plains and the mountains. It is fish, birds, animals and plants. The biosphere is just twenty kilometres thick, no more than a thin shell around the mortal life found in the earth's interior, but still it is what we think of as our earth, all that is alive and beautiful, that which keeps us safe.' She glanced up at him. 'You're not working.'

'Oh, yes, sorry.' He stuck his hands into the soil and searched along with her.

'The biosphere is you and me and everything else that is alive, everything created by photosynthesis. The biosphere is also that which distinguishes the earth from other planets, at least the other planets we know about.'

He held an artichoke up to his nose. It smelled good, nutlike.

She laughed at him kindly, pulled the clean sleeve of her jumper over her hand and wiped dirt off the tip of his nose.

'But life could exist in other places,' Tommy said.

'Yes, it could. But we will never find out. There are only two thousand other stars within fifty light years of our earth and no life was ever discovered on them, back when humans had the resources to research such things. The others out there are so far away that we cannot possibly make contact with them. Maybe one of our radio signals is on the way to some of them now, but the amount of time it will take to arrive is so monumental that several thousand years will pass before we achieve anything resembling a brief exchange of ideas. Outer space is basically too large for communication to be possible.'

She laid the artichokes in a heap, took out a small brush and started brushing the soil off them. 'Once there were people who tried to create a biosphere in a biosphere. And do you know what they called it?'

'No.'

'Biosphere Two, of course.'

He laughed.

'It was an artificial world. Built in Arizona, a contained ecological system, with a rain forest, an ocean with pump-driven waves that broke over a coral reef, a mango orchard, a savanna and a large agricultural area. Biosphere Two was a beautiful world, also on the outside. A pyramid of glass, blinding white with Babylonian cupolas and chambers, reminiscent of the way the future is depicted in the science fiction comic books in the library. You have read them, haven't you?'

'I can't be bothered to read comic books any longer.'

'But you *have* read them ...' She paused for a moment as she inspected an artichoke with particular care. 'Do you think we should eat it or plant it?'

'How should I know?'

His voice cracked at the end of his sentence and he blushed.

'But of course you should know, you must know such things,' Grandmother said. 'We must put the largest and the nicest plants back in the earth so they can form new roots.'

'Fine, plant it then.' Fortunately, this time he was able to keep his voice under control.

She nodded and put the artichoke to one side. 'Yes, I agree.'

Then Grandmother continued telling him about Biosphere 2. It was a world that produced everything life on earth needed to survive, even its own oxygen. The inhabitants were four women and four men: they were locked up inside and at the same time protected. They really *were* their own world. They created an ecosystem that ensured that all the inhabitants, whether they were humans, animals, insects or plants, would have the food and water they needed. Inside everything was run by humans, which is why the winds were never too strong, the heat never too intense, the rainfall never too hard, the waves never too powerful. More than 3,000 species coexisted under the shelter of the cupolas, wheat, beets, bananas, figs, onions, beans, potatoes and rice. They never used toxic substances, the farming was organic and they had thought of everything, even creatures to take care of the destruction, decomposition and recycling of organic materials, such as flies, ants and cockroaches.

'Biosphere Two was more beautiful than the world it resembled. A cocoon: a simpler, more peaceful place,' Grandmother concluded.

'And safe?'

He doesn't remember if he actually asked this last question. Or if he did, how she had answered. But he does remember that he walked right over to the library afterwards to read more about Biosphere 2, that the conversation, in spite of the reluctance he had shown Grandmother, put him on the trail of something. The way their conversations so often did.

And wasn't it this afternoon that he almost smashed into Rakel on his way home? That's how he remembers it. He was walking with his head in a book. She came running, bid a laughing goodbye to someone further down the road behind her, and didn't look where she was going.

He lost hold of the book, watched it fall and hit the muddy ground, so it was covered with muck.

'Oh, sorry,' Rakel said, snatching it up quickly.

He accepted it without reply and tried to wipe off the mud stains with the sleeve of his jacket.

'It's not that big a deal,' Rakel said. 'See, you're getting most of it off. And you can still read everything that's written there.'

'Sure,' he said curtly.

Then she walked away, leaving him standing there looking down into the book. Yes, he could still read the text, but a large splotch of mud now covered up the biosphere's cupolas. He wanted to shout something to Rakel but didn't know what to say.

*

Rakel, the school's leader, the girl who did not excel academically, but nonetheless won recognition because she excelled at that which was really of importance. And because she was who she was. A sun, he thinks, a sun the other children were drawn to. Sometimes he could see that she used it, that she asserted herself, dominated others through her words and body language, looks and small grimaces, through who was graced by her gaze and who she ignored, by offering approval and then suddenly withdrawing it. Rakel was very demanding and she occupied a lot of space. Completely different from her sister. Runa was like a plant that required little care, deriving energy from a few rays of sunshine and preserving those rays inside her as a power source throughout the entire winter. While Rakel made demands all the time. She had lost so much that she thought she was entitled to something in return. To everything. Even though everything is far too much. But Rakel didn't understand that. No, she wasn't like a sun, but a generalist, who thrived everywhere, like a dandelion: adapting to the changes in climate, popping up between stones, in places where one wouldn't think that anything could grow. When a species dies out, the generalists take over, step in and adapt. They survive, regardless, and ensure that their descendants prevail. Maybe she was a better adapted plant than he was, maybe that was why she called for help.

But, he asks himself, isn't that a contradiction in terms? She was a strong survivor, but she was also broken.

Was she broken? Is that really what he thought of her, something so ugly, so irrevocable?

Rakel is gone now and it is his fault. The least he could do is to stop thinking about her in this way.

He gets up suddenly, throws his book down and walks over to some pots on a table. Without knowing what he will do with them, he lifts one and carries it to a table at the other end of the greenhouse. The pot is heavy, his back complains. And it helps.

He keeps investing all his energy in avoiding her, as he did during the first days in the cottage. He left when she entered a room, he turned away when she looked in his direction. He spoke little with her, except to give her practical information. At all times he made sure to stay at least two metres away from her, took care to seat her on the opposite side of the table, assigned work tasks so they never ended up doing anything together. If she was picking mushrooms, he took care of the snares; if she offered to make dinner, he quickly volunteered to chop wood, or vice versa. Preferably the latter; he was better in the kitchen than he was with an axe. At all times he was angry with her because Grandmother had sent her here, invited her to invade his family. Because Grandmother has shared more with her than with him.

He didn't think about this then but has later wondered about his influence on her. If his evasiveness had provoked her, or perhaps confused her, if his evasiveness had given him power over her, control.

Finally, she was the one who took the initiative. Tommy was trying to skin a fox when Rakel came out of the cottage. The others were inside. The children had found an old deck of cards and Rakel had taught them a game that she called Beartrap and now they were completely obsessed with it. Now and then he heard cries of irritation from inside and triumphant cheers.

Rakel stood watching him, assessing his movements, the knife in his hand, which became cumbersome under the weight of her attention. He fumbled, cutting wrong.

'Did you want something?' he asked.

She came all the way over to him, standing close enough

that if he were to reach his arm out all the way, she was within the knife's radius. He noticed her sharp gaze, but tried to continue working, sort of effortlessly.

'You're clever, Tommy,' she said.

He didn't reply, and tried working faster, taking hold of the base of the tail and pulling the tail out of the skin, wanting to finish. He knew that they really shouldn't eat fox, that the meat could be contaminated, but perhaps they would have to all the same, if they couldn't find anything else.

'Do you think it has stockpiled a lot?' Rakel asked and pointed at the fox.

'For sure,' he said.

Foxes gathered and hoarded. What they did not eat in the summer, they saved for the winter. Several times he had found eggs hidden in the ground, the fox's winter storeroom.

Rakel turned towards the cottage.

'It's one week until twenty-third August.'

She didn't say anything else, but he knew what she meant. The midnight sun disappeared on 23 August. After that, the hours of daylight diminished rapidly, as darkness rushed in.

'Aren't you thinking about that?' she said after a while, and now the hint of a smile in the corner of her mouth had disappeared.

'That it will be dark? I don't go around thinking about it all the time, no.'

'That we don't have enough food.'

'That's why I'm standing here skinning this fox.'

'But we need much, much more.'

He shrugged.

Rakel studied him. 'Tommy,' she said slowly. 'You and I, we haven't exactly been best friends.'

'No,' he said. 'We haven't.'

'I hope you're not cross because I used to tease you sometimes.'

'No,' he said quickly.

'You know it's just nonsense, everything I said and all that, that I was just winding you up? You know how I am, I wind everyone up.'

'Yes. Of course.'

He just looked at the fox, at the knife and tried to conceal the trembling of his hand. He didn't understand what she wanted him to say. Why do you have to talk to me, he thought, bother me. Can't we just keep working?

'Tommy.'

She placed a hand on his arm.

He looked up and observed her. Her eyes, which were usually narrow, dark streaks, were rounder, more open. Her mouth was also open, not much, but a crack, the lips divided so he could glimpse the teeth inside. Her hand squeezed his arm lightly. Her touch sent sensations spreading through his entire body like ripples across a pond.

He turned towards the carcass again.

'It's fine,' he said. 'And you're right. I would rather just sit in the library with my books.'

'That's what I thought,' she said and smiled. 'That you like the books better than you like us.'

'No. It was just the library was the only place where I got some time off,' he said.

'Time off from what?'

Her voice was warm. The sincerity of her interest caused a lump to form in his throat, though he didn't understand why.

'You know what. My brothers, the responsibility, everything,' he answered softly.

'Yes,' she said.

He nodded.

'But you have perhaps not been very good at asking for help,' she continued.

'Help? There has been nobody to ask.'

'There's always someone, you just have to find them.'

He didn't know how to respond.

She squeezed his arm in encouragement before letting go and taking a few steps away. 'You're coming with me now, aren't you? Because there have to be two of us.'

They walked inland, along the Advent Valley, Rakel in front, him behind, away from the cottage, and even further away from Longyearbyen. She moved lithely and quickly, while he struggled to keep up. The children had stayed behind in the house; it was just the two of them. The feeling of her hand on his arm had left a mark, a beautiful scar. He couldn't rid himself of the image. His bare arm, her hand stroking his skin lightly, as she pulled him to her.

He remembers this moment so well, this image, the first of many, an expectation that was planted inside him. The boys had talked about Rakel, she was someone many boys had wanted. But he had never thought about her in that way, hadn't had the time to think in that way about anyone. And especially not about Rakel, whom he hadn't even liked.

Had it only happened because they were alone?

The Bolterdalen Valley came into view before them; a light wind from the south hit him in the face.

'There,' Rakel said and pointed.

About 100 metres away from them were two grazing reindeer.

'If we are quiet now, they won't notice us.'

He nodded. The reindeer at Svalbard were often completely

unafraid of people, but they could also be startled away. They feared bears.

The polar bears had formerly hunted at the ice edge; they were especially fond of seal. And when the sea ice disappeared, the bears starved and struggled to reach their winter lairs. But in the 2020s, the bears began attacking reindeer. The she-bears taught their cubs to hunt reindeer, and the calves in particular were their prey. The Svalbard reindeer had been without enemies in the natural world; they moved about alone for the most part, grazing peacefully, often in close proximity to humans and other animals. Reindeer still wandered down the streets of Longyearbyen. They were not particularly afraid of humans, in spite of their rifles and hunting guns. But the reindeer had learned to fear and flee from the bear and as the autumn and hunting season progressed, the reindeer also became increasingly afraid of humans.

Rakel crouched down and slowly moved towards the reindeer with her knees bent, as close to the ground as she could get. Despite the knapsack on her back, her movements were silent and smooth, every step steadily following the last. Nobody could hunt like Rakel, nobody could blend into the landscape like her, become silent, become invisible.

For his own part, Tommy felt that his movements were choppy and strained, his steps made too much noise, and as he crept clumsily forward, he lost his balance.

The buck continued grazing, did not notice them.

As they came closer, Rakel signalled to him that he should move towards her and then she lay down on the ground. He lay beside her, so close that he could smell the scent of her, the scent of a girl.

He could raise his hand now, place it on her arm, the way she'd placed her own on his. He could caress her through the fabric of her jacket, allow his hand to move towards her cheek, carefully move his fingers across her face, ears and neck, stroke her throat with his index and middle fingers.

Stop it, Tommy, he said to himself.

She began crawling forward, approaching the reindeer. He followed behind her, but was unable to keep up, the stones on the ground hurt his knees and thighs.

Then he saw her move her finger to the trigger.

The silence was shattered, like a flash of lightning across a pitch-black sky. It overwhelmed the senses but the sound was gone almost before it had come. And the buck lay lifeless on the ground.

'Yay!' Rakel cheered.

For a moment she turned to face him and flashed a smile, her eyes and mouth forming an ordinary impulsive expression of joy.

'We did it!' she whispered, although they no longer needed to whisper. And even though 'we' was, strictly speaking, only her. 'Can you grab the knapsack?'

She climbed to her feet and was over by the buck in a few strides. He picked up the rifle and ran after her. By the time he reached her side, she had already stuck the knife into the deer's jugular.

'But what about the bucket?' he said.

'Yes, take it out,' she said.

He began digging through the knapsack, but the plastic bucket was stuck inside and it took a while for him to pull it out. Finally, he had to fold the fabric to one side to extract it, and he noticed that his hands were shaking.

The ground was already red with blood, but then she placed the bucket under the buck's neck and the knife so the blood poured into it instead.

'Do you like blood sausage?'

'No.'

'Me neither,' she smiled.

She whipped the blood so it wouldn't coagulate and poured a little sea salt into it from a cloth pouch. When she was done, she put the lid on the bucket.

Together they rolled the reindeer over onto its back and cut out the entrails. They put the heart to one side. Then Rakel stuck the knife into the animal's mouth and cut out the tongue. It was greyish-purple, full of blood and fat.

They continued to work in silence. A few times Rakel stopped, drew a breath, seemed about to speak but then stopped herself. They went to the brook and rinsed off the entrails, plunging their fingers into the icy meltwater from the glaciers on the mountain, and observing how the water was stained red and then gradually became clear again. Then they wrapped up the entrails in pieces of old tarp and pushed them down into the knapsack. Afterwards they tied the carcass to a pole, which they would carry between them back to the cottage. Rakel pulled the knapsack onto her back before he had the chance to offer to carry it. Should he say something? Was he expected to carry the knapsack in addition to the pole, since he was a boy? But she was every bit as strong as he was, if not stronger.

He said nothing.

They lifted the pole and started to walk, him in the front, her in the back.

He couldn't see Rakel but felt her gaze on the back of his neck. Or perhaps he was just imagining it.

They continued walking for a few hundred metres. He was warm, the pole weighed heavily on his shoulder.

'You've always been the favourite,' he heard Rakel say.

'The favourite?'

He tried looking behind him but couldn't see her without turning around and he couldn't turn around without stopping and putting down the reindeer. So he just kept walking.

'You are the real grandchild,' she continued, in a voice more subdued than was usual for her. 'Blood is thicker and all that. But it's not just because of that.'

She was silent for a second, perhaps waiting for him to reply. Low hanging clouds of fog slid into the valley; they should hurry back before it settled in.

'I've never thought about it as a contest,' he said.

'But you don't think she should have saved us,' Rakel said. 'Runa and me. You think we should have stayed back there with the illness and died along with the others.'

'I never said that.'

'No,' she said. 'But you haven't said the opposite either. And it's not hard to figure out that you think we're a nuisance. That you don't think Aunt Louise should have sent us here.'

'She's not your aunt,' Tommy said but the words sounded petty.

He tried to find a place to rest his gaze, but the fog wiped away all the edges and details, made everything blurry, including his thoughts.

'I'm scared about food,' he said after a while. 'The more of us there are, the less we have.'

'Are you just scared about food?' Rakel said. 'I'm scared about everything.'

Henry came running towards them. He was far away from the cottage, his eyes burning.

'Where have you been?!'

He didn't say anything more until he reached Tommy's side.

He pressed his face into his big brother's jacket and threw his arms around him. Tommy's hands were full so he could not reciprocate.

'What is it?' he asked. 'Calm down.'

He could feel Henry's back shaking. He lowered the pole from his shoulder, heard Rakel protest weakly, but ignored her and bent down towards his little brother.

'Can't you tell me what's the matter?'

Henry lifted his face towards him. Tears and snot were dribbling down it. He was sobbing so hard he was barely able to speak.

'I've been waiting ...'

'And?'

Another sob.

'I was standing by the window ...'

'Yes, Henry?'

'I just stood there ... it took so long ... finally ... I thought you weren't coming back ... I thought you were gone, Tommy. I was sure you were gone.'

At that moment, Hilmar came out of the cottage and walked towards them. There was something abashed about his gait, the way he held his head.

'Did you know how upset Henry was?' Tommy asked.

Hilmar shrugged. 'He was just crying.'

'And what did you do about it?'

'I told him to pull himself together. He had to, didn't he? He was being foolish. I just told him the truth, that you were out hunting. That you would come back. But he wouldn't listen to me. It was like he'd just made up his mind. He went completely nuts, Tommy. Completely nuts.'

'And when it didn't help to "tell him the truth", what did you do then?'

Hilmar looked at the ground, staring fixedly at a stone. 'I told him to shut up. I said that if he didn't stop, you wouldn't come back.'

'And I'm guessing that didn't help much either?'

'I couldn't take any more. I said, fine, they're gone. Live with it.'

Tommy felt Henry's tiny body shaking silently against his own. He held his arm around him for a while without saying anything.

Then he stared at Hilmar. 'Next time you have to try a little harder. Okay? A little harder, you can do that.'

Hilmar stared back at him, showing no signs of looking down.

'Did you hear what I said to you?' Tommy said.

Hilmar shrugged. 'Whatever.'

'Behave!' Tommy was shouting now.

He released Henry and took a step towards Hilmar. The middle brother continued staring at him.

Tommy clenched his fists, his heart pounding.

Suddenly Henry was beside him, tugging gently at his sleeve. 'Tommy, please.'

'He has to behave!'

'It's fine. I wasn't *that* scared,' Henry said and Tommy could hear the tremor in his voice.

*

The day when the midnight sun disappeared – 23 August – came and went. Every day was like the day before, the same weather, the same cold wind. But the darkness gradually gained ground.

Tommy was the first to wake up every day. In this way he avoided the discomfort of Rakel and Runa entering the sitting room while he was still asleep, the feeling that they were looking at him, that he revealed something private about himself. He forced himself awake, even though he really needed to sleep more, disentangling himself carefully from Henry's arms – because his little brother would often come out to him in the course of the night – and setting his feet on the morning-cold floorboards, he pulled on his socks, trousers, jumper and shoes.

The first thing he did was walk down to the road, continue northwest for a short distance out of the valley until he could see Hotellneset and the outskirts of Longyearbyen.

Every morning he walked until he was warm. To reach the top of the slope he had to pass an aerial tramway pylon. He looked up, taking in the sight of the structure. The woodwork was so rotten that it was uncertain whether it would survive the next winter storm. That's how it was with all the remaining signs of human life on Svalbard. Nature had claimed possession of the materials, made them its own, fungi and rot ruled over them now, and sun, rain and wind wore away at them every single day. He didn't understand why somebody had wanted these old pylons to be preserved. Nature took over anyway and made everything its own, sooner or later. Preservation was a Sisyphus-like task, but in the last century there had apparently been time for such things.

Sometimes he climbed up one of the few aerial tramway pylons that was still successfully resisting the wind and weather. He sat on top, ten metres above the ground, dangling his legs. He was always breathing hard – from the climb but also because of his mounting anxiety. He feared the absence of signs of life.

But the smoke was there every single morning, a slender, grey streak, curling upwards through the air, a soft shape, a line in movement.

He was unable to make sense of the smoke rising so resolutely, what it meant. He was unable to conceive of what it would mean if it should stop. He only managed to handle the fact that it was still there, and that as long as this was the case, nothing had changed. As long as the smoke from the crematorium kept rising into the sky, he still had a grandmother, a father, there were still people alive in Longyearbyen. The smoke meant only one thing: that they should wait, not think, that the standstill would continue.

Then that morning arrived.

Tommy got up first as usual and went outside. The red cottage was at his back, and the others were all still sleeping. The Advent Valley lay below in silence.

So silent.

He kept walking. He walked closer than he usually did.

Quickly he climbed an aerial tramway pylon. Left hand, right foot, left foot, right hand, quickly, quickly.

He reached the top. Hotellneset lay before him. It was a clear day, his eyes weren't playing tricks on him. The absence of life was chilling.

No streak of bluish-grey smoke rising from the crematorium to be seen. The valley was lifeless, the road as well. Something moved far in the distance, by Isdammen reservoir, but it was just a reindeer.

His hands shaking and legs trembling, he climbed down again.

Without looking back, he ran to the cottage. He slammed the door shut behind him. Then he stood in the middle of the sitting room and tried to catch his breath. He heard the sound of movement in the boys' bedroom. The slamming of the door must have woken them.

Henry came shuffling into the sitting room. He sat on the sofa, yawning loudly, scratching his shin beneath his wool sock. Tommy could hear his nails scraping against his skin. The sound was amplified, unreal.

'Did you sleep well?' he asked. But his voice seemed to come from far away.

'Mm,' his little brother said.

'I'll make breakfast now,' Tommy said.

'Yes,' Henry said.

But his hands wouldn't move and Tommy just remained standing in the middle of the room.

Henry looked up at him.

'Your face is all red,' he said.

'Oh,' Tommy said. 'Right.'

He placed his hands against his cheeks, feeling how hot they were.

'You look like you've been out for a run,' Henry said.

'Maybe I have,' Tommy said.

But he couldn't remember at that moment whether he had run back to the cottage; maybe he had. Yes, he had sprinted with his heart in his throat.

Henry got up off the sofa, taking Tommy's duvet with him. He held it around him like a cape and trembled a bit underneath it.

'It's cold,' he said. 'It's autumn.'

'No,' Tommy said. 'It's not autumn yet.'

'But it's getting darker,' Henry said. 'That means autumn is here. Weren't you going to make breakfast?'

'Yes.'

'It's not happening very quickly, from what I can see,' Henry said, imitating Tommy's own voice.

Then he turned towards the sofa and put the duvet back on it.

'I guess I should get dressed,' he said. 'Then I can help you.'

'Wait a minute,' Tommy said.

'Why?'

Tommy walked over and sat down on the sofa, pulling the duvet around him, the way Henry had done.

'Come here.' He nodded towards his little brother.

Henry hesitated momentarily, but then he did as he was told. Pattered over and sat down. Tommy draped the duvet around him as well, so they were both sitting under it with only their heads sticking out.

'You're shaking,' Henry said.

'Yes,' Tommy said.

Henry took hold of one of his hands, squeezing it with one of his own small hands.

'It will be all right, you'll see,' he said.

'Yes,' Tommy said. 'But ... do you mind if I cry a little bit?'

Henry glanced up at him. 'No. Why?'

Tommy didn't reply because if he were to try to speak now, only deep sobs would come out of his mouth and then he would wake up the others and he had to make sure he didn't do that, had to be sure to avoid Rakel right now, so he could think, figure out what he should say. The tears ran down his cheeks and he trembled faintly, but Henry clutched his hand as tightly as he could and wiped away the salty tears with a corner of the bedding.

Now things are skidding out of control. That was what he thought, now things are skidding out of control and it's important that I don't show the others this, that Henry and Hilmar don't understand that everything's skidding out of control, like a huge chunk of glacial ice sliding down a mountain and out into the ocean where it is taken by the waves and quickly melts.

Tao

The van moves down destroyed roads, surrounded by darkness. They take turns at the wheel, often driving all through the night. Sometimes they stop at disused farms, find a mini power station and recharge. Other times they must use the van's back-up wood gas engine and the exhaust hangs like a tail in the air behind them.

They seldom run into people. Rivers once ran through this landscape like glittering blood vessels. Now their source in the mountains has disappeared, there are no glaciers to keep them alive any longer and without water neither is there any basis for human life here. The arid landscape awakens something inside her and it takes her a while to understand what it is: a faint sense of anger. Stupid, stupid humans, she thinks, who destroyed so much.

The convoy creeps upwards, further away from the ocean all the time, driving through the desert, steppes, passing mountains, through sand and dust, in increasingly cold temperatures and darkness.

Henry, Runa and Hilmar sleep sitting up, their heads slung on thin necks, from side to side, every time the van veers to avoid a pothole. The rear compartment of the vehicle is outfitted with benches on which they had laid loose cushions, far too thin, so their backs hurt constantly. Henry's little body constantly threatens to tip over. She wants to lean forward and straighten him up but is afraid of waking him.

The children speak to each other in Norwegian but say little to her. Only Runa tries to smile her polite smile and always says thank you for the food she is given.

During the first few days, Henry often asked about Tommy. He asked to be woken when it was time to take out the radio, sat beside her, his eyes eager and his body agitated. But eventually, when his brother didn't reply, he gave up.

It is as if the dust from the road has settled upon him and the other children, making their eyes dull and bodies sluggish. She tries to tell them about the place that will be their new home, the fertile Sichuan, where insects buzz in the forest, where the birds twitter and the summer is long and sunny. The children listen politely but never ask any questions, don't seem interested. They are so different now from when Tao arrived in Spitsbergen. At that time they were enthusiastic, all of them talking at the same time, interrupting each other, eager to show her their home.

'Welcome to Longyearbyen,' Rakel said when they had made their way up the road from the beach. She threw out her arms. 'Yes, this is Road Four Hundred, or the Mine Seven road, as it is also called.'

There was something so awkward about her movements that it pained Tao.

'This road continues inland along the Advent Valley,' Rakel continued in a melodramatic storytelling style. 'And there you will find Svalbard's fresh water source.'

'The Isdammen reservoir, right?' Tao said, remembering the name from the old maps she had studied.

'Yes, correct,' Rakel said. 'And the road up to the right,

Road Five Hundred, leads to Road Two Hundred, or Hilmar Rekstens Road, which is the former main street of Longyearbyen. If this were one hundred years ago, you would have stayed there for sure, at the Polar Hotel.' She pointed at a large building.

The others gathered around her. Tommy said something to Rakel in Norwegian, clearly irritated. She answered irately and turned away from him, ignoring him.

'Up there we had a hospital and the greenhouse is there, too.'

'A greenhouse?'

'Yes.'

'Can I see it?' Tao asked.

'Of course you can see it. How nice that you're interested in our greenhouse.'

For the first time Tao noticed Tommy looking at her.

'It's not a big deal,' he said. 'Just a few plants and a little soil. You have forests where you come from so it won't impress you.'

His modesty was touching; she wanted to reassure him but couldn't find the words.

'Besides,' he continued, and now his voice was harder, 'we're going to leave it behind.'

Tao turned to Mei-Ling, who had cleared her throat several times. Now she pulled Tao impatiently to one side.

'What are you waiting for?' she asked.

'I am just giving them the chance to welcome us properly.'

Mei-Ling looked at her in dismay. 'It's not as if we've sailed across the sea like Columbus bringing glass beads and other trinkets. They are the ones who invited us here.'

'They're just children,' Tao said.

'Exactly.'

Tao turned to face Rakel again, who was waiting for them with a hesitant smile on her face.

'We would like to go up there right away.'

'To the vault?'

Tao nodded.

'Are you going to take the seeds already, today?'

'Yes. The sooner we get back the better.'

Rakel laughed suddenly. 'So you're thinking we should go there right away?'

Mei-Ling sighed in irritation. 'We should have gone *yesterday*.'

Rakel said something in Norwegian to the other children. They started chattering eagerly in response. Only Tommy remained silent.

Then Rakel turned to face Tao. 'It takes a while to get up there, but I can go with you.'

Tommy interrupted her. '*We* can go with you,' he said. 'We'll go together, all of us.'

And so they started walking, not towards Longyearbyen, but out along the fjord on the only road there was. The children took the lead, straggling and excited. Rakel kept turning around to make sure the adults were keeping up.

Henry and Hilmar had brought a ball. Now and then they kicked it back and forth between them. She noticed that Hilmar especially had good control of his feet. She thought about the boys who used to play ball back home and for the first time she pictured the children from Svalbard in her own country.

She later saw Henry pack the ball in the bag of toys he brought with him on the boat.

The bag is in the back of the van now. But Henry hasn't opened it since they left Longyearbyen. She hasn't seen the children play at all during the past few days.

The van hits an especially large hole and Henry's head knocks against the wall, waking him up suddenly. He whimpers, looks around, disorientated.

'Tommy,' he says.

Then he holds his head in his hands and starts crying woefully.

She reaches back towards him, wanting to comfort him, but he twists away and the tears stop as suddenly as they started. 'I'm fine.'

She holds her scarf out to him. It is large and soft.

'Why don't you rest your head against this?'

'No,' he says. 'I'm fine, I said.'

Tommy

He hears Hilmar's footsteps; he is running in front of him on the road. He can feel Henry's hand in his, how his brother pulls him onwards. His brothers are tugging at him, all the time, the way they have always done. They are still with him, even in their absence, and that makes it difficult to sit still. His back aches, the muscles in his neck are so stiff. His stomach is upset, labouring away, something inside there constantly churning.

He wanders towards Bjørndalen. A sudden thaw has hit Spitsbergen. The snow is melting, the air is humid. But a huge, low-hanging and waning moon illuminates the landscape.

In some places, on steep sections, the earth is bare. He sees the remains of a landslide far out in the valley. Loose sediments set into motion by millions of drops of water, which penetrate the ground, and literally move mountains.

Tommy walks all the way down to the shore. A pod of beluga whales are frolicking along the coast. It has been a long time since he has seen these small, white whales here in Isfjorden. The ocean is gradually becoming too warm for them.

He can make out eight, perhaps ten backs, an entire family. The white backs move in and out of sight amidst the waves. The swells break against the shore and he notices the taste of salt.

He is damp, everything is damp and even though the moon is shining, drops of moisture strike him. He doesn't know whether they come from the ocean or from a cloud he can't see.

He turns away from the ocean and starts walking, remembering another evening, another rainstorm. Raindrops were bouncing loudly off the cardboard on the roof of the cottage. It was at least fifty years old, that cardboard. In a couple places they had to nail it in place and it leaked in the corner by the front door. The drops hit the water in a bucket erratically. It was half full.

Runa, Hilmar and Henry were asleep and he and Rakel were sitting in front of the stove. The coal inside was glowing and Rakel lifted her wool sock-covered feet towards the heat. He could not understand how she could bear to hold them so close to the fire.

It was dark outside, as dark as it gets when the sky is overcast and the sun has disappeared far below the horizon. It would soon be back, he tried to console himself, daybreak began at three in the morning. The absence of the sun was still brief, but long enough to remind them of the steady advancement of the polar night.

When Rakel awoke and saw him sitting on the sofa with Henry, crying, she understood where he had been and what he had seen. She often walked along the road herself to look for the smoke from the village.

The whole day had gone by without their saying anything. He had dried his tears, got to his feet, made breakfast and then gone out to skin yet another reindeer they had shot. Afterwards he and Rakel had used a block and tackle system to hang it high up on the meat frame, so the bears would not be able to reach it.

It was hard work – the reindeer was fat after a long summer of grazing and weighed almost as much as Tommy. They struggled with the big, dead carcass, sweating and toiling, and it forced them to think about something else.

But now, now finally the children were asleep ... the children, that was the word he used. As if he and Rakel were father and mother.

Rakel stared into the glowing embers with rapt attention. He didn't understand why she didn't say anything, why she didn't express an opinion, she who always had so many of them.

She wrinkled her brow, opened her mouth and then shut it again. It was as if she were arguing with herself.

'Aren't you getting hot?' he asked.

'What?' She looked up.

'Your feet? They must be burning up when you hold then so close.'

'I want to get hot. That's *why* I hold them so close.'

'Okay,' he said. 'Fine. But take care that you don't catch fire.'

'Fine,' she said. 'Thanks for your permission to warm my feet, Tommy.'

'I didn't give you permission,' he said, his voice growing louder. 'I just said that your socks could catch fire.'

'I would feel it,' she said. 'If my socks got so hot that they caught fire. Don't you think I would feel it, Tommy?'

He stood up without replying and walked over to the bucket of rainwater in the corner, picked it up and emptied it into the utility sink. The metal bucket clattered rudely against the sink.

'Be careful not to wake Runa,' Rakel hissed. 'She's a very light sleeper.'

'Yeah, yeah,' he said.

'And why are you emptying the bucket anyway? It's not even half full.'

'I'm emptying it because I am going to bed,' he said, and used a rag to wipe up a few drops of water that had hit the floor when he'd taken away the bucket, before putting it back in place.

'So you're going to bed *now*?' Rakel said and her voice was suddenly hard.

'Yes, I'm tired.'

Tommy stood in the middle of the room, feeling empty-handed without the bucket.

'Tired? Well then, obviously you must go to bed!'

'Yes?'

'Yes!'

She abruptly got to her feet, stood facing him.

'Go ahead and go to bed. I really think you should do that.'

He walked over to the sofa and started taking his duvet out of a box on the floor. Rakel followed him. She waved her arms. 'Won't it be great to fall asleep now!'

'Hush!' he said. 'Now you're the one who's waking up the others.'

He pulled the sheet out of the box. It was covered with stains and smelled sour. They hadn't washed it when they got here, still hadn't washed anything, even though they had running water from a hose that ran from the brook. They should make the most of it now, it occurred to him, before the brook froze over. Everything would be more difficult after the first frost.

'But what are we going to do now, Tommy?'

Her voice cracked suddenly. He looked up from the sheet and into a face now drained of all anger.

'I don't know,' he said.

'But what do you think it means?' she said. 'Does it mean that there aren't any more people who are sick? That they have recovered? Or that everyone is dead?'

He shrugged, not in a gesture of feigned toughness, but because he was unable to speak. If he tried to say something, he knew that he would start crying again.

'Shouldn't we go into the village, and see?' Rakel asked softly.

'I don't know,' he repeated.

'We needn't go all the way in,' she said. 'We can keep a distance and check if we can see something using the binoculars.'

'But what if someone sees *us*?' he said.

'Does it matter?'

'No, perhaps not.'

She grasped the other end of the sheet and they began making up the sofa together. Her body was suddenly awfully close to his and it was cramped and warm in the cottage. The sofa – his bed – was there between them. She could just lie down on it, they could lie down on it together. His hands under her jumper, a girl's skin under his fingers, her breasts, the contours of which he could see, in his hand, stroking her abdomen gently, allowing his hands to slide downward, hearing her whisper his name.

No. Get it together. How can you think like this, how can you think like this now?

'Tommy?'

'Yes.'

'Are you okay?'

'Sure.'

He turned away.

'Maybe we should just wait a while, then?' she said.

'Yes,' he said. 'Perhaps it's best to wait a while.'

'A couple of days then, or what do you think?' she said and he could hear the impatience in her voice.

'Yes?' he said. 'I don't know.'

'Tommy,' she said, and the irony was back. 'You're really a man of action.'

She went to bed without saying goodnight. The door to her bedroom banged loudly behind her and it was sheer luck that she didn't wake anyone. He was left standing there, heart pounding, racing.

He crept under the duvet, lay on his side, but was sickened by the sour odour of the sheet. He turned over onto his back and lay staring up at the ceiling.

The knots in the woodwork stared back at him like dark eyes. Yellowed pine from the old days, back when Svalbard had materials shipped in from Norway. He tried to imagine how the trees had once looked, how close together the branches had been, how thick they had been. He wished the planks were a forest, he wished he were lying in the forest now, on a floor of moss, beneath a canopy of live tree crowns with the sound of the wind in the leaves around him.

Trees, trees, he tried to cling to images of trees. And even though he lay in a box made of pine, it was leafy trees he dreamed of. Ash, birch, aspen and maple.

He turned over on his side again, finally managed to ignore the sour odour, took one of the sofa cushions between his arms and hugged it hard against his body, as if it were a tree.

Two days passed. Three, four. Both Rakel and Tommy often went down to the road to look towards Longyearbyen, but nothing changed. They raised the binoculars, stared until their eyes became dry, but didn't see any signs of life, no smoke from the smokestack of the crematorium, and no smoke from any other chimneys either. On the fourth morning, Tommy thought he detected some movement down by the ocean at Hotellneset. He stood staring for a long time, his eyes open wide, without blinking, in the hope of identifying what he thought he had seen. But nothing more happened. Everything seemed dead.

Rakel filled the days with activity, she was good at that. And she had begun talking about the winter, that they had to prepare themselves, make long-term plans. He perhaps should have felt grateful that she was able to look ahead, that she worked from morning until night setting out snares, hunting, and gathering coal from the mines under the aerial tramway, but the intensity of her compulsion to stay productive took his breath away. She shot geese, sat out in the sun and plucked their feathers with abrupt, staccato movements and a deep crease between her brows that made her look older than her seventeen years. She gathered scurvy weed, crowberries and bog bilberries and served these to the three children, pronouncing the word *eat* severely, even though they made faces over how sour the berries were. And she bossed them all around. Her bustling industry filled the cottage, forced the four others to work. It was not possible to sit still around a person who was always in movement.

Rakel and Tommy did not go out hunting again. They already had a lot of meat. The hides of the two reindeer were hung up on the roof, like large screens. The two carcasses hung on the meat-drying rack outside the cottage. The only time he saw Rakel stand still was when she stopped and gazed happily at the meat. It seemed like the sight gave her a sense of security.

But the carcasses could also put them in danger. They had experienced this many times in Longyearbyen because Spitsbergen had many hungry inhabitants. And meat hung out on display was an invitation.

The bear came in the afternoon. It was a warm, windless day. Henry, Hilmar and Runa were playing tag in the sun and Rakel was sitting bent over a dead grouse. He was about to carry in the last cord of driftwood from the shed on the south side of the cottage.

'We should gather more,' he said to Rakel in passing and heard that it sounded like a reproach.

'We should also put out a net,' she replied sharply, without looking up from her work.

He regretted having said anything and did not continue the conversation. She was right. They needed fish to stay healthy throughout the winter, but could not walk down to the fjord, because the village lay in between. They were cut off from the ocean, from fishing, from everything the ocean washed up onto the beaches. They could move inland, up into the mountains and of course they could reach the ocean if they took a long detour around Longyearbyen, but that would take at least half a day each way.

'Bear!' they heard Runa cry suddenly.

The three children came running towards Rakel and

Tommy, simultaneously pointing at something behind them, behind the cottage.

'Get inside, get inside!' Rakel said and was on her feet.

The basin holding the grouse tumbled to the ground, and flipped over, blood and entrails falling out and staining the ground red.

Tommy took a few steps to the side so he had a view of the area behind the cottage and there it was. The bear's head swayed from side to side, its snout searching, sniffing, headed for the meat-drying rack. It ran fast. He had never seen a bear run so fast before.

'Tommy!' In two bounds, Rakel had gone inside and retrieved the rifle. 'You get inside, too!'

He moved towards the door, tripped over the basin on the ground and almost fell, but he managed to stay on his feet. Then he stood motionless, with his hand on the door handle.

Rakel held the rifle against her cheek, aimed at the bear, moving at all times to keep it in her sights.

The bear moved closer.

And then it stopped, just a few metres away from them.

'We're in the way,' he whispered. 'We're between the bear and the meat.'

Then Rakel aimed the rifle into the sky and pulled the trigger. The shot splintered the air, echoing in his ears.

And it frightened the bear.

It lowered its head, observing Rakel. The small, black eyes, the snout in movement. Slowly it opened its mouth, bared its teeth, its huge jaws.

'We have to let it have it,' he whispered. 'Just let it take the meat.'

'Are you an idiot?' Rakel whispered as her fingers around the stock of the rifle whitened.

The bear took a couple of steps towards them, testing, assessing.

'Well, shoot it then, at least,' he hissed.

Even though he knew they weren't supposed to shoot polar bears. The bear was here for human beings; it was the bear that *was* Svalbard. It owned this land, the people on it were only visiting. And the bear had learned that reindeer made an excellent meal. Even better when it was already skinned and cleaned, hanging on a meat rack like now.

Rakel took a step towards the bear, which stared at them fixedly, while moving its head slightly in reaction to her movement.

'Go away,' Rakel said. 'You can't have our meat.'

The bear didn't move.

Suddenly Rakel aimed the rifle upward again and fired another shot.

The bear flinched with its whole body and retreated a few metres, but then, again, it stood still.

'Don't tell me I have to shoot you,' Rakel said.

It wasn't until then that Tommy noticed that the door to the cottage was ajar. Three pairs of eyes were peering out at them.

'Tommy,' he heard Henry say. 'What's happening?'

'It'll be on its way soon,' Tommy said. 'It's not dangerous.'

But the bear held its ground.

Again Rakel placed her finger on the trigger. This time she aimed right at the bear.

'I know I'll hit it,' she mumbled. 'It will die immediately.'

A grouse flew through the sky above them, softly calling to its dead companion on the ground. For a second the bear turned its head towards it. Rakel seized her chance and took a step forward.

She lowered the rifle and stood holding it in one hand.

If the bear decided to attack, she wouldn't even have time to aim.

Then she raised both arms.

'Get lost,' she said. 'Get out of here.'

But she didn't shout the words loudly enough. It didn't sound like she meant it. The words were feeble, delivered without force or courage.

Rakel turned towards him.

'Help me.'

Tommy knew that he should move to her side, that they should make themselves large together. But his legs refused to obey.

Instead he remained where he was, waving his arms half-heartedly and trying to shout.

'Go on, get out of here.'

The air swallowed up his words.

It isn't possible to predict the polar bear's actions. This had been ingrained in them since the time they were small: the polar bear is unpredictable, unreliable, its behaviour seemingly without rhyme or reason – sometimes it will attack suddenly and brutally. Grandmother used to say that it was difficult to know whether the bear was smart or stupid. The only thing she had really understood about them was that it was impossible to anticipate their next move. The polar bear could turn around and leave, only to come back again because it had discovered where the food was, or it might immediately lunge at that food, lunge at people. It could even attack the cottage, hitting the walls with its huge paws or breaking a window to get to those who were inside. Runa, Henry and Hilmar.

And then it took yet another step closer. Rakel had time to raise her rifle again, press her finger against the trigger.

'We have to shoot it,' she murmured.

She squeezed one eye shut again and aimed.

But then a figure came running up out of nowhere, roaring and waving its arms, rushing to get between them and the bear. It took a few seconds for Tommy to understand who was roaring and whose arm movements they were.

Grandmother!

Strong Grandmother, suddenly much larger than he remembered.

She stood in front of them, in the line of fire. A rifle hung over her shoulder, but she would not have time to get it up on her shoulder were the bear to attack. All the same she stood between them and the bear, unarmed and yelling.

'Uaaaa!' No words, no orders, just a huge, dark, terrifying scream.

Then she started walking towards the bear, one step at a time. She continued roaring; the sound was deep, raw, he didn't know her voice could sound like that, and her arm movements were dramatic and violent.

And finally the bear reacted.

First, it shook its head vaguely.

Then it turned and lumbered away.

Nobody moved. They watched the bear's movements as it continued into the valley, away from the cottage. Towards the mountains.

Grandmother turned and looked at them. First at Rakel, who was still holding the rifle aloft, then at Tommy.

Then she walked over to Rakel, motioning to Tommy as she did so, wanting him to come. She hugged both of them, holding them tightly against her body. Grandmother was shorter than both him and Rakel, but her arms still offered the greatest feeling of security he had experienced in a long time.

They remained huddled together without moving for several minutes.

Then all three went inside.

There Henry and Hilmar threw themselves at Grandmother.

'Where's Daddy?' Henry asked, clutching the hem of Grandmother's jacket, as if to confirm that she was real.

She let him hold her tightly.

'He fell ill,' she said simply. 'He is dead.'

Father is dead, he thought in the days that followed. These three words, over and over again. Father is dead, as if it would become more real if he only repeated it enough. Father's face filled his head. He tried to picture every single tiny detail, burn them permanently into his memory. His round chin, the narrow nose, the shaggy eyebrows casting shadows over his eyes.

Svalbard took Father, Tommy tried to think, the way Svalbard has taken so many far too soon. But the truth forced its way in. Because Father *gave* himself to Svalbard, he sacrificed himself and left the boys on their own. He made a choice that put them second. Maybe he thought they would have Grandmother, that she was enough, as she had been enough for him ... But she *hadn't* been enough for him. That was what he blamed her for, that it wasn't until they arrived in Svalbard that he was given the village he needed.

'Where have you been this whole time? What have you been doing?'

Grandmother and Tommy were sitting in front of the fireplace. The little ones were asleep. Rakel had gone to bed with Runa.

'I stayed in Bjørndalen most of the time,' Grandmother said. 'In the old cabin.'

She shovelled coal into the stove. They had almost run out, would have to find more before the weather turned colder, before winter came. The old windmill did not produce enough electricity to keep them warm. He felt a jab of anxiety, but then he remembered that Grandmother was here now. They would be fine, everything would be fine.

'Bjørndalen?' he asked. 'But why couldn't you stay here with us?'

'I wanted to keep an eye on things,' Grandmother said. 'I went into the village often, hid myself and observed them from a distance.'

'But ...' He thought for a moment. 'We are closer to Longyearbyen here than in Bjørndalen. Why couldn't you stay with us? Hilmar and Henry have asked about you, every day, they've been crying and afraid.'

'Out of consideration for all of you,' Grandmother said, who always had an answer. 'I was afraid I'd contracted the illness. That I came close enough to have been infected.'

He was not satisfied with the explanation but didn't know what else to say.

'And besides,' she said slowly, 'I needed a little time alone. After David ...'

She said no more. It took a moment for him to understand what she meant. That she had needed time to be alone with her grief. And perhaps also with her anger and frustration.

Tommy had once read that the loss of a child is the worst thing a person can experience. It goes against the nature of things. The eldest is supposed to die first. He tried to picture it, Grandmother alone in a cabin, wailing, furious with her son, with the illness.

But he was unable to put Grandmother's face into this image, unable to picture her lying there in that way, picture her surrendering. And no matter what the reason was, he still didn't understand why she had left him and his brothers alone, afraid, grieving.

He believes that this, in particular, is something he will never be able to understand.

'You were away for so long,' he said. 'What were you doing all that time?'

She studied him inquisitively.

'Perhaps I haven't been myself these past few weeks.' She searched for words. 'Or ... the person I had been was altered.'

She paused, reconsidering. 'I think maybe that I am still altered. I don't know.'

Her words made him uneasy. Grandmother was supposed to be Grandmother, the person she had always been. And she noticed his uneasiness because she leaned forward and stroked his cheek with one hand. 'Don't give it another thought, Tommy. You don't need to think about it.'

'But what happened?' Tommy asked. 'What happened to everyone?'

Her hands lay motionless in her lap, her focus inward.

'I walked to the village every day. I saw the bodies they carried in, I saw how those who initially were transporting others later became those who were transported.'

'Could you see Father? Among them?' he asked.

'No,' she said. 'The majority were covered up. At least, to begin with. Eventually it was as if they gave up on everything, that included. No sense of dignity remained. It was just a matter of getting them into the oven, getting rid of the corpses and the illness that could still be alive in the blood and flesh.'

He didn't understand why, but he was relieved that she hadn't seen his father's body, that she couldn't describe to him what his corpse looked like, what the illness had done to him. Not because Tommy believed that Grandmother would have shared this kind of information, but because knowing that she could have such images of Father in her head would also make Tommy think about what those images *were* and maybe ask, pester her for more details. That Grandmother hadn't seen Father made the circumstances surrounding his death abstract.

Yes, his death *was* abstract and, for a while, Tommy tried to create a story about Father, to tell himself that he had miraculously escaped infection, that he had found his way to safety, isolated himself before it was too late and that he, like the children, was living somewhere else in Svalbard, alone in a cabin, like a trapper, that he had made his way to Fredheim, had become a kind of Hilmar Nøis or a Henry Rudi, a polar bear king in Bjørneborg. He is doing just fine in his cabin, he shoots reindeer and grouse, he lives on what nature provides for him, his eternal hunting grounds are a cabin located on a peninsula, beneath the snout of a beautiful blue glacier.

But the story was not believable. He knew that his brothers would not accept such a fantasy, either. They were accustomed to how death could at any time take away anyone at all, including mothers and fathers. That's how life had always been in Svalbard.

'In the end nobody was brought to the oven any longer,' Grandmother said. 'Every day I walked into the village, lay down on the ground just above the aerial tramway station with my eyes glued to the binoculars, observing the silent streets. But I saw no signs of life.'

'And then?'

'Then I ventured all the way in ...' Her voice trembled. 'Oh ... Tommy ...'

He didn't know what to say, if he should comfort Grandmother. She had become so pale and thin, had dark circles under her eyes and protruding cheekbones. His hands in his lap felt empty and ineffectual. A bit awkwardly, he lifted one hand and this time it was his turn to stroke her cheek.

His touch startled her. She grasped his hand and held it in her own.

'It was so empty, everywhere,' she explained. 'I didn't dare enter any of the houses, knowing that they could still be contaminated, and that I might also find people dying. But everything had fallen apart, everything was abandoned. I have seen many empty cities in my life, in the past, before I came here. But this was different. Because here everyone had disappeared, almost simultaneously. They had sort of dropped whatever they were doing and gone to die.'

'But did you see anyone, then?'

She shook her head. 'No, nobody.'

'And then you came here?'

'Not until I was sure that I was healthy. I went out to Bjørndalen and stayed there for a little while longer.' She suddenly released a hard little laugh. 'Every day I thought I felt symptoms of the illness, every morning I woke up and thought I had a fever. I had heart palpitations and headaches. But it was all just my imagination, a kind of anxiety.'

'Are you sure?' he said, because she really did not look well.

'Of course I'm sure,' she said.

They sat in silence for a moment. She continued to hold his hand between hers.

'Do you know when we can go back?' he asked.

'Not yet,' she said. 'But maybe later . . . yes, I believe we can go back soon.'

Then he remembered something.

'But what about the seeds, Grandmother?'

'What about them?'

'Who's taking care of the seeds now?'

'The seeds are fine,' Grandmother said. 'The seeds are safe there inside the mountain.'

She pulled her hands away, and once again her gaze grew distant. She was searching inward, sifting through her memories. 'Do you remember how he used to whistle?'

'Father?'

'Yes, my son, David.'

'Yes . . . I think so.'

'He whistled softly and pretty badly. It was impossible to determine which song he was trying to produce, even though I believe there was a symphony orchestra in his head and the whistling was an expression of the orchestra's music.'

'I think his whistling was just fine.'

She smiled. 'You whistle in the same way, did you know that?'

'No.'

'Yes. You do.'

'Maybe I whistle, but not like Father. My whistling has no melody. It's just a steady stream of sounds coming out of my mouth and it's something I do just because . . . because I miss him.' Tommy's throat suddenly thickened.

She leaned towards him, as if she wanted to comfort him, but he didn't accept her hug.

'I've been thinking about what he said about you,' he said.

'What's that?'

'The words he used: enlightened despotism.'

'I can't remember that.'

Tommy was certain that Grandmother was lying. She certainly wouldn't have forgotten something like that.

'Your father was modest, but he never gave up,' Grandmother said. 'He was a resistance movement that had gone underground, that worked in silence, but slowly had its way, without anyone really being able to understand how it happened.'

'But he did not get his way. He died.'

'He died with his flock, Tommy.'

'But,' Tommy said, and again it was difficult to speak. 'We were his flock.'

'Yes,' she said. 'We were as well.'

'I don't understand what you man.'

A feeling of uneasiness forced him to his feet. He no longer wanted to hear Grandmother's words, but she continued all the same. 'What I am most proud of,' she said, 'is that David had something I never had myself. A big flock.'

'A flock? But everyone died! We are the only ones who survived and he abandoned us.'

'Yes, Tommy, I know.'

For a moment, he wanted to hit her, stand over her and scream, you can't defend him, he chose to leave us! But instead he turned on his heels, went into the bedroom and closed the door hard behind him.

She made no attempt to stop him.

He lay down beside Henry. His little brother was breathing evenly and heavily, but it did not calm him down. Tommy lay awake in the semi-darkness. He found his father's face amidst the knots in the ceiling boards, traced it and sought comfort in it. But when he had found it, he was unable to look at it for more than a few seconds before it became too much for him. And then he tried to think about trees, about how the wind whispering in the leaves would sound, tried to imagine the sound, the movement of the branches, tried to let *that* image, of the leaves and branches in the wind, dissolve into nothingness.

Each day was twenty minutes shorter than the last. They were approaching the dark season. None of the children asked Grandmother about her plan, about how long they would stay in Todalen, or if they would venture back to Longyearbyen. Tommy didn't talk to Grandmother about Father any more, avoiding all subjects that could upset him.

For a while he was relieved about the standstill, relieved that nothing happened. He liked that the days were the same, predictable. Runa, Henry and Hilmar played beside the cottage. Rakel, Grandmother and Tommy worked. They hunted, prepared meals, gathered coal. Grandmother assigned tasks and they did as they were told. Nobody argued in the presence of Grandmother. Nor otherwise, since her return. Grandmother needed a great deal of rest; increasingly he would find her on the sofa when he came inside with a basket full of coal for the stove, increasingly she went to bed before everyone else, and increasingly she would stop working, was far away, inside herself. There's nothing abnormal about that, he thought. She's just tired. That's probably just how elderly women are. And the brooding expression he so often saw on her face, doubtful, introspective, had to be grief over the son she had lost.

Then it grew colder, the snow covered the ground, the carcasses on the meat-drying racks froze into stony statues, the water in the hose from the brook did not melt even when the sun shone on it, so they had to carry water in buckets. And the sun released its grasp.

*

One day in late October they were woken by the sound of Grandmother packing, rummaging noisily, stuffing things carelessly into their backpacks. The windows were still dark. The day was just a couple of hours long.

'We will leave today as soon as it's light,' she said, without looking up.

'Back there?' he asked.

She nodded.

Rakel had also come out into the sitting room.

'But why now?' she asked. 'How can we be sure it's safe?'

'We can't,' Grandmother said. 'But it's not safe here, either.'

Rakel opened her mouth, about to say something else, but Grandmother interrupted her. 'We could perhaps manage to trap and hunt enough meat, but the electricity from the windmill is unstable, we don't have enough coal and the snow makes it difficult to gather more. When the brook freezes over, we will have to melt snow to make water and I don't trust that the snow is clean enough. Besides, we can't eat only meat. We need access to fish and we need a greenhouse. If we stay here, we will slowly but surely develop scurvy.'

She paused, looking at the doubtful faces.

'Yes,' she said, as if she could hear the questions they were asking themselves. 'There's a certain risk that the infection is still alive there in the village, but that is just a chance we will have to take.'

Rakel didn't say anything else. She merely stood looking at Grandmother, who ignored her.

Tommy took out his backpack and started pushing his wool jumper into it, to show Grandmother that he was with her, no matter what.

Then he realised that he would need to wear the jumper when they left and pulled it out again.

'What are you doing?' Rakel asked.

'Packing,' he said.

She raised an eyebrow.

'Fine,' she said, and went into the bedroom where her little sister was sleeping.

'Runa, you have to get up. We're leaving now.'

We're alone, he thought, and looked around him. Six small figures, on the road, almost invisible. The landscape grew around them, the mountains darkened, looming.

They were all carrying heavy backpacks, loaded with meat, food. Rakel and Tommy also carried a reindeer carcass on a pole between them. They would go back and retrieve the other one later. The weight of it pulled him towards the ground; every step was hard work. It had grown colder and there was a light snowfall. The flakes settled onto his eyelashes, and he blinked them away. As they approached the village, the overcast sky cleared. The sun no longer rose high enough in the sky for them to see it, but it emitted a pale light from its hiding place behind the mountains.

The road was covered with fresh snow that the wind had not yet swept away, offering additional resistance to each step they took. They walked in two lines, Grandmother and Rakel leading the way, making tracks in the snow for the others to walk in, Tommy behind Rakel, Hilmar behind Grandmother, and Runa and Henry last.

'It's hard,' Henry said.

Tommy stopped and turned around.

'I know,' he said.

'I can't walk any more,' Henry said. His face was hidden by his hat and a large scarf. Only his tiny red nose stuck out. The cold made it runny and he sniffled.

'Come on, yes you can,' Tommy said. 'Come here.'

Nobody spoke. Henry just sniffled again and clung to Tommy's hand.

They passed Isdammen reservoir and the old dog kennel. And then Longyearbyen came into view before them. Everything looked the same as before. And everything was different. Because not a single human being was in sight, no smoke rose from the chimneys, not a sound was heard. Longyearbyen, as Tommy had known it, his home, had disappeared.

Walking became even more of a strain. He was barely able to lift his feet. He sucked air down into his lungs, gasping, the cold air burned or perhaps it wasn't the air that stung.

Then it all came tumbling down inside him, all the people, all their faces hit him, his classmates, the neighbours, Berit, Georg, Martin, Glenn, Manfred and Marie, Cora, Grete, all the children of the Christie family , Emily, Mikkel, Wilma, Gerda and Brett. And Father.

He stopped, unable to lift his feet any longer. The pole carrying the reindeer carcass slipped off his shoulder, falling against Rakel's back.

'Ouch! What the hell?'

Then she also dropped her end of the pole and looked at him.

'Are you okay?' she asked over the carcass in the snow.

'No.'

He shook his head and saw that the movement did something to Rakel. Her eyes were bright and cold and everyone had stopped walking now, Grandmother, Runa, Henry and Hilmar.

'Are you crying, Tommy?' Henry asked and threw his arms around his big brother.

Grandmother was immediately at their side; she put her arms around them. Hilmar followed suit and then Rakel and Runa joined them.

There they stood, a small circle of human beings, warming themselves against one another, their cheeks and arms and the material of their garments touching. Tommy could hear muffled sobs and sniffling, the squeaking of jackets, feel their warmth. They were a small group of a few survivors, the six of them, as they stood on the road with their arms around each other beside a frozen reindeer carcass – a small handful of people in a large, deserted landscape, the only remaining flesh and blood, the only beating hearts.

The only heart beating in Svalbard.

A naked heart beats as he wanders down the roads, walks between the shelves of the library, stands by the fjord and looks out at the waves' glittering phosphorescence in the black night and the Northern Lights turning the sky inside out. He can set his watch to the steady rhythm of the beating of his heart, hours, minutes seconds. 08.00 make lists, 09.00 work, 12.00 eat, read, work, eat sleep. Repeat.

He is imprisoned by his watch; it offers him the security of prison walls.

Did Vavilov have routines in *his* prison?

In 1940 he was arrested. Four men dressed in black picked him up and took him away, under the pretext that he was needed in Moscow. For the entirety of his adult life, Vavilov had through painstaking labour and scientific methods fought to bring an end to the famine that was wreaking havoc on his country. Nonetheless, the country's leader had given the order to arrest him for espionage. Hour after hour he was interrogated and tortured. In the end his legs were so swollen that he could not walk. Eleven months, 400 interrogations, 1,700 hours.

That must have been quite a battle, Tommy thinks, as he reviews the translation of the interrogations. The charismatic, committed botanist against the legendary Lieutenant Khvat, a man feared for his malicious nature.

In one of the books, there is a photo of Vavilov in the prison. Tommy often finds himself studying it. He is unshaven and battered, his face bloodless. But he's alive, Tommy thinks. He doesn't give up.

He reads the interrogation transcripts and pictures a cell without windows. Vavilov sits hunched at a table, the gruesome Khvat looming over him.

'You are arrested as an active participant of an anti-Soviet wreckage organisation and a spy for foreign intelligence services,' Khvat states. 'Do you admit your guilt?'

'No, I do not admit my guilt,' Vavilov responds in a clear voice. 'I was never a spy or participant of an anti-Soviet organisation. I have always worked honestly for the benefit of the Soviet state.'

'You are lying,' Khvat says. 'The investigation is now aware that during a long period of time you headed the anti-Soviet wreckage organisation in the field of agriculture and you were a spy for foreign intelligence. We demand truthful information.'

Vavilov sits up straight and looks Khvat right in the eye. 'I categorically declare that I was not involved in espionage or any other anti-Soviet activity.'

But Khvat, of whom Tommy has found no photographs, but whom he is sure had pig eyes and a combover, leans even closer to Vavilov.

'The investigation knows you as a man who is principally hostile to the existing regime and the policies implemented by Soviet power, particularly in the area of agriculture,' he hisses.

Vavilov gets to his feet then, pounds his hand against the table. 'I maintain that the investigation possesses one-sided materials that cast an erroneous light on my activity and, evidently, they result from my disagreements regarding scientific and administrative work with a whole number of people who have described my work tendentiously, in my opinion. I maintain that it is nothing but slander.'

But Khvat is unrelenting, and over the course of the next two weeks, Vavilov is subjected to a total of 120 hours of interrogation. Khvat is assisted by Major Shwartzman, an experienced torturer, who is also famous for falsifying inter-rogation reports.

It is David against two Goliaths.

On 24 August, after ten nights, which he has been forced to spend on his feet and during which he has barely slept, Vavilov finally makes an admission.

'Yes, I am guilty of being a member of a right-wing organ-isation functioning under cover within the Commissariat for Agriculture,' he says softly.

This is the only confession he ever makes: that he belongs to an organisation that both he and his torturers know doesn't exist.

It is the ultimate theatre performance, with life and death stakes.

Vavilov never conceded that his research was incorrect, or that he had promulgated a false doctrine, never agreed that Lysenko's pseudoscience was valid. Throughout the duration of his years in prison, he held the banner of science high. He never acquiesced to the pre-eminent, grandiose lies.

Was Vavilov naive? Tommy asks himself.

Why didn't he flee the Soviet Union before war broke out? There had been no shortage of warnings. Why didn't he just toe the line and say that Lysenko was right?

Vavilov had collected 380,000 seeds, which were stored in Leningrad's vault. And his work could have saved millions of people from starvation. If he were to give in, it would amount to stating that nothing of what he had done was significant, that the seed collection was worthless.

It was all about the seeds. He protected them with his life. He stayed behind and fought, he chose the difficult path.

It would have been so easy to accept defeat.

To leave Russia, run away, abandoning the seeds and his faithful colleagues.

Take the few possessions he thought he would need and a few mementos of his parents. His favourite books from the library.

And then climb into a dinghy, row slowly out to sea. Climb on board a ship, be assigned a cabin, put down his possessions, go up on deck, watch the anchor being raised out of the water, glittering with droplets, turn to face his homeland, his gaze fixed on the wharf, the houses, the hotel, the valley, feel the ship moving. Look away, look ahead, towards Isfjorden, only to turn back one final time and discover that Longyearbyen, Advent Valley, Platåfjellet Mountain were already smaller. Simply observe the movement as the ship sails away, the way everything shrinks, his world becoming tiny, until he can no longer see the place he called *home*.

A good life. Simpler. Food served on a plate, food he didn't need to work for. A library, the peace of mind to spend the whole day there, reading instead of working.

A life together with Hilmar and Henry.

Tao

The winter sun hangs low in the sky above the mountain plateau. All that is left of the road are faint wheel ruts in front of them, overgrown and barely visible. They drive over dead grass, sand, soil and rocks, they drive night and day while the winter draws steadily closer.

Then they stop to stretch their legs. The crew spills out of the vehicles, and the cook hands out biscuits. Shung takes a look at the neck of the seaman, who pulled a muscle during the night.

Henry plays alone, roaming about and talking to himself. Tao finds herself watching him, his body language and movements. His mouth, which he sometimes closes in a determined way, the nose he wrinkles when he is curious. The tiny figure against the enormous landscape. He moves with quick agility over the rocks, flexible, gliding; his body is so accustomed to assessing the small hindrances that appear all the time, to overcoming them, his gait is designed for the uneven, rough terrain. And this quickness of his, the body that never relaxes, prepared to flee at all times.

But he also has a child's ability to forget, at least for fleeting moments. He stops beside a mud puddle that has a thin layer of ice on the surface, rosettes of frozen water, art by nature's hand, incomparable. He studies the ice for a while, then he braces himself and hops onto it. It cracks beneath his feet as the rosettes are shattered.

He smiles in satisfaction. Then he turns around and notices Tao.

'Hi?'

'Hi, Henry.'

She looks at the puddle, pokes the ice with her foot.

'You forgot something there.'

He hesitates. Then he hops again, with less force this time, to destroy what remains of the ice image.

She turns and points.

'There's one over there too.'

He presses his lips together as he stands and assesses the situation.

Then he walks over to the next frozen mud puddle.

'Are you coming?' he asks.

'Yes.'

She walks over to stand beside him. The puddle is oblong, large enough for both of them.

He bends his knees and motions for her to do the same.

They stand side by side, their knees bent and then Henry summons his strength and jumps onto the puddle. The ice splinters into hundreds of tiny pieces.

Then she jumps. It feels like hitting glass. The ice makes thin crackling sounds beneath her feet when she moves them.

Henry moves to one side again and looks at the puddle from above. Parts of the ice are still intact. He crushes these quickly with his foot.

Then he turns around and looks at all the other frozen puddles.

'Longyearbyen,' he says softly.

She nods. 'It resembles it.'

She walks over to a large, frozen puddle nearby. 'Shall we do one more?'

But the moment has passed. He has remembered who she is, where he is. He shakes his head and his face becomes shuttered. Then he turns his back on her and walks away.

A little while later, Mei-Ling comes over to her. She checks her watch.

'We have to get moving.'

'They're probably waiting for you at home now,' Tao says.

'My family? They are always waiting for me,' Mei-Ling says. 'Whether I'm here or somewhere else. Being married to me or having me as a mother *means* waiting. And I can promise you that when I've been home for a while, they expect me to leave them again, because before long I start behaving like a caged animal.'

She kicks at a stone, tries to aim at a larger stone further away.

'They're patient, then, those awaiting your return at home?'

Mei-Ling laughs curtly. 'Unlike me, yes.'

She kicks yet another stone. Her aim is better this time.

'Was this just another job for you?' Tao asks.

'The seeds? No! Are you crazy?'

'But you didn't come because you thought we would find them.'

'What do you mean?'

'You didn't think we would find them ... and because of that ... because of that perhaps you don't feel like such a failure because we failed.'

'A failure because we failed?' Mei-Ling laughs at her choice of words. Then her smile fades. 'Lo and Bong, my sons, we hear all the time how they are short for their age.' A painful grimace appears on her face. 'Their growth is stunted.'

'I heard the same thing about Wei-Wen,' Tao said. 'I think most parents have received the same feedback.'

'After the last check-up, the boys each came home from school with their respective growth curves. They could see for themselves how flat their curves were, compared to what they call normal. When the Committee contacted me the next day and told me about the seeds, there was never any doubt about whether I should go. And yes, there have been brief periods when I have allowed myself to believe that we could find them.'

They stand for a moment without speaking. Then the silence is broken by a low rumbling in the distance. They listen, puzzled, turn around and see that all the others have also stopped whatever they were doing and turned their faces towards the noise. A low thundering sound of rapidly moving hooves against the ground. And then: the sound of neighing.

Above the hill to the south, where the sun is hanging low in the sky, a cloud of dust rises. Then they see the silhouettes of wild horses, a herd of eight to ten animals. For a moment it seems as if the animals are headed straight for them, and they can see them more clearly. Powerful bodies, shiny coats and quite short-legged. They don't resemble the horses at home. Tao squints to get a better look at them.

But then the animals change directions, forming an arc, and continue westward.

Tao and Mei-Ling watch the herd until it disappears and only a faint cloud of dust remains suspended in the air.

'Did you see that!' Hilmar says, and comes running over. 'Horses! I've never seen horses before.'

'Neither have I,' Mei-Ling says. 'Or, yes, I've seen horses. But never horses like those.'

She gazes with wonder at the spot where the animals disappeared. Then she catches herself and turns to address the crew. 'Come on! Let's get going now! I want to cover another twenty or thirty kilometres while it's still light.'

The children crawl into the back. They chatter together excitedly in Norwegian. Tao tries to catch Henry's eyes. 'Wasn't that nice,' she says.

'Yes,' he says, without looking at her.

'Can you believe we saw horses!'

'Mm.'

It's Tao's turn to drive. She starts the engine, glances quickly at Henry in the rear-view mirror. He is staring straight in front of him and his face is closed. It resembles his brother Tommy's face, the same tenacity, the inscrutability.

Tommy

Stepping carefully, almost stealthily, they walked back along the road and into Longyearbyen. Tommy caught himself looking for the footprints of shoes and boots other than their own, but saw only tracks from birds, fox paws and reindeer hooves.

There are no longer any carriers of the infection here, he thought, and felt ashamed when he realised that the absence of people was also a relief.

Henry and Hilmar began running eagerly as they approached the path leading up to Road 232 and their house.

'Wait,' Grandmother said.

She stopped, considering. 'I don't want to go there. I want to start over somewhere else.'

Henry and Hilmar turned around.

'Aren't we going home?' Hilmar said.

Grandmother shook her head, and a smile spread across her face. 'I thought it might be fun to try another house. And maybe we can find something larger, nicer!'

The brothers seemed to accept her answer.

This struck Tommy as odd and at first he wanted to object. But it occurred to him that maybe Grandmother feared that Father's body was lying inside the house. But he didn't dare ask, not wanting to know the answer.

They walked towards the centre of the village, pass-ing house after house, discussing damages and repairs, destroyed roofs and broken windows. A few times they went inside a house and checked the electrical system.

Finally, they stopped at a relatively new house in the Skjæringa area, just below the old aerial tramway station, with a view of the harbour and Isfjorden. On the roof was a solid windmill spinning in the breeze. The Lauritzen family had lived there. A father and four children, grandmother and grandfather. Tommy had not known them well, but his impression had been that they were pleasant, decent people. Moreover, the house was big.

'Here,' Grandmother said. 'Here we will be safe from avalanches and landslides. The house looks like it's in good repair, don't you think?'

It wasn't a question. She had already decided.

Several of the neighbouring houses had been inhabited. They could bring in wood from the piles outside and enter the houses later to help themselves to furniture, plates and whatever else they might need, Grandmother said. Tommy felt a surprising puff of joy at the thought: that all the other houses were now at their disposal, that they could find vir-tually everything they needed, pilfer at whim, the warmest duvets, the least threadbare clothing, the most solid kitchen appliances. The boy Glenn from his class had had such a nice bicycle. It was less rusty than the other bicycles on the island. He had taken good care of it. The bike can be mine now, Tommy thought. He could just go over and take it, and nobody would ask about it. He could ride it back and forth on the road from Elvesletta and down to the water, or all the way out to Bjørndalen. The thought of the freedom the bicycle would give him made him happy. But then he remembered that Glenn was dead, lying inside the oven, that all that was left of him was ash. And his happiness was replaced by nausea.

They went into the Lauritzen house. It was freezing and damp, smelled old and stuffy. Grandmother checked the batteries and the fuse box in the hallway, nodded quickly, and went from room to room turning on all the heaters. Henry and Rakel went to stand in front of one of them, took off their mittens and held out their hands.

'Does it work?' Runa asked excitedly.

'Listen!' Henry said.

The heater emitted a ticking sound.

'Hurrah!' Henry said, and hopped into the air.

Grandmother nodded in satisfaction. 'But we should supplement it with another windmill. And there are many to choose from. Maybe one of you would like to help me with that job, Rakel or Tommy?'

'Yes, I'd be happy to!' Rakel said before Tommy could reply.

'And the greenhouse,' he said. 'We must begin to work in the greenhouse as well?'

'You know very well that we must,' Grandmother said.

'Then I can help you out there,' he said while observing Rakel.

Grandmother cracked a small smile and Tommy simultaneously knew that she saw right through him, that his jealousy was every bit as visible as if someone had painted his face green. But he did not relent: 'And then there's the seed vault. We must go to the seed vault soon, right?'

He wanted to say more, to stress that she had said he was going to take over, point out the bond between them, created through the seeds.

But Grandmother replied quickly: 'The seeds are just fine where they are. But you can start working in the greenhouse in the morning.'

He nodded and said nothing more, feeling vexed over the blush he could feel on his face.

The sequestered gardens had lived their own lives despite the lack of any upkeep by human beings and had become wild and overgrown. Tommy spent more or less every day there, all by himself. He cleared and swept in the Four-season Room, salvaging any fruit that was still edible. The Summer Room was a jungle. He threw stringy radishes, rotten pumpkins and squash into the compost heap, pulled ripe potatoes and winter carrots out of the soil. Then he tied up cucumber plants. These fast-growing, sprawling plants were some of the last he had repotted in large, 10-litre pots before they left Longyearbyen. Now they had grown long and wild and were a bit scrawny because they were in need of fertiliser but they had many blossoms. He moved the pots and placed them by a wall with a trellis of reinforced steel, carefully weaving the long, stringy tendrils between the rusted bars.

Plants must know what gravity is, Grandmother told him once when they were here in the Summer Room together. 'Otherwise they would not have managed to grow upwards. Because they aren't just reaching for the light; they are stretching away from the earth.'

She put down her spade and walked over to a record player she kept in the corner. There she took out a 100-year-old vinyl record and placed it on the turntable. Music by Bach flooded into the room. Tommy knew the Mass in B minor inside out. They didn't have many records to choose from.

'And plants have a sense of smell,' Grandmother continued, raising her voice so she could be heard over the music.

'No they don't, actually.'

'How else can you explain that the pears ripen more
quickly when we put the tree next to the apple trees? The
apples emit ethylene, which all fruits and vegetables react to.'

'You probably also think that plants can express love, then?'

'Yes, of course. For example, there is a parasitic plant that
only leans and stretches in the direction of certain plants,
based on whether they are a species it likes. It reaches out its
long arms towards tomatoes but not towards wheat.'

'So you are saying that it loves tomatoes but hates wheat?'

'I can understand that. Wheat is no match for tomatoes.'

The record started to skip and Grandmother went over to
lift the needle off the surface and lower it again, at a point further in on the spinning vinyl disc. Then she pointed towards
the lamps in the ceiling, smiling slyly.

'And plants can see, because they respond to light, stretch
towards light. Thirteen point five hours of light every day
is perfect in here. I have experimented with both more and
less light, and some plants like more, others want less, but
thirteen point five is a good common multiple for all plants.'

'I understand that they like and need light, but I wouldn't
call that seeing.'

'There are many ways of seeing, Tommy.'

The record started skipping again.

Tommy looked askance at the record player in resigna-
tion. 'Do we have to listen to that broken record over and
over again?'

'It's not for us, it's for the plants, son,' Grandmother said.
'Plants hear through vibrations in the air and soil. They are
always listening. The vibrations are registered by all the cells

in a plant. The plants like the music and they show their gratitude by producing more abundant crops. But the music should be low frequency to ensure the fastest growth.'

'Do you really believe that?'

'I don't believe it, I have observed it, Tommy.'

This comment irritated him. He felt she was being pedantic. But now, back in the greenhouse after having been away for a long time, he had to smile. The record player was still in the corner, and the records beside it were stacked neatly. He was headed across the room to put on a record when the door opened. It was Rakel, her cheeks red, and on her hat and shoulders was a heavy layer of snow. The greenhouse was without windows, shut off from the world; he had no idea what the weather was like today. In the morning, the stars and moon had dominated the sky, but it must have clouded over since then. Rakel took off her hat and shook it. The snow dropped into small melting piles on the floor. Then she suddenly stopped mid-movement and pointed.

'Does it matter?'

'What's that?'

'Water on the floor.'

'Not at all. There's often water on the floor here.'

He was puzzled. It was unlike her to show such deference.

Rakel came over to him and looked around.

'You've done a lot.'

'Yes. Have I?'

In the middle of the greenhouse, like a hole between all the crates and pots containing plants, was a table and two wooden chairs. Rakel went over and sat down on one of them.

Tommy kept working, removing suckers from a tomato plant just a few metres away from her. He tried to concentrate on the plant, not looking at her, knowing that she wanted something, was here for a reason, but figured she would have to tell him what it was herself.

'Tommy?'

'Yes.'

'Do you have a minute?'

'Not really. You can see how overgrown everything is here.' He waved his hand. 'And since none of you help out, that means a lot of work for me.'

'Can't Runa and Hilmar come?'

'They just mess around. Playing between the rows, running and shouting.'

'I'll have a little talk with Runa. Usually she's a good little worker. Maybe it's because of Hilmar that she—'

'Hilmar is usually a good worker too.'

'I know, I didn't mean it like that,' she said quickly. 'Just that sometimes they're a bad influence on one another.'

'Bad influence – good God, you sound like Greta.'

Rakel laughed warmly. 'Maybe you're right about that. I sound just like Greta. She often said it to me, you know, she used to make me stay after school and she would sit at a desk in front of me.' She pointed at the empty chair on the other side of the table, as if their teacher were sitting there. 'Greta was like that; she wouldn't sit at her desk, she wanted us to sit facing each other, as if we were on the same level, like two . . .'

'Equals?' he said.

'Yes. As if a teacher and a pupil can ever be equals. And then we sat there, and eventually I was as tall as she was, taller even, so in that sense we were equal at least, and she stared at me as if she felt sorry for me, and then she said I was a bad influence on people.'

'Oh,' he said.

He realise that he had stopped working and was standing

there with a tomato sucker in his hands. He dropped it hurriedly in the waste bin and resumed pruning the plants.

'Who did she mean?' he asked.

'What?'

'*Who* was it that she said you were a bad influence on?'

'Everyone.'

She took hold of her hat, smoothed out the brim and shook it above the table so drops of water showered off it, at all times without meeting his gaze. There was something about the movement, the sort of impulsive way she shook the hat that made her look younger, gentler, made her resemble Runa.

'I haven't always been fond of Greta,' Tommy said.

Then Rakel turned to look at him. 'You have too.'

'No. Not always.'

'You're the one who was several years ahead of the rest of us, who was given special assignments, homework just for you, the one she asked to stay behind in the classroom during recess so the two of you could "talk". You *were* an equal, Tommy. Had you been a little older and better looking, I'm sure she would have fallen in love with you.'

'Yuck!'

'Greta and Tommy, that would have been something.'

Rakel's smile reached her eyes. He couldn't help smiling back.

'Yuck,' he said again and stepped towards her. 'Keep your sick fantasies to yourself.'

She laughed. 'I'm a bad influence, Tommy, I told you. On you, too.'

He put the lid on the waste bin, walked over, pulled out the other chair and sat down.

'Yes,' he said. 'So here we are.'

'Like two equals,' she said.

They fell silent. She was no longer looking at him and was still fiddling with her hat, rolling it up into a sausage on the table.

'How long do you think we will stay here?' she said finally.

'Here? In the greenhouse?' he replied, although he understood that she was asking about something else.

Rakel lifted her head and looked at him, completely serious now. 'Hasn't she said anything to you?'

'No? About what?'

'About what she's thinking, if we are just going to stay here, the six of us ... about, like, what's going to happen later?'

'No,' he said. 'I mean, I haven't thought about it. We have only just come back, moved in, I've just started working.'

He gestured towards his surroundings to indicate that he meant working in the greenhouse.

'But have you really not thought about what's going to happen later?'

Her gaze was open and wide-eyed.

'No,' he said. 'No, I've just thought about, I don't know ... electricity ... that we actually have electricity ... that we have warm duvets for Henry and Hilmar, for Runa ... and food, that we have enough food. The greenhouse here, all the vegetables, I was just so happy to see that they have grown so well, that the kids will get the vitamins they need to stay healthy. Now that we don't have to share with anyone, we have an abundance. We have so much now, is what I've been thinking, that suddenly we are fortunate, even though things are the way they are. And then ...'

He swallowed. Rakel watched him with the same open gaze and for once he felt that he could be honest with her. 'I have been thinking about Father. I think about him all the time.'

It was difficult to say any more.

She squeezed the hat.

'That's okay, Tommy, I understand that you're thinking about him. About everything that has happened.'

'Yes,' he said. 'But?'

'But it's just that ... I wonder what's going to happen. And I think you should start thinking about it. With time.'

'I think about it all the time. About the winter. About food.'

'About what is going to happen *after* the winter,' Rakel said. 'In a year. In two years.'

'Have you talked with Grandmother about this?'

'I've tried,' Rakel said. 'But she ducks the question, evades it. All I have managed to get out of her is that she doesn't want to make any decisions. That you and I must decide.'

'What? Did she say that?'

Rakel nodded.

Tommy hesitated. 'But does something have to happen?'

Rakel got to her feet so abruptly that the chair almost tipped over. 'Yes. Something has to happen,' she said. 'We can't just stay here for ever. And when you "feel ready", I hope you will let me know.'

Then she pulled the wet hat down over her head, so it almost covered her eyes. And she left without another word.

He noticed that he was sweating. Rakel was a polar bear, a young she-bear, he never knew what she was thinking and he didn't understand why time and time again he *thought* he could trust her. Yes, she was a she-bear; the only thing she protected was herself and maybe her little sister, as if she were her own offspring.

Something had to happen. But what was that supposed to be?

Did she mean that they should leave here? Set out on the

ocean? In what vessel, then? The electric motors on the fishing boats would not carry them far enough. But there were
several sailing boats. Maybe she meant they should sail away
on one of them. Out on the ocean, alone, when none of them
knew how to sail. And to where? Foreign destinations and
foreign people? The thought was chilling.

But maybe that wasn't what she had meant, that they
should leave. She just meant that they could not continue like
this, alone, the five children and Grandmother, that one day
or another something would have to change.

And it could be that that was true. But why did Rakel
think that it was something he should think about? And why
now, already?

Besides, he and Rakel couldn't make such decisions. That
was something only Grandmother was able to do.

Usually Grandmother got up first, along with Henry and Runa. It was the three of them who made bullion and put smoked meat and cold, boiled vegetables on the table, which they would heat up by dropping into the bullion. The bed had asserted its power over Tommy since their return; sleep was like a rope that bound him tightly, from which it was almost impossible to liberate himself. He was therefore accustomed to the others having more or less finished their breakfast by the time he finally came downstairs.

But one day everyone was seated at the table, except Grandmother. Henry and Runa's cups were almost empty, while Hilmar was digging around in his cup with a spoon.

'Where is Grandmother?' Tommy asked.

'She doesn't want to get up,' Hilmar said.

'Doesn't want to? Is she sick?'

Hilmar shrugged. 'How should I know? When I tried to wake her up, she just said that she wasn't getting up today.'

Tommy turned and walked quickly up the stairs leading to the bedrooms. Grandmother's door was ajar and her room was dark. He opened it so the light from the hallway shone onto her bed, where all he could see of her was a bulge under the duvet.

'Grandmother?'

The bulge moved slightly.

He carefully walked over to the bed and perched on the edge, lifted his hand and patted the duvet.

'Are you awake?'

For a few seconds, she was silent.

'Grandmother?'

Then she finally replied. 'If I wasn't awake before, I am now at least.'

'Sorry,' he said. 'I just wanted to tell you that breakfast is ready.'

'Yes,' she said.

And then she said no more, but he could hear the sound of her breathing, heavy and jagged, under the duvet.

'Are you ill?' he asked.

She moved again, pushing the duvet away so he could see her face.

'Yes,' she said. 'It seems I am ill.'

And once she had replied, he saw her suddenly, really *saw* her.

There's a book in the library about optical illusions. Every drawing is a code because the illustration hides more than it reveals at first glance. A woman's body is also the profile of a man's head, a rabbit is a duck, a young woman is an old, witchlike crone with a wart on her nose. Some people are only able to see the female body, others the man, some see only the rabbit. But it *is* possible to see both, if you just look long enough, and that is why Tommy likes the book. He knows that there are two truths in every single picture. When you can see both of them, it is like a revelation. And once you have seen it, the rabbit in the duck, or the woman in the man, you can't erase the picture's other meaning, it will always be there and you don't understand how you hadn't noticed it before.

That's also how it was with Grandmother. It was only when she was lying there in bed in front of him that his eyes were opened to the knowledge he had repressed for several months: that there was something inside her that had taken control over her body, that was eating her up. The cheeks that had once been round and soft were hollow, the colour of her skin, which previously was healthy and tan, was now a brownish-yellow, and she had dark, greyish-blue shadows under her eyes. And she was so thin, her flesh drawn taut over her cheekbones, her shoulders bony, and her collar bone protruding.

Grandmother never got out of bed again. She must have known for a long time that she was ill, but had held on, he thinks; she must have found a reserve arsenal of strength to draw from that enabled her to do everything she needed to do before leaving the children for good. And now she had ensured their survival, their safety. Now she could give up.

Grandmother became more and more withdrawn, slept a lot, and when she awoke, it often took her a while to understand where she was. She spoke about experiences in other places. She was often back in the life she had lived before coming to Svalbard. She talked about being a migrant, about a road without an end, about moving on. She spoke as if she were not the only one who had to move, that all of them had to keep moving. They were supposed to move on, all of them, keep walking, because movement in itself was the point.

'That's the beauty of wandering,' she mumbled, her eyes glassy from the fever. 'It's without destination.'

'Ssshhh,' Tommy hushed her reassuringly. 'You aren't going anywhere, nobody needs to move, just lie there, we'll take care of you.'

And her body convulsed yet again with pain.

Tommy and Rakel tried frantically to find out what was wrong with her.

'Cancer,' Rakel said.

'Haemorrhagic fever,' he said.

He consulted a medical encyclopaedia at the library, but it didn't give him any answers. Regardless, he soon understood that answers wouldn't change anything.

They begged her to eat, drink, try to sit up, came up to her bedroom with the best cuts of meat and fresh berries. He asked Henry to remember to hug Grandmother in the morning, midday and evening. He helped her down the stairs and into the sitting room, so she could watch Henry and Hilmar perform a play they had made up themselves and listen to Runa sing, her voice as clear as a bell. And he seated her in front of the picture window facing the fjord, so she could enjoy the dance of the Northern Lights that she loved. He stood watching her while the Northern Lights cast a green glow upon her face. She was so exhausted that she was unable to keep her eyes open. They kept sliding shut and he knew that the Northern Lights didn't help. That the children's play didn't help, nor all the hugs they gave her. Still, they kept trying.

His memories of the final days will not release their grip. The pains that tormented her, the moaning, her loss of control over her bowels, the nappies they had to change, how they tried coaxing her yet failed to get her to eat. Henry who stood at her bedside with a glass of water in his hand and begged her to drink, his voice trembling, and how she, because it was him, made an effort to comply but did not have the strength to swallow. The water dribbled out of the corner of her mouth and mingled with the tears on her cheek. She slept more and more all the time and they felt a sense of relief over this in particular, that she found peace, because when she awoke, she had room only for the pain, and not for the children. He wanted to forget all of this. These days, this end point, this standstill had nothing to do with Grandmother's life. Because she was the opposite of a standstill; she was life, forward momentum and growth. Movement.

It was night-time and his turn to watch over her. She was sleeping peacefully on her side. She had shrunk; the head on the pillow resembled a child's.

At one point she turned over, half awake, and saw him sitting there.

'Tommy,' she said softly.

'Yes, Grandmother?'

He leaned forward and tucked the duvet snugly around her body.

Then he placed his hand over hers. It was like a tiny animal in the protective cavern of his fingers. He looked at her slender wrist, the blue blood vessels still pumping life through her body. But her blood was flowing more and more slowly.

She lay in silence for a long time, breathing shallowly. Finally, he couldn't hear anything. He was terrified. There were so many things he'd wanted to ask her about, so much she still had to teach him. The boys, his brothers. She couldn't just leave them in his care. And the seeds, the vault, there were certainly a thousand things he needed to know.

'Grandmother?'

But, fortunately, she opened her eyes and tried to smile at him.

'Did you think ... I was dead?'

'Not at all.'

'I'm still here.'

'I know.'

She moved her hand slightly.

'As long as you are holding onto me, I can move forward.'

'I'm holding on tight,' he said. 'But, Grandmother, we have to talk about the seeds ...'

'It will be fine, Tommy,' she said. 'It will be fine.'

'But I am wondering about so many things ...'

She inhaled, wanted to speak but emitted only a few, barely audible sounds.

'What did you say?' he said.

'I,' Grandmother said. 'I just want ... you all to be fine. That's all that matters.'

And then she said no more. All she was able to do was draw air slowly into her lungs.

Afterwards, when he was sure that she was sleeping, he went to stand in the hallway outside her room. Beneath him he could hear Hilmar and Henry roughhousing. It was the sound of a play-fight that would soon teeter out of control, the sound of laughter mixed with tears, tears mixed with laughter, laughter on the verge of tears. I have to pull myself together, Tommy thought, and wiped his cheeks with his hands. I have to pull myself together.

But the pain continued to invade him. He squirmed, as if changing the position of his body might squelch it. It didn't help. He held out both his arms, hitting the walls on either side of the hallway, stood with his palms against the walls, pushing against them as hard as he could, challenging the solidity of the walls, tensing all the muscles in his body, wanting to burst his way out of the house, away from everything.

Then he heard a thud from the ground floor and Henry screaming.

'What are you doing? You brat!'

'I'm coming,' Tommy called. 'What's going on? I told you no fighting!'

The pains that tormented her, the moaning, the nappies the children had to change. Henry standing at her bedside with a glass of water in his hand, her struggle to swallow.

Did she give up in the end, Tommy asks himself.

No, the children became spectators to a battle. Only Grandmother could fight this battle, and she could not win. But she kept fighting anyway. Because somewhere or other deep inside a human being there is always something that holds on tightly, even when we know that all hope is long lost and perhaps it is exactly that, the indomitable nature of the human spirit, that is life itself.

There was frost in the ground so they couldn't bury her and Tommy refused to have her cremated. The oven was repugnant to him. He couldn't imagine how they would manage to let Grandmother's body disappear in the flames, let her become one of the many carcasses that had ended up inside there and, afterwards, sweep out the ashes and think that this was Grandmother, this was Louise, and now they were supposed to honour her memory and say goodbye to a grey powder that could just as easily have been the contents of a fireplace nobody had bothered to clean out for a while.

For the first few days after her death they laid her body in a bed in a neighbouring house that was airtight and cold. The children were going in circles. They didn't know what to do, and it wasn't until the fourth day that they realised that they should wash and dress her. Rakel filled a bucket with hot water and found a washrag. Tommy brought a hairbrush and a clean shirt he had found in the cupboard. They walked over to the house carrying the steaming bucket between them, and washed Grandmother, removing her filthy jumper and replacing it with the clean shirt, which was blue and which Tommy knew that she'd liked. They brushed out her dark hair until it shone. He trembled as they worked, as much from the cold as from grief, and also in fear, because he had never before touched a dead human being.

But Rakel was calm the whole time. With slow movements, she wrung out the washrag, as clouds of steam spread through the room.

'Can you lift it?' she said, and pointed at an arm she wanted him to hold so she could gently slide the washrag over it. 'Help me turn her over,' she said, when it was time to wash her back.

When they were finished, they stood looking at the body lying in the bed. The cold of the house had preserved it and she looked the same. It was still the person Louise who lay there before them. She didn't look as ill as she had done while still alive. She was thin, yet she looked like herself. Her skin was smooth and pale in contrast to her dark hair, which they had combed and brushed away from her face. She reminded Tommy of Snow White, an ageing Snow White in a coffin of ice and, without thinking, he leaned forward and kissed her on the forehead.

When his lips touched the hard skin, he flinched and pulled away immediately.

'Cold?' Rakel asked.

'Yes.'

'She is dead, after all.'

'I know that.'

Rakel pulled up the blanket she had laid over Grandmother, rearranging it a bit, so it reached the middle of her chest. She then took the arms and bent them, so they lay on top of the blanket with the hands over her heart.

'Are you going to fold her hands?' Tommy asked.

'No. Why? It wasn't exactly as if she believed in God.'

'No,' he said.

And even though he was not a Christian either, there was something in him that still wished that the thin hands before him could be folded.

'She didn't believe in any *afterlife*,' Rakel said. 'And now she's dead. There's nothing left of her, nothing but this body ... That's why it's really important that we do something nice with it.'

He nodded.

We agree, he wanted to say, how good it was to agree, but it felt like commenting on it would be too much, that if he said something, made reference to their consensus, he could easily end up ruining it.

He watched Rakel's movements as she folded up Grandmother's old jumper and put it in a bag, as she quickly went out and emptied the bucket down the drain, as she wrung out the washrag and hung it over the bucket. He saw the clouds of frost made by her breath and thought: you are alive. You are alive and now it's just the two of us. And my brothers, your sister, they need us more than ever before.

Her strong body, designed for hunting and fishing, for long treks on foot, the restlessness that propelled her forward at all times. Nobody was better suited to life up here than she was.

Together with you, he thought, together with Rakel I can do this.

They said goodbye to Grandmother while a light wind danced across the water and the moon was high in the sky. Rakel and Tommy bound her body securely to an old sledge and pulled it down towards the ocean, as close to the water's edge as they could get. Her rowing boat lay on the shore, and they lifted the body into it, sweating and struggling as they balanced the corpse between them, and Tommy could not help thinking about the reindeer carcasses.

They laid her in the bottom of the boat on a blanket, tucked the body under a thwart and spread yet another blanket over her. Finally, when she was lying securely in the boat, they went to fetch the children.

Hilmar, Henry and Rakel were each carrying an oil lamp and they climbed into the boat and placed the lamps around Louise. Runa had found some artificial flowers in the Polar Hotel which she placed between the cold, dead hands, and Henry had brought along his toy rabbit.

He was the last one to get into the boat. He perched on the thwart, looked at Louise and looked at the rabbit.

'It will take care of her,' he said.

'Are you sure?' Tommy asked.

'I'm too big for it now anyway,' Henry said. 'It's been a really long time since I've gone to sleep with it.'

And that was maybe true, even though the rabbit had accompanied them to the cottage in Todalen and back again.

'Besides,' Henry said. 'When you're dead, you've sort of gone back to the place where you were before you were born. You're sort of little again. And then it might be nice to have a toy?'

Then he put the rabbit beside Louise's head.

Afterwards the five of them stood on the beach looking at her.

'Doesn't it look a little strange the way we've put her halfway under the thwart?' Tommy asked.

'No,' Henry said. 'I don't think so.'

And Hilmar agreed.

'Bye-bye,' Rakel said.

'Goodbye, Aunt Louise,' Runa said.

'Goodbye Grandmother,' Henry, Hilmar and Tommy said.

Together they pushed the boat down towards the water. The ice on the beach crunched under the weight of it. Then the hull hit the water.

An offshore wind was blowing. Soon the wind took hold and pulled the boat out into Adventfjorden. The children stood in a row, Rakel and Runa standing to one side, Hilmar, Henry and Tommy on the other, together. Nobody said a word. They saw the boat grow smaller, the light of the oil lamps fade.

His brothers stayed by his side; Tommy could feel their bodies against his own. Then he felt their hands, too, first Henry's, then Hilmar's.

Thick mittened hands in his own padded fists. It was difficult to hold them, the slippery material kept sliding through his fingers. But he clutched them tightly all the same, both of them.

That night he dreamed that the Northern Lights came and tried to capture them. Long arms of light reached down from the sky and grabbed hold of his brothers, wanting to take them away to the mute ocean of light above, turn them into something alien, have them dissolve in the unknown.

They screamed as the light pulled at them, the coiling tendrils of light like bean stalks from a faraway place. But Tommy held on, at all times he held on tight, remained calm throughout the entire dream and when he awoke the next day, he was proud of himself because he had never let go.

But it was only in the dream that he was able to hold onto them. He has actually released his grip on his brothers and has been left alone.

You are never alone, Tommy, Grandmother would have said, or maybe she actually said that once, he can't remember any more – you are never alone, I hope you know that.

What an idiotic thing to say, he should have replied. Look at me now. The closest human beings are tens of thousands of kilometres away. There are few people in the world who are as alone as I am.

But there are many ways of being alone, she would have answered. You can also be alone when you are with others.

It's not the same and you know that very well.

Had Vavilov felt alone?

Tommy is sitting at the table in the greenhouse and holding one of the books about the seed collector in his hands.

On 9 July 1941, three generals spent five minutes deciding Vavilov's fate. He was found guilty on all charges, including espionage against the Soviet Union. He was sentenced to death, but he appealed. He asked the state to consider whether they might not have use for him after all, in the years ahead. He begged them to consider that his knowledge might still prove beneficial.

What did Stalin say when he learned of Vavilov's request? Did he laugh? Did he mock the scientist?

Or perhaps, with German troops knocking on the door, he had other things on his mind.

In the autumn of 1941, thousands of political prisoners were gathered at Kursk railway station. They were to be evacuated from Moscow because the Germans were drawing closer.

'On your knees!' they were commanded. 'Don't look up!'

The first snow had fallen and it melted under their knees. But they still had to wait in this position, trembling with cold, eyes on the ground, for six hours. Moscow's evacuated residents passed by, screaming and threatening them: 'Spies! Traitors!'*

Finally the trains arrived. The prisoners were loaded in together, twenty in compartments designed for five. The trains started to move out of the station on a journey that lasted for several weeks.

Vavilov was among those who survived the trip. He ended up in prison in Saratov, the city where in 1918 he had been appointed professor of agriculture. He shared a cell with a philosopher and an engineer. They took turns sleeping on the one plank bed. A single lightbulb hung from the ceiling, a lightbulb that remained lit, day and night. The prisoners were dressed in canvas sacks and wore shoes of bark on their feet.

They were fed three times a day: two spoonfuls of kasha in the morning, a small cup of soup at midday and a spoonful of kasha in the evening.

'Still, we can't give up,' Vavilov said to his cellmates. 'If we stop working, we will die.'

Every day they held lectures for one another, about history, biology and the logging industry, about which the engineer

---

* Pringle 2008, p. 270.

knew a great deal. Vavilov was also an inexhaustible source of exciting anecdotes about all his travels to exotic locations.

But they could not live on knowledge alone. Vavilov gradually became more undernourished. The hunger was a storm in the body. All his muscle mass melted away, he suffered from chronic diarrhoea, developed a rash on his legs. Finally he was transferred to the hospital. He was pale, emaciated, had difficulties walking and breathing, but all the same introduced himself properly when he arrived:

'You see before you, talking of the past, the Academician Vavilov, but now, according to the opinion of the investigators, nothing but dung.'*

Then he was confined to a hospital bed.

He never left it. On the morning of 26 January his heart stopped beating in his emaciated body. The seed custodian, who had dedicated his life to work against famine, had starved to death.

Tommy pictures the skinny corpse in the hospital bed, dressed in the filthy canvas sack. The body that is lifted by two guards weighs so little that carrying him requires almost no effort. The canvas sack is removed. He is tossed onto a wagon belonging to the funeral director Aleksey Novitsjkov. Other bodies are laid on top of him. All of them are naked; all of them have a metal name tag tied to one of their feet. But Novitsjkov doesn't look at the tags. He is only interested in the payment he will receive. A bottle of liquor for each prisoner. Then he drives off and the corpses are hurled around on the flatbed. They are so light that they are tossed back and forth, one hand slips over the edge.

Vavilov is dumped in an unmarked grave in the cemetery.

---

* Pringle 2008, p. 278.

The seed custodian's body is nothing more than human remains, flesh that slowly hardens in the winter cold.

All the bodies.

The sound of the wagon on dusty roads.

They are stacked on top of each other.

The undercarriage of the wagon creaks. It stops by a hole in the road. Can they get around it? No, they will push through it.

The wagon's right back wheel slips into the hole. The bodies on the flatbed start sliding.

One bare foot peeks out, the flesh purplish-blue.

Emily's face comes into view.

Her body, stiff, blue.

A house that had once been yellow, the sounds from inside, the kind of pain that causes humans to stop being humans, turns them into animals.

Five-year-old Wilma. They are just lying there. I have called for them but they don't hear me. She was wearing only one shoe. Won't you come inside with me? Please? Mum is just lying there, please. Mum.

The metallic of blood, a familiar scent, from hunting and slaughtering, but unfamiliar all the same.

The view. The smokestack. The smoke rising.

The howls from the yellow house.

The howling gets mixed up with Grandmother's moaning during her final days. Take it away, she hisses, you must take it away for me, cut it out, make it stop. I can't, he says, I'm so sorry, I can't do anything. Daddy, Grandmother says, where are you, I can't see you, Daddy, help me, please, Daddy, Mum.

Mummy.

The memories are bones in the ground. He has buried them himself and makes sure they stay there. Every time it rains or the wind blows, they are uncovered: a leg sticks out, a vertebra, and he hastens to shovel more soil on top. He has been doing this for his entire life.

And it has settled into his body, all the work of digging, the shovel grows heavier and heavier, his shoulders have stiffened, pain shoots up his spinal cord, penetrating his neck, his upset stomach, spreads into his lungs, making his breathing laboured, to his heart, which beats increasingly hard and painfully, even when he is sitting still.

It no longer helps to divide time up into precise hours, minutes, seconds, to fill every segment of it with work.

Although he falls into bed exhausted every single evening, he is unable to sleep. He has eaten too little, hunger gnaws at his stomach. The mattress is uncomfortable, he can't make contact with it, his body just wants to keep running. And he gets up again, wanders about the room, looks at the bed, at the duvet he has thrown aside, jumps, because isn't there someone lying there?

'Henry?'

He prods at the pile on the bed but it is only a duvet, no little boy is hiding there any longer. The warmth they created together is gone.

'I can't sleep.'

Every evening Henry stood in the doorway. He would come just after Tommy had gone to bed. Tommy didn't know if he had lain awake waiting, or if he slept lightly and had become accustomed to being woken by the soft noises his big brother made when he turned in for the night. Even though Tommy tiptoed, and didn't turn on the light, even though he brushed his teeth in the kitchen instead of in the upstairs bathroom, Henry heard him and would come.

'Tommy, I really can't fall asleep.'

'Come and get into bed here then,' Tommy said.

He pulled back the duvet for Henry and tried to conceal his irritation.

'Did you have a dream?' he sometimes asked.

'No,' Henry replied. 'I don't remember.'

'Have you slept at all?'

'I don't know.'

Always the same two answers: I don't remember and I don't know.

'It's just that my bed is so big,' Henry said the first time he appeared, and that was the closest he ever came to an explanation for why he couldn't fall asleep.

'Perhaps you should have had a smaller bed, then,' Tommy said. 'One that fits you better.'

'Yes. Perhaps.' Henry said.

And then he crept up against Tommy, into his bed, which was absolutely *not* too big. And all night he lay there, his sharp elbows and knees jerking in sudden movements and poking into Tommy's stomach and an open mouth breathing heavily, sometimes snoring, because his nose was often a bit stuffed up, and the smell from his mouth that had begun to change – before it was sweet, and now it smelled more like the sleeping breath of everyone else, a little sour. It was a sign that he was getting bigger. It also felt as if he grew larger in bed as well – every night his body occupied a bit more space, he slept a bit more restlessly, he made himself just a bit more at home. Once in a great while Tommy would shake his little brother, wake him, pull him up into a sitting position, help him out of bed onto the floor and lead him into his own room. But only a few minutes would pass before Henry was back again, squeezing into bed beside him. Once Tommy tried sneaking away. He climbed over his little brother, crept quietly out of the room and lay down in his bed. But when he woke up the next morning, Henry was lying beside him there as well.

Tommy had never before thought about all the things that made up the bodies that were his brothers. He had merely thought of those bodies as small. But now they were there all the time, with their sharp corners and smooth skin and cheeks, the softness of which never failed to surprise him, with their big feet and skinny calves, their rounded backs and their flexibility, as they rolled around in the snow, play-fighting, falling down and getting up again.

They fought over his hands, often wanting to lead him somewhere by the hand. Tommy was a magnet for the two, skinny boy bodies. He was their north pole, the direction in which their inner compass always pointed.

No matter where Tommy was, at least one of them followed on his heels.

*

He was in the kitchen. Hilmar came in.

'Hi,' Tommy said.

'Hi,' Hilmar said and came over to stand beside him.

His little brother studied Tommy's movements as he used the knife. His arms hung limply at his sides.

'Are you just going to stand there?' Tommy said.

'Yes . . . no?'

'Look here. You can slice the potatoes.'

'Okay,' Hilmar said.

'Sit at the table. There's lots of room there.'

'Yes.' But he remained where he was, right beside Tommy. 'There's room at the counter, too, isn't there?'

'Yes,' Tommy said.

He was headed outdoors. It was so warm inside. The children were playing upstairs, the thuds and howls they produced echoing through the house. He quietly removed his jacket from its hook, knotted his scarf around his neck. But when he sat down on the bench in the hallway to tie the laces on his winter boots, the bench creaked.

The commotion above him ceased.

And shortly thereafter Henry came running down the stairs.

'Where are you going?' he asked.

'Out,' Tommy said.

'Can I come?'

'Weren't you playing with the others?'

'We're done now.'

'Go back and play some more. I just need to get some air, I'll be right back.'

'Are the Northern Lights here?'

'Yes, I think so. But you know I don't like the Northern Lights.'

'Can't I come with you anyway and look?'

'I'll be home again before you know it. I'll be back before you have had time to get dressed.'

'But I'll hurry. Look, I already have my jacket on!'

He sat on the sofa, darning socks in the light from a lamp.

Hilmar sat beside him reading a book. His body against him.

Moving his arm became difficult. His elbow hit his little brother every time Tommy lifted the hand holding the darning needle.

Tommy moved a couple of centimetres away.

A few seconds passed. Then Hilmar slid over, closing the gap between them.

Tommy cleared his throat.

Hilmar kept reading.

Tommy wanted to move again, but he knew what would happen. He stayed where he was, darning quickly, with his arms squeezed tightly against his upper body.

Hilmar did not seem to notice the sharpness of his movements.

But then Henry would trip on the stairs and hurt himself or Hilmar would cut himself on a knife and start bleeding and all he wanted to do was hug them, make sure that everything was all right, that they were still in one piece. And when he held them close, he felt a sense of relief. His brothers were still here. They would make it through the winter, all five of them. They had enough food, they had electricity, and even though Longyearbyen was a ghost town, it was still not a frightening place. Because everything there was at their disposal. The houses and streets did not feel deserted; they looked more like the inhabitants had gone out for a walk, had gone fishing down at the shore, or were out on an expedition on the mountain plateau to hunt reindeer or grouse. Books still lay open on the tables, jackets hung over chairbacks, in the hallways the shoes remained where they'd been removed helter-skelter. And everywhere there were things the five of them could use, things they needed. The frugality the children had grown up with was over; now they finally had everything they wanted.

Hilmar and Tommy retrieved Glenn's bicycle, dragging it through the snow. They tested the brakes on a hill where the wind had blown away the snow. The brakes squealed; he would have to oil them. But otherwise the bicycle was every bit as wonderful as Tommy had remembered and he felt a fleeting puff of joyful anticipation, of looking forward to spring.

The bicycle, the cups, the shoes in the hallways, it all reminded him of one thing: they had survived.

Every day he went to the greenhouse. The plants in the Summer Room lived in accordance with their own seasons, overlapping and criss-crossing; each plant had its own season, depending on when it was sown. While Rakel was the one who brought home meat for their table, Tommy came home every day with vegetables and berries. *Home* ... yes, it wasn't long before he started thinking about the house they inhabited in Skjæringa as a home.

Henry was the one who most often accompanied him to the greenhouse. Afterwards they would stop by the library. The room was freezing. Tommy had not attempted to turn on the electricity and they fumbled around looking for something to read in the dim light from a rechargeable torch.

He wanted to give the children lessons, gathered books, went to the school, heated up a classroom and gave Runa,

Henry and Hilmar classes. He started with the basics – geography, history, biology. He encouraged them to read texts alone, got them started. They liked his school, laughing and chattering, and were surprisingly attentive when he assumed the role of the teacher, especially Runa, who encouraged the other two to do as he said. But it was time consuming. He received no help from Rakel, who barely knew the multiplication tables and after the first couple of weeks he had to scale back the hours of school, because there was too much work to be done in the greenhouse. One evening he summoned his courage and asked Rakel if she could take over some of the work in there, so he could have more time for the children.

'It's important to keep up their schooling,' he said. 'That they keep learning.'

'Why is that?' she asked.

'They've missed almost a year of school,' he said.

Then she just laughed loudly, pulled the rifle off the rack on the wall in the hallway and went outside.

Every evening Tommy and his two brothers crawled into Hilmar's bed. He would read to them for an hour, sometimes longer, and they never got bored. The boys sat with their mouths open as he took them to other worlds, where everything was possible. They wanted so badly to be in there, all three of them, in the story.

Tommy was aware of a river of relief that occupied increasingly more space inside him. We are the survivors, he would say to himself, we have enough food, we have electricity. I have Henry and Hilmar, Runa and Rakel. If we just work and wait, work and wait, existence will slowly begin to resemble the old days. We have been given the gift of life and we can get our life back.

Sometimes he would pause, in the middle of a task, as he tossed dead plants on top of the vermicompost heap or sowed cabbage in one of the elevated beds and stood lost in thought for a moment, thinking about Henry and Hilmar and how they were doing. He sometimes felt terrified by the thought that maybe one of them had fallen on the ice in the freezing rain or that they had wandered too far up into the valley, where there was a risk of a landslide. And then he found himself longing for them, missing their voices and bodies, which were at once both soft and angular. He remembered the feeling of the last hug he'd received from Henry, or the sincerity of Hilmar's chuckle when Henry read aloud from a book of jokes the night before and how much better that laughter made him feel.

Wash your face, get dressed, eat breakfast.

Every morning he jots down new items on the list of tasks to be done and crosses out everything he did the day before. But more and more often, the items from yesterday remain on the to-do list. He is accumulating a growing pile of work.

One morning in November he sits looking at the slate and the white, sloppy letters. Words taken out of context, *repot, weed, pollinate, harvest, compost, stratify, cultivate, prune, cut, chop, cover.*

He is unable to combine the words into anything meaningful, picture what it was he actually did the day before. Had he even done anything at all?

Or had he merely sat at the table in the greenhouse, reading and staring out into space?

He puts down the slate, gets up, leaves his breakfast untouched. Steam rises from his cup, but he doesn't want to drink it down; even swallowing liquid is unpleasant now.

If he is industrious, works hard all day, gets through the list, crosses out every item, then the good tiredness will inhabit his body, his appetite will return, he will be able to eat normally, without stopping for every single bite, turning the food over and over in his mouth for far too long, without fear of swallowing. And he will be able to find peace in the evening, fall asleep and know he has been productive. That is the best thing there is, resting his head on the pillow and knowing that before him are many hours of darkness and oblivion. During these hours he is not alone.

He dresses quickly and goes outside, hurrying up the hill to the greenhouse.

The snow squeaks beneath his boots, his hunger makes him dizzy and the sound of his footsteps echoes in his ears. It is Rakel who is walking beside him again, the way she did on that day one year ago, the first time he really said no to her.

He hadn't noticed that she had followed him, until suddenly she was walking beside him. Her cheeks were red from the cold, she was a little short of breath, as if she'd been running. The warm air from her lungs misted into clouds between them. Rakel pulled her zipper all the way up to her chin, tugged her hat further down over her ears and tightened her scarf.

'Brrr,' she said, with a demonstrative shiver.

'Fourteen below.'

'And look at the clouds behind Operafjellet Mountain,' she said. 'Do you think it will snow?'

She was behaving sort of flirtatiously, her voice higher than usual, a bit childish. She was sweet-talking him, and although he didn't understand why, he was flattered.

'Maybe.'

'And warmer weather?'

'Could be.'

He observed her. Where was all this talk about the weather coming from?

She continued walking beside him in silence. Several times it seemed she was about to speak, as if she had something on her mind.

'Where are you going?' he asked finally, to help her out.

'I wanted to talk to you,' she said. 'Without the kids around.'

'Ah. Yes, I understood that something was up.' He noticed

that he blushed, surprised and pleased under his scarf. 'So, what is it, then?'

'The same as before,' she said, and now her voice was deeper.

'As before?'

'Yes, Tommy. I wonder what you are thinking is going to happen.'

'Happen? Right now I'm going to work in the greenhouse. You are going out to put out some snares, maybe? And then we'll see each other at home and eat together, the way we usually do. This weekend it's maybe about time to start thinking about the spring, start making plans. I thought we should try and plant potatoes again, grow some barley.'

She nodded and looked at him with an expression he didn't understand. 'This is really what you want,' she said. 'For us to piece together a life now, just the five of us. That we will be here next year.'

'Yes,' Tommy said and stopped. 'Of course we'll be here?'

'Yes,' Rakel said in a voice that was barely audible. 'Clearly, we will. We will be here next year, and the year after that and the year after that.'

She took a step towards him. 'We will be a family, the five of us, that's what you've envisioned, isn't it, Tommy? You and I are the mother and father, and Runa, Hilmar and Henry are our children. And we will live happily ever after here in Longyearbyen. That's what you want.'

The question was a trap, he was a grouse and now the noose tightened around his neck.

'I ... I don't know,' he said. 'No ... listen, Rakel, I just want things to be like they used to be, we were very happy. Longyearbyen was a good place to live.'

'Was it really? Compared to what?'

'Well sure, you heard what the old timers used to say? About the world? How it was?'

She made a face. 'The old timers . . .'

'What use do we have for the world out there?' He searched his memory for Grandmother's words. 'We are the ones who live the way one should live. We have achieved something up here, something the human race has never before managed to achieve. We are the only ones who put *the great love* for the world, for nature, before *the little love*.'

'Yes, it was all just marvellous,' Rakel said, and now her voice was cold. 'But you are forgetting about the seeds.'

'What do you mean?'

'We have something up here the entire world owns.'

'*Owned*,' he said. 'Not *owns*. The seeds are ours now, nobody else's. The world abandoned both us and the vault. They have themselves to thank for that.'

Her words kept buzzing in his head all the way up to the greenhouse. *We have something up here that the entire world owns.*

He continued their conversations in his mind, argued with her, thought of everything he should have said. If there is anyone still alive out there, he should have said, who is supposedly interested in the seeds, they only wanted to save themselves and their descendants. They would use the seeds to remake the world in their image and that image depicts the world as it was one hundred years ago, a globe on which there was scarcely any wild nature left at all.

He opened the door and entered the warm interior. Her words slowly released their grasp. It did him good to work, to be amidst all the greenery and light.

He took out three small plastic pails containing seed

capsules from cabbage, broccoli and lovage, gathered several weeks ago and put aside, from the healthiest plants he had. The capsules had been drying for a long time and now he went to work on opening them.

Creep inside this. Live here.

The Summer Room could be their own biosphere. He had to smile at the thought. *Biosphere 3*. Waking to the sight of the plants when the light switched on every morning and to the scent of soil, leaves and mild decomposition. Going to sleep here every night, hibernating along with the plants when the light went out after thirteen and a half hours. Every day the same, no distinction between winter and summer, the dark season and the midnight sun, nothing mattered, expect what happened in here, the sprouts pressing through the walls of the seeds, up through the soil, up into the light, dividing into two small leaves, and continuing to divide, stretching, the leaves that expanded, curled back, like hands opening, the blossoms that were first visible as small buds and then, slowly or rapidly, depending on the species, burst open. To burst open, *burst*, as if it were something done quickly ... but the bursting of the buds took place so slowly that it was invisible to the naked eye, the change noticeable only when he returned after a brief absence. The blossoms expanded, along with the leaves, which grew larger and larger, the colour darkening, an almost invisible abundance of pollen covering the heads of the blossoms. And then fruit and vegetables, sour, hard, small, but with time, large, sweet and full of juice. Or like large roots deep in the ground, potatoes, carrots, parsnips, beets and turnips. And finally, the decay, which was also a part of the growth cycle, the sweet scent of fallen fruit in the pots, the leaves that dropped to the floor and were swept up into large piles, the decomposition in the compost system inhabited by earthworms tunnelling through it at all times, in movement, eating and processing, where the micro-organisms worked, transforming old plants into the foundation for new.

They could have lived in here, amidst all of this, here they could have lived well, here Runa, Henry and Hilmar would be safe. Here Rakel would be happy.

Tommy lifted one of the buckets of seed capsules, shook it, picked up a few with his fingers and crushed them gently, so only the seeds remained in his palm. He went to get a large, white plate, walked over to the table and sat down. He carefully crushed more capsules with his fingertips, rubbing the dry dead blossoms between his fingers so the seeds felt out and onto the plate, cleared away debris and pushed the seeds into a pile on one side of the plate. He liked the feeling of the plants between his fingers, liked seeing how the seeds detached themselves from the capsules.

Finally, he brushed the seeds into a small paper bag and put it aside. He would store them in the cold room beside the greenhouse, his own little seed bank.

Tommy had grown warm as he was working and pulled off his sweater. He picked up the other bucket of capsules and continued. He held a couple of the small seeds in his hand, black specks on his white palm, so tiny that they were barely anything at all, barely visible, but nonetheless behind the shell of every single seed was the fertilised basis for a plant, ready to grow if it came into contact with soil and water, ready to develop into something powerful, large and green: a field, or a forest, ready to take over a landscape, suppressing everything else.

He stayed far too long in the biosphere.

When he came home, the house was dark. He went into the

kitchen and ate the cold leftovers from the evening meal. The light and heat of the greenhouse were still inside him. Was it Runa who had made dinner? Or Hilmar?

He did the washing up quietly and went upstairs, checking in on the children, listening to their breathing from the doorway, tiptoed over the threshold, adjusted the duvets around their bodies.

Then he went out again. On his way towards the stairs, he passed the door to the bathroom. It was ajar. A rhythmic sound was coming from inside, and it took him a while to understand what it was.

He carefully pushed the door open. Rakel was sitting on the floor with her back to him and her head in her hands, crying.

Tao

They keep trying to make the children laugh. Tao digs up old jokes from her memory: *Why do birds fly south for the winter? It's too far to walk. How can you tell that a hen has a fever? She lays hard-boiled eggs. Where did the muddy footprints come from? I don't know, they follow me everywhere.* Mei-Ling makes faces and walks on her hands across black ice until her fingers turn numb from the cold. Shun dons a hazmat suit and staggers around like a ghost.

Runa is the only one who laughs. Only Runa, the polite one, claps her hands and urges them to continue. Henry and Hilmar also clap obediently, but never ask for more. And the smiles they serve up are so polite and stiff that Tao gets a stomach ache.

All the vigour in the small bodies is gone. When they are let out of the vehicle to stretch their legs, they move heavily, like old men.

And she can't get hold of Tommy. She tries every evening, taking into account the time difference. She always calls him when it is 5 p.m. where he is, late in the evening where she is. Sometimes she wonders whether she is mistaken about the time but consoles herself with the thought that the radio is set on listening mode, so he can reach them at any time. The door is open for him, she is there for him, as she has always tried to be. But he has never been willing to trust her.

They searched for the seeds for six days before Tommy and Rakel disappeared. Long, exhausting days, during which they searched through Longyearbyen's houses and warehouses. Mei-Ling grew more stressed with every passing day, talking about how each subsequent day was twenty minutes shorter, about the winter that was on the way. And Tao could feel how the captain's uneasiness increasingly become her own.

Tommy was at all times taciturn and dismissive. Only once did she manage to have a proper conversation with him. It was the fourth night. It was late in the day, but instead of getting into the boat and rowing to the ship with the others, she walked up to the place she knew usually calmed her: the library.

Upon entering, she stopped and viewed the room with surprise. So many books, an abundant collection. The children were fortunate to have grown up with all this knowledge at their fingertips.

Then she heard a sound from one corner and someone stood up from their seat beside a table. It was Tommy.

'Hi,' Tao said. 'Forgive me for disturbing you.'

He shrugged. 'The library is public space.'

She walked closer, looked at the piles of books he had stacked in front of him and the slate on which he made notes.

'Do you spend a lot of time here?' Tao asked.

Tommy nodded.

'Alone?'

'Now? Yes, of course. Sometimes Henry and Hilmar are here but, otherwise, alone, yes.'

'And before? When there were many people here?'

He nodded. 'Then too.' He thought for a moment, then tried to explain. 'It wasn't that the other children didn't read books. The local government advocated it, that we should read and learn, but it was more that I read a great deal *more* than the others ... and that the things that interested me didn't interest them as much, so then I would end up in here.'

'Or maybe it was that the things they were interested in didn't interest *you* all that much?' Tao asked.

'What's the difference?' He thought for a minute. Then he nodded. 'You're trying to say that it wasn't the others who avoided me, that I avoided *them*.'

'Something like that, yes.'

A flicker of a smile softened his face but he quickly became aware of it, because he blushed slightly, stood up and walked over to a bookshelf where he began taking out books at random.

'I grew up in a library myself,' Tao said.

'Really,' he said, and studied the pages of a book, although he didn't appear to be reading.

'But it was a school library. They had just a fraction of the number of books you have here. I ended up reading the same books over and over again.'

'Maybe this wasn't what you expected,' he said. 'To come to the end of the world and find such a huge collection of books?'

'No,' she said and ventured a smile. 'You're right about that.'

He placed the books back on the shelf and began walking between the rows of bookshelves into the library. She followed him, but in the next row, so she caught only intermittent glimpses of him between the books as they walked.

'The other children,' he said. 'When you were little, was that how it was for you, too – that they went in for things that didn't interest you very much?'

'Yes,' she said. 'That's exactly how it was.'

'I thought so,' he said.

For a while they were silent.

'Paper and ink,' she said. 'Imagine. Books are nothing but paper and ink.'

'Trees,' he said. 'Books are trees. They used to use spruce and pine. But also eucalyptus and acacia. And in some countries, bamboo and bagasse.'

She detected a trace of enthusiasm in him and seized it. 'During the past few years, they have produced a few books of paper again. You can look forward to smelling the scent of a new book again. And to hearing the creaking sound the binding makes when you open it. It's one of the nicest sounds I know.'

He didn't respond to this and turned his face away from her.

The books were organised by subject and alphabetically. She found a shelf of books about nature and ecology and, on an impulse, she looked under *S*.

And there it was – not just one, but three different editions, in English, German and what she assumed was Norwegian. She took the English edition off the shelf. The pages were dog-eared, the edges of the cover worn, the pages fell open easily, the entire book was pliable and soft, as if it had been opened many, many times. She ran a finger over the tiny black bee printed on the green cover below the title: *The History of Bees*.

Tommy came over and saw which book she was holding in her hands.

'Have you read it?'

She nodded and leafed through the book. It was the first time she had seen the original English edition. Then she found the quotes that had once made such an impression on her:

'Without knowledge we are nothing,' she read. 'Without knowledge we are animals.'

Tommy nodded and recited: 'In order to live in nature, with nature, we must detach ourselves from the nature in ourselves. Education means to defy ourselves, to defy our nature, our instincts.' A smile lit up his face. 'I read Savage as soon as I could,' he continued. 'Devoured him, like just about everyone else up here.'

He paused, walked over to the shelf and pulled out the Norwegian edition. Several pages slid out and fell to the floor when he opened it. He bent down and began picking them up, handling the pages with deference.

'We had our rules. But, actually, this book was the closest we came to a law text.'

Tao glanced at the title page. 'Thomas Savage. Thomas. Tommy. Are you named after him, perhaps?'

'Thomas? No.' He reconsidered. 'Actually, I don't know. I always thought I had been named after a trapper.'

He looked down at the name, astonished, as if he had discovered something new about himself.

'Do you think you were living in an ideal society?' Tao asked.

He turned to face her once more. 'An ideal society?'

'Yes?'

His gaze became fiery. 'The human race had evolved into a species that had to exploit others to survive. The human race was not satisfied with living a life of balance, it demanded more all the time. But we, up here, rose above all that, we rose above human nature. Yes. It was the ideal society.'

Perhaps you're right, Tao thought, the ideal society, for a short while, until you no longer existed.

'You don't believe me,' he said.

'Yes, I do,' she said. 'I believe that you achieved that. That you lived a good life up here. But maybe it wasn't enough since you were all alone?'

'We had each other.'

He placed the Norwegian edition carefully back on the shelf. Tao was left holding the English edition. She ran a finger over the cover.

'This book changed my life,' she said. 'And it changed the life of everyone at home. We have heeded its message, we have allowed nature to claim its rightful place. When you come back with us, you will see. That we have managed to achieve that.'

'I don't believe you,' he said.

She was startled. 'What?'

'If you really meant it, you wouldn't have come here to get the seeds.'

'I don't understand what you mean . . .'

'We survived without them. We never used what is in the vault. And that's how it should be for you, too. You shouldn't need the seeds.'

'No,' she said, and noticed that his words had hurt her. 'I understand why you would think that. Nobody should actually need the seeds, the world shouldn't have become the way it is today.'

'Nice that you understand what I mean,' he said coldly.

'But this can't be changed. And now we need the vault,' she said earnestly. 'There are so many species that have disappeared.'

'Amusing choice of words. "Disappeared." As if the species had chosen to disappear on their own. *Were wiped out*, you mean. By humans.'

'Yes, you are right, we have wiped out so many species,

but with the seeds we can once again create an abundant world and a more robust natural world, for plants, animals and humans.'

'There are only agricultural seeds in the vault,' he said, and his voice was hard. 'Robust agriculture is good for human beings, but animals, plants, everything else has no need for your agriculture.'

'But Tommy.' She tried to speak calmly. 'You're a smart boy. You know that it's all connected.'

'*The world is, like the beehive, a super organism: everything is connected to everything else,* yes. Savage, page a hundred and forty-three.'

He took the book out of her hands, as if she didn't deserve it, and put it firmly back in its place on the shelf.

Tommy

He was unable to find a way to reach Rakel. He should have done more. Even though he tried.

Once he asked Runa, Henry and Hilmar to manage on their own for a few hours and invited her to accompany him to the library. Tommy had a couple of books in mind that he wanted to show her. Perhaps there was something in the library he could recommend, something that would induce her to start reading.

If he could just manage to introduce her to the world of books. Through them she would be able to experience the world out there, take the journey she dreamed of, and perhaps it would calm her. Perhaps the books could bring them closer together. He pictured himself selecting quotes, Rakel standing beside him and leaning over the book with him, her finger tracing the words, pointing out sentences, and that he lifted his hand and pointed at the same sentences and their hands met, in the air above all the words.

That's what he envisioned.

When they entered the semi-darkness of the room, she wandered between the shelves, looking. Sometimes she stopped and pulled out a book, read the title and wrinkled her nose.

'Where is your favourite, then?' she asked after a while.

'My favourite? Of the books? I don't have one, I have many.'

'Are you afraid to choose?'

'No ... but all the books are different. It would be like choosing between Henry and Hilmar.'

'So you compare books to human beings?'

She shoved the book she was holding back onto the shelf, walked over to the sofa and sat down.

'No. Of course not.'

He followed her, ended up standing beside her, and didn't know what to do with his hands. He stuck them in his trouser pockets. He pulled them out again.

Then he sat down directly facing her.

'Yes,' she said. 'What is it you really want?'

'I just wanted to show you the library,' he murmured.

'But I've seen the library before,' she said. 'And you know that I don't like to read.'

'Yes. I know.'

'You will never turn me into a reader, Tommy. That's not who I am. I just don't like it. I don't like books. I don't like being in here. It smells stuffy – don't you notice it – like old paper.' She stood up quickly. 'It's an uncomfortable place, you must see that – dark, mouldy. And all the bookshelves, it feels like someone is hiding behind them. Imagine if a bear came in here, without your noticing, and stood behind all your beloved books, waiting, silently. Imagine if it attacked you as you came around the corner. Tore you to pieces while you were standing with a book in your hand, and also tore that to shreds.' She made a sudden hand movement. 'Nothing but blood and paper!'

'It's not possible for a bear to get in here. Just look at the door.'

'But it's a creepy place. It spooks me, makes me imagine spooky things. I don't like the library, Tommy, don't you understand that?'

To hell with you, he thought.

She took a step closer to him. Tommy glowered at the floor, not wanting to look at her.

'We have to get out of here,' Rakel said, and her voice was quieter now. 'We must try to ask for help.'

He behaved as if he hadn't heard her, and simply got to his feet and pulled his hat over his ears, tightened his scarf around his neck and walked towards the exit.

'Louise wanted that, too,' Rakel said to his back. 'Aunt Louise said we should get out of here.'

The words pulled him up short. He spun around. 'She did not.'

'She wanted us to be fine ... we aren't fine now.'

'But you don't understand! We have to work for it then, work to be fine.'

It was impossible to look at her any longer. Rakel was beautiful, she always had been and it caused him despair.

She slowly shook her head. 'Do you really believe that, Tommy?'

'You won't even try. We have to try. It has to turn out all right; it will turn out all right. Everything will be fine.'

Did things improve? He didn't know. He didn't want to think about it. Every day was like an isolated unit. They had to make every single day function. That was the most important thing. That they had food, that Runa, Henry and Hilmar were healthy and happy. He dedicated all his time to the children. Especially his brothers.

*

Henry's hair dropped to the floor, one lock after the next, with every clip of the scissors in Tommy's hands. Henry squeezed his eyes shut.

'Does it look good?'

'Yes,' Tommy said.

'It's short, at least,' Hilmar said, who was standing beside them watching.

'Watch yourself,' Tommy said. 'You're next.

Then he placed a hand lightly on Henry's neck.

'Bow your head a little. Yes, like that.'

Henry's neck was so thin – strange that it was able to support his huge head – and dirty, embedded with filth that became even more apparent as his hair was removed.

'Afterwards you have to take a bath,' Tommy said.

'I don't want to take a bath.'

'But you must.'

'Because Grandmother would have wanted me to?'

'Yes. And because Tommy wants you to.'

'Tommy mommy. That rhymes.'

'Yes, so it does.'

He continued cutting his brother's hair in silence for a while.

'Ooh, it tickles.' Henry snickered as Tommy took the hair behind his ears between his fingers and tried to cut it as short as possible.

In the evening, both brothers lay in bed in their rooms, with their new haircuts and their bodies warm and clean from their baths, two round heads beneath the big duvets. Tommy heard them chuckling softly about something as he opened the door.

It had been three months since they'd learned that Father

was dead, and just a few weeks since they'd sent Grandmother out to sea. All the same, his brothers managed to smile and laugh. That's how children are, I guess, Tommy thought. Here, in the moment, every single moment a sealed chamber. For them time was made up of a series of such chambers, rooms along a long corridor. They could enter one and forget everything outside and if there was something in there that made them laugh, if a clown was in the room, a clown who with great physical precision performed his tricks, then they saw only the clown. It wasn't until they moved on, opened the door to the next room and were confronted with the monster inside that they entered another feeling. But then their fear was so strong that they had long since forgotten how much the clown had made them laugh.

It was a matter of keeping them in the room with the clown. That was all it took.

A perpetual calendar hung on the kitchen wall. Every morning, when Henry came downstairs yawning, his eyes like slits and with grooves from the pillow still on his cheek, he walked straight over to the calendar. He searched with his finger until he found the right date. Then he turned around and told everyone in the room what day it was.

'November the twenty-fourth! Just a month till Christmas Eve!'

The darkness of the polar night was dense, almost tactile. The sky offered them no assistance. Outside Tommy could discern heavy snowflakes in the dim light emanating from the window.

'A month is a long time,' Tommy said. 'And now it looks like one of us must go outside and shovel snow.'

'We need a Christmas calendar and Christmas jumpers and Christmas decorations,' Henry said.

'And torches,' Hilmar said. 'We're going to walk in the torchlight procession, aren't we?'

'I don't know . . .' Rakel said.

'Sure we are,' Tommy said. 'Of course we'll walk in a torchlight procession.'

Then he got to his feet and walked over to the calendar. He lifted a hand and traced all the days that had passed with his finger. Where had the days gone?

He stopped at 12 November: that date had passed without his noticing. He was several weeks late.

'And you're right, Henry. We need our Christmas decorations.'

Henry slipped his hand into Tommy's as they walked up the hills towards Gruvedalen. Neither of them spoke. They were wearing head torches. The beam on the ground before them bounced up and down in time with their steps, Henry's slightly more erratic and quicker than his own.

'Have you been there?' Henry asked. 'In our old house?'

'No,' Tommy said. 'When would I have been there?'

'How do you know what it's like in there?'

'I don't know. The way it always was, probably. Cold.'

Henry nodded and continued walking for a few moments in silence.

'What really happened to Daddy?' he asked.

'He died. He got sick and died.'

'But, where?'

'We don't know.'

Henry slowed his steps.

Tommy glanced down at him. 'Are you afraid of . . .?'

'No.'

His reply came a bit too quickly.

Father lying on the sofa, his face stretched into an enormous, mute scream, lifeless, wide-open eyes, or perhaps he was sitting at the table in the kitchen, his head resting in his arms, and a pool of dried blood under his chair.

'He's not there,' Tommy said.

'Are you absolutely sure?'

'I promise that he's not there.'

'Okay.'

That's how easy it was to convince Henry. That's how blindly he trusted Tommy.

Henry picked up the pace again, drawn towards the house.

Tommy's eyes came to rest on the familiar facades of houses along the old route home.

With every house they passed, he remembered the people who had lived there.

The Hermansen family and their white husky Pippi, a dog who loved people and whom they could not bring themselves to put to sleep, even though she didn't have the strength to pull a sled any longer. Pippi's leash hung from a hook on the wall beside the entrance door. He wondered where she was now and if the other huskies from the kennel had survived.

The Christie family, who'd had six children in as many years. Outside their house toboggans, sledges and bicycles were piled on top of each other in a heap and everything was covered with a light dusting of snow.

Henry sat on a sledge, placed his hands on the steering bar, twisted it and made a whistling sound, as if he were sailing down a hill.

'Do you want it?' Tommy asked.

'I don't know.'

'Take it if you want it.'

Gerda and Brett, an elderly couple who had been friends with Grandmother. Gerda loved fishing and beneath the overhang above the entrance door hung a long row of stock-fish. Brett would often bring the rocking chair out and sit in it knitting, in front of the house. The rocking chair was still by the front door. Tommy walked over, brushed off the snow, rocked the chair.

'It's nice that it rocks,' Henry said. 'Can we take it?'

'We can pick it up later,' Tommy said. 'We'll have too much to carry. We came for the Christmas decorations, remember?'

They continued walking up the hill, shuffling through the

snow that grew increasingly wet. Henry pulled the sledge behind him for a while, but finally left it in a ditch. Tommy's back was sweating and his cheeks were warm when they finally arrived.

For a moment they stood looking at the front door.

'It looks just like it always did,' Henry said.

'Yes,' Tommy said. 'And it is.'

To prove to his brother that what he said was true and that there was nothing to worry about, he walked up the four steps, put his hand on the handle and pushed it down.

But the door was not like before. The house, or perhaps the doorframe, had warped. The woodwork was accustomed to the house being heated and had adapted in response to the cold and dampness that now reigned both inside and out. Tommy had to lean his shoulder against the door and, when it finally opened, he stumbled into the hallway.

'Oops!' Henry said.

Tommy tried the light switch on the wall, but it was not working. He could hear Henry's shallow breathing just behind him, rapid and anxious.

'There's nothing to be afraid of,' Tommy said.

'No, of course not,' Henry said, and slipped his hand into Tommy's again. 'I'm not afraid.'

The house was shell, a box, which, more than keeping out the cold, preserved it inside. Their breath misted into clouds before them in the beams of the head torches, the air was raw and smelled different than before, stale and abandoned. But he could not smell death.

He's not here. Of course he's not here.

Tommy walked quickly through the rooms, pulling Henry behind him. Everything was unaltered but distorted all the same. The furniture was smaller than he remembered, arranged differently, pushed against the walls so the floors were cleared, highlighting the large, hard surfaces. He couldn't remember that there had been so much floor space in this house. He remembered it as being cramped and cluttered, full of people.

He opened the door to his room and quickly went over to the bookshelf to look through the books. There were books here that he would like to read again, but he couldn't take them with him now. That would have to wait until later. Then he pulled open the lowest drawer of the chest of drawers and dug out the Christmas jumper that had lain at the bottom for one year. He held it up before him. The sleeves were shorter and the jumper narrower over the shoulders. He should check Father's wardrobe, see if he could find his jumper instead, but he couldn't bring himself to go into that room. He could manage the other bedrooms, but not Father's.

Rudolf grinned at him from the front of the jumper and the bells Grandmother had sewn onto the antlers jingled faintly. She wasn't the one who had knitted the jumper. She hated knitting and had hired Brett to make it, in exchange for some vegetables, but Grandmother herself had added the bells. It struck him, as he stood with the jumper in his hands, that sewing on the bells had perhaps fooled her into believing that she had made the jumper for her grandchild, that she could take the credit for it.

Tommy stuffed the jumper into a canvas bag he had brought along and turned towards Henry.

'Go into your room and get your jumpers, too,' he said. 'And I will look for the Christmas decorations.'

'Yes,' Henry said, but he didn't move.

The beam from his head torch trembled slightly on the wall in front of them.

'Do you want me to go with you?'

'Yes please.'

His hand was there beside him at all times. Every time he released it to do something or other, his little brother stood holding it out, waiting to reclaim his own the split second it was free again.

'I can't hold your hand all the time,' Tommy said.

'No, I know,' Henry said.

But the waiting hand didn't disappear.

They found the jumpers, Henry's with a smiling Christmas bauble and Hilmar's with a leaping elf, and from the hall cupboard Tommy dragged out some Christmas decorations and a driftwood structure they used to decorate and call a Christmas tree.

'We can carry all of this back,' he said to Henry. 'Don't you think?'

'Yes,' Henry said, and Tommy could see that he was smiling beneath his head torch.

'Now there's just one more thing I want to find. Do you have time to wait?'

'Sure,' Henry said. 'More Christmas decorations?'

'No. Keys.'

'To the seeds?'

Tommy nodded.

Henry wrinkled his brow. 'Was that why you really wanted to come here?'

'No, it was because of the Christmas decorations.'

'It was because of the keys,' Henry said.

'First and foremost, the Christmas decorations.'

Henry's expression as he stared at Tommy made it clear that he didn't believe him but he said no more.

They walked out into the hallway and Tommy opened the

key cabinet on the wall. It was old and mostly for decorative purposes. Nobody locked their doors in Longyearbyen because, if a bear showed up, it was important to be able to seek refuge in the nearest dwelling. The only two keys that were actually used normally hung in the cabinet.

'Empty,' Henry said.

The brothers continued into the kitchen. Henry discovered a basket of old children's books and began eagerly examining the contents, while Tommy opened the large corner cupboard. Here they kept everything in the way of random items, everything that couldn't necessarily be filed away under a specific category: pieces of twine, folded up pieces of old aluminium foil, a plastic toy horse that had lost one leg and was to be repaired, but which Henry had long since grown out of and therefore had been forgotten. Clothes pegs and an empty perfume vial, a few of Grandmother's or maybe Mother's hairpins, ribbon for wrapping presents, a solar cell panel the size of his hand, an old padlock with the key in it. Here there were old children's books with pages falling out that should have been glued back in place, and several sheets of paper with recipes on them, which Father had given to Tommy when he taught him how to make dinner.

He ended up standing by the cupboard for a long time, holding each individual object, noticing how the objects also had a hold on him. Because the objects were openings to memories of images and scenes. He and Hilmar making an aerial tramway out of clothes pegs and twine. Henry tugging so hard on the one leg of the plastic horse that it broke off. Grandmother and Tommy at the cabinet down by the wharf, where they take out life-vests before setting out on the water. It is cold on this day, his teeth are chattering and Grandmother takes off her scarf and winds it around his neck while she scolds him for not having dressed warmly enough. Father, who comes in through the door and registers to his dismay that Tommy is not even halfway through making dinner, who asks him how much time he had planned and if he started when he said he would and Tommy who lies, and Father who looks at him and Tommy knows that he knows that he's lying, but still Father doesn't say anything. That moment, when they share the lie and they both, simultaneously, decide not to say anything: he not to confess, Father not to pursue it. Was that a typical moment for Father and Tommy? He doesn't know. Maybe it was just a typical moment for people who love each other.

'Tommy? What's that?'

Henry had stood up and come over.

'Nothing.'

Tommy finally managed to shut the door to the cupboard and stood in the middle of the room struggling against the pressure in his chest, before pulling himself together and going up to the first floor with Henry on his heels.

There was no key to be found in Grandmother's room, either. Not in her clothes, nor in any of the drawers in the desk by the window.

They walked quickly through the rest of the house, the boys' rooms and Father's, checking the bathroom last. Nothing.

They ended up back in Grandmother's room.

Henry opened the drawers of her chest of drawers one more time. For him this was a fun game, a treasure hunt.

But Tommy was certain that the keys weren't in here. He sat on the bed.

Where are they, Grandmother? Where did you put them? Her cold body under his hands when they washed her.

Rakel and Tommy had taken off her jumper, dressed her in a clean shirt and clean trousers. Was it possible that it had gone with her out to sea in the end?

He tried to picture her, on the boat, as the boat drifted out across the fjord – not the pale face, the hair that Rakel had arranged in a fan around her head, but her thighs, the trousers, her pockets.

He couldn't even remember which trousers she had been wearing.

But maybe he didn't need any keys. Maybe she had actually left the door open, to be on the safe side, for him, the seed custodian.

Tommy is standing in the greenhouse, his shoulders tense, his back aching, as he clenches his fists in anger.

All of life in your hands, she said to him back then. But she hadn't meant it. She died and the only thing she cared about during the last days of his life was that he would be fine. He doesn't give a damn about being fine. Vavilov must have known that Stalin would imprison him. Still, he stayed in the Soviet Union, he did not flee. Because the seeds were what was most important, always the seeds. Being fine was not something Vavilov thought about, neither in the years before the war when he was fighting Lysenko's idiocy, nor while he was being tortured by Stalin's men in prison. Nobody who has achieved anything here in life has ever had *being fine* as their primary objective.

And, besides, why wasn't his well-being important for her until the end of her life? She hadn't been interested in making sure he was fine previously, all the times she disappeared and left him alone with all the responsibility for his brothers on his shoulders.

She could have just given him the key.

All of life in your hands.

They are standing over there by the bench, he and Grandmother, working side by side.

Why didn't you give me the bloody key, he should have asked.

You know me, she would have answered, with her fingers in the soil. I have never liked simple solutions.

His open hand. In the palm, five tiny tomato seeds.

He moves them around a bit with his index finger.

Their conversation surfaces from the depths of his memory one sentence at a time. He was sixteen, maybe seventeen. It was after she'd said that he was to be the seed custodian. And he wasn't angry the way he is now, but calm and happy, because he remembered that he'd had a good day, that he liked being in the warmth of the greenhouse and that he liked being in proximity of Grandmother's strong and agile little body and he liked listening to all her words, to the instruction he understood she was carrying out.

She pointed at the seeds in his hand.

'You plant them,' she said. 'And tomatoes will grow on every plant and inside every tomato are seeds for very many new plants.'

'Yes?' he said. 'And?'

'You could also throw them away,' she said. 'You might throw them into the ocean and they would be forever destroyed.'

'Why should I do that?'

'It's incredibly simple to destroy something so small,' she said.

'It's simpler to plant the seeds,' he said. 'Because then I don't have to go outside.'

He raised his hand closer to his face, stuck his left index finger into the seeds and moved them around.

'Your hands in all of life,' Grandmother said.

He glanced at her. 'What do you mean?'

'No,' she said. 'Truth be told, I don't know.'

He began carefully pressing the seeds down into small seedling pots full of damp soil.

'We talked about what death is,' Grandmother said. 'Do you remember that?'

'Death is the absence of life.'

She smiled. 'But what actually is life? Do you know the answer to that, smarty?'

'Yes ... or, no?'

'Life is process,' she said. 'Life is movement, life is that which distinguishes organisms from minerals, the state that distinguishes organisms from inert objects.'

'Life is both a process and a state? Isn't that a contradiction in terms?'

Grandmother smiled a crooked smile. 'Like I said. Smarty.'

'I know.'

She took the tray of seedling pots from him and filled a spray bottle with water. 'Usually one defines life according to three processes. The first process is metabolism, that you in one way or another eat and exude waste.'

'I know what the metabolism is.'

She squirted water carefully on every single little pot, making sure not to overwater or the seeds would be washed away and accumulate around the edges.

'The second is reproduction. You know what that is, at least.'

He blushed.

'And the third is evolution,' Grandmother said. 'Adaptability.'

'So what you're saying is that those individuals that don't adapt won't survive? I can think of a few old men who ...'

She laughed. 'The adaptability of the species over time, Tommy, not the individual organism's ability to adapt.'

He blushed even more, this time over his own stupidity, about making a mistake about something so elementary.

'And life is the opposite of chaos,' she said. 'While what is dead gradually disintegrates more and more, decays and dissolves, life creates systems and structures. Life is development.'

'But how did life start then? Life itself, with a capital L?'

He took out another tray of seedling pots and began filling them with soil.

'The very first form of life? That arose on the earth three point seven billion years ago.'

He nodded. She took out yet another tray and they worked side by side at the large work bench in the greenhouse.

'The very first form of life,' she said, 'arose in the ocean, safely protected from the radiation on the surface, in hydrothermal vents at the bottom of the ocean. The first amino acids were formed out of ammonia, hydrogen and methane.'

'I know that. But how?' he said, impatient now. 'How did it start? *What* triggered the creation of life at the very beginning?'

'That is life's great mystery,' Grandmother said with a smile, and brushed the soil off her fingers.

'So nobody knows?'

'No. Some people think it was an extremely auspicious coincidence and that it has only occurred here, on earth. Others think, and have even proven, that when ammonia, hydrogen and methane are exposed to electricity and radiation, amino acids will always be formed. And out of these, life will again emerge. I like that theory best, that this can happen everywhere, in the entire universe, if only the proper conditions are in place.'

'Why?'

'The opposing view, that life on earth is an insane, isolated coincidence makes me feel lonely.'

'But ... I don't understand. You said that no matter what, it would be impossible to make contact with anyone else, because outer space is too enormous.'

She turned to face him. 'Don't you think the idea that the rest of the universe is a desert of stone, fire and gas is a lonely thought?'

'Well, yes. Maybe.'

She swept off the surface of the table with a brisk hand movement. Small clumps of soil rolled off the table and onto the floor.

'And then there's the third theory.'

'What's that?'

'A theory that, in a sense, can be combined with the other two.'

He considered this for a moment. 'Oh, you mean ... God?'

She nodded.

'The creation of the first form of life on earth ... *there's* an argument for faith,' Grandmother said.

'So suddenly you're a believer?'

'No, that's not what I said. But if you need a reason to become religious, it is found in precisely that moment, the origin of life on earth.'

'Needing a reason to become religious is not enough. You have to believe in the fairy tale, too. Actually, we are all alone.'

'You're never alone, Tommy. I hope you know that.'

He doesn't know where the time goes. The days melt into each other, time is made up of slippery fragments that slide around in his hands, escaping between his fingers, Like Runa's hair when he tries to twist it into plaits.

Happy Christmas, Tommy.

He pulls the cloth bag out of his pocket and places it on the table.

Dessert. From the greenhouse.

Then he opens it and pours some of the contents into his hand.

Raisins?

He nods. Raisins are essential. At Christmas time.

But it's not Christmas yet, Tommy, pull yourself together.

No, it's only November, but who cares anyway, November or December, the darkness is intense. Darkness, never daylight and therefore never night.

He has walked up to Svalsat several times, stood in the corridor outside the control room, even put his hand on the door handle. But each time he has turned around and left without having called her. Turned around and left before finding out whether she has tried to reach him.

He has the seeds. He must remind himself that the seeds are what is most important. His brothers are merely individual human beings, connected to him through signals in the brain, nerve fibres and hormones. The seeds are a legacy for eternity.

But he is tired.

Bones in the earth, he digs and digs, but the wind blows more fiercely all the time. It settles in his body, all the digging, an insidious pain in his back, stiff muscles in his neck, his heart pounds hard and fast, even when he is sitting still. And at all times hunger gnaws at his stomach.

He picks up a raisin, chews slowly, moves it around in his mouth as it gradually dissolves.

Finally he takes the chance of swallowing. It slides down his throat, offering no resistance.

He picks up another one, chews it just as carefully.

Slowly he eats the raisins, one by one, allowing the memories from the very last Christmas to invade him.

They awoke on the morning of Christmas Eve to a light snowfall.

Tommy had got up early, lit the stove, hung a few more balls on the tree and put water on the stove for hot peppermint tea. Henry and Hilmar came padding down the stairs in their pyjamas, and Runa followed shortly thereafter. He gave them cups of steaming tea and wrapped them up in blankets on the sofa.

'Butterflies in your stomach?'

'Yes.' Henry smiled.

They looked like three butterflies in blanket cocoons, silently waiting. Runa's smile was not polite; it was genuine.

'I found more oil lamps,' Tommy said. 'One for each. They will be every bit as nice as torches. We can go after we've had breakfast.'

'Mmm,' Hilmar said.

'And then we can make snow angels!' Tommy said.

They nodded on the sofa and drank small sips of hot tea.

*

Rakel stayed in bed until late morning and when she finally got up they were already out in the hallway and Tommy had commenced the process of getting all of them through the door.

'Mittens,' Tommy said. 'An extra pair of socks ... look, Henry, you need a scarf too, it's windy, and Hilmar, your hat is here. Yes, you need to wear a hat.'

Rakel stood watching them.

'Are you really going to go through with this?'

'What do you mean?' Tommy said, although he understood what she was saying.

'Do you have torches?'

'We have oil lamps,' he said. 'They will be every bit as nice as torches.'

He smiled at her, his tone of voice light. Don't ruin this, his smile said, don't take this away from them.

'But it won't be as nice as torches,' Hilmar said and stared at him.

'It will be nicer,' Tommy said and turned to face Rakel. 'Right, Rakel?'

She held his gaze for a few seconds, and then apparently made up her mind, because she turned to Hilmar and pulled the corners of her mouth up into something meant to resemble a smile.

'Of course it will be nicer.'

They walked along the fjord, two by two, with Tommy leading the way alone. He opened his mouth and started to sing 'Silent night, holy night'. Runa joined in, but with less force than usual. He didn't hear a peep from Rakel and Hilmar. But Henry chimed in, his high voice loud and a bit out of tune.

They sang a verse. They sang two. But he couldn't remember the third, so he started singing the first one again.

Their voices were thin and faint between the tall mountain-sides. Tommy could glimpse the outlines of the mountains above them. The moon shone brightly, illuminating the polar night. And the oil lamps were not the same as torches; they were paler, sadder.

They walked a bit further. Tommy started singing another Christmas carol, but it was now more difficult. How many songs had they usually sung in this procession? How had they had the patience for this every single Christmas? And the courage ... because the mountains were menacing and perhaps it would take nothing more than the sound of their voices to shake the mountainsides into movement, set the snow in motion, or the heaps of stone underneath that covered layers of ice due to the sudden twenty-four-hour spell of rain they had had during the last week.

Finally, after a third verse of 'Hark! The Herald Angels Sing', Tommy stopped and turned around.

'Are you cold?' he asked.

'Yes,' Rakel said.

The others mumbled their agreement.

'Maybe we don't have to walk all the way out to Hotellneset,' he said.

'Fine by me,' Hilmar said.

'We can go back now,' Runa said.

Only Henry hesitated.

'Is that okay, Henry?' Tommy asked. 'If we turn around now?'

'Yeah ...' Henry said, but Tommy could hear from his voice that he didn't mean it.

'I have raisins,' Tommy said. 'In the greenhouse.'

*

He brought his little brother along to retrieve the raisins and fresh vegetables for their Christmas dinner.

When they were about to leave, he noticed that Henry was standing in the far corner by the ash tree. The branches butted against the ceiling. The tree had grown as tall as it could within the parameters of the room.

Henry looked upwards towards the top of the tree.

'Poor thing.'

'Oh?' Tommy asked. 'Why is that?'

'It can never leave here.'

'No. It doesn't have feet.'

Henry chuckled.

Tommy walked over to a drawer and took out a cloth bag, opened it and shook some seeds out into his palm. 'These came to Svalbard on a tree when I was a little boy.'

Henry looked down at the seeds.

'How little? Like me?'

'Even littler.'

'Was that all the seeds?'

'No, we had many. And Grandmother and I planted some of the seeds. This little tree comes from a big tree.'

Henry carefully poked at the seeds with his index finger.

'They have wings.'

'Yes, they do. That's so the wind can lift them easily and carry them away to a place where they can find good soil and put down roots.'

'Have you let them fly away outdoors?'

'No, there's no point.'

'Why not?'

'I think you can guess.'

'Because trees don't grow in Svalbard.'

'That's right. Because even if the seed landed in a spot

where it had both fertile soil and enough water, even if it started to sprout, it would never be able to grow. The winters are too dark.

'And too cold.'

'The summers are too light, too, for some plants.'

'Can it be *too* light?'

Tommy nodded. 'But in other places in the world, the summers and winters are just the way the trees like them. There are enormous forests made up of thousands of trees. And these seeds can survive there, they can sprout and eventually become small plants. And in the end, maybe trees.'

'Big trees? Bigger than this?'

'Enormous.'

Henry gazed at the seeds in amazement.

'But what is the best way for them to be sown? To plant them in the earth or let them fly away on the wind?'

'The best way is to plant them in the earth.'

'Okay ... but it would be fun to let some of them fly away on the wind, too, since we have so many?'

Tommy smiled. 'Yes, I agree with you.'

Then he put the seeds back into the bag, reconsidered briefly, and gave it to his brother.

'They're yours.'

'Mine?' his brother said happily.

'Yes. Happy Christmas, Henry.'

The moments in the greenhouse are a memory full of light. Of all the events of this Christmas Eve, it is in this memory that he tries to find peace. Not what happened afterwards.

The children were in bed. He was sitting in front of the fireplace. Rakel was puttering with something or other in the kitchen.

Then she came into the sitting room. He heard a clinking sound. She placed a bottle and two glasses before him on the table.

'Happy Christmas,' she said.

'What's this?' He picked up the bottle. 'Alcohol?'

'It's Christmas. I intend to celebrate.'

Without asking him whether he wanted any, she poured some drink into both glasses. Then she lifted her glass to her lips and swallowed a huge gulp.

They sat like that for a while. She drank down the contents of her glass and poured herself another, but he didn't touch his.

Though he could feel her eyes burning into him, something prevented him from asking any questions.

'How do you think that went?' she said finally.

'What do you mean?' he asked.

'Christmas. The celebration. Do you think it went well?'

'I think it did,' he said.

'Be serious, Tommy,' she said through pursed lips.

'What would you have suggested instead?' he asked. 'No celebration at all?'

She didn't reply, squeezing her glass.

'Henry was happy today, couldn't you see that?' Tommy continued. 'He was thrilled about his presents. And Hilmar, too, he laughed many times. I don't hear him laughing all that often any more. But today he laughed. They liked the jokes, you saw that.'

'Nice tradition,' Rakel said, her voice icy. 'It was something new, wasn't it? You've never hidden jokes under the plates before. You should do it next year too, then, isn't that what you are thinking?'

'And the dinner,' said Tommy. 'It was the best Christmas

dinner I've had for years. Even though we didn't have porridge, the raisins were even sweeter than usual. The grapes
we have in the greenhouse are growing better all the time.
Grandmother said they would, that the grapes will just
improve and that's how it is with a lot of the produce in there.
Both the vegetables and the fruit have increasingly more
flavour, sweetness, the bushes are growing, the apple trees
in the barrels, too.' He could hear how his voice was rising.
'And next year, next Christmas we will have even more and
in the spring I will plant potatoes, and I will sow barley, we
can grow barley again, on the slope facing south, we will
have porridge on Christmas Eve, just the way we always did.'

'Yes, Tommy,' she said. 'It's going well, all of this. You
are good at this, Tommy. Everything will turn out the way
you want.'

Rakel was about to pour herself even more, but her hand
glanced against the glass and it rolled across the table. She
caught it just as it was about to fall to the floor.

'Be careful,' he said and touched her arm in warning.

'I'm always careful,' she said.

He had removed his hand immediately but the sensation
of her arm against his palm remained.

'You've never had a drink, have you?' She spoke slowly.
'You've never tasted a drop, because you never went to the
parties, you never joined us, not on the beach all the spring
evenings, not when we went up to the top of Platåfjellet
Mountain for midsummer's eve.'

'No,' he said. 'You're right. I never went to any of
those things.'

'Because you were at home. Playing family. A good boy
then, just like now.'

For a second, he thought he heard sympathy in her voice.

She pushed the full glass she'd poured for him across the table, towards him.

'Take as much as you want.'

And then he accepted the glass. He could smell the sharp, familiar odour of potato spirits, but he didn't drink.

Rakel took an even larger gulp, then she wiped off her mouth.

'What is it, Tommy? Don't you want any? You must have been curious, all those times, about what you were missing?'

'I never had the feeling that I was missing much.'

'You're lying. I saw you, Tommy, lingering stares in our direction every time we did something fun, every time we laughed.'

'That's not true.'

'Try it, then. This is the only fun we have up here.'

'I don't think being drunk seems like all that much fun.'

'There's no harm in a little taste.'

'I know that.'

He should have protested, he should have said that drinking meant relinquishing control and if there was one thing he couldn't do, it was that.

But she was right. He *was* curious.

'Just taste it,' she said.

He raised the glass and then he took a sip. The flavour was strong and unpleasant, more or less the way he imagined alcohol would taste, only worse.

They sat in silence for a while, each holding their glass.

'Do you remember the arguments every spring?' Rakel asked, and started imitating. 'Potatoes are to be eaten, not used for alcohol.'

'My father used to say that,' Tommy said.

'Your father was the sanctimonious type.'

'What do you mean?' Tommy put down his glass.

'And he loved Svalbard.' Rakel continued.

'I don't think we should talk about my father.'

'He probably would never have wanted to leave, either.'

That did it.

Tommy got to his feet, turned his back on her, went out into the kitchen, poured himself a glass of water and tried to rinse away the taste of alcohol in his mouth. But the tingling sensation on his tongue was still there.

He brought the glass of water with him and placed it in front of her. 'I think I'm going to turn in.'

'Do that,' she said, and stood up. 'You can dream about the future. All the years we will have together, the five of us.'

'Goodnight, Rakel.'

'The family we will be. And the family we will create. It's a good thing the children aren't siblings and certainly a good thing that they aren't all the same sex.'

She lifted a hand, slid it across her body, drawing body parts. 'Fantastic that Runa is a girl, right, so she can have children. Are you thinking she will do it with Henry or Hilmar? Do you think she should mate with the youngest or the oldest, or maybe both? And what about you, Tommy, maybe you will also do it with Runa, get her pregnant? She is a beautiful girl after all.'

'What are you talking about?'

'I'm messing with you, Tommy. I know that's not what you're thinking. You're thinking that you'll do it with me.'

'What are you talking about?' he said again, but his voice was faint, no match for hers.

Because she was standing so close to him now, and beneath the scent of drink he could smell the scent of a girl, see the details on her face, her mouth that was a little crooked, her dark eyebrows, and the tiny, down-like hair along her jawline.

'We have to hurry,' Rakel said. 'We must start right away. Runa is not sexually mature yet, but I'm ready. You can get me pregnant. Many times. Then we will propagate, breed, until there are so many of us that we are a village again. We will be like Adam and Eve, you and I, in a rocky and freezing cold garden.'

'No,' he said and tried shaking his head. 'No ...'

But he was unable to say any more. His brothers were sleeping. The sitting room was warm, it was just the two of them and she was standing so close to him. And when she stood like that, up against him, everything changed. She was about to speak, but he saw that his body affected her, the way hers affected him. The hardness in her eyes disappeared, like a light mist blown away by the wind.

'Rakel,' he said.

'Yes?'

He reached out his hand, and gently stroked her cheek.

Their gazes remained locked.

He let his hand come to rest on her face and thought he could feel the weight of her head, a faint pressure from her chin, as if she released her weight into his hand.

She turned her head slightly, and her lips came even closer to his fingers.

And then it was as if she suddenly had no time to lose.

She placed her hand on his fly; the light pressure caused him to gasp.

She held it there, for a moment, rubbed up and down, once.

Then she started unbuttoning.

'Are you sure ...' he said.

But she kept going, pulling off his trousers and pants at the same time. As he stood there with them around his ankles, he felt suddenly embarrassed and wanted to cover himself with his hands, but they would not obey. Rakel took hold of one of his hands and guided it under her jumper.

And his hand around her breast was paralysed. He couldn't feel whether the breast was large or small, whether it was as he had imagined, felt nothing. And then she fondled him and he gasped again.

She started moving her hand, up and down, clumsily, and it occurred to him that she was perhaps not as experienced as he'd thought.

But then, as if in response to the thought, she pulled him over to the sofa, and pushed him backwards, so he stumbled and fell, lying with his legs half on the floor.

He lay there without moving as he watched her remove her jumper, singlet, trousers, leggings, wool socks, socks, under-pants, so many garments. Finally she was completely naked in front of him. He said nothing more, thought nothing.

She lay down on top of him, struggling to find the right angle, but then he was inside her and he looked up at the Christmas tree, at the lustre of the ornaments, at the angels Henry had cut out of thin sheets of aluminium that they'd found on the shore, while he squeezed her and felt her hands all over him and caressed her, all of her, soft and smooth as they moved together. She made some unfamiliar sounds and writhed above him, and she smiled at nothing, in a way he had never seen her smile before.

Everything is going to be all right, he thought.

We are going to be fine.

But afterwards, when it was over, she sat up, pulled on her clothes again, at all times with her face averted.

'Rakel?'

She didn't reply.

He repeated her name.

'It didn't mean anything,' she said.

'No,' he said. 'I know.'

'Will you turn off the lights?'

She started walking towards the stairway leading to the first floor and didn't wait for him to reply.

As he was clearing the table, his water glass slipped out of his hands. It sailed through the air and fell to the floor where it shattered, and water splashed all over the place.

He bent down and started picking up the broken pieces of glass, carefully, one piece at a time and deposited them in the rubbish bin. Then he took out the broom and dustpan and carefully swept the entire kitchen floor. He pictured Henry's bare feet, how he might get up early and walk barefoot down to the kitchen, and step on a tiny sliver that would lodge itself in there, in the soft flesh of a child, that Tommy wouldn't be able to get it out again and it would get infected, enter his bloodstream and give him blood poisoning.

He swept every single corner of the kitchen floor. Afterwards, he got down on all fours and washed the floor with a rag. The floor was grotty; there were sticky bits of food stuck to the floor under the kitchen table. They should do a better job of cleaning, he should do better.

He rubbed and rubbed at every spot until it disappeared.

Three days later, Tommy took down the Christmas decorations. He placed the tree baubles and the homemade angels in a box, which he put in the storage room. The tree took up a lot of space, the decorations gathered dust; Christmas on the whole made it difficult to breathe, and nobody had gone to the trouble of organising a New Year's Eve celebration.

Henry and Hilmar objected loudly and claimed that he was ending Christmas far too soon. But they relented when he shouted at them, telling them to shut up.

'What's bothering you?' Hilmar said softly, and led Henry up into their bedroom.

Tommy was left to do the cleaning up by himself.

He had to do most things by himself. Dinner. Laundry. His attempts to keep his brothers relatively clean.

He seldom asked Rakel for help. They lived side by side in the house, with the three children, but rarely spoke, except to communicate simple messages. She often stayed outdoors for long periods time and spent less time taking care of the children.

The images from Christmas invaded his thoughts constantly. When he was standing in the greenhouse with his hands in the soil, her body was beneath his fingers, when he walked down the road and felt the fabric of his trousers rubbing against his crotch, he twitched, and the twitch was a thrust into her body. Was what had happened on Christmas Eve his fault or the alcohol's? Should they have refrained? And could it happen again? Should it happen again?

He tried to speak with Rakel on several occasions, but she avoided him, just said the same thing, that the incident hadn't meant anything.

Every time it happened, he grew angrier with himself. What had taken place was not important, it meant nothing, she was right.

Some other words had also started echoing in his head.

We have something up here that the whole world owns.

What did she mean? Was Rakel capable of deciding to visit the vault by herself?

Owned, he had answered. The world had abandoned both Svalbard and the vault.

The seeds were his responsibility now and he hadn't taken care of them the way he should have, hadn't looked after them.

He walked up there alone. He didn't tell the others where he was going – this was his affair. When his brothers were in bed, he packed up his tools and a spade in his knapsack and got dressed to go out.

The cold had crept in during the afternoon. The grains of snow were tiny and sharp, drifting on the hillsides, forming snowbanks. Tommy moved with stooping shoulders up the hill to the vault, pulled Father's old balaclava all the way up over his nose, so his entire face was covered except for his eyes.

Large banks of snow had accumulated in front of the vault, but there was a ramp leading to the entrance door and he crossed without great difficulty. Then he pulled out the spade and began shovelling off the snow blocking the entrance.

He cursed the weather, which had decided to work against him. The snow settled everywhere, covering every single surface; even the barely visible edge on top of the hinges was coated with a thin layer of snow and the white crystals stuck to the shiny, smooth steel.

The entrance door was actually two doors, which he remembered opened outwards. The left door was a hard, unbroken surface, while the door on the right had two key-holes, a door handle and a long, vertical steel handle running from the top to the bottom.

Tommy was sweaty and breathless by the time he was finally satisfied with his snow shovelling. And luckily the sky was starting to clear up. He clapped his mittens together a couple of times to rid them of snow, before grasping the door handle. He was able to push it down, but when he pulled, nothing happened.

Then he grasped the long steel handle on the door to the right.

The door didn't move.

He tried again, placing his left foot and hand against the door on the left, bracing himself against it.

He pulled and tugged but still the door didn't budge.

A frustrated sigh escaped his chest and he sat down in the snow. Why did she just die without giving him the key?

The cloud cover broke apart over his head. The Northern Lights rippled dramatically across the sky, shimmering turquoise and green.

Are you up there now, Grandmother, he thought, and turned his face towards the sky. Are you coming to get me with long tentacles of light?

He whistled, in sheer defiance.

But the sound was feeble and weak, the landscape swallowed the faint whistle. The Northern Lights blazed. He shuddered. He still carried inside him the scars of his childhood fears.

Then he stood up again and studied the hinges. Solid bolts held the doors in place in the steel frame, and the bolts were fastened with equally solid studding. Maybe he could screw off the studding, he thought, and studied the screws. With the right tools, it might work.

He bent over his knapsack. As quietly as he could, he opened it and took out the set of Allen keys he had found in one of the workshops.

He tried several before finding the right one, and took off his mittens, but his hands quickly began to freeze. He fumbled with the slippery metal. Then he tried unscrewing but could not get the Allen key to grip. It kept slipping and his fingers refused to obey him.

He put on his mittens again, tried once more, but he couldn't get a firm grasp on the Allen key and it slipped out of his fingers, falling down into the snowdrift beneath the ramp on which he was standing.

'Fuck!'

He crept down from the ramp, squatted in the snow, switched on his head torch and swept the beam across the white surface, searching for the hole the Allen key must have made when it hit the snow. But he couldn't see anything. He dug through the snow with his hands, swore again, but couldn't find it.

Finally he ended up just sitting in the snowdrift listening to his own breathing. He tried to calm down and again turned his face towards the Northern Lights.

If you're up there, Grandmother, it would be nice if you would give me some kind of sign. What is your plan, really? What in hell have you done with the key?

He puckered his lips, whistled again, as loudly as he could, a long, piercing note.

The Northern Lights continued rippling across the sky, electric particles from the sun colliding with the earth's atmosphere. That was all it was.

He had only himself.

Tommy ran his hands quickly through the snow and there, finally, he encountered something hard.

He jumped up onto the ramp again and with a strength he didn't know he possessed, went to work with the tool.

The screws loosened one by one.

Soon the upper studding released its grip.

And then the lower.

He took hold of the steel door and pulled it towards him. It gave way.

In front of him was a narrow opening.

He was just able to squeeze through.

Tao

Tao will never forget the sight of the vault.

Tommy had trailed behind them on the walk up, but as they approached the narrow building in the hillside, he took the lead. He was the one who was supposed to show them the seeds, he said, and sent a cold glance in Rakel's direction.

The road surface was a thick layer of mud, a quagmire of resistance.

'It's been raining for weeks,' Rakel said, and looked apologetically at Tao's boots and white trousers. 'Sorry. Your nice clothes.'

'It's fine,' Tao said quickly. 'It isn't your fault that it's wet.'

They walked all the way up to the door. Tommy walked over to it, leaned down, studied the hinges and then he turned back to face the others.

'Somebody has opened it already,' he said.

Rakel walked over to join him. She had her hands in her pockets, as if she were holding on tight to something, but then she pulled them out and looked first at Tommy and then the door in astonishment.

Everyone congregated around him, the children peering with curiosity at the hinges that had been unscrewed.

'None of you have been up here lately?'

Rakel shook her head.

'Never.'

'No,' Tommy said. 'We've had our hands full with other things.'

Mei-Ling and the first mate shoved the door all the way to one side, and they entered one by one.

It was cramped in the corridor. The children tripped over each other, somebody clearly stepped on somebody else's foot and Mei-Ling cursed.

'There's a switch there,' Tommy said to Tao, and pointed.

Tao pressed it and the ceiling lights began to tick. Everyone tilted their heads backwards to look up at the lights.

'They're the original lights,' Tommy said. 'We use them so seldom that they never break.'

Tao shivered. 'It's really cold.'

He nodded towards the ceiling fans. 'They are still running, too. Like clockwork.'

Tommy gave a sign that he was about to go inside and the others followed him. Henry trotted right behind his big brother, excited and cheerful.

Their footsteps were loud. The fans couldn't drown out the sound of the large group. The further inside they got, the colder it got, and Tao noticed that Mei-Ling's teeth were chattering.

'You two should have dressed more warmly,' Tommy said. 'You knew it would be cold.'

Rakel muttered something curt and angry to him.

He didn't reply.

Nobody said anything more until they were standing in the cross-corridor. Tommy switched on the light here as well.

Tao was breathing heavily and a bit erratically. She was

cold and felt a growing sense of discomfort over being so deep inside the mountain.

'How many thousand tons of rock are there above us now?' she asked.

'Just think about the miners,' Tommy replied. 'Every single day they crawled all the many kilometres into the mountains.'

He led them over to the middle door in the corridor.

'The majority of the countries are in here,' he said.

He pushed down the door handle with a sudden movement.

The door opened easily. Tao entered first. The din from the fans grew louder. She squinted as she searched for yet another light switch on the wall and pressed it before the others had made it over the threshold.

Then she froze, blinking.

'But . . .'

Behind her she heard cries of astonishment from the others.

'There's nothing here,' Mei-Ling said.

'No,' Tao said, because she didn't know what else to say. 'Apparently not.'

She took a few steps into the hall, walked between the rows of shelves, expecting to see a few forgotten boxes in there, but nothing appeared.

She turned to Tommy. 'Where are the seeds?'

He didn't answer.

'Come on,' Rakel said. 'Aren't there two more doors?'

She walked quickly out into the corridor and opened the door to the eastern hall.

Empty shelves there as well.

They hurried over to the door furthest west. Rakel's desperation was evident in her movements.

Nothing.

Tao rushed out into the corridor again, glanced into the

hall in the middle, then walked to the eastern hall, as if by double checking she would conjure up the seeds. Her heart was pounding, she was boiling hot, despite the cold.

'They're not here,' she said. 'Not anywhere.'

It sounded feeble and silly.

'We can see that,' Mei-Ling said. Her voice was unusually hard. She turned to Rakel. 'You said you had the seeds. We came all this way to get the seeds.'

'I don't know where they are,' Rakel said, obviously distraught. 'I have no idea.' Then she turned to face Tommy. 'You must know something? You are the one Aunt Louise called the seed custodian.'

He answered her immediately, his words sliding out so quickly that it sounded like he had learned them by heart: 'Seed custodian? I was a little kid. That was just something she said to be nice.'

Tommy

He is standing in the Polar Hotel's great room. Empty chairs everywhere, some overturned, as if the room had been evacuated in a hurry. A jacket hangs over the back of a chair, a child's hat is slung on another. Did they use the room when everyone got sick? The thought makes him shudder.

He walks over to the bar in the corner. Every single one of his movements makes noise. His jacket squeaks, his shoes pound across the floor.

Several of the bottles are still half full. He lifts one, doesn't look at the handwritten label, knows that it will be just as foul regardless of what they have named the contents. Then he lifts it to his mouth and takes a swallow. It tastes disgusting. He plugs his nose, takes another large gulp and then another.

He sits on a chair. Waits.

The effects of the alcohol hit him immediately. A vague dizziness. He lifts a hand, and notices it is more difficult to control it now. His head buzzes, his thoughts become jumbled.

You see, Rakel, now I'm drinking, the way you said that I should.

The alcohol makes his cheeks tingle the way sunlight will

do, in response to the warmth it generated when he and his brothers saw it return for the very last time.

The polar night's total darkness slowly released its grasp. First, the light solely produced a faint alteration in the quality of the night, later a more obvious adjustment, as if someone were turning a switch, first slowly, then more quickly.

Pastel winter was what they had called these weeks, when the sky was flooded with shades of pink and blue that washed over the mountains, when the light from the sun, which had not yet risen above the horizon, highlighted all the contours of the large, white surfaces. Not twilight, but blue light, because the days were hours of blue, and the world re-emerged, but in dreamlike shades, as if not fully awake.

One afternoon when the sky was clear, he left the greenhouse early to arrive in time to watch the dawn. He stood looking towards the mountains, remembering how happy Father always was at this time of year, how much he wanted to share the experience of the light returning with the children, how he always pointed, exclaiming about the pink, the golden and the bright blue, all the colours hidden in the white, barren landscape. And Tommy remembered how this beauty had not made much of an impression on him as a child, that he thought his father was tiresome. The light gave Tommy lucidity, opportunities, freedom. That was all. But perhaps one needs experience, he thought now, to understand the beauty of a landscape. He turned his face towards a shimmering moon in a pink sky. Maybe I am in the process of becoming like him.

Then he picked up his knapsack and walked home. He had brought cabbage with him today, wrapped up in thick layers of an old sheet to protect it from the cold. He looked forward to taking it out and making dinner. The knapsack thudded against his back but wasn't heavy. And then he noticed his shadow on the path, the moon shadow which would soon be a sun shadow. There was no room for fear right now, or self-pity; joy had simply come running towards him, become one with his shadow, because apparently joy could only arrive in this way, on its own volition. And his shadow was a gymnast, a dancer, lighter and more flexible than he was, who could dance on the path before him, turn cartwheels or leap across the ground, able to do all the tricks he could not.

He pulled the door open and went inside without bothering to watch his step and almost tripped, because the floor was covered with shoes the others had left lying there. Tommy bent down and placed them on the shelf, one pair at a time, and then shouted into the sitting room.

'Hey, I can't be the only one who tidies up in this house.'

The others had clearly already had their dinner. Henry, Hilmar and Runa were seated close together on the sofa, each reading a book, their hunger appeased, their eyes drowsy. Henry's eyes drooped shut.

Only Rakel stood by the window, staring out into the darkness.

'Hello?' Tommy said.

'Hello,' the children on the sofa said.

Rakel didn't respond.

'Did you have a nice day?' he asked.

'Yes,' the three children said without looking up from their books.

Rakel tapped her fingers against the windowsill and sighed. Then she leaned her head against the pane and stood there like that for a moment before pulling away again, leaving behind an impression of her forehead on the glass.

Runa glanced up from her book and looked at him. She tried to smile at him, sort of an untroubled smile. See, her smile said, everything is normal, there is nothing here that is worrying me.

But there was something and he knew that Runa had long since noticed it. She had been seeking Tommy out more than usual. A few days ago, when she was dressing to go outside, the zipper on her snowsuit got stuck. She came into the sitting room to ask for help. Rakel was lying on the sofa, but it was Tommy whom Runa approached. He spent a long time coaxing the fabric out of the zipper while her soft curls tickled his chin. The next day, when she was about to set the table, it was the sleeve of Tommy's jumper she tugged when she needed help reaching the plates on the top shelf. And the past few nights she had given him a goodnight hug. Quick, small hugs, pressing her cheek against his own, never her body, never embraces, just this small, smooth cheek against his.

Rakel turned towards the others. Runa quickly hid herself in her book. Henry had fallen asleep and Hilmar was absorbed by his old, dog-eared, superhero comic book, which he had to hold with both hands at all times so the loose pages wouldn't fall out.

'A good book?' Rakel asked.

'Yes,' Runa said without looking up at her sister.

'And you, Hilmar,' Rakel said.

'What?' He looked up with the dazed expression typical of someone who is living more in the plot of the story he is reading than in the real world.

'Good book?'

'Yes,' he said and wrinkled his brow in an attempt to understand the situation. 'Sure.'

'Good,' Rakel said. 'Terrific.'

Hilmar returned to his book but Runa sat covertly observing her sister.

'All right then,' Tommy said, stretching his mouth into a kind of grin and clapping his hands. 'It looks like I missed my dinner, but perhaps somebody would like a bedtime snack?'

Rakel did not say a word while he prepared the snack for the children, not a word when he carried Henry up to his bedroom and scolded the other two into bed. She sat on the chair closest to the stove, feeding it driftwood from time to time. The light from the flames flickered across her face.

'Now it's coming!' Henry shouted. 'Look! I see it! There it is!'

The sun's very first rays spread across the snow-covered landscape.

Tommy closed his eyes for a moment and tried to feel the faint warmth that reminded him of the time of year they had ahead of them, tried to let it comfort him, allow some of the children's enthusiasm to fill him. But he felt no warmth, the sun was cold and clear. Why wasn't Rakel here now? I am just trying to create some kind of life, he thought, why can't she ever help me, why won't she try as well? We could have done it, the two of us, if only she were willing.

The rays broadened. The light was so strong that they all had to squint. It wasn't just the light that was unfamiliar, but the shadows, too. The uniform, diffuse natural landscape had suddenly acquired hard contours, keen-edged lines and sharp contrasts.

'The sun!' Henry said.

And then he clapped his hands.

'Welcome, Madame Sun!' Tommy said and applauded along with him.

He heard that his voice sounded overly enthusiastic but continued anyway. 'You are most welcome!'

Hilmar and Runa also joined in. The only sound that could be heard was the muffled clapping of their mittened hands.

They were sitting on the old hospital steps by the church ruins. This was where they usually went on 8 March, where they usually gathered to watch the sun's return, above the mountains furthest inland in the Longyear Valley.

Just like before, he thought, the sun comes back the way it always does. We are sitting here and waiting for it, the way we always do.

Before them lay the weeks of the year he liked best of all, when every twenty-four-hour period contained both a day and a night. The day gained ground; every twenty-four hours it ate up almost twenty minutes of the night, until finally the night had to surrender, but many weeks still remained before that day. When he was younger, he had wondered a lot about how it must have been to live somewhere else in the world, along the equator, where the night and the day were the same length all year round, where every day was like the vernal equinox, or in a boat at one of the earth's poles, where every night and every day lasted for six months. The North Pole had always frightened him, not the swirling ocean of midsummer or the free-floating ice in the winter, but the light up there and the darkness. It seemed so absolute.

'It stings my eyes. It's too bright,' Henry said.

'You mustn't look at it, dimwit,' Hilmar said.

'I know that,' Henry said.

'Would you like some peppermint tea?' Tommy interrupted before an argument could break out between them.

He had brought along a Thermos and four cups and poured tea for all of them.

Hilmar and Henry considered the contents of both the cups and Hilmar was the quickest.

'I wanted that one,' Henry said.

'It makes no difference which one you get,' Hilmar said, and smiled in satisfaction over having received two drops more than his little brother.

'There you go,' Tommy said and poured an extra dollop into Runa's cup.

'Thank you,' she said, and accepted it with both hands.

Steam rose from the cups, mingling with the mist of the children's breath. Runa and Hilmar puckered their lips and blew carefully on the hot drink, but Henry took a big gulp of his.

'Ow!'

'You have to blow on it first,' Hilmar said.

'I did!'

'Look,' Tommy said. 'Now it's disappearing again.'

Because the sun was growing fainter, smaller, the rays pulling away, like a fishing net being drawn into shore, and soon it left them behind, in the soft, blurry landscape bathed in gently shimmering pastels.

Tommy emptied his cup. It was ten below and the tea had already become lukewarm. Lukewarm, the way everything was. Not cold, not black, not white. Just lukewarm and grey. And he was stuck in this lukewarm state, suffocated by steel-coloured, slack water.

As they approached the house, Rakel came outside. She was wearing her outdoor garments and carrying a fishing pole.

'You missed it,' he said.

Rakel shrugged.

Then she turned to Runa and forced the corners of her mouth outwards into a smile. 'Did you see it?'

'It was brilliant,' Runa said and disappeared into the house.

'Cold, cold, cold,' Henry said and scurried in behind her.

Hilmar was the last. He looked at Rakel.

'What is it?' Rakel asked.

'Nothing,' Hilmar said, and went inside to join the others.

Rakel and Tommy stood outside the house for a moment. She gave him the once over and he tried to avoid meeting her eyes. This lukewarm feeling, this greyness, it's her. It comes from Rakel, she is what is holding me back, what is holding all of us back. She counters every attempt to find joy and lightness with heaviness. She behaves as if we're waiting for something and so we wait. But I don't want to wait. I just want to follow the rhythm of the sun, and the growth of the plants. And the growth of Runa, Hilmar and Henry. I just want to enjoy my life.

Rakel lifted the fishing pole onto her shoulder. 'Want to come down to the water with me?'

'I have to stop by the greenhouse,' he said.

He was about to leave, but something about her gaze stopped him.

'Fine. Just for a little while, then.'

They walked down to the beach in silence. It was quiet; he tried whistling.

Rakel glanced at him and laughed softly. 'Marvellous.'

She was right. It sounded as pitiful and forlorn as when he whistled beneath the Northern Lights.

They walked down the beach. The frost had hardened the sand and the rocks were slippery. Several times he almost tripped.

'This is where you were lying, Tommy, do you remember?' Rakel asked and pointed. 'I remember that when I found you, at first I was frightened.'

'You were frightened?'

'I thought you were stuck. Under the tree. I couldn't under-stand why you would want to hug a tree. I mean, why would a little boy lie down on a cold beach and hug a tree?'

'For the reason you just gave. I was little. I didn't think about what I was doing.'

They continued walking beside the fjord.

Rakel shoved his shoulder, jostling him. 'Come on, are you still cross about that?'

'If you were frightened, then I don't understand why you teased me.'

She shrugged. 'Maybe I was relieved when I understood that nothing was wrong and then I had to think of some-thing to say.'

'Think of something to say?'

'Yes.'

She made it sound so simple.

He started walking faster. 'Are you going to cast from the wharf?'

'Where else?'

'Why don't you just put out a net?'

'I feel like casting.'

'And you do whatever you feel like doing.'

'Yes, Tommy. I do whatever I feel like.'

Suddenly she stopped, threw the fishing pole onto the ground, took hold of his arm again and forced him to stop as well, to look at her.

'I do whatever I feel like. I am here with you and three little kids. I will continue being here, I will see them grow up. I will have a child with you or many children, I will fish, hunt, accompany you to the bloody greenhouse, I will work, struggle, at all times thinking only about survival, that's

how my life will be, until one of the following things finally
happens: I will die in childbirth, like your mother. I will be
killed in a landslide, like my own parents. Or I will be struck
down by an illness, like all the others, an illness for which
we have no cure, cancer or blood poisoning, or some kind
of blasted pneumonia ... Oh and by the way, there's also a
fourth alternative. That I will be "fortunate" enough to live a
long life, that it takes a really long time, that in the end I will
die of old age, pass away in my sleep. Then I will have had the
honour of having lived a really long life up here and of seeing
our children grow up and start doing it with each other and
then subsequently doing it with their siblings and maybe I
will be so fortunate that I will see the results of inbreeding,
too. And we are accustomed to inbreeding. But the conse-
quences might be horrible, it might not be the way it was for
Inga, who just had a little trouble learning to read. It can lead
to illnesses and missing arms and legs and what do I know.'

'You make it sound grotesque. But it need not turn out
that way.'

'Yes,' she said. 'That is just how it will turn out.'

Her hand squeezed his arm and when she exhaled her
breath formed clouds.

'I know you don't like me, Tommy,' Rakel said.

'I like you.'

'Don't lie.'

She released his arm, picked up the fishing pole again and
sighed heavily. He didn't know if the sigh was unintentional
or if it was a deliberate signal meant to communicate how fed
up she was with him.

He was so unspeakably tired, so sick of her, sick of having
to find a balance, relate to her; he just wanted to sleep, he
felt so heavy, as if he could lie down there and then and fall

asleep immediately, on the beach, lie down beside the tree again, put his arms around it, hold on tight and feel the sensation of the comforting bark against his cheek.

'There is something you need to know,' Rakel said. She sat down heavily on a rock, staring at the ocean before them. 'There's something I have to tell you.'

'Yes?'

'Some time passed before I found out, before I noticed,' she continued. 'I have never been one to pay close attention to such things. I suppose that's because I've never had anyone to teach me to pay attention. But when I finally started thinking back, counting the days, remembering, then ...'

She didn't finish the sentence, but the realisation of what she had just told him caused everything else he was feeling to vanish and a landslide of joy tumbled through him.

'A baby?' he said. 'Are we going to have a baby?'

'No, Tommy,' she said. '*I'm* going to have a baby.'

Tao

No cameras, no celebrations, no children holding flowers await them when they finally arrive in Sichuan. Li Chiara hasn't even summoned Tao for a meeting, merely given orders that the children were to stay with her for the time being, until they decide what they are going to do with them. Tao has enough room, doesn't she?

Mei-Ling drops them off outside the apartment complex.

'Do you need help carrying your things?'

Tao shakes her head. 'No, we'll be fine.'

She turns to face the children. 'Won't we?'

Only Runa answers, politely. 'Yes, we'll be fine.'

Mei-Ling gets out of the van and looks at Tao.

'All right then,' she says. 'That was that.'

Tao nods. 'Thank you for everything. It was quite a trip.'

Mei-Ling grins. 'Was it?'

'No, perhaps not.'

Then Mei-Ling become serious. 'I will never forget it.'

Tao nods.

'And good luck,' Mei-Ling says, and points at the children who have stepped away. 'With the children.'

'Thanks,' Tao says.

They fall silent. Neither of them knows what else to say. Mei-Ling scrapes her foot against the ground.

Then suddenly she throws out her arms and embraces Tao. Mei-Ling is a head taller than her and her body is muscular and hard. Safe, Tao thinks. I was safe with you.

'Take care of the children. And yourself,' Mei-Ling says in a voice that is uncharacteristically gruff.

'You too,' Tao says.

'Never,' Mei-Ling says, and the cocky expression is back on her face. 'Bye now,' Mei-Ling says. 'See you.'

Then she drives away. Tao knows that Mei-Ling has already been notified about her next job. They will probably never meet again.

She lets the children into the apartment, which is oddly empty and smells stuffy. Tao lets Runa have the little room that was once Wei-Wen's. Runa stands looking around her and then sits on the bed, running her hand over the mattress.

'Do you think it will be okay?' Tao asks.

Runa nods but turns her face away.

Then Tao opens the door to her own bedroom and shows it to the brothers.

'You two can sleep in here.'

'In the big bed?' Hilmar asks.

'A grown-up bed,' Henry says.

'Yes, you'll have to share it.'

For a moment, the two boys forget themselves and dive onto the bed, rolling around with the pillows and rejoicing together. Tao allows them to carry on while she unpacks their clothing, putting garments into the large chest of drawers against the long wall.

She smiles to herself over the wildness of their playful tussle. But only a few minutes pass before Hilmar leaves the room, book in hand. Henry stays behind.

He walks over to the window and stands there for a while, his face pensive.

'Why is it light?' he asks.

'What do you mean?'

'I thought that when we arrived it would be dark.'

'It's light in the daytime and dark at night. Just like it's been during the voyage.'

'But it's winter!'

He is pale, a little red under his nose, snivelling and sickly.

'Yes, that's how the winter is here.'

'But how can it be Christmas when it isn't dark?'

The room is west facing. Outside the clouds are breaking apart in the sky and rays of sunlight hit his face. It is expressionless.

'How will Christmas come?' he asks again, without looking at her.

Then he moves away from the window and walks out of the room.

She hears him padding around in the apartment while she puts the rest of the clothing into the drawers.

She puts the boys' clothing where Kuan used to keep his. She holds up a jumper, knitted from several different types of wool. The colours don't match. She must find more clothing for the children, she thinks. New, clean, cotton garments.

When she has finished, she goes out to the kitchen. The short-wave radio is on the table. Henry is sitting on a chair beside it. Listening.

She tousles his hair.

'Come on,' she said. 'It's bedtime.'

He gets to his feet obediently and without any objection goes into the bathroom.

*

Afterwards, when he is lying in bed, freshly bathed and wearing clean pyjamas, she sits on the edge of his bed. The two of them are alone in the bedroom. Hilmar has not yet gone to bed.

'Goodnight, Henry.'

'You can tell me that story now,' he says.

'What story?'

'The one about how the world was made.'

'Are you sure? Aren't you tired?'

'Yes, you can tell it now.'

'Fine. Then I'll start ... Once upon a time there was an egg,' she says. 'It was enormous and black, almost like the coal in Svalbard.'

Henry sits up a bit, pushing the pillow up against the wall for support. 'Did it come from the mines?'

She thinks for a moment. 'Yes, maybe that's right. Exactly. It was an egg that had been lying in the depths of the black mines.'

'Which one of the mines?'

'Hm, I don't know ... maybe mine number seven?'

'No, I don't think so. I think the egg was lying inside the vault.'

'Yes, it must have been in there, where it was safe. And sleeping inside the egg, was the god Pangu.'

'I don't believe in gods,' Henry says. 'Tommy says that ...' He searched for the right words. 'Tommy says that believing in god is the same as believing a fairy tale.'

'But then maybe this is just a fairy tale.'

'Okay, then.'

'Okay?'

He nods. 'Yes. You can continue the story now.'

'Good. Then I will. Pangu awakened after eighteen thousand years.'

'He'd been sleeping for eighteen thousand years?'

He sits up all the way and looks at her sceptically.

'Yes. And he felt pretty cooped up in there, you can understand why. He was actually lying inside an egg, inside a vault.'

'For eighteen thousand years.'

'Yes, for eighteen thousand years. Then he found an axe.'

'Did he have an axe inside the egg? Didn't it rust after eighteen thousand years?'

'I'm not the one who made up the story. But, yes, it seems he had an axe. And he used it to chop a hole in the shell. Light poured out of the egg.'

Henry wrinkled his brow. 'So there was light inside the egg?'

'That's right. A very strong light. And the light turned into the sky and the egg turned into the earth and Pangu stood holding them apart for another eighteen thousand years, while he grew. Finally, he was so tall that the sky and the earth were separated for good. And then Pangu died.'

'Why?'

'I guess he was worn out.'

'I can understand that.'

'But when he died, he didn't disappear. Because his breath became clouds and wind. One of his eyes became the moon, the other the sun. His body became tall mountains, his muscles fertile soil, his tears rivers, his blood water and his sweat rain.'

'Gross, his sweat became rain?'

'Remember, it's just a fairy tale.'

'Yes but ... what about his hair?'

'His hair turned into stars.'

'Oh. That's nice.'

'My mother used to tell me this story,' Tao says. 'And when I had a son, I told it to him.'

'And now you're telling it to me,' Henry says.

He scoots down in bed again and pats his pillow into a more comfortable shape.

'Yes, now I am telling it to you.'

Henry thinks a bit. 'But Tao, what if the egg is still lying there?'

'In the vault?'

'Maybe someone has hidden the egg deep inside the vault and Pangu is completely safe in there and will come out in eighteen thousand years. Maybe none of this has happened yet.'

'That would be nice,' Tao says.

'Yes.'

She ventures to stroke his forehead. Gently. For a brief moment she has contact with him. But then his gaze slides away, and he is gone again.

Afterwards she lies awake, tossing and turning in bed. She keeps seeing Tommy's face. His surprise inside the vault seemed genuine, she believed him. But at the same time, she had doubts, because she didn't know him, didn't know how everything he had experienced had affected him.

And what about Rakel? Hopeful Rakel, carrying a new life. From behind it wasn't possible to see it on her. She moved lightly, her steps catlike, and seemed wholly unencumbered by her belly.

On the way down from the vault she apologised over and over again. By the time they reached the beach, the children were hungry and Tommy took them home without a word.

Mei-Ling and Tao were left alone with Rakel. She had tears in her eyes.

'Sorry,' she said again. 'I ... it never occurred to me ... I thought that ... I have no idea what happened.'

'Have you ever seen the seeds?' Mei-Ling asked.

Rakel shook her head, staring at the ground.

'You tricked us into coming all this way for something you have never even seen?'

Rakel sank onto a rock, supporting her back with one hand, her face white as chalk.

Tao gave Mei-Ling a stern look. 'Watch it,' she muttered softly.

Then she put her hand on Rakel's shoulder in a gesture of support.

'It's no wonder that you're tired. Do you know when the baby is due?'

'In just a few more weeks. Twenty-fourth September.'

'Nine months after Christmas Eve?' Mei-Ling said.

Rakel nodded.

'So at the very least you had an enjoyable Christmas celebration,' Mei-Ling murmured.

'Please,' Tao said.

'And now you'll give birth on the road,' Mei-Ling. 'Because I guarantee we won't make it back before your due date. You had better prepare yourself for a childbirth in a remote part of the deserted steppes of Russia, in a car. If we've even made it that far.'

'Mei-Ling,' Tao said. 'That's enough.'

Still seated on the stone, Rakel flinched, pulled her legs under her and hid her face. Tao remembered her own pregnancy, the back pains, the cramps in her legs, all the restless nights. She continued patting the young girl's back reassuringly. How would it be when they brought the child back with them? Would they set Rakel and Tommy up alone in a flat with an infant? Two teenagers with narrow shoulders, carrying traumatic memories from a nightmare and with hormones raging through their bodies – how were they supposed to take care of a child? Poor little one, Tao thought, and didn't know whether she was thinking about Rakel, first and foremost, or the little mite she was carrying.

'It's not your fault,' she said.

'No,' Mei-Ling said, clearly trying to control her rage. 'Maybe not. But the seeds aren't in the vault. And *that* is somebody's fault.'

'Ask Tommy,' Rakel murmured.

'We have already asked Tommy. He's been here all along,' Mei-Ling said.

'Ask him again.'

Tao and Mei-Ling exchanged glances.

'Go ahead and try,' Mei-Ling said. 'I'm far too angry right now.'

Rakel took Tao up to the house. Tommy was in his room and the children were having dinner in the kitchen on the ground floor. Rakel sat down with them and let Tao go to find him by herself.

He was sitting on the bed, surrounded by clutter.

Dirty plates covered the desk. A cup emitted the aroma of soup. There were books everywhere, on the floor and the table, many of them open, as if he were in the middle of reading them. There was a heap of dirty clothes on the only chair in the room and dirty socks were scattered across the floor around the bed. A young boy lived here. Would Wei-Wen's room have looked like this now if he were still alive?

Tommy stood up and removed the pile of clothing from the chair so she could sit.

'Sorry,' he said, while looking around for a place to deposit the clothes.

She waved away his apology with a flick of her hand.

Once he had put the clothes in a wardrobe that wouldn't shut, he sat on the edge of the bed, facing her and leaning forward with his hands folded over one knee, almost as if he were striking a pose, she thought.

'You don't believe me,' he said. 'You think I know where the seeds are.'

'I don't know you,' she said, trying to soften her words so they sounded kind rather than harsh. 'But I would like to believe you.'

'I've only been in the seed vault once before, a couple of years ago. I went with Grandmother on an inspection. Then it was full of boxes of seeds from every country in the world. I haven't been inside there since, and I don't even know where the key is.'

'Have you looked for it?'

'Of course I have. But I believe it went with Grandmother into her grave.'

There was a certainty about him more typical of an older person but, at the same time, he was vulnerable. She was speaking with someone who was simultaneously an old man and a little boy.

'And where was she buried?'

'We buried her at sea.'

'But could she have . . .'

'Listen,' he said. 'The last year has . . . been pretty unusual.'

'Pretty unusual' was an enormous understatement, in her opinion, but she let him continue.

'Everyone died. We were attacked by a polar bear. Then Grandmother died, too. On top of that, Rakel got pregnant and then suddenly you were all headed here.'

'Rakel was the one who wanted us to come,' Tao said. 'I understand that you feel like you've been tricked.'

He turned his face away. 'That's right. I didn't want you to come.'

'But why not?'

'Do you really need an explanation for that?'

His animosity fed the growing impatience inside her. 'You understand that it's difficult to believe that you don't know where the seeds are?'

'Because I didn't want you to come?'

She nodded.

'No.' He stared at her again with the same defiant gaze. 'No, I don't understand that those two things have anything to do with one another.'

She took a deep breath. 'Fine ... but you must have some thoughts about where they could be?'

He shook his head and sat in silence for a while.

'I think it must have been Grandmother,' he said, finally. 'When we were hiding from the illness, she was gone for a long time. She said afterwards that she stayed by herself to protect us and because she needed time to grieve. But I believe she may have spent those weeks moving the seeds. And if Grandmother hid them, it was because she didn't want them to be found.'

Tommy got to his feet and stood in the middle of the room, his mouth a firm line, his eyes narrowed.

'Whoever has hidden them, doesn't want them to be found,' he said, his voice louder now. 'Not by anyone.'

She stood up as well, but she was shorter than him and felt small facing the large and limber boy's body. He must have noticed it, because he took a step towards the window, as if wanting to seem less menacing.

'Tao,' he said. 'It's not that I have something against you. Or any of you. But Grandmother was the seed custodian. She made this decision.'

'What if she was wrong?'

'She was seldom wrong.'

'I don't have anything against you, either, Tommy. And I'm sorry we came here without your consent, but we're not leaving here without the seeds. And we would appreciate it if you would help us search for them.'

'"Appreciate" ... my father also used that word. It always meant that I had to do something or other.'

'I don't know what the alternative would be.'

'The alternative is that you respect Grandmother's decision, that you go back to where you came from and let us go on living our lives, just like before.'

'We're not leaving Svalbard without the seeds.'

'Or I'll take off and leave you behind here. I'm starting to get pretty sick of Longyearbyen.'

He turned his head towards the window. The light fell upon his face, revealing his vulnerability.

'I don't think you're going to do that,' Tao said calmly. 'Where would you go?'

'A hunting cabin. In Grænfjorden or Colesbukta. There are a lot of places to go. I'd manage.'

'Alone?'

He raised his head, standing tall, trying to swagger. 'I'd manage just fine.'

She felt sorry for him. 'No ... you won't run away. Not as long as you have your brothers here. And a child on the way.'

He flinched.

'Tommy, you have to help us, do you understand?' she said. 'Would you please help us find the seeds?'

Tommy

When he thinks back on the final days, when they searched for the seeds, it is his conflicting emotions he remembers.

The problem was that he liked her, he liked Tao, and part of him wanted to be co-operative, polite, easy-going and helpful.

Another part of him just wanted to tell her to go to hell.

But he decided to pretend that he was helping them. It was easier than working against them in the search and it also gave him control over their movements.

They started in the buildings located closest to the seed vault: the airport and the old warehouses by the harbour. They entered them one by one, trying to search every room, every workshop, every hall. In some place walls had tumbled down, in others the wind had blown off the roof. Father had forbidden the brothers to enter most of the buildings; only Rakel and her friends would go inside the old buildings. In a couple of places, Tommy and the foreigners found evidence of their parties, empty bottles and the remains of bonfires.

He had never before thought about how many buildings there actually were in Longyearbyen. Most of the houses were not fit for habitation but could still be used as hiding places.

He was on his feet all day long and every night he came

home exhausted, often long after Henry and Hilmar had gone to bed. He went into their bedroom to check on them, stood in the room listening to their breathing. Otherwise he barely saw them.

They worked their way from the harbour area to the cliff by the shore, inspected all the buildings in Gruvedalen and Skjæringa, broke into what remained of the collapsed research centre building, and went through every single room of the Polar Hotel.

On the fifth day of searching in vain, Tao pulled him aside.

'Do you really believe that the seeds are hidden in one of the buildings?' she asked.

'I don't believe anything,' he said. 'I'm just looking, like you said I should.'

'But don't you think if someone has hidden them, he or she would want them to be preserved?'

'Like I said . . .'

'You don't believe anything.'

She studied him, a bit irritated, or so it appeared. 'You're an intelligent boy, Tommy. The seeds will be ruined if they aren't kept in cold storage.'

'Sure,' he said. 'It could be that Grandmother, if she was the one who hid them, has put them somewhere cold.'

'And where could that be?'

'In a freezer?'

'Tommy.'

'I don't know,' he said.

She sighed heavily. 'There's still permafrost in the mountains, isn't there?'

'Deep below the surface.'

'And the mines? There must be roads inside them?'

'The mines are sealed,' he said. 'By both concrete and frost. Nobody's been inside there for almost a hundred years.'

She studied him for a long time. 'Fine. But the ice caves then. I've read that there are ice caves in the glaciers up here. Could the seeds be there?'

He shook his head. 'We can't get inside them. At least, not at this time of year.'

'But you've been there?'

'All glaciers have caves. They are created by underground rivers every summer and they are constantly changing. Once upon a time the glaciers up here were so big that their snouts extended down into the Longyear Valley. Apparently then people went on Sunday treks up to the caves in the winter. Then they started to melt and many of them disappeared. You don't see any glaciers in the valley now, do you?'

'But they exist? At higher altitudes?'

He shrugged.

'Take us to the closest one tomorrow.'

He walked over moss and heather. The foreign visitors were panting heavily as they ascended. Tommy moved more quickly and had to stop and wait.

They followed a riverbed upwards; before them lay only green mountainsides.

He stopped again and turned to face Tao.

'It must have retreated even more since I was here last.'

'But it's there?'

'No idea.'

She started walking again, increasing her pace, overtook him and continued walking beside him.

'How do we know where the entrance is?'

'We don't. They change constantly, I told you that. And they are only safe in the wintertime.'

'You said that, too.'

She wasn't watching where she was going and stepped on some moss that collapsed under her foot, emitting a damp squelching sound.

'Did you get your foot wet?'

'No.'

But he could hear her shoe squishing as they resumed walking.

'What's it like there, inside the caves?'

'Dark, mainly.'

'And if you've brought along a torch?'

He heard how she was restraining herself, in an effort to keep her voice calm.

'It is I guess what people call incomparably beautiful. Like a cathedral. The ice creates the most breath-taking formations. And inside the walls the remains of plants are mummified in the frozen water.'

'It would be a great place to hide the seeds?'

He didn't reply, just kept walking.

Finally, they saw the snout of the glacier protruding into the valley far above them.

Tao's forehead was sweating, Mei-Ling was red in the face and Shun kept stumbling.

'It has shrunk,' Tommy said. 'A lot.'

Nobody spoke as they continued up the side of the valley. The river ran placidly beside them. The ice was the source; it was the water inside the glacier that had created the caves.

They reached the moraine. The going was more difficult now, the ground beneath their feet was made of ice, sludge and stone. It threatened to give way beneath their feet with each step.

Mei-Ling gazed dispiritedly upwards at the sheer ice.

'Where's the entrance did you say?'

'I said, many times, that I have no idea.'

They walked in silence for a while, then Tao stopped and picked something up. A pattern was engraved in the stone she held between her hands.

She admired the clear traces of a leaf that had lived millions of years ago.

'Fossils,' Tommy said. 'The moraine is full of them.'

'How lovely.' She stroked the fossilised leaf lightly with her finger.

Afterwards, she walked holding the stone in her hand. Sometimes she bent over and picked up another, like a child.

Tommy could feel how this irritated him. 'If you're going to bring all of them, you'll have a heavy load to carry.'

Tao looked at him, a little embarrassed, he thought, because she put the stones down.

The trek grew steeper, heavier. They climbed another few metres. He could hear from their breathing that they were struggling and noticed that Mei-Ling and Tao exchanged glances.

'How many glaciers are there in Svalbard?' Mei-Ling asked.

'They stopped counting almost one hundred years ago,' Tommy responded. 'That was the year twenty-one hundred.'

'And now?'

'You're asking how many of them have melted? Do you really think I know the answer to that?'

Amateurs, he thought as they walked back. You should have seen them, Grandmother. Amateurs.

*

By the time they made it home to Longyearbyen it was evening. Mei-Ling and the rest of the crew rowed slowly out towards the ship, but Tao stayed behind, standing beside Tommy on the beach.

He presumed that it was a kind of planned strategy, that once again she would try to gain his trust and pump him for information.

Tao gave him a lingering and pleading look before having another go.

'You must think, Tommy. Please.'

She ran her hand through her sweaty fringe. Her face was dirty, and grey with exhaustion. A part of him felt sorry for her.

'Sorry,' he said. 'But I'm out of ideas.'

'All that's left are the mines,' she said. 'We can't leave here without having tried.'

He spoke slowly, with exaggerated clarity, as if speaking to a child: 'Like I said: the mines are sealed. It's the same as the ice caves. Only worse. We can't get inside, not in the summer and not in the winter.'

She studied him for a long time. Tommy could see that she didn't believe him.

'Fine,' he said finally. 'Maybe we can try Mine Seven. That's the mine that was in operation the longest.'

'But isn't it located way out in Advent Valley? I've seen a map. Mine Three is much closer, just above the vault?'

'Like I said, it's sealed.'

'We'll go there tomorrow morning.'

'Okay,' he said. 'Tomorrow. Then you can see for yourself. That's fine.'

He started walking towards Skjæringa. She called after him: 'Tommy?'

'Yes?' He turned around.

'Thank you.'

She looked so defenceless down there, thin and forlorn.

Where was Rakel while they were searching? What was she doing during those six days, while they ransacked every possible and impossible hiding place in Svalbard? Tommy didn't know, but he believed she stayed at home, cooked meals for the children, continued packing for the new country or was down by the ocean fishing. And he saw that in the afternoons she often talked to Tao or Mei-Ling, wanting to know everything that had happened in the course of the day, where they'd been, what they'd tried and their plans for the time ahead. For his own part, he still did what he could to avoid Rakel. He shrank from her searching gaze, certain she could tell that he was lying. But even though he avoided her, he had a feeling that she grew increasingly attentive to what he said, what he did, and that she knew where he was at any given time.

It is evening. Tommy packs up for the day, puts on his coat and goes outside.

The wind hits him from the side, a powerful gust. He pulls his scarf up over his face, leans into the wind and begins walking home quickly.

When he rounds the corner of the greenhouse and starts heading towards Skjæringa, the weather gets even worse. The wind whips up the snow, blinding him. The light from his head torch is no help; before him is a wall of snow. All the same, he keeps walking for a short distance.

When he turns around again, the dark shadow of the greenhouse is no longer in sight. And in front of him there is no road, no path, no navigation points whatsoever.

He doesn't dare take another step, draws a breath, is still warm but knows that in this cold, the heat will quickly drain out of his body.

If I turn around now, he thinks, and walk straight ahead as best as I can, retracing my steps, then certainly I will find the greenhouse?

He looks down at his feet, calmly turns around 180 degrees, with the utmost care, ensuring that he is moving in exactly the opposite direction. And then he begins to walk back.

Ten steps, twenty.

How many metres has he walked?

He tries to find the greenhouse, to imagine its location in relation to the terrain, to the road. But the white darkness chases every image out of his head.

'Where is it, then?' he mumbles in desperation behind his scarf.

But the wind whisks away his words.

One foot in front of the other. Thirty steps. Forty.

His fingers are prickling from the cold, he shoves his hands in his pockets, tries to wiggle them, notices how the cold is seeping up from the ground and penetrating his winter boots.

A powerful wind blast rushes across the landscape, forcing him to stop. He stands crouched against the wind. Hell no, he thinks, you bloody well can't have me.

He starts walking again, has given up on finding the greenhouse now, but sooner or later a building has to appear, somewhere he can seek shelter, just until the worst of the wind has passed. He moves more quickly. You can't have me, no, you can't.

And then, right in front of him, so close that he almost crashes into it, the wall appears.

He is so relieved that he wants to sing, wall sweet wall; he strokes it with his hands. The safety of a few weather-beaten boards.

He slowly moves along the wall of the house, leaning one shoulder against it at all times, as if he could hold the wall in place with his body.

And finally the door appears. He tears it open, tumbles inside onto the floor, a wet and freezing cold heap of clothing, snow and ice.

In one corner of the greenhouse he makes a nest out of his outdoor garments and a few burlap bags he has found in the storage room. He drifts in and out of sleep as the storm continues to rage outside.

When he wakes, the wind has grown even stronger. It

makes the building shake, something has come loose, he can
hear it banging against the building, but he doesn't know
what it is.

But I'm safe, he thinks, this building is designed to withstand storms.

He pulls out his watch again. It is five to seven.

In the morning?

Or could it be evening?

Then he realises, of course it's morning, he has slept in his
tiny nest all night and now it's a new day.

Thursday, 4 December?

No. Friday, the fifth.

It is the morning of Friday 5 December 2111, and it's time
he got started with his day.

Work, read, try to eat something, while the storm
rages outside.

A deafening uproar. The wind pounds, bangs, hurls objects
through the air, a threat to all living creatures. Like in a war.

It is a war. His own siege.

It lasted for 900 days, the Siege of Leningrad, and one and
a half million human lives were lost.

Although the world-famous art treasures at the Hermitage
Museum had been removed from the museum through
a large-scale operation and hidden in cellars and secret
storerooms, the seeds in Vavilov's vault at Saint Isaac's
Square were left behind. The approaching German troops
knew what the seeds were worth and the seed bank was an
objective behind the invasion. Hitler had even appointed a
designated tactical unit, an SS Sammelkommando, to attend
to the task of gaining control over the seed bank. But this
made no impression on Stalin. Only Vavilov's own men and
women cared about this treasure.

None of his colleagues knew anything about what had happened to Vavilov. The news they received was that he had been taken to an *important meeting* in Moscow. Then silence.

They were without public funding and without a leader. But they kept working all the same. Vavilov's people barricaded themselves inside the freezing, dark building. They worked in shifts, so someone was guarding the treasure at all times, the barrels of seeds, roots, potatoes, rice, beans. There was no food to be found in beleaguered Leningrad. Even the rats were starving. People died in the streets; everything that could be digested was eaten: farm animals, dogs, pigeons and cats. Everything that could be burned was thrown into the stoves: furniture, books, art. But Vavilov's colleagues stood their ground against the cold, the Germans and the desperate residents of the city. They stood their ground against the rats. They stood their ground against their own hunger.

They began standing guard in pairs, to make sure that nobody succumbed to temptation and helped themselves to the treasures in the vault. The temperature dropped to 40 below. They burned all the furniture they could find. The rats grew bolder all the time, running across floors and tables. But Vavilov's people did not give up, even though they were on the road to self-obliteration.

In the summer of 1942 they grew potatoes and cabbage in the cemetery of Saint Isaac's Cathedral, not for food but to replenish the seed collection. The tiny shoots were guarded as if they were their own children. One of Vavilov's men was later asked whether it had been difficult to resist the temptation to eat what they cultivated. 'It was hard to walk. It was unbearably hard to get up in the morning, [even] to move your hands and feet ... but it was not in the least difficult to refrain from eating up the collection. What was at stake was the meaning of life, the meaning of my comrades' lives.'

Not a seed was touched throughout all the months the siege lasted, not a grain of rice, a bean, a kernel of corn, a potato. The botanist Alexander Stchukin died while sitting at his desk. In his hand he held a bag of peanuts.

The world's leading rice authority, Dmitry Ivanov, starved to death surrounded by grains of rice.

The archivist Gleiber died surrounded by Vavilov's field notes.

The oat expert Liliya Rodina also starved to death behind the walls of the vault.

Along with Steheglov.

Kovalesky.

Leontjevsky.

Malygina.

Korzun.

A total of nine of Vavilov's colleagues sacrificed their lives for the seeds.

Tommy puts down his books. He listens to the war raging outside. Of course I can do this, he thinks. I have heat. I have food and drink. I just have to stop feeling sorry for myself.

Then he walks over to his nest, lies down, curls up in a foetal position and falls asleep. There, in his sleep, he fumbles for her, tries to find his way back to her body, but he never reaches her.

Her body, her skin under his hands, imagine that something could be simultaneously so good and so evil. And that just a few minutes, seconds, could change an entire life.

It's irreversible and we must just figure it out, he thought. And when the baby comes, for sure we will manage to do just that. We will love it together. We will have something in common to love. The child will be exactly what we need.

Spring had arrived without his having noticed when it supplanted the winter. An uncommonly rainy, dark and wet spring. He sowed barley, hilled potatoes, picked small, new spring dandelion and goutweed leaves from south-facing slopes, shot barnacle geese and plucked all their feathers before lighting a fire behind the house and grilling them on a spit, to the children's delight.

The three children were doing well. Sometimes he heard them talking about the little one who was on the way, but for them the pregnancy was still too abstract to be real. They were too busy being children themselves. Runa stepped in to create a buffer when conflicts broke out between the brothers, was gentle and conciliatory. Every time an argument threatened to heat up, she instinctively directed their attention to something else through play. They dared to be children, could permit themselves that, as long as they, or at least he, assumed the responsibility of being an adult.

But *am* I an adult, he asked himself. When do you become an adult?

In the books he read, he caught himself searching for answers to these questions.

Runa, Henry and Hilmar viewed him as an adult. Because they took it for granted that he would take care of them. That was why they could be children, because they knew he shouldered the responsibility. Responsibility and care, two sides of the same coin. He was an adult because the children needed him.

He went back to the old house and consulted the books Father had kept on his bedside table: *Living with Teenagers* and *How to Connect with Boys in Puberty*. Father read these books because in his mind it was necessary for him to be a good father. When it came to taking responsibility for them, and doing it in a good way, he was not driven by desire but by necessity. The road between necessity and obligation was a short one. Had father felt obliged to take care of them? Or perhaps he just clung to the knowledge, to the 'good parenting lessons' – which involved all these actions that had virtually become automatic for him: patting a child on the head, showing approval, telling them that he loved them – maybe he clung to this lesson and worked so desperately to fulfil it to the letter, as a means of placating his guilty conscience about not actually being present?

When does one become an adult? What does it mean to become an adult?

To make decisions that affect others.

To make decisions out of consideration for others, more than for oneself.

To protect those weaker than you, act as a wall between the dangers of the world and the children.

But it was more than that.

Responsibility, necessity, protection, a guilty conscience . . .

the answer to his questions lay somewhere in between these words.

Tommy tried: one becomes an adult when one takes responsibility for others out of necessity, and when that necessity is inextricably connected to the guilty conscience one knows will arise if one *doesn't* take responsibility.

Something like that?

A guilty conscience is the same as pain.

But there is some joy there, somewhere or other, the word joy should also be included, and empathy, no, perhaps mutual love.

Henry and Hilmar and their hands in his, how he held them tightly.

That was the opposite of pain.

He protected his brothers by holding onto them tightly, by keeping them here.

The way he also protected the seeds.

And the child on the way.

'I don't dare,' Rakel said. 'I don't dare give birth.'

They were sitting alone in the sitting room. The children had gone to bed.

She leaned forward, placed her hands on the table, opened them, as if asking for his understanding.

'Tommy, I'm afraid,' she said. 'I'm afraid of giving birth up here alone, I'm afraid of having a child.'

Then she stood up and began pacing around the room.

'Look at me, Tommy, look how narrow I am over the hips. It's no good, it's not possible. Please, Tommy. I won't manage it, you won't be able to help me. We have to get out of here!'

She looked at him and her gaze was beseeching. Or she tried to make it beseeching, he wasn't certain.

Tommy didn't say another word, and also got to his feet. He often ended their conversations by going to bed. Rakel would sometimes call for him and it happened that he halted on the stairway, listening to the pleading in her voice, acknowledged the desire to go back to her, put his arms around her, tell her it would be fine, she just had to trust him, she just had to trust them. But he never did because he knew that she wouldn't listen to him anyway. And that she didn't want his arms around her.

And the next morning, when the children got up, he was able to tuck all her words away in the small nooks and crannies of his brain. He got started with the day's work, as if the argument of the day before had never taken place and the only thing he told himself, to the extent that he even allowed his thoughts to gravitate towards the brain's nooks and crannies, was that yesterday's exchange of fearful thoughts and harsh comments would be the last, that this evening would be nice, that now Rakel had stopped worrying, had begun looking forward to the new life on the way, both the child and the life they would have together.

What had Rakel been up to this spring, while he was sowing barley, hilling potatoes, shooting barnacle geese and taking care of the children? While the rain poured down for weeks on end? He had tried to picture her many times, tried to understand the choices she made, understand their source. As if understanding her would change something.

She had started showing, a clear, curved swell where her body had once been flat and hard. And she had started feeling the baby's first kicks. It felt like a seal, she said to him, a baby seal sliding around inside there, slippery and round. Sometimes she felt what must have been a foot or a shoulder, but she was unable to think about it in terms of body parts on a human being, a child. For her it was at all times an animal.

The arguments in the evenings grew worse. She followed him, from room to room, told him that she dreamed about a slaughter scene on the ice, red drops on the snow, her uterus tearing as the life inside pressed its way out, slid out of her, through a river of blood. Tommy picked up the animal, blood-covered, slimy, and then he gave it to her. The animal's round head and black button eyes staring into space resembled a seal. It howled the way an animal does – there was nothing human about that howl – and squirmed in her hands, was so shiny and slick, trying to escape her grasp at all times, drop onto the ice, injure itself, and she was unable to hold onto it, didn't even know whether she *wanted* to hold it.

She had the dream again and again and soon she was woken by it every night.

He no longer saw her crying. Perhaps she believed that her tears had no effect on him. But he knows that she went to the library. Maybe she searched for a long time before finding the book she needed. Of all the books in there, this one had to be the driest, the most boring, but she forced herself to read it all the same.

He can picture her reading, maybe several nights in a row. Then she got up, while the household was fast asleep, got dressed quietly and tiptoed outside before he could catch her.

It was light when she walked down the road beside Adventfjorden, it was soon light around the clock, as if nature had decided that they should no longer be allowed to hide. Rakel followed the road along the fjord to Mine 3. There she took a left in the direction of the vault. Maybe she was thinking of him, Tommy, as she passed it. The seed custodian. He had been so proud of the title, but then the key had been missing. It was pretty comical, actually.

She kept walking, all the way up to Platåberget Mountain. For once she was perhaps out of breath by the time she reached the top, her nose stuffed up. It was the baby in her belly that made her like this, she said, slower, full of mucus at all times. Her entire body sort of moist, her eyes shinier.

Why had she made love to him? Such an old-fashioned expression, 'to make love to someone'. They were his words, she would never have used such an expression. Hadn't she wanted to become pregnant? No, her desperation indicated that the pregnancy had come as just as much a surprise to her as it had to him. Because she could? Because he wanted it? Because she wanted to exercise her power over him? Punish him for never listening to her?

Because he always met her with a torrent of words, knew more, mastered more, was more articulate? Or because she felt love for him?

'Mayday, mayday, mayday. Five children alone. Seventy-eight degrees north, fifteen east. We need help. Can someone hear us? Please come. Seventy-eight degrees north, fifteen east. Mayday, mayday, mayday.'

He has understood that a good deal of time passed before they answered, that initially the only response was a crackling vacuum.

'Mayday, mayday, mayday. Five children alone. Seventy-eight degrees north, fifteen east.'

Probably she sat at the big table in the control room. The chair was rotten and mouse-eaten, the room every bit as cold as the day outside, because the air flooded through the broken windows.

A small glitch in the crackling? Wasn't there a small irregularity there, a skip or a brief pause, maybe?

'Mayday, mayday, mayday.'

Always three times. She had most likely read that in the book she had left behind, three times, so the words would not get lost along the way.

Her voice must have sounded so small out there as she repeated the same sentences again and again. Rakel's strong voice no more than a thin, invisible thread sent out to the rest of the world. And the words formed a kind of rhythm, a song, which she performed for an audience who wasn't listening; no, to an empty auditorium.

A frail girl's body with a seal writhing in her tummy, a voice sent out into the world, long, invisible threads being spun out of her, whirling without direction upwards and away, in the hope that someone would receive them, catch hold of them on the other end.

Weeks must have passed, when the only thing she encountered every time she switched on the radio was the crackling vacuum: sounds that weren't sounds, only something flowing, inaudible, which entered the room and disappeared, sounds that weren't really noticeable until she turned off the radio again, and the contrast to the actual silence became evident. But Rakel did not lose heart. He believes she sat by the radio for hours, imbibing the white noise as if it were an intoxicating beverage. The electric sound of nothing was better than nothing, because the sound carried with it the expectation that at any moment something could break through, manifest itself out of thin air, a voice, another human being, proof that somebody else was out there.

He knows now that she went up there every morning. She never told him what she was up to. But he noticed that she no longer went fishing, no longer went hunting.

It must have been like scuba diving. The sound filtered out all other sounds and hanging over it was perhaps the thought he believes she feared most of all: that the five children were alone, that there was nobody else out there, on the other end, that there were no other human beings in the world.

Then after many days with nothing to show for her efforts, she returned to the library and filled her bag with dictionaries. He found them later, in stacks by the radio. German, French, Spanish and, of course, Chinese, which she had never bothered to learn in school. For the first time in her life she was interested in languages and grammar. Because the words could save her, save her from herself, from Tommy, from the animal in her tummy.

He remembers that she started coming home late in the

evening. She lived up there now, repeating her long songs in different languages, with a pronunciation she probably didn't trust.

Her hope was a grain of sand in an hourglass. Every day a few grains ran from the top down into the bottom and soon there were no more grains of sand left. Only the emptiness existed, the same vacuum she heard over the radio.

And her desperation spread into the vacuum's narrow, empty container.

He could see it on her. She no longer met his gaze. Didn't wash, ate little. The seal flailed with increasing restlessness inside her, she told him, sometimes her whole abdomen was stretched taut, became a mountain of flint and the pain made her gasp.

'What is it?' he asked.

'It's hurting me,' she said. 'It has to stop, I want it to stop.' She placed her hands on her tummy in a movement that was almost aggressive, as if she wanted to strike the baby inside. And she told him that the animal kicked her everywhere, her ribs, her bladder. Soon it was so strong that it would cause her pain.

She was grey in the face. Even though her tummy was expanding, it was as if she was shrinking.

He wished he had asked her what was happening. He believed that it was all due to the baby, that there wasn't anything he could do.

And then, on one of these bleak sun-filled nights when she was sitting with the volume on the radio turned all the way up, she must have understood what she needed to do. That if there was anyone out there, they would never respond, because there was no *reason* for them to respond. Maybe they had been listening all along, both to Rakel and many others. She was definitely not the only person sitting in some deserted spot somewhere on earth and calling for help; no, probably she was far from the only one, there were certainly thousands of them. Throughout the entire history of the world, children in distress have called for help, in all kinds of ways, but they have seldom been heard. The difference between Rakel and all the others was that she had a bargaining chip.

'Mayday, mayday, mayday! Five children alone. Seventy-eight degrees north, fifteen east. We need help. Can someone hear us? Please come. Seventy-eight degrees north, fifteen east. We have the Global Seed Vault. Mayday, mayday, mayday. Seventy-eight degrees north, fifteen east. The Global Seed Vault.'

And then, finally, she received a response. A voice sliced through the buzzing like a sharp knife.

'Hello? Hello?!'

'*Nǐ hǎo!*'

'Yes, yes!' she said, her arms flailing as she searched for the sheet of paper containing the translations, even though she had long since learned them by heart. '*Wǔ gé háizi yīgè rén.* Five children alone. We need help!'

'Yes, we hear you,' the voice on the other end said. 'You have the Global Seed Vault?'

'Right,' Rakel said. 'Yes!'

'Stay there,' they said. 'We are coming. Please just stay there.'

Tommy sat on the ground in Skjæringa, where he could feel the warmth of the sun on his face. Then he let himself slump backwards, and lay prone for a while, his eyes closed. The sunlight was so strong that it shone through his eyelids.

He turned over onto his side and lay there with one cheek against the grass and heather, against sub-arctic buttercups and moss silene. He could feel the warmth from the sunlight stored in the earth beneath him and the support the soft, cushiony ground provided for his body.

Then he opened one eye, just one. The world he saw was flat. In this position, he lost the ability to judge distance and dimensions. He squinted at the small plants on the ground and when he lay like this, just like this, the plants looked like trees. Like pine, birch and ash, trees that stretched up to the sky. We also have trees, he thought. I must show my brothers this, our little forest. And then, a new thought, I must show the baby this; one day I will bring the child that has not yet been born out here and show him or her this forest.

Suddenly the warmth from the sun disappeared, a shadow fell over him. He opened his eyes and was unable to see her face, but he could hear from her voice that she was smiling.

'They're coming,' Rakel said. 'I've made contact.'

He sat up. 'What?'

'They're coming to rescue us. They will soon be on their way.'

'Who?'

'They didn't hesitate,' she continued. 'They responded immediately, once they understood what we have to offer.'

'What do you mean? Rakel, what have you done?'

There was no point in screaming at her. The rage he launched at her like hard lumps of ice melted upon contact with the heat of her enthusiasm. He tried, for a whole day, an evening. But she accepted his anger with a smile, with restrained small talk, with plans. He wanted to run to Svalsat, instruct them to turn around, but she made him understand that this could not be undone. Now that she had told them about the seeds, they would come, no matter what he said.

The next morning he ran up to the vault and sat down on the clean, ice-cold floor with his back against the innermost shelf, as frustration caused his stomach to turn over.

She had promised them the seeds, as if they were ordinary wares at a market, as if this inheritance were hers to barter with as she pleased in a cheap transaction.

The people who were coming here, who were on their way, they wanted nothing but to save themselves and their descendants. He knew that they would use the seeds to destroy the natural wilds. They gave the little love precedence over the great love, they would consume the contents of the vault, squander the treasure. These were the kinds of people who had destroyed the earth and these were the kinds of people the population of Svalbard had hidden from up here in the north. And now she had called them. She had betrayed their plans, Henry, Hilmar and Runa, she had betrayed everything Longyearbyen stood for. She had betrayed the unborn child and she had betrayed him.

Tommy jumped to his feet. He started walking beside the long rows of seeds. At the top of the closest shelf was a crudely constructed wood crate labelled Afghanistan; below it, Albania, Algeria, Angola and Argentina.

Eight crates, one on top of the other, or fewer, if the crates were bigger. He ran his hand lightly over Belgium, Belize and Benin. Patted El Salvador, Eritrea and Estonia.

Then he started moving more quickly.

Fiji, Finland, France.

He tripped over his own feet.

Jamaica, Japan.

He almost fell but recovered his balance just in time.

Namibia, New Zealand, Nigeria.

Nation states that no longer existed. The names no longer referred to land territories and border posts, to citizenships and each individual's possession of a nationality. They were just words.

But the seeds existed. The different countries' unique botanic character had not been lost.

A million species.

Vietnam, Yemen, Zambia, Zimbabwe.

Tommy stopped beside the final, innermost shelf and took down the top crate. Venezuela. The label on the crate specified that it contained 183 different species.

He took off his mittens, hands shaking. Inside the crate was a plastic container. He knew that he shouldn't, that he risked damaging the seeds, but he just had to see, had to check one container, to confirm with certainty that everything was as it should be, that nobody had taken the seeds out, stolen or destroyed them.

And they were there. Large, shiny, sealed plastic bags, containing many small seed bags of paper. All the bags were labelled with the name of the seeds, in both Latin and Spanish. When he shook the bag, he heard a light rattling sound. He squeezed the plastic gently and could feel the shapes of the tiny plant families inside.

A genetic diversity, vast riches, an abundance of new life. With these seeds, everything was possible for the human race, with this treasure it could be reborn, the human species could increase, proliferate anew. It will be possible to sow grain everywhere – wheat, oats, corn, specialised species that were adapted to even the smallest, most remote corner of the earth. Genetic opportunities for wholly new species, new adaptations. A rousing farewell to the generalists. And a unique form of security for human beings.

No, because the people who were alive today were the descendants of those who had destroyed everything.

This was the human race's vault, its agri-food. The agri-cultural revolution was the beginning, and the vault was the conclusion. And after the conclusion would come a new beginning, which the seeds would provide for them. The survival of the human race – that was all this vault was about.

They can't have them, he thought. The foreigners will make their way here, they will invade us, but they can't have the seeds. I will take care of you, I will watch over you for the rest of my life. Like Grandmother.

Then he walked out through the first door, closed it behind him and hurried down the long corridor. A shivering chill surged through him. The closer to the exit he came, the more his breathing normalised.

He closed the door behind him and stood gazing around him as the warmth returned to his body. His eyes swept over Hotellneset and the old warehouses.

Then he turned around, looked towards the mountain-side. Deep inside there, it was still cold. Not eighteen below, but cold enough for the seeds to survive. The deeper inside the mountain, the greater the security for the seeds. And Platåberget Mountain was riddled with tunnels, like a rotten old tree trunk, full of hiding places.

He packed a knapsack with tools and broke into the old building adjacent to Mine 3.

Some broken helmets were still lying on racks on the shelves. A pair of worn old overalls dangled from a nail on the wall. In a corner beside a table was a decrepit kitchen fixture. On the walls hung faded photographs and framed newspaper articles, the words of which were impossible to read.

He walked through the room and entered the old workshop halls. Svalbard's inhabitants had helped themselves to many things from here over the years, they had taken machine parts, tools and scrap metal and for the most part the rooms were empty.

From there he followed the rails towards the entrance to the mine itself. The floor was stained black from coal dust. He knew that the mine extended several kilometres into the mountain. It followed the coal that once had been excavated from here.

He picked up the sledgehammer he'd brought along and pounded the concrete that had been used to block the opening to the mine. A large unbroken surface. And behind it, he knew there was a plug of ice, created by meltwater that ran in during the summer and hit the permafrost still found deep inside there. It would take him weeks to break through.

Besides ... wasn't the easily accessible Mine 3 one of the first places they would look?

He wandered around the old building for a while. Everywhere he could see remnants of coal, of the forests that had once been here. The trees were still here, in another form.

If he closed his eyes, he could hear the music of the leaves, the birds twittering, the insects buzzing. A lush forest, perhaps near a coastline, when Svalbard once lay somewhere else on the globe: animals and insects, marshes, swamps and forests. Tall, swaying trees, hardwood forests, maple, beech, horse chestnut and the ground covered with horsetail plants. All these living things lived through photosynthesis, relied on the sun. He opened his eyes, bent down, picked up a small lump, took off his mitten and touched it. It was dead, dry and black, but nonetheless it stored the energy of the sun. There was nothing about it reminiscent of a tree. He dropped the lump of coal, it fell soundlessly, landing beside the other coal fragments on the floor, every one of them, equally uniform and dead. I dream about a forest, he thought, but all I find are pieces of coal in a workshop.

The smell suddenly made him queasy; the coal dust stuck to his tongue.

He turned around and walked towards the exit. First through the workshop halls, then the breakrooms and a changing room.

In the breakroom something caught his eye.

He stopped by a wall. Between the photographs and newspaper clippings hung a framed image that was dusty and faded. A vague memory emerged. He had been in here before, with Grandmother; she had stood and pointed at this picture in particular. He walked over and wiped the dust off the glass. It was still possible to discern the faded map underneath.

It was a map of the mine, showing both the tunnel that continued for several kilometres into the mountain and the different fields in the seam of coal, which resembled cake filling that ran through all of Platåberget Mountain. From the main tunnel that went from the entrance and the adjacent building, he counted a total of ten ventilation shafts. Only two of them continued all the way to Bjørndalen. They were used both for ventilation and as escape routes for the miners, a narrow path into the light, out of the darkness where they often worked lying on their stomachs for many hours at a time.

Tommy remembered that Grandmother had pointed at the tunnels.

'Look how far they go,' she had said. 'Like a spider's web into the mountain, and all the way out again on the other side. You can enter here and walk with a roof over your head all the way to Bjørndalen.'

The way she said it made him think of the tunnels as something magical, like portals into another world. Tommy was maybe ten at the time and had devoured all the fairy tales that were to be found in the library. Then he had a quivering sensation that if *he* were allowed to walk through the entire mine system, he wouldn't come out the other side and just be in Bjørndalen; no, the tunnels would take him to a place that resembled Narnia. In a flash he pictured centaurs and elves, dancing in the light of a sunset, before this image was replaced by another that was even more beautiful. He imagined that the tunnels would lead him to a secret forest. A forest that was his alone, where warm sunlight filtered through shimmering leaves, where there was birdsong and the sound of insects buzzing, of leaves rustling softly against each other, the gentle movements of branches, of trees dancing.

On the way back from the mine he eagerly shared his fantasy with Grandmother. She didn't say much, but he could see that she was smiling.

*

With the map in his hand and knapsack on his back, Tommy trotted down the well-trodden path where there had once been a road winding around Vestpynten and the ruins of the old lighthouse. At all times he had his eyes on the mountain to his left, his gaze searching.

But all he saw from a distance was stone and soft, green vegetation. He swerved off the path and moved closer to the mountain.

Tommy knew that he had seen the two entrances before, though he had never really given them much thought. There were many such signs of the mining that had been done on the island, sealed ventilation shafts and openings marked with rotting logs, just as grey as the surrounding stone and blending almost seamlessly into the landscape.

He found one of them first and when he knew what he was looking for, he soon discovered the other. They lay side by side in the mountainside, their location determined by the coal seam in the mountain.

He quickly climbed up to the first, slipping on stones and loose soil, his foot getting caught once, whereupon he stumbled but did not slow down. By the time he arrived he was breathing hard. A wooden panel covered the entrance. He pulled the crowbar out of his pack and attacked the panel. The rotten boards creaked but the panel was nailed solidly in place. He tried coaxing the hammer under some of the rusted nails and then once again put all his strength into the crowbar.

This time he managed to loosen the panel.

Behind it he saw a wall of stone, gravel and ice.

He hurried to the next opening, working more quickly this time, as he tried first to loosen some nails with the hammer before leaning all his weight onto the crowbar.

But here as well he met a wall of frozen water and loose sediment behind the boards.

He threw down the crowbar and sat down beside the entrance to the tunnel, cursing to himself.

Then he took a sip of water from the bottle, opened his backpack and studied the map from the picture frame again. Only the outside building and these two tunnels provided access to the mines. If he was going to get inside, he would have to go through the ice.

He climbed to his feet again and walked back to the other entrance. There he took out the sledgehammer.

The ice sprayed in all directions when he hit the wall in front of him, small fragments hitting him like hail in the face.

He raised the hammer and hit the ice wall. Again and again.

And then he could feel the ice wall giving way, that it wasn't as thick as he had first believed.

He was able to create a hole and kept hammering around the edge of it. He put all of his eighteen-year-old force into each blow; his arms and back were burning, but he scarcely noticed. Because the hole was growing.

And then it was large enough for him to enter.

His hands were shaking as he pulled the torch out of his pack, switched it on and beamed the flickering light on the black walls of rock.

The tunnel was open before him.

He started walking.

The reflection of daylight from outside quickly disappeared. The beam from his torch was diminished to a fragile sword of light braving the darkness inside.

The walls were black with coal but the darkness also came

from the mountain itself, from the tons of rock above him, beneath and around him, huge jaws that swallowed him.

It became gradually colder, as he entered the permafrost, his breath forming clouds of frost in the air, and with every step he took, he walked into this cloud, advancing towards the cold and safety.

In the days the followed, it was during the nights that he lived.

As soon as he was sure that the others were asleep, he got out of bed. Outside the old kennel by Isdammen reservoir, he found a cart with wheels, the same kind previously used to transport corpses. He adapted the harness and fastened some old straps over his shoulders, turning himself into a draught animal.

Then all the many trips commenced. Up the hill to the Seed Vault with an empty cart, in through the door, down the tunnel. Stack the boxes on the cart. He was able to bring six to eight each time, mostly, they weren't heavy: the contents weighed almost nothing. The trip down from the vault was easy, even though the road was muddy and in several places there had been landslides.

It seemed that the rain would never cease. Torrents of water rushed down the mountainside, seeping into the loose sediment. He stopped from time to time, took in the sight of the mountainsides, feared another landslide, and then he continued, walking even faster.

The road out to Bjørndalen and the tunnel was the most taxing and the most boring. But he didn't notice it. All through the sunlit and rainy summer night he pulled the cart behind him, stopping only once in a while to take a sip of water. Otherwise he was constantly in movement.

He worked alphabetically, carrying the crates deep inside

the tunnel, where he was certain the cold temperature was stable, and created stacks four crates high.

Time worked in his favour. It took weeks for the foreign visitors to plan their expedition, Rakel told him, such a long time in fact that in the end he started to wonder whether it was all a lie. But then one day she declared that they were actually on their way. They would travel through Russia and then north by car, and the final stretch from Archangel by ship. It was a long, arduous journey, but she told him that they were well equipped and prepared, that they would manage this.

With the exception of the times he sought her out to ask for news about the visitors, Tommy tried to avoid Rakel. The disappointment he felt every time he saw her was uncontrollable. He didn't know what to do with it, where he should put his hands.

The only thing he wanted from her, the only thing that perhaps would have helped, was an apology. But Rakel was apparently a person who never said sorry. He doubted if she knew that the word existed.

Neither did it appear to occur to her that she owed him at the very least a show of remorse. He'd never before seen her so excited, so happy. Rakel and the three children made it their mission to pack thoroughly. Henry filled up his large toy sack, while Hilmar's selection was more random: a pair of shoes, some books, a battered deck of cards. Rakel and Runa walked through Longyearbyen collecting clothing, Runa mostly for herself, the most beautiful garments she could find in her size. Rakel searched for baby clothes. Every evening she would deposit the day's take on a table in the sitting room. Tiny threadbare garments of cotton and wool. She sorted the clothing into piles, according to size, wanting to make sure that she had enough for the first year of the baby's life.

He listened for the sound of their footsteps, their voices and laughter – because she often laughed, now that she believed help was on the way. When he could hear that she was in her room, he hurried down to get something to eat. When she was in the bathroom, he stayed far away from the hallway, afraid of running into her. If that were to happen, if he should meet her in the hallway or downstairs in the kitchen, or on the way in or out of the loo, then he didn't know what he might do. He often thought about how he was stronger than her, fantasised about shaking, hitting, throwing her against the wall, screaming. But then he would catch himself and shut down such thoughts immediately, because her belly was there, his child.

Henry and Hilmar understood that something was wrong but they were unable to grasp what it was.

'Why do you stay in here so much?' Henry asked one evening. 'Why do you sleep all the time?'

He had just entered the house, had not yet taken off his outdoor garments, smelled of wind and rain and mud and was full of excitement over a dam he and Runa had built on the lower side of the house.

Tommy unzipped his rain jacket and took hold of one of the sleeves as he twisted out of it, spraying drops of water around him.

'I've always liked being in my room,' Tommy said. 'And maybe I'm not feeling very well these days.'

A sudden fear appeared on Henry's face. 'Are you sick too?'

'No, absolutely not. I'm just tired.'

Henry released a sigh of relief.

'What do you think it will be like, when the foreigners arrive?' he asked.

'I don't know,' Tommy said.

'Aren't you looking forward to it, like Rakel is?'

'It will be exciting.'

'But you haven't packed anything.'

'I haven't had time. Be quiet now. I'm so tired.'

'Yes. But ...'

'Shhh ...'

They sat down on the bed together. Henry placed the pillow against the wall and leaned against it. Tommy pulled him close. Henry curled up snugly in the crook of his big brother's arm. Tommy could feel the warmth of his body through his jumper, and hear his agitated, rapid breathing.

I want to be you, Tommy thought. I want to be little again, no decisions weighing on my shoulders. Be led away submissively, like a stick in a brook, allow myself to be carried downstream by strong water currents.

He pulled his little brother even closer to him and absorbed his brother's tranquillity. For a while they just sat like this in silence, breathing in unison, the two of them just children, as close to being one and the same person as brothers can be.

The evening Rakel told them that the ship had cast off from the harbour in Archangel, he moved the few remaining crates out of the vault. The beam of his head torch swept across the walls of the tunnel for the very last time. Then he directed the beam towards the exit and started walking. A chill shivered through his body and, as he neared the exit and warmth, he began breathing more easily.

The summer sky was overcast with heavy rainclouds. He heard thunder above the mountains.

He stood for a moment looking up at the sky, before

hastening to nail as best he could the partially demolished boards over the entrances to the tunnels to close them up again.

He saved a single piece of wood, which he drove into the ground like a post a few metres below the tunnel, packing stones and gravel around the base for added support. When he finished, the first raindrops fell on him. For the first time in all these weeks, he bid the rain welcome, turned his face towards the sky and accepted it.

Tao

The children have started school. Tao accompanies them every morning. They walk ahead of her on the road, seldom saying anything, neither to her nor to one another. Henry holds his big brother's hand. Hilmar drags him along, at all times obliged to adapt his strides to Henry's shorter steps. Sometimes Runa turns and smiles at Tao, politely and wanly. Her smile never lasts long.

While Tao is with the children, watching them, sometimes an unusual feeling comes over her. She gets angry. When she sees the children eating every single grain of rice as if it were the last on earth, when she pricks herself with the needle as she is patching a pair of trousers, when she glues Hilmar's shoe for the third time, when they must stop and seek shelter on the way home, because the street is flooded by a rainstorm so powerful that it washes away crops and fills cellars with water, when she stands with the children, drenched to the skin, her teeth chattering and doesn't know how they are going to make it home – she gets angry and she doesn't know with whom.

Tao expects that Li Chiara will contact her and put her to work again but hears nothing. At first, she is impatient, surprised by the silence. But eventually she stops waiting.

They manage to fill the days. There is school, there are meal-times and homework. But the evenings are long. Often she finds Henry in front of the radio in the kitchen. He listens in vain to the humming. And sometimes he wakes up in the middle of the night when she is trying to call Tommy. He stands beside her, jiggling his legs, his whole body full of restlessness. The first time she asked him to stand still, but then he started picking at the worn wood veneer surface of the kitchen table, until he got a splinter in his index finger and started to bleed.

Tommy never responds. She doesn't know if he understands what he has done to his brothers.

He doesn't see them. And neither did he see them during the days they waited for him and Rakel, during the days they searched for them in vain.

Several times she found one of the brothers in Tommy's empty bedroom. They were digging through his things, as if the objects could give them answers, or they were just standing there without moving, and clinging to a garment belonging to their big brother.

On the last night she stayed in the house until they fell asleep. She tiptoed upstairs and peeked through the door into their room. They were sleeping close together. Hilmar lay with his back to the door, and his arms around Henry, who had kicked the duvet off his body. She ventured over to the bed and laid it over him again.

Afterwards she went downstairs to the sitting room, sat down by the big window and looked out, feeling how infinitely tired she was, in her body, in her mind. They had searched for Rakel and Tommy for four days and they had continued to search for the seeds. She and Mei-Ling went out to Mine 3 the morning after Tommy disappeared, but all they found there was a wall of concrete and ice. Mei-Ling attacked the one wall with a sledgehammer, but quickly understood that it was futile. Afterwards they had walked around aimlessly, glancing at the huge mountains as if they might move at any moment, feeling small and defenceless in this daunting landscape, not daring to venture too far outside of Longyearbyen, or too far from the coast, fearful of what they might encounter.

Tao was not accustomed to moving in this way, through such brutal nature. It settled into her body; her joints and muscles ached. She leaned back in the chair, noticing that in this house for once she felt safe and warm and for a brief moment allowed her eyes to fall shut.

The next morning they awoke to frost. When Tao came out on deck after breakfast, she saw Mei-Ling standing and staring at the snow-covered mountains.

'I don't dare wait any longer,' she said without turning to face Tao. 'I said we were going to stay here for two days. Ten days have passed now. I have a responsibility to bring the crew home. And the children.'

'But something has happened to Rakel and Tommy,' Tao said. 'We must keep searching.'

A snowflake fluttered through the air.

The captain swore. 'You see.'

Several light flakes floated towards them, landing on their outstretched palms.

'Rakel and Tommy have abandoned their little siblings,' Mei-Ling said. 'They've run away, taken off – it's completely obvious – and left them with us. We have no other choice. We are leaving tomorrow.'

'And the seeds?' Tao said.

'There never were any seeds.'

*

They rowed to shore at dawn in two boats. The first mate and a sailor stayed behind on the beach, while Tao and Mei-Ling went up to the house to get the children. There they were invited to come inside.

'We aren't quite ready yet. But I can heat up some broth?' Runa said. 'You can have a cup while we finish packing.'

'Actually we just came to help you carry your things,' Mei-Ling said impatiently.

But Tao elbowed her gently in her side. 'Let them finish at their own pace,' she whispered. 'A few minutes more or less won't make much difference.'

Runa opened the door and showed them into the kitchen.

'Sit down here while I prepare the broth,' Runa said to them and indicated some simple wooden chairs by the kitchen table.

Then she discovered that there were some food stains on the table and she quickly wiped them off.

'Sorry, apparently there's a lot here that's not ready yet.'

'Ready? For what?' Mei-Ling asked.

'I don't know . . . I just think it should be tidy here when we leave. Tommy always makes sure that it's tidy.'

'But he's not here any more,' Mei-Ling said.

'If he comes back, he will be very happy to see that you have tidied up,' Tao hastened to say.

The aroma of the broth spread through the room as Runa heated it. Steam rose from the saucepan. She took out two cups from a cupboard but replaced them with two others when she discovered that they were chipped. Then she poured the broth into the cups, but her hand shook and she spilled it.

'Sorry, pardon me, I really didn't mean to do that.'

They drank in silence. Tao could hear the two boys

rummaging through the other rooms, discussing and moving things around, zipping and unzipping a bag.

Mei-Ling puffed at the broth impatiently. She took a sip and clearly burned her tongue because she cursed softly.

Then Henry came in, carrying an overloaded backpack. He eased it off his shoulder and put it down on the floor in front of them.

'Toys,' he said, and opened it so they could see.

'I don't know whether you can take all of that with you,' Mei-Ling said.

'Sure he can,' Tao said. 'No problem.'

'I hope you've brought along some clothing, too,' Mei-Ling said to Runa.

She nodded. 'We've packed the best we could but we didn't know what we should bring with us.'

'What you need,' Mei-Ling said and got to her feet.

'Yes,' Runa said. 'Rakel helped me pack and I think Tommy helped the boys ... but we didn't have a chance to finish. So we tried to pack the rest by ourselves.'

'Whatever you haven't brought we will take care of when we arrive,' Mei-Ling said, although she knew that there was a clothing shortage at home. 'Just show me what needs to be carried, and we'll get going.'

The children didn't say a word as they were putting on their coats, nor as they pulled on their enormous backpacks.

Then the children walked out and closed the front door for the last time. Once outside they didn't move. Henry, Hilmar and Runa tilted their heads upward simultaneously to look at the first floor, as if they expected to see Tommy or Rakel appear in one of the windows.

'I don't mean to nag,' Mei-Ling said, 'but we actually have to go now.'

The children walked in front of Tao and Mei-Ling on the road leading down to the beach. The morning sun shone on the three figures; Henry's tangled hair turned golden in the light. They walked with short steps beneath the weight of their heavy loads, but steadily, almost sleepwalking and without protest.

Once Henry turned around and looked back at the house again. Then his eyes slid across the mountain and the valley behind them, until falling to rest on Tao.

'Tommy?' he asked.

She shook her head in reply.

Only when they had come down onto the beach where Shun and the first mate were waiting by the two boats, only when the baggage was loaded on board, did it seem as if the children came to and really understood what was happening.

The brothers stood close together on the black sand, Runa a metre away from them. None of them moved towards the boats, none of them moved at all.

And then, without warning, Hilmar began to cry.

He wailed while he repeated his big brother's name, Tommy, Tommy ...

Henry stood beside him. Then he slipped his hand into Hilmar's and leaned his face against his jacket. Tao could hear woeful, pent-up sobs.

Runa dropped her backpack onto the ground with a sudden movement and threw her arms around both the boys. The three of them stood huddled together, their backs shaking.

Tao looked at the others. Neither Mei-Ling, Shun nor the first mate made any sign of moving. They looked at one another in bewilderment.

Hilmar wiped his face with the sleeve of his jacket, trying

to pull himself together, but the tears kept running down his face. 'Tommy has to come with us.' And then he sobbed in despair. 'I thought he would come.'

Mei-Ling looked at Tao and whispered, 'What should we do?'

Tao walked over to the children and laid a hand on Runa's shoulder. She shook her gently, in part to comfort her, in part to encourage her. Runa released Hilmar, looked up at Tao and nodded.

'Yes . . .' was all she said. 'I'm coming now.'

But the boys stayed where they were, Henry with his face hidden in his big brother's jacket.

'Hilmar?' Tao said.

He didn't reply, simply bent down towards Henry's head, burying his face in his hair.

Mei-Ling, Shun and the first mate were still standing stiffly behind them. Shun had tears in his eyes and Tao registered a wave of irritation over their passivity.

'Hilmar? Henry?' she said softly.

Then Hilmar straightened up and nodded. 'Yes, we're ready.'

Runa had already begun walking towards the boat and Hilmar made an effort to extricate himself from Henry's arms so he could move towards the water, but his little brother held him tightly and sobbed.

Hilmar carefully wormed out of his grasp and squatted down facing Henry. He dried his tears and spoke calmly.

Henry cried and cried. His skinny body trembled.

'Tommy,' he sobbed. 'I want him to come with us. He has to come with us.'

But Hilmar continued speaking to him patiently. It was as if he'd forgotten his own tears.

Finally, he managed to coax his little brother to walk to the water's edge and helped him on board. The tears continued to stream down Henry's cheeks, but Hilmar was completely calm. He put on the life vest the first mate handed him and paid close attention as he showed him how to fasten the belt. Then he helped his little brother with his vest.

Nobody said a word when Mei-Ling shoved the boat off the shore.

The children sat up straight with their faces turned towards Longyearbyen as the boat slowly glided through the water.

Tommy

Tommy has never believed in anything or anyone. Life is just the body, cells, nerve signals and when the body is gone, there is no longer any life.

The human body is the result of evolution. Evolution's will is the only force that exists, nothing else controls us. There is nobody who sees us, who has control, who monitors us or sends us signals. By watching and observing nature, its changes and development, we can experience and draw conclusions about our actions. Nature has no opinion, nature doesn't explain, nature doesn't judge, nature just is.

As long as nobody knows about it, there is nobody to judge him for what happened to Rakel.

He is lying on the floor in his nest, doesn't know for how long he has been lying there like this, while his thoughts leap about like wild reindeer running amok.

Rakel's face as the ground crumbled beneath her feet.

The howling from the yellow house.

Grandmother moaning.

All the dead bodies.

The boat disappearing out on the fjord with his brothers on board.

Then he sits up. You have to get your act together, Tommy,

shape up, it's a matter of structure, you can do this, you just have to stick to the time schedule.

He pulls back the sleeve of his jumper and looks at his watch. Twenty to three.

He lifts the watch to his ear and listens.

It's silent.

He shakes his wrist. Come on!

But the second hand remains motionless.

The watch slips through his fingers as he tries winding it. It doesn't want to work; the watch will not obey.

Finally he throws the watch down on the hard floor. He hears the glass shatter.

Then he collapses into the nest again.

Don't think, be soft, limp, pull the darkness over you.

And there, deep inside the bottomlessness of sleep, there is someone puttering around him. First, he hears the faint clicking of knitting needles, then he feels the warm light from the fireplace on his cheeks, then he hears a basin being filled with water, he inhales the scent of something familiar, something clean, and then he feels the wet, warm washcloth against his face.

Mum, he whispers.

Yes, I'm here, little one. I'm here.

He wants to hold her, feel the washcloth against his face, the cool hands stroking his forehead, but sleep is a traitor, it abandons him and, when he wakes, she is gone. Only a faint scent lingers, an echo, a feeling in his hands, as if he were holding something that slips through his fingers.

He gets to his feet. His legs are trembling, but he forces himself to stand, to walk, to work. This is his biosphere, he says to himself, the storm can rage for as long as it wants, he needs nothing but this room, the greenhouse, in here he can survive for hundreds of lives.

But the spade keeps slipping out of his hands. He drops the pail on the floor, spills soil, wastes seeds because his fingers won't obey him.

And then Grandmother's voice is there, he can distinguish the echo of it from the roaring of the storm, it increases in volume, until it is as clear as it would be if it had been real.

Biosphere 2 didn't work out so well, Grandmother says. You know that very well. Don't you remember what I said?

Shut up, Grandmother.

There's no such thing as an island.

Yes, he insists, there *is* an island, and we were doing just fine on our island. And if only the others had stayed, the five of us could trust each other. But the outside world . . .

Honestly, you know nothing about the outside world, Tommy, you were raised in the most protected society imaginable, you know nothing about the world, about man's true nature. And if you don't remember what happened to Biosphere 2, I will tell you about it.

I don't give a damn about Biosphere 2!

Be quiet, Tommy, and listen to your grandmother,

I don't want you to tell me, Grandmother, I have read everything!

Yes, he has known it all along, how the story of Biosphere 2 ended.

On 26 September 1991, the eight inhabitants entered the bubble. They had no user's manual to explain how they should live in this new world, but they were proficient. Among them there was a botanist, a marine biologist, a general practitioner and a physicist. They were going to produce all the food they ate, and slaughter and process farm animals. In order to ensure that they would have enough food, they adhered to a strict diet – 1,800 calories a day. Eventually, as they produced more, they increased this to 2,200. It was the doctor among them, Roy Walford, who set up the diet and decided how much they could eat every day. He was the eldest, but exercised so much and had such a healthy diet that he was convinced that he would live until he was 120 years old. Walford maintained that through calorie restrictions, all human beings could drastically extend their lifetimes. The biosphere's inhabitants became his guinea pigs.

It wasn't long before hunger became a ubiquitous inhabitant among them, impossible to ignore. It turned them against one another, teased out their worst sides, caused them to seek conflict. They divided up into two groups, four against four. The controversies were related to the road ahead, whether they should focus more on the scientific portion of the experiment or continue as they had done until then. Some of them wanted another leader, several were sceptical of John Allen, who sat on the outside of the bubble and controlled everything like a Big Brother figure, via video conference. The antipathy towards him grew. It was easy to put the blame on a person you had never met in flesh and blood, but only saw on a screen. The climatic conditions in the biosphere were harmonious, comfortable but, even so, a chill seeped under the domes and penetrated the body and mind.

The participants considered themselves to be peaceful human beings, pacifists; nobody resorted to blows, but their language with each other grew harsher and several times someone spat gooey, nasty, gobs of spit in the direction of an opponent.

Breathing became more difficult.

Group therapy, somebody suggested, we must find a compromise through discussion. They read books in search of knowledge, did roleplay exercises, tried to understand the dynamics of the group they were all a part of. And they found hope in the discussions, told each other we will get through this, maybe we will even come out of this stronger.

But then their world, the biosphere, began to collapse. The microbes in the soil produced carbon dioxide more quickly than the young plants were able to produce oxygen. The oxygen level dropped from the initial 20.9 per cent to 14.2 after sixteen months. Instead of doing something, the inhabitants decided to allow nature and the experiment to take its course.

They struggled through the days through the sheer force of their wills, despite the body's protests, the headaches, the nausea. Even the smallest of tasks became impossible to carry out; their muscles would not comply, their thoughts went in circles, and breathing – at all times they inhaled air deeply into their lungs, but it didn't help. Even while resting, their lungs laboured mightily, even while sleeping.

Only when their lungs began to rattle, when their faces swelled up and they were barely able to stand, did the trailers arrive. Large oxygen tanks. The inhabitants saw the hoses being hooked up outside, the umbilical cords that gave them life.

And then, finally, they were able to breathe again, finally they could run, finally they had the strength to laugh, to dance. A dark cloud was lifted. They became friends, they celebrated the oxygen, feeling reborn, praised the life-giving gas and all the world's plants and algae, which at all times supplied the human race with sufficient quantities of it and which made Biosphere 1, the earth, so green and so alive.

They thought, nothing can stop us now.

But the oxygen was not enough. The natural environment inside the closed-off world had already given up and this development could not be halted. The birds died. The bees died. The flowers waited in vain for visiting insects. There were no longer any creatures there to carry out pollination.

Only a few species survived, were able to thrive where others perished, and soon the cockroaches took over the biosphere.

Crawling, breeding.

They are crawling all over him, cockroaches and dead bodies. But he does not try to escape from them. He wants to hold someone close, grabs hold of something, it is Henry. He hugs his little brother tightly, strokes his head and cheeks, opens his eyes, wants to look at him and then he sees that it is only his jacket that he is clutching against his body.

He throws it down.

Grandmother. I'm here now. Talk to me, please.

But the only response is silence.

Even the wind has vanished.

Tommy opens his eyes, sits up, listens.

Yes, the storm has really subsided.

He climbs to his feet, finds his jacket, scarf and hat.

Every step is an effort, but his body obeys as he walks towards the door, takes hold and pushes hard.

The fresh air hits him, giving him strength.

It is only a few degrees below zero, the ground is covered with a light powdering of snow. The full moon hangs high in the sky and emanates a light so intense that it could have been daylight, overpowering the Northern Lights. You see, he says to the Northern Lights, which are little more than a faint green shimmer, you have no power, not against the moon.

The door slams shut behind him. He pulls up the zipper on his jacket, knots his scarf snugly around his neck and then he starts to run.

It is the same route he ran on the night everything was destroyed. Along the coast towards the disused airport. On the fjord, the ship's lights were glowing, but otherwise it was dark. He jogged until he was certain that nobody could see him any longer, then he continued walking quickly out to Bjørndalen and the entrance to the ventilation shaft.

He had lain awake after the others had fallen asleep. They had searched for the seed vault for six days to no avail, but in the morning they were going to check the mine, Tao had said. In the morning they would begin to talk about all the tunnels inside the mountain there, in the morning there was a chance that they would make the trip out to Bjørndalen.

When Tommy was certain that everyone else was asleep, he got up. He checked on his brothers, who were sleeping deeply, Hilmar on his back with his arms behind his head, secure even while asleep. Henry was on his side, curled up in a ball under the duvet, his hair alone visible.

As Tommy ran, it started raining again. The air became saturated with humidity, his boots made sucking noises in the mud with every step he took. Torrents of rain rushed down the mountainsides, trickling into loose sediments.

The post was where he had left it. Far too visible: how could he be so stupid? And by the entrance to the tunnel, the vegetation was trampled, thousands of signs, left behind by him, all of them. When they came out here, they would see the hiding place immediately.

He yanked the post out of the ground and, using it as a

shovel, dug up the soil, trying to conceal the prints left by his boots, spraying muck everywhere, until he was covered with mud and filth as he tore up tufts of grass and moss and laid bare the barren topsoil beneath. But it didn't help, it actually made things worse, the destruction highlighted the signs of human impact. He took a few steps away. It was even more visible from a distance. Only a human being could have produced such a wound in the natural landscape.

He stood holding the post in his hand, resisting the urge to throw it down and scream at the top of his voice. His arms just hung limply at his sides.

Then he raised his head and stared upwards. There, 500 metres above him, was Platåberget Mountain. As solid as a mountain, he thought, and suddenly he smiled. What a foolish expression. None of the mountains of Svalbard were solid.

Again he walked over to the entrance to the tunnel, again he drove the post into the ground. To be on the safe side, he took off his scarf and tied it around the post like a flag.

He walked quickly along the shore and back towards Vestpynten. Near the old harbour the road forked; one of the roads led to Longyearbyen, the other to the mountain. Tommy headed for the mountain.

It will take too long, he thought, checking the time on his watch constantly, I have to make it before they wake up. His chest was burning, his heart pounding in his ears. When he finally reached the top, he stopped momentarily to catch his breath and take in the view of his village. The houses far below resembled grey stones, which were already in the process of being conquered by nature. Then he turned away and kept walking across the mountain.

Isfjorden lay before him. The water was choppy around the point, the swells colliding, but above him the sky was calm.

He walked to the spot where the mountain dropped straight into the fjord. Below him he could see his scarf on the post waving on the wind.

He picked a stone up from the ground and threw it down over the precipice. It triggered other stones along the way, and soon they too were tumbling down the mountainside, more and more stones all the time. It took so little, the ground was saturated with water, a landslide could be activated by nothing, by a large stone, by a movement, by standing here and jumping up and down.

And that's what he did. He started jumping. Up and down, waving his arms, without making a sound; he became a bizarre jumping jack up there on the mountain.

It wasn't long before the stones started sliding; the loose sediment did exactly what he wished. Soon it would grow, soon the mountainside would be torn away, just a little bit more.

That was when somebody came running, her body heavy because of her condition, but nonetheless quickly.

'Tommy! No!'

Nobody could hunt like Rakel, nobody could blend into the landscape like she could, becoming invisible.

He kept moving, further and further out onto the edge, the ground sliding away between his feet, he could feel that soon the ground would no longer support him.

'No! No. I know what you're doing, and you can't, I won't let you! Stop!'

She pulled up short a few metres away from him, not daring to come any closer.

'Think about Louise,' she said. 'About your grandmother.'

Again he jumped, breathlessly. 'That's exactly what I'm doing.'

She hesitated. 'You have no right to determine the fate of the seeds, Tommy,' she said calmly. 'You're just a stupid kid, just like me!'

A cold thought paralysed him, causing him to stop.

'What do you mean? Did she give you the key?'

'What?' Rakel said, and suddenly she was confused. 'The key? No.'

She took a step towards him. 'Tommy, listen to me. She didn't give either of us the key. Seed custodian? That was just something she said to be nice! She would never have asked a child to be a seed custodian!'

'Shut up!' he shouted.

And then he started jumping again.

'Stop!'

She stormed towards him and grabbed him, putting her arms around him, trying to restrain him, to make him stop.

She stood there just holding him, gaining control over his body, and he noticed how it responded immediately, as if his body wanted something other than what his head wanted, as if his body wanted her to soothe him.

He could hear the sound of her breathing in his ear, felt it against his cheek and it soothed his own respiration, as did her stomach, large and round against his body.

'What are you doing, Tommy?' she said, her voice compassionate. 'What is it you're doing?'

He leaned his forehead against her shoulder, closed his eyes and realised that he couldn't hide anything from her. She was too sharp, too alert. Of course she had followed him, seen what he was up to; she knew where the seeds were and even though he would manage to hide the entrance to the tunnel, she would take the foreigners there and show them the place, show them where they should dig. Because she hadn't lost the fight. People like Rakel never lost. Rakel would always do what was necessary to ensure that she and her descendants survived.

Slowly, she relaxed her grip, but she kept her arms around him, and arms that had been reins and ropes now became supportive, holding him upright.

And then she started talking. She talked about the baby they would be having, she put his hand on her tummy, feel how it's moving, our little sprout has become a whole child, *our* child, and he could feel it kicking inside, a foot, a shoulder, now we are going to take it with us to the other side of the ocean, to the other side of the world and there the six of us will live together, you and me, Henry, Hilmar and Runa, and the baby, and we will be safe, we will have enough to eat, we will stop fighting, and above all we will no longer be alone. We will be a part of something, move through the world in interaction with other people. Take my hand now, Tommy, and we will walk down from here together, we will tell the others where the seeds are, that we have found them together, we can say that, that we were out here looking together and then we found Grandmother's hiding place, and afterwards while the others carry them out of the mountain, we will finish packing, close up the house, walk down to the boats and leave Svalbard.

They stood completely still, his heart beating more calmly. He wanted only to remain inside her voice, inside all her reassuring words.

They stood completely still on the edge of the precipice, but even though they didn't move, the ground they were standing on was already in motion. Stones and gravel accumulated more stones and gravel, Tommy's movements were no longer of any importance, the landslide moved the landslide, stones building upon stones, spreading like ripples across water. The mountain was alive.

Rakel released him abruptly, gasped when she saw what was happening, stepped aside.

'Be careful, Tommy!'

They stood side by side, a few metres apart. She reached out her hand and now it wasn't to stop him but to hang on.

But they were too far apart and the distance between them expanded, as the ground beneath her feet crumbled.

'Rakel!'

She slid away even though she did not move a muscle. For a brief moment she stayed on her feet, as if surfing on a wave of soil and stones. Then she disappeared.

He didn't hear her fall; he heard only the din of the landslide.

'Rakel!'

And then silence.

A black chasm in the mountainside below him. An alteration in the landscape. The post had disappeared. Every living thing that had once been growing down below, which had spent years putting down roots in the barren earth, was gone.

The hours that followed are now disconnected images. He is squatting beside the landslide, digging with his hands, he is screaming Rakel's name. She is lying here somewhere, how long can a person who is buried beneath gravel and dirt survive? Several days if she is lucky. The ground is wet, she can find drops of water. She is lying down there, her mouth is open, and life-sustaining water will keep her firmly in this world and he must just dig, he must keep searching, he will manage it, he will find her, he can't go back without her, can't look Henry, Hilmar and Runa in the eyes and tell them that she is gone. They will think that it's his fault, was it his fault, he must just keep digging. And the hours pass, the days, he loses all contact with time, everything disintegrates, all that exists is dirt, stone, gravel, mud, the pouring rain, waves pounding against the coastline, two reindeer run past behind him but he doesn't look over his shoulder, never turns around, a few times he seeks refuge in Grandmother's cabin, collapses and sleeps for a couple of hours and then he is back on his feet again. At one point he thinks he hears the foreigners' voices, he is lying on the cot, his body aching, he thinks he hears Tao, but from a great distance and now they are coming, now they will see him and understand what he has done and it wasn't his fault. But then the voices fade away, they are gone, he tiptoes outside and can't see them. He runs back to the landslide, has dirt under his fingernails, cuts on his hands, his back is aching, he is covered with mud but just keeps going. It was his fault. Rakel, Rakel.

And then, a sharp noise from the fjord, the beating of a sail. He turns around and sees the boat, in the middle of the fjord. The wind is filling the sails, it heels gently, and the dark solar cell panels along the hull glitter in the sunlight.

He climbs to his feet, unable to believe what he is seeing. Henry? Hilmar?

They are out there and the boat is headed out to sea.

The realisation is like a boulder against his chest. All the choices he has made, tiny mutations, all of this has led inexorably to precisely this moment. And like a mutation, it has not been anyone's fault. It has all just happened. The culmination of everything that has brought him here, and now it has happened, the worst thing of all, he has lost what is most precious.

He runs towards the shore, screaming his brothers' names. 'No! Stop!'

He thinks he can see somebody on deck, a small figure against the grey sail.

'Henry?'

He thinks he sees his brother, thinks he hears him and his shouts carry, but not far enough, because neither of them can hear the other.

Tommy collapses into a heap, closes his eyes, and then his brothers are there, in his arms. Henry small and soft, Hilmar angular. He holds them tightly, both of them, they are an inseparable lump of arms and legs. It is excruciating to hold them against his body for the very last time. His hands are in pain as he strokes their hair, again and again, as he embraces them. His cheeks ache as he presses them against theirs, especially against Henry's, which are so soft that he sinks into them. Inhaling their scent is painful. Henry's soft, little boy scent, Hilmar's which has changed in the past year, in the process of entering a new phase. You will grow up, Tommy thinks, and rests his nose against his brother's neck, you will grow up and I won't be there. It is difficult to embrace them both at the same time. Even though they are thin and stand completely still, it's as if they are fighting over the place in his arms and soon they slip through his fingers and he opens his eyes and they are gone.

And maybe it isn't Henry he can see way out there, on deck, maybe it's one of the sailors, and now the person disappears below deck, hasn't even seen Tommy here on the beach.

Because nobody has seen him. They don't know that he's alive, and he can still stop them.

He gets to his feet. Again he waves his arms.

The wind swallows his voice, yet he keeps shouting their names.

'Henry! Hilmar! Come back with my brothers!'

'It was my fault. That I lost Henry and Hilmar, it was my fault.'

The radio hums. He leans closer to the control table.

'Please, Tao? Can you hear me? It was my fault. Rakel died, our unborn child died, you all left, I lost my brothers, Henry and Hilmar lost me. It was all my fault.'

The room is cold, his breath mists into clouds. Dust floats through the strip of light falling from the window.

'Tao?'

His fingers shake as he switches on the heater. I must stay here, he thinks, I must just stay here, until she responds.

He keeps calling her, again and again, trembling from the cold, but stays seated, his eyes on the radio, terrified that if he should even blink, he will miss her.

And then, all of a sudden, he hears a scraping sound, faint, but clear, and her voice emerges. It is every bit as clear as if she were in the room, close and physical, he can almost touch it.

'Tommy?'

'Yes, Tao, I'm here!'

She laughs in relief. 'Tommy! You're alive!'

He's alive, she is with him, and now the words tumble out of his mouth. He tells her about the landslide, about Rakel. He tells her about how they held each other, how she said that everything would be all right, and how he believed her for a fleeting moment, but then he lost her again. And if he hadn't been up there on the mountain, if she hadn't followed him, if he hadn't caused a landslide, she would be here now.

Rakel is dead, he says. It was his fault, he whispers the

words over and over, my fault. Just come and pick me up, he says, please just come and pick me up. I want to be picked up, he sobs, begs, pick me up, pick me up.

When he finally falls silent, Tao answers him calmly.

'Everything will be all right, Tommy, it will be all right now, you will be fine.'

He nods and clings to her voice, it is the thread holding him firmly in place.

'Are you there?' she asks.

'Yes,' he says.

'You know what I have to ask you now,' she says.

'Yes,' he says. 'You have to ask me about the seeds. Whether they exist.'

'Tell me about the seeds. Tell me what happened to them.'

Her voice is a tightly drawn string, the joy over what she hopes to hear wrestling against her fear.

'The seeds exist,' he says. 'They are in the mountain beneath me.'

'Will you give them to us?'

'I don't care about the seeds,' he says, struggling to suppress the tears. 'Just come and get me.'

'Dear, dear Tommy,' is all she says.

Then silence. He leans towards the speaker.

'Are you there?'

'I'm here,' she says, but her voice is fainter, as if she is moving away from the microphone. 'And Tommy, we will talk more, a lot more and we will figure everything out. But first there is someone else who must hear your voice.'

'Yes?'

He squeezes the microphone and doesn't move.

Tiny sounds can be heard over the radio, on the other end, sounds of somebody moving.

'Tao?'

He twists the volume button, turns it up all the way, wishing he had the hearing abilities of a dolphin.

And then he hears the clear sound of footsteps on the other end, not hers, but lighter, and a little erratic, as if they can't quite make up their mind about where they are going.

Then the sound of someone sitting.

A scraping of chair legs. The person on the other end fumbles with the microphone.

'Is this how you do it? And talk into here?'

He hears Tao murmur a reply and pictures her standing in the background, instructing the boy who is speaking to him.

'Hello? It's me. It's Henry. Tommy, are you there?'

Tommy leans as close to the radio as he can get, wants to come right up against the voice, embrace it.

'Tommy?'

Then Henry seems to turn away from the microphone, because the sound fades. 'He doesn't answer.'

I'm here, Tommy wants to say, but his lips won't form the words, it was my fault, you must be angry with me, Henry, for letting you leave, for letting you down.

'Just keep talking, Henry,' Tao says in the background.

There's a silence, as if Henry is searching for words.

'Sure. What should I say, then?' He hesitates. 'Right, Tommy, I'm fine. We had carrots for dinner. They were good . . . but not as good as the carrots from the greenhouse at home.'

Again he falls silent. Tommy can hear the familiar sound of his rapid breathing.

Keep going, he thinks.

'The library here isn't very big,' Henry says, 'but we go there a lot anyway. Tao reads to me. She tells me fairy tales, too.'

Behind the scraping noises and the distance, Henry is the same as always. Tommy hears him clearly, through his choice of words, his pauses, and the hint of curiosity, even when he is not asking questions. Tommy looks at his hands, how he holds them around the microphone, squeezing it. Keep going, he thinks again, just keep talking to me, Henry, it makes no difference what you say, tell me about carrots, about the weather, tell me about what you did today, about the walk home from school, about anything at all, as long as I can hear your voice.

But Henry has fallen silent.

Little brother clears his throat.

'I don't think he hears me,' Henry says, finally.

'Yes, he does,' Tao says. 'Try again. He's there.'

'Are you sure? Okay.'

Then it's as if Henry holds the microphone even closer to his mouth.

'Actually, I just wanted to wish you a Happy Christmas, Tommy.'

Is it Christmas?

'Here it's light in the daytime even though it's Christmas. I don't think it's a proper Christmas when it's so light out. Are you celebrating, Tommy? Have you gone in the procession?' Henry asks and his voice is suddenly higher. 'Did you walk in the torchlight procession to Bjørndalen?'

Yes, it is Christmas Eve. Time is a huge animal that has picked Tommy up in its jaws and run away with him, tossing him around and finally swallowing him whole.

'I miss you,' Henry says. 'I miss you, Tommy.'

I miss you too, Henry. I'm worn out from missing you.

'Can you answer, please?'

You are the first thing I think about when I wake up and

the last thing I think about before I go to sleep. I want so much to see you, hug you, my brother, dear, dear Henry.

'You don't have to say a lot. You can just say hi, that's enough. So I know that it's you.'

Tommy squeezes the microphone and nods, smiling at his little brother's voice.

'Tommy, if you hear me, can you please just say hi?'

Tao

District 242, Shirong, Sichuan, 2111

Sometimes I become infuriated. When I see the fields crack open and the soil turn to dust. When the colour of small, green shoots fades into dullness and they whither, are torn out of the earth and are blown away by the wind. When the children must go to bed hungry.

I am infuriated and I have slowly come to understand at whom my anger is directed.

At those who lived before us. They chose their own lifetimes, the few years they had, the few months, weeks, minutes, instead of all the time to come after their lives had ended. I want to punish them, send them into the future, into my time, I want them to see what they have done. I want to scream at them, as if they were children, look at the mess you've made! And they really *were* children, they thought like children, made choices like children. I want to bring them to court, without a defence attorney, you deserve no defence attorney. Stupid, stupid people.

But then I force myself to make an effort.

All we have here is that which we can see, hear, taste, smell and feel. All we have here is life and death. And life is found in death as death is found in life, because all living things are moving towards death at all times, through decay. A living creature is always in the midst of this process of dying, just as that which is dead always moves towards life. A living leaf on a branch takes nourishment from the dead leaves on the ground under the tree. In this way, the same leaf moves up and down, to the soil and from the soil. This is what I believe in. But I also believe in something more, I believe in knowledge about life and about death and the connection between the two. I believe in books. The library is my house of worship ... no, my seed vault. Because in the same way that the seeds are distillers of nature's knowledge, the books are the distillers of human beings. All knowledge is stories, and I really believe in stories.

If I were the defence attorney for the human race, this would be my closing argument: Given the fact that the earth is the only planet on which life has arisen, given that humans are the only species that has been capable of abstract communication, given that the Holocene is the only geological epoch providing such prime conditions for life that a wholly unique species diversity emerged and with it, the conditions for modern man, given that during this one moment alone, in the entire universe, there has been a basis for the survival of a species not only able to describe nature's richness and beauty, but also to capture these descriptions, these emotions, this knowledge in words printed on paper, aren't then the books themselves evidence of our value?

Is that a good argument?

Do I believe this?

Or was Tommy right, how he thought of us before?

I don't know.

And then there is no need to think any more; I don't have time to be angry, because suddenly Henry is there, and he wants to show me something, his voice full of excitement. Or Hilmar; he tugs at my jumper, competing with his brother for my attention. Or Tommy's voice over the radio, when he describes his day to me in detail, because this gives him something to hold onto, while he counts the days, hours and minutes.

It is spring. There's snow on the ground in Svalbard, Tommy says, but the midnight sun is shining and on slopes facing south the earth is bare.

What do you think the ocean is like now, he asks me, do you think the drift ice is still floating on the currents from the North Pole? And what do you think your mountains look like, he asks, he calls all the mountains located between him and us *my* mountains, do you think the road is visible? Do you think it's ready for you?

Soon, I say, just a few more days now, we must allow spring to settle in properly.

And then the warm weather arrives. In the course of a week, the temperature rises dramatically and the trees are filled with leaves so quickly that we can see the difference from one day to the next. The spring is more explosive than I can remember it ever having been, everything about its being is surprising.

They walk towards me, all three of them. Runa first, the two boys behind her. Henry notices a boy from his class who has just left the school building. The boy stops and makes a silly hand gesture at Henry. Henry responds in kind and then they both laugh. Hilmar pokes Henry in the back and then points at me. Then he takes Henry by the hand and leads him in my direction, while Henry shouts something to the other boy and laughs even more. Hilmar pulls his brother along. The two brothers still hold hands, but increasingly it is Hilmar who takes the initiative, who takes his brother's hand while Henry has begun to forget and sometimes is even irritated by the hand that at all times is searching for his.

We stroll home on an afternoon that has become so hot that I must take off my jacket. The boys fall behind, stopping to look at things along the way, earthworms, a large puddle and a long stick. They chitchat, mostly in Norwegian, this sing-songy, strange language that is so difficult to learn – but the more time we spend together, the more frequently I hear them switching over into my own language.

Runa leads the way beside me. We don't say much, but it is a comfortable silence. Runa is a person you can be silent with. She has become more careless about the way she dresses, doesn't always remember to say thank you and doesn't smile as often as she used to. But she laughs more and twice we have had arguments. The last time she said I was dumb. Dumb, a small, simple word, but large coming out of her mouth. I had to turn away and hide my smile of joy over precisely that word.

It's been a long time since I asked her whether she misses her sister.

Runa seems to trust me. She is serene and knows this will all work out just fine. While the boys have first and foremost been attached to one another, I think Runa has made a conscious choice to form an attachment to me. Maybe for pragmatic reasons, it is the simplest and safest, maybe out of a sense of relief. I don't think she has had an adult she could call her own, but still I'm certain that she must have had a strong tie to someone at an early stage of her life, as an infant maybe, that she has been held, that someone has hugged her tightly and met her eyes and murmured words of kindness in her ear. Besides, I think she feels that I see her. And she dares to be seen. She has stepped out of the darkness and into the light, become visible for other people, not as a cheerful, good little doll, but as the person she is.

We still live together, all four of us, in the apartment where I once lived all alone. The presence of the children fills me with a strong sense of astonishment. I wake up and a couple of seconds pass before I remember how different life is and then the surprise is there, it takes hold of me, a prickling, tickling sensation that continues all day long, until I fall asleep with a bewildered smile on my lips. While life with Wei-Wen was filled with the intense and joyful worries of parenthood, and life after his death by an all-consuming grief, this new life, this new period, is the age of astonishment.

We arrive at our house. Henry has been dragging a long stick the whole way home.

'Can I bring it inside?' he asks.

'No,' I reply. 'It's too big and too dirty. But put it here against the wall, no doubt it will still be here in the morning.'

'But I want to save it until Tommy comes. What if somebody takes it?'

'Nobody is going to take a stick,' Hilmar says.

'You don't know that,' Henry says.

'Aren't you a little too old for sticks?' Hilmar asks.

Henry's face turns red but he doesn't answer. He merely leans the stick up against the wall and looks at it for a long time before walking over to the front door.

The two boys have started bickering recently. It's new and unlike them. Tiresome and enervating. And a relief. Their squabbling irritates me but also makes me strangely happy.

I let us into the apartment and the children disappear into their respective bedrooms. I can hear Henry and Hilmar playing in there, because they can still play together, although Hilmar has almost outgrown Henry's adventures and sometimes pulls away. Luckily, Henry is able to continue by himself. He has a great imagination, nourished by countless books. I hear him living on a deserted island, in a black egg, in a submarine in the ocean or in an amphitheatre. I hear him sword fighting and picking hour-lilies, I hear him battling with dragons. While Henry plays by himself, sometimes Hilmar comes out to look for me or he wanders around the apartment a bit restlessly, until I ask whether he wants to play a game or help out in the kitchen. The newly expanding distance from his brother makes him ambivalent, relieved and also anxious. But every night the boys go to bed at the same time, every night they sleep with their bodies snugly entwined. There is no ambivalence when they are asleep.

I sit at the kitchen table drinking a glass of water. The sound of the children fills the apartment. Runa is singing softly in her bedroom. Henry and Hilmar are playing noisily and their movements are so rambunctious that I can feel them through the floorboards. I hear furniture creaking, footsteps across the floor, laughter. The echoes that previously filled the apartment have been swallowed by children's bodies, by clothing, all the things with which they surround themselves.

Then it is bedtime. The children talk to Tommy before they go to bed, early. They are tired after a week at school. I make up a bed on the sofa in the sitting room for myself. I try to stay awake, just to be present in the room and in my new life. But usually sleep comes immediately, spreading over me like mulch that shuts out all the light. No dreams, only rest.

Of all the events of the past thirteen years, there is nothing that I miss. Not the looks, not the attention, not Li Chiara's many requests, nor being in a position of such proximity to power.

She hasn't contacted me a single time since I came home. In my absence, Li Chiara has found other symbols to use in her communication campaigns. Wei-Wen is still a key figure, his computer-generated face is still everywhere. But the Mother has disappeared. I don't think anyone misses me. I am starting to get too old. My face is sharply lined and I am no longer the young, sensitive woman whom everyone loved. My grief and I are both outdated. It's a relief. And it is true. Many years have passed since I stopped knowing where my own grief ended and the cameras' grief began, whether I was actually sad or just performing pain for their benefit. Wei-Wen is always with me; he will be for as long as I exist. When I retreat into myself, I always see him. But I am facing outwards now, reaching for the light.

The children have the day off school and we are walking through the forest, strolling slowly down the wheel ruts behind Field 748. Henry, Hilmar, Runa and I.

They stroll with their heads tilted back, their gazes focused at all times on the crowns of the trees. They have been here many times in the course of the winter, but this is the first time since the trees began to bud.

'It's so green,' Henry says, looking up at the tree crowns. 'The trees look like they're lit up.'

He has brought along the long stick, dragging it behind him.

'The leaves *are* actually green,' Hilmar says.

Henry turns his head towards his brother in irritation. 'I know that.'

Around us, spring's song can be heard, the humming

of insects, the twittering of birds, the gurgling of a brook. Everything is as it should be. We are four and I am part of a *we*. The most beautiful word in the world.

We keep going until we reach a flat piece of land between the trees. I have brought a blanket, which I spread out on the grass and then I take food out of a bag.

Runa sits down with me while the boys run back and forth between the trees.

Then my stomach growls.

Runa chuckles. 'Are you hungry?'

I have to laugh. 'Yes. Are you?'

'Very,' she says.

I take out plates, open a bottle of fruit squash and pour it into the glasses. Then I call the boys.

'Coming,' Hilmar says from somewhere between the trees.

He comes quickly to join us and throws himself down on the blanket with such force that one of the glasses of squash almost tips over.

'Careful,' I say. 'Where's Henry?'

'I don't know. He said he was going to take care of something.'

I stand up and walk towards the grove.

'Henry?'

A wave of anxiety clutches me, stemming from another spring day out here, the day I lost Wei-Wen.

'I'll be there in a minute,' I hear the child call.

Because this is not that day and I am not going to lose Henry.

I walk closer and catch sight of him in the grove. He is sitting in a clearing where the sunlight is dancing against the foliage, the rays flickering all the way down to the dark soil on the ground and Henry's soft neck. His fingers are in the soil, covering up something or other, his hands are dirty as if he has been digging. Beside him lies a small cloth bag. He picks it up and empties something from it into his palm, stands up, walks a few steps and opens his hand. He blows at it, and something organic soars upward. I can see small, narrow petals like wings. They swirl through the air and disappear.

Only then does he turn to me.

'Hi,' he says.

'Hi. What are you doing?'

'Nothing.'

'Do you want to eat something?'

'Mm.'

He comes over and stops in front of me, leaning his head backwards and looking up. The rays of the sun beat down through the fragile, budding leaves and strike his face. He squeezes his lips together in a small frown, not dissatisfied, more an expression of confirmation.

'Tao,' he says.

'Henry,' I say.

He takes another step towards me, standing so close to me that I can feel the presence of his body, the scent of him, of a child's hair and soap and something unmistakably Henry. I get the urge to stop, squat down, pull him into a hug and bury my nose in his hair.

Henry makes a small movement with his shoulders.

'Do we have anything good?' he says and starts walking.

'Not much. But we have squash.'

'Plum squash?'

'Yes.'

I walk beside him, trying to adapt the length of my steps to his.

His hand dangles at his side, right next to mine, but I don't take it.

Later, perhaps. We have time.

Acknowledgements

I would like to extend my gratitude to the many helpful individuals who have read, offered comments and thought aloud with me during the writing process: biologist Anne Sverdrup-Thygeson, biologist Dag O. Hessen, historian Ole Georg Moseng, author Line Ylvisaker, climate scientist Ketil Isaksen, biologist Dagmar Hagen, special adviser at the Norwegian Polar Institute Kim Holmen, biologist Tommy Presto, geologist Lars Erikstad, landscape architect Marianne Lesner, the gardening apprentices Live Kjolstad, Bjorn Myrvold and Thomas S. Knutsen at Norsk Radio Rale Liga, zoologist Peter Bockman, botanist Reidar Elven, the general manager of Mine 3 Havard Fjerdingoy, Benjamin L. Vidmar at Svalbard Permaculture Solutions, operations manager Maja-Stina Ekstedt at Svalsat, biologist Eva Fuglei, Trine Krystad at Visit Svalbard, property manager Jan Myhre, botanist Kristina Bjureke and the coordinator of the Svalbard seed vault Asmund Asdal.

Further, I would like to thank PEN Norway and SvalbardArtica for making my writer's residency in Longyearbyen possible.

I would also extend my gratitude to Aschehoug forlag

and Oslo Literary Agency, especially my wise editor Nora Campbell, who has been by my side ever since 2014, when *The History of Bees*, the first novel of this quartet, was still only a manuscript.

Finally, I would like to thank all the people working in the sciences to counteract the climate and nature crisis, who in their openness to change, take the lead and pull others behind them, whether this be in local communities, nationally or globally. We need you more than ever before.

Sources of Inspiration

Arlov, Thor B.: *Svalbards historie*. Fagbokforlaget, 2019.

Attenborough, David: *Et liv på vår planet*. Cappelen Damm, 2021.

Bjørnstad, Åsmund: *Korn: frå steinalder til genalder*. Tun Forlag, 2006.

'Cosmos: Possible Worlds' Vavilov. Fox, 2020.

Ekko. NRK, 26 November 2020.

European Environment Agency: *Climate Change, Impacts and Vulnerability in Europe 2016*.

Færøvik, Torbjorn: *Midtens rike*. Cappelen Damm, 2009.

Fowler, Cary: *Seeds on Ice*. Prospecta Press, 2016.

Hanssen-Bauer, I., Førland, E. J., Hisdal, H., Mayer S., Sando, A. B. & Sorteberg, A.: *Climate in Svalbard 2100*. Norwegian Environment Agency, 2019.

Harari, Yuval Noah: *Sapiens*. Cappelen Damm, 2016.

Hart, Tony: *Mikroterrorister.* Tun Forlag, 2004.

Hermansen, Pål: *Frø til verden.* Kom Forlag, 2013.

Hessen, Dag O.: *Carl von Linné.* Gyldendal, 2000.

Hessen, Dag O.: *Liv – historien om universets mest spektakulare oppfinnelse.* Cappelen Damm, 2021.

Hovelsrud, Kjell Reidar: *Svalbard: Et eventyrlig polarliv.* Orion 2000.

Ingebrigtsen, Hanne Margrethe, Midthun, Heidi Meyer & Spjelkavik, Sigmund: *Longyearflora.* 2017.

Jahrenm, Anne Hope: *Alt jeg vet om planter.* J.M. Stenersens forlag, 2016.

Knarvik, Julie C. & Jarild, Sverre Chr.: *Jeger i Svalbards villmark.* Ildvik forlag, 2010.

Kovacs, Kit M. & Lydersen, Christian (eds): *Svalbards fugler og pattedyr.* Norwegian Polar Institute, 2006.

Lauritzen, Eva Mæhre: *Seks planter som forandret verden.* Akademika forlag, 2012.

Mancuso, Stefano & Viola, Alessandra, *Smarte planter.* Bazar, 2013.

Mathismoen, Ole: *Varm is.* Kagge, 2020.

Moseng, Ole Georg: *Pesten kommer.* Kagge 2020.

Nabhan, Gary Paul: *Where Our Food Comes From.* Shearwater Books, 2009.

Næss, Arne: *Dyp glede.* Flux Forlag, 2008.

Pringle, Peter: *The Murder of Nikolai Vavilov*. Simon & Schuster, 2008.

Ritter, Christiane: *Kvinne i polarnatten*. Polar forlag, 2002.

Skjaraasen, Martin & Helledal, Eline Johnsen: *Frø i fare*. NRK.no. 21 March 2021.

Stange, Rolf: *Svalbard, Norge nærmest Nordpolen*. 2017.

Sverdrup-Thygeson, Anne: *På naturens skuldre*. Kagge, 2020.

Wolf, Michael: *Spaceship World*. Impact Partners/ RadicalMedia/Stacey Reiss Productions, 2020.

Ylvisåker, Line Nagell: *Verda mi smelter*. Samlaget, 2020.

Zimmer, Carl: *The Lost History of One of the World's Strangest Science Experiments*. nytimes.com, 2019.

The following works have been cited in the novel:

Pringle, Peter: *The Murder of Nikolai Vavilov*. Simon & Schuster, 2008.

Ende, Michael: *The Neverending Story*. Ralph Manheim (trans.). Penguin Books, 1983.